Caeldighn

JENNIFER LEITZMAN

This is a work of fiction. Names, characters, places, events, and incidents are either the products of the author's imagination or used in a fictitious manner. Any resemblance to actual persons, living or dead, or actual events is purely coincidental.

ISBN: 1511927909
ISBN-13: 978-1511927901

TABLE OF CONTENTS

DEDICATION

This dedication will be vague,
specifically very vague,
and come to no real conclusion.

It is for you.

CHAPTER ONE

Jaea Harbor walked up to the familiar glowing obelisk and leaned her forehead against its translucent crystal. "Hello again, Lady Nirah."

"Hello again, Jaea-Shaper. And happy birthday," Nirah answered. Jaea had long ago grown accustomed to the way the melodic feminine voice filled the clearing in which she sat, coming from both the stone and inside her head simultaneously.

"Thanks! Twenty-two today." Jaea turned and sat down, leaning back against the monument. She stared into the thick fog that obscured the surrounding area, searching for clues out of habit. Nothing made itself visible, but that wasn't surprising.

"I have not had your company as much these last couple years. I have missed our talks."

"And I have missed you, old friend." Jaea reached behind her and placed one palm against the smooth crystal. "I have missed this place, strange as it is. I always feel at home here."

"I am glad you came today for I have news for you," Nirah said amicably.

"News?" Jaea asked. "How can you have news for me? You said most dreamers just drift through here on accident."

"I also told you there are some that are pulled here," Nirah reminded her patiently. "And that is my news, dear one. I have

1

finally solved our two biggest puzzles! I know why you come here so often, and why you once sought your friend here."

"You do? That's great. Maybe." Jaea tilted her head back to look warily at the crystal behind her. She noticed that the monument was glowing brighter and the smoke inside the clear stone was swirling faster. Jaea knew this only happened when Nirah, the being somehow trapped inside the crystal, was very happy." Do I really want to know what, you, the lady stuck in a stone in my dreams has figured out about me?"

"Yes, you do," Nirah responded matter-of-factly. "As you have told me before, curiosity-"

"Killed the cat." Jaea laughed and waved her hands in defeat. "Okay. Lemme have it."

"Jaea, this place so often calls to you because you were born here," Nirah said excitedly. "You were born in my world, not on Earth."

"Impossible." Jaea laughed nervously. Knowing that would be impossible didn't stop the shiver that shot down her back. She sat straight up and half turned toward Nirah, intending to object to her friend's absurd claim.

"There is more. Listen, Jaea," Nirah insisted. "You were born here in Caeldighn, and the friend you once sought lives here still."

"My imaginary friend lives in Caeldighn, a world I visit occasionally in dreams and was somehow born in?" Jaea repeated uncertainly.

"Maya is not imaginary," Nirah rebuked. "She is your sister, your twin. You were searching for her the first time you dreamt of me. I think it is your tie to her that pulled you here."

Standing now and fully facing the monument, Jaea tried to make sense of the absurd claim. "I have a twin sister? Here?" Thoughts racing, she paced to the edge of the wide path and back. Returning to stand before the monument, she rested her

2

forehead on the cool stone. "How does that make any sense?" she whispered, half to herself.

"I think you went through a gate when you were young, to the land you live in now. Ponder that later," Nirah said impatiently. "Remember, you have a sister! Maya wanted to tell you -"

"Happy birthday!" yelled a loud voice, startling Jaea from her dream and causing her to fall to the floor in a tumbled heap of blankets.

Jaea stared at her bedroom ceiling trying to collect her thoughts. Reeling from what Nirah had said, she was in no hurry to get up. Maya had something to tell her. *Jeez. Maya is real!* Jaea rubbed her hands over her face. *And she is my sister. I have a sister!* For someone who had grown up an only child in a small adoptive family, the idea was baffling. *Maya remembers me, and not only that, she has a message for me?* Jaea shook her head as though trying to clear it, then narrowed her eyes as she remembered that she had been yanked from her dream by some idiot yelling. She untangled herself and prepared to give that buffoon a piece of her mind. That is until she recognized him. Dark hair, gray eyes, cocky grin; Tharen McKenna, her best friend and one of very few other Shapers she knew. She stood up, holding her pillow.

"Tharen! I am so glad to see you!" Jaea exclaimed before she thumped him with her pillow. He just continued to sit on the edge of her bed laughing. So she thumped him again and felt a little smug when his attempt to block the pillow resulted in him falling to the floor with a loud thud. She walked around the foot of the bed to stand, hands on hips, looking down at him.

"Glad to see me, huh? I can see that," Tharen said. He got to his feet and sent Jaea his most winning grin. "It's good to see you, Jaea."

"Likewise." Jaea laughed. "But what are you doing here? I thought you were still in Ireland."

Tharen threw his hands in the air in an exasperated gesture. "I

3

am here to surprise my best friend on her birthday, and help her haul all her college stuff home in a couple days. Because she is graduating tomorrow!"

"But you said just last week that you wouldn't be home in time," Jaea argued as she started to make her bed.

"If I had said otherwise it would not have been a surprise, now would it?" Tharen tossed Jaea her pillow.

"Well, did you have to wake me up like that?"

"Not my fault you were asleep at three in the afternoon," Tharen teased.

"It's called a nap. Without them, hundreds of college students would drop dead every year," Jaea retorted. She pulled her coal black hair into a ponytail. "And now that I'm awake," she said, narrowing her eyes at Tharen, "I am in need of something else vital to college survival: food."

"Opal was taking cookies out of the oven when I got here." They looked at each other for a minute then darted down the stairs to the kitchen.

Jaea and Tharen collapsed, still laughing, into kitchen chairs just as Opal was setting a plate of cookies on the table. Opal was the closest thing Jaea had to a grandmother. She looked the part with her rounded frame topped by a cap of silvery hair and laugh lines etched into her kind face.

"You kids haven't changed a bit." Opal chuckled. She kissed the top of Jaea's head. "Happy birthday again, sweetheart. Better yet, happy end of finals week! Oatmeal chocolate chip cookies really are the best way to celebrate, don't you think?"

"Definitely." Jaea smiled and picked a cookie of the plate. "Thanks, Opal. You're the best."

Tharen tossed a whole cookie in his mouth. He shrugged when Opal raised her eyebrows at him and continued to chew contently.

"Glasses in the cabinet by the sink. Milk in the fridge," Opal

4

informed Tharen. "After you wash that one down, try tasting another. I've changed the recipe since you were home last, and I want to know what you think."

Tharen rose to fetch a glass of milk. He filled one up for Jaea, too.

"They are perfect," Jaea praised.

"Well, you two have a lot to catch up on, and I need to get a few things for dinner," Opal told them. She pointed a finger at Tharen. "The spare bedroom should be all set up for you."

"Alright. Thanks, Opal," Tharen said.

"No need to go thanking me. I don't mind company when it's folks I like," Opal retorted. "You two gonna be here for dinner?"

Mouths full of cookie, Jaea and Tharen nodded their heads.

"Then I will see you both later this evening." Opal took the grocery list from its place on the fridge and headed out the door.

Tharen smiled at the bells jingling from the just closed door. "I've missed her."

"She has missed you. I think she is tickled pink that you are staying here for a few days. She figured you planned to settle back into your old room at Doc's," Jaea explained. 'Doc' Bailey, Opal's brother, had taken Tharen under his wing years ago. Jaea took Tharen's guilty expression to mean he hadn't kept in touch with his old mentor either.

Tharen arched an eyebrow at Jaea. "Are you trying to make me feel guilty for being gone so long?"

"Maybe a little," Jaea admitted. "You are not the best pen pal, you know. I feel terribly behind in your life story."

"Maybe I just don't have much to write about." Tharen took another cookie from the plate.

"Right," Jaea said. "Absolutely nothing interesting about living in a foreign country."

"It rained a lot. And I worked a lot. I also ate and slept."

"Tharen, you went to university abroad! You then graduated

5

early and later spent over half a year doing photography stuff with some museum dig thing? See, I don't know even know enough to explain it properly."

Tharen focused on picking up cookie crumbs from the table, looking down sheepishly. "You may have a point. I'll get you caught up. But for now, what's on the agenda until dinner time?" Jaea barely managed not to frown as Tharen changed the topic. "We could walk around campus, I suppose. It isn't very far. Or we could just sit in the garden and talk more." Jaea gave him a pointed glance. "Since you still have to fill me in on what in the world you have been up to between the few and far between postcards and letters."

Tharen ignored the jab and brought his and Jaea's empty milk glasses to the sink. "I vote for talk more. On the condition that we only delve into more Shaper related topics." He rinsed the cups out before turning back to Jaea. "It is easier to discuss such matters when there is no one around and since you are something of a celebrity this week, it is hard telling when we will get the chance again. Besides, I have a theory to run by you and I want to hear the latest from Nirah."

"To the garden then," Jaea decided. She grabbed two clean glasses from the cabinet. "We should bring some iced tea with us though. The latest from the Lady is going to take some telling."

Tharen set his glass on the table, taking a second to admire the sight of Jaea reclined on the porch swing. With one of Opal's many plants winding its way up the swing's A-frame and his friend looking so content, it was an idyllic picture. Of all the people he knew, no one looked so comfortable in their own skin as Jaea. Then again, not many people were able to change their skin the way she could. "You look lovely," he told Jaea as she kicked off her shoes. Tharen wanted to kick himself as soon as he said it. Seeing Jaea stiffen, he worried he had crossed some newly drawn line in their friendship. Thankfully, Jaea's face quickly relaxed into a smile, and Tharen felt the knot in his chest loosen.

"You have your poet face on," Jaea said amused. She patted the empty seat beside her on the swing. "Snap out of it friend. I would like to hear this theory of yours. After you tell me what you have been up to."

Tharen smiled and took a seat. "Oh, not much really. I studied. I worked. Traveled, mostly just for the sake of seeing a new place. I have a ton of photographs to show you. Ireland especially ate a lot of film. Met some people, tried some new food. Researched random things, added to our Shaper theories. It will be easier to tell you about places when I can show you the pictures I took. Unfortunately, they are all packed in my luggage right now."

Jaea shook her head. "You aren't getting out of this, mister. But I guess I can wait to hear all about it when I see the pictures. Go on then, tell me this new theory."

"Well, it has to do with why we haven't encountered many other Shapers."

"Many? Between the two of us, we barely know of a handful. And one is a selkie, not really like us at all," Jaea pointed out.

"Exactly. That is part of the reason I think that I may be onto something. In most of the research I have done, the magic or supernatural element of the story is from somewhere other than the story's setting," Tharen explained. "It comes from some other time, country, or world. I met a guy in Ireland who is trying to connect that element of elsewhere in stories with the existence of aliens, which convinced me even more that I am onto something. I do not believe the Shaper people originated here, on Earth, at all."

"Oh dear," Jaea said quietly.

"Jaea, are you okay? I expected you to laugh at first, not go pale on me." Tharen jumped up to get her glass of iced tea.

Jaea took a drink and smiled at Tharen. "Thank you. Now sit back down and quit looking so nervous. Women hardly swoon nowadays and me least of all. I just wasn't expecting you to echo Nirah like that."

Tharen was unconvinced. "What did Nirah say that lines up with my thinking we may be descended from aliens?" he asked as he resumed his place on the swing.

"That I was born on another world in a land called Caeldighn, that Maya is my twin sister, and that I probably walked through some inter-planet gate from Caeldighn to Mom and Dad's."

"Oh dear," Tharen repeated.

"Yep." The two were quiet for a moment, each processing the implications of this news.

"No wonder we could never pinpoint where Nirah is," Tharen said suddenly.

"No kidding," Jaea said. "How many maps and pictures have we poured over trying to locate a place with similar characteristics. Well, what characteristics we could gather. Nothing in art or architecture ever quite matched up with Nirah's stone."

"There were similarities though, lending to the theory that if we are not native, we are at least not alone here in this planet's history. At some point, there were enough of us to impact human culture. Maybe Shapers were once from here and moved on a great deal back? But from or to where? And how?" Tharen asked in amazement.

"I don't know exactly. What you just said does make some degree of sense though," Jaea said. "It feels right, which is strange. According to Nirah, I am from Caeldighn. If I traveled through a gate as a kid, our ancestors could have used a similar gate to come to Earth. And if I walked through a gate from there to here then it should work in reverse. In theory anyway." She shrugged.

8

"In theory, I suppose," Tharen said. "Wait. You're going to try to go back, aren't you? I can see it on your face."

Jaea reached over to return her glass to the small table beside the swing. "Yes," she said decisively. She squared her shoulders and raised her head defiantly. "I am going to try to find the gate. I have an idea where it might be." She leaned back and set the swing in motion again with her feet.

"When did Nirah tell you this that you made up your mind already?" Tharen asked, giving her a sideways glance.

"Right before you woke me up. Don't look at me like that. I needed to process it a bit, and we were talking about other things earlier," Jaea said defensively.

They sat in silence for a few minutes, each lost in their own thoughts. Tharen stopped the swing and turned to look at Jaea.

"When?" he asked, the solitary word seeming to hang in the space between them.

Jaea shrugged. "I don't even know if I will be able to find the gate. And I have goodbyes to say before I try for it, just in case."

Tharen felt his anger rising even as his heart plummeted. He must not have succeeded in keeping it from his face because Jaea laid a hand on his arm.

"Tharen, what is the matter?"

Tharen stood and took a few steps away from the swing. "When Jaea?" He felt like there was an invisible boa constrictor tightening around his chest.

Jaea wouldn't meet his gaze, locking her eyes on the ground instead. "I was thinking next month."

"Next month?" Tharen repeated incredulously. "So you graduate and then just drop of the face of the earth? You aren't planning on going by yourself are you? That really doesn't sound safe."

Jaea patted the swing seat. "Sit down please."

To humor Jaea, Tharen returned to the swing.

"Correct me if I'm wrong, but this is my best chance to learn about my family. It is also our best lead on information about Shapers in general. We know next to nothing. We've tried to dig up something on people like us for years. I'd have to be insane not to jump at this opportunity."

"I suppose you have a point," Tharen said. "But leaving Earth! Weird fantasy or sci-fi travel through gates..." He shrugged. "Kind of a big deal. Those are the sort of plans one usually discuses with friends and family before acting on."

Jaea gave Tharen a sour look. "Do I look like I am embarking on a trip right this second? I'm not even wearing shoes. And this conversation, about said trip? I was under the impression I was talking it over with a friend."

"How did I so quickly lose this argument?" Tharen asked.

Jaea shot him her most winning smile. "There's my grumpy sarcastic buddy!"

Tharen decided not to grace that comment with a reply .

Jaea turned to face him, tucking one foot under her. "I have two questions."

Tharen arched an eyebrow. "Only two?" He grinned when Jaea rolled her eyes. He turned, mirroring her pose. "Two for me you mean. Ask away."

"Will you help me piece this together? Finding the Gate and Caeldighn?" Jaea asked nervously.

"Of course. If you really want to leave."

"I have to try to find my sister."

Tharen nodded, then hung his head. "I know."

Jaea tilted Tharen's chin up so that he was looking at her again. "Come with me?"

Tharen didn't answer, didn't move; just stared at her. He was afraid to reply. There was a good chance he had just heard what he wanted to hear and not what Jaea had actually said.

"Tharen, will you come to Caeldighn with me?" Jaea

repeated.

Tharen grinned. He started to lean forward to kiss Jaea before remembering he wasn't allowed to do that anymore. "Of course," he said pulling back. He cleared his throat. "Someone has to keep you out of trouble, right."

Jaea nodded, her reluctant smile telling Tharen she noticed what he had just done. He hoped it wouldn't be this awkward between them forever.

The front door set of a cheerful jingle of bells that Tharen assumed meant Opal was back from the store.

"We should head in. Opal may need help with dinner," Jaea said quickly.

He saw hope flared in Jaea's eyes as she grabbed the excuse like a life preserver. "Right. Okay." Tharen rose and straightened his shirt.

Tharen followed her back to the house, hurrying to hold the door for her when they reached it. "Birthday girl first," he said politely. He smiled, hoping to ease the tension he had created between them.

"Thanks." Jaea smiled back as she walked in and deposited her shoes by the door.

After dinner, Jaea and Opal went through their usual routine to clean up. Opal let Jaea help clear the table and load the dishwasher. In return, Jaea let Opal chase her out of the kitchen after those few allowed tasks were completed. Once Opal had finished tidying up, she wandered into the living room where Jaea and Tharen were sitting on the couch, pouring over a book.

"What are you two up to now?" Opal asked as she sat down in a recliner by the window.

"Tharen was showing me some pictures he took in Ireland. They are beautiful," Jaea answered getting up to bring the album to Opal. "This one is my favorite so far." Jaea pointed to an image of a boy and his dog.

"Is it the only one with a critter in it?" Opal teased.

"No, there are a couple in there," Tharen said. "That boy and his dog followed me around for most of two weeks though. His parents ran one of the inns I stayed at."

"What is the plan for tomorrow, chickadee?" Opal asked as she continued to flip through the photos.

Jaea picked a graduation announcement out of the basket of papers near the phone and flopped back onto the couch. "Commencement at one p.m. I have to be there by noon. Mom and Dad said they plan on being here around eleven. The whole thing is set to end at three, but it will take at least half an hour to meet up again, say a quick goodbye to the department, and shoo the proud parents and their picture taking on out the door. Then we all head back over here to socialize and be merry, while Mom and Opal ban us from the kitchen to whip up a small feast!"

"Sounds good to me," said Tharen heartily.

"We will do a quick lunch then, before we head out. We can't have you passing out on us halfway across the stage," Opal decided. She handed the photo album back to Tharen. "You have got some beautiful shots in there, kiddo."

"Thanks, Opal."

"Oh, before I forget, Jaea, what time are you meeting Caleb on Sunday?" Opal smiled as she stressed the name Caleb in a way that made it clear she thought him a suitable match for Jaea.

Jaea rolled her eyes at the teasing tone in Opal's voice, but answered the question. "We are meeting at eleven thirty at the pizza place by campus. I don't know if I will be back here by dinner or not. I want to run a theory or two by him while we are both still in town, and you know our debates can get lengthy. Would you mind if he came over that evening?"

"Of course not, the more the merrier. Just give me a call Sunday afternoon and let me know if I am cooking for just

Tharen and I, or for you two also."

"Actually, I was hoping Tharen would join us for lunch. I know Caleb would like meet him. If you're up for it, Tharen."

Tharen nodded. "I am not aware of any pressing plans that day, but I don't want to intrude on your time with Caleb. He may not appreciate the additional company."

"Are you kidding? He will be ecstatic. Especially since he thought he wasn't going to get the chance to meet you, what with you being in another country and all."

Opal laughed. "Well that settles it, four for dinner Sunday. You lot don't have a smidgen of a chance of being done with all your chit chat by dinner." Satisfied with that conclusion, she reached for the television remote. "Now, I am going to watch Jeopardy. You are welcome to join me or move your conversing elsewhere. No hard feelings either way."

"I think we will hole up in the study and talk a little longer. It's been a while," Tharen said as he rose from the couch. He kissed Opal on the cheek. "Thanks again for putting me up. Good night."

"You are always welcome in my home, and you know it. Now scoot before I miss the next clue."

Jaea followed suit by pecking Opal on the cheek and quickly moving out of the line of sight for the TV.

Settling into a chair in the study, Tharen looked questioningly at Jaea. "So tell me more about this Caleb fellow. And whatever it is we will be discussing."

Jaea let her hair down. She stuffed her hair tie into her pocket and crossed the room to the big armchair next to Tharen. Once seated with her legs folded under her, she arched an eyebrow at Tharen. "What do you want to know? His level of intelligence or our level of intimacy? I'm not sure either is any of your business."

"Are you dating him?" Tharen asked.

"No."

"Opal seems to think differently."

"Opal likes Caleb. He is a likable guy. He drove me home after a lecture one night and won a spot in Opal's heart forever."

"So why are we having lunch with your 'not boyfriend'?" Tharen asked, confused.

"Because he is a friend, and I enjoy good company," Jaea said simply. "He is also something of a rival of mine, academically. We have had a number of classes together and we have similar focuses, despite him not being an English major."

"What did he major in that had so many similarities to literature?"

"History." Jaea smiled. "Anyway, I think he may be able to help us with the gate issue. The three of us together ought to be able to come up with at least a couple viable theories based on what we have run across in our studies."

"Is he a Shaper?" Tharen asked, intrigued about the idea of finding another person with his and Jaea's ability.

"Not that I am aware of. He doesn't know that we are either. I am just really comfortable with him. He has been a good friend. And he is brilliant. Caleb is the one that did the paper arguing that alternate planes could exist for that science class I hated. By the end of his presentation even that cranky professor agreed that Caleb's theory would be difficult to disprove."

"No kidding? This kid is starting to sound more and more interesting," Tharen said.

Jaea nodded. "He is a good guy. A little distant sometimes, but a great sounding board. The only trick will be enlisting his help without unintentionally revealing our secret."

"We should come up with a solid story. We could probably chalk all our interest up to academic curiosity. It seems the both of us have done research on similar topics so it shouldn't be hard to at least appear detached from what he would see as

14

hypothetical."

Jaea nodded her agreement. "Won't be difficult. Rather used to hiding the truth by now, aren't we?"

Tharen knew that having to hide being different had never settled easily with Jaea. They had argued the point until each of them had given up trying to change the other's mind. To Jaea, it would always seem like she was lying. She agreed with Tharen and her family that it was necessary, but she hated it. So Tharen wisely left the comment alone and changed the subject. "Any chance we could schedule in a trip to the beach before we head to your parents' place? I was thinking we could go by there before we try to locate the gate, give ourselves a chance to practice a bit of Shaping. It won't do to enter some other world only to find our abilities rusty from disuse at the first sign of trouble."

"Good idea. I don't see why we couldn't. We have a few days before I head home. I wanted to make sure I had plenty of time to pack without being in much of a hurry." Jaea sighed and ran a hand through her hair.

"What's wrong?" Tharen asked.

"I don't think my parents are going to like this. They have been unbelievably cool about the Shaper thing, you know. I mean they raised me, some random kid that wandered into their life one day, even after they learned I was different. I don't want to hurt them, Tharen. And just thinking about leaving them hurts me. It's not fair that I have to leave them to find my sister." She threw her hands in the air. "And how sisterly can two people be when they have been apart almost twenty years?" She shook her head. "What if I can never come back? I don't know how to tell them goodbye, Tharen."

A teardrop raced down the left side of Jaea's face, quickly followed by one on the right side. It hit Tharen suddenly how hard this was for his friend. He didn't have family ties like she did. He knew that Jaea's family, the Harbours, Doc, and Opal, cared about him. Tharen cared for them too, but they were her family much more than his. Tharen only felt that close to Jaea. And he was one of the few people Jaea let see her emotions. She had learned early to keep a tight reign on them and to mask them from other people, partly to keep from accidentally Shaping.

Tharen walked over to Jaea and pulled her out of the chair into a hug. "We will figure this out, Jaea. It won't be goodbye," he promised. "Now, Miss Graduate, you should put this from your mind and get some rest. Big day tomorrow. Funny hats and flowers and all that important stuff."

Jaea laughed and gave Tharen a shaky smile. "Thanks. For everything." She hugged him again. "Night."

"Good night, Jaea."

CHAPTER TWO

The next couple days seemed to fly by in a blur. Jaea remembered frantically getting ready for graduation and her dad ushering her teary-eyed mother out of the house. The ceremony itself didn't quite seem real at first with all her professors and classmates parading into the stadium in formal black gowns, the colors denoting their fields and honors scattered among them like an upturned box of crayons. Speeches were made, and degrees were awarded. Jaea cheered for her friends as they proudly crossed the stage and blushed when they applauded her in turn.

After the tassels were turned and everyone paraded back out, Jaea found herself bustled along in a sea of people hurrying to tell fellow classmates and their favorite teachers goodbye. Well wishings, plans to meet later, teary partings with promises to keep in touch, and laughter in abundance filled the air. Mixed in with the odd melody were the clicks, beeps, and flashes of cameras trying to catch it all. Jaea's pride in earning her degree was diminished some by the knowledge that she may not get a chance to use it, but she pushed that from her thoughts as best she could, determined to enjoy this time with her family.

Sunday morning a very apologetic Caleb called Jaea to let her know that he wouldn't be able to make lunch because his family was taking him out to some fancy restaurant. He was so happy when Jaea suggested he join her and Tharen for lunch and some mild debating later in the week that Jaea wondered if she should brush up on her old 'Myth, Legend, Lore' notes. They set the date for one o'clock Wednesday, and Jaea spent the day packing up some of her room instead. Tharen tried to convince Jaea that she should tell her parents and Opal her plan to leave before they met with Caleb, but she decided to wait until the weekend to break the news. She wanted to wait until Saturday, after the party her mom had planned to celebrate her birthday as well as her graduation. That way everyone she needed to tell would be in one place at the same time. Tharen finally agreed that might be best and helped her plan out the rest of their week. They decided to leave for Jaea's parents' house Friday which, with the Caleb lunch planned Wednesday, gave them three days to have things packed and a solid argument for leaving ready to present to Jaea's parents.

Monday dawned dreary and rainy with the promise of a good storm coming in. Fat raindrops splattered against the window Jaea was staring out, trying to hold her excitement in check. She smiled when she heard Tharen come into the kitchen and greet Opal. She turned to look at Tharen, her eyes blazing with anticipation. "Ocean," she said. "Ten minutes. You may want to put on a shirt. It's chilly." Then she took the picnic basket Opal had insisted on packing and made for the truck.

Tharen joined her outside just a few minutes later.

"Mind if I drive?" Tharen asked.

"Fine by me." Jaea tossed him the keys and walked around to climb in the passenger seat.

Tharen navigated through town without once having to consult Jaea on directions. Jaea hadn't quite decided if she appreciated his memory or if it annoyed her that he could recall these roads so easily. It had been her town much longer than his, she reasoned.

"I like this truck," Tharen said, breaking the silence. He brought the Ford F150 up to the highway's speed limit and changed the setting of the windshield wipers. "You've had it, what, three years now?"

"Almost four," Jaea said. "Doc kind of got it for me. Not long after you left. I wrote you about it."

"I remember. Sometimes your letters were so full of news I could imagine I was still at Doc's."

Jaea looked away from Tharen's smile to hide the hurt of being reminded how few of those letters he had answered. The quiet took a turn toward awkward.

"Will there be trucks in Caeldighn?" Tharen wondered aloud.

"You know, I have no idea," Jaea said surprised. "We'd better enjoy it while we can."

"Absolutely. The radio work in this thing?" Tharen asked.

"Would I have survived years of driving between campus and home with a busted radio?"

"Point taken." Tharen laughed.

Jaea turned the radio on and immediately began to sing with the song playing. She made dramatic faces at Tharen, who in turns laughed or pantomimed along with her. When the song ended and a more laid back tune came on, she turned the volume down and laid her arm along the window feeling the cool of it against her skin. She let her mind wander the rain-soaked roadside. *Would Caeldighn look like Earth?* Thinking about appearances reminded Jaea that she didn't know how Maya looked, since twins weren't always identical. *For all I know Maya is short and blonde. How am I going to find her in a completely foreign world?*

"Penny for your thoughts?" Tharen asked.

Jaea shook herself out of her reverie at Tharen's question. "Sorry, wandered off for a bit there I guess."

"What were you thinking about?"

"Everything and nothing. Mostly though that I am glad you

are going with me."

"Well, I could hardly pass up the chance to Shape," Tharen said.

"Not today, you goon, I meant to Caeldighn. I am glad you will be going with me. Or helping me find it anyhow. Though I am looking forward to Shaping with you today, too," Jaea told him.

"Jaea dear, if you try to leave without me, I will follow you," Tharen assured her. "Any idea how we are going to go about locating the place?"

"Not much," Jaea admitted. "So far the plan is as follows: some quick researching, try to dream of Nirah again, tell the folks goodbye, seek out the gate I walked through originally somewhere in Mom and Dad's woods."

"And Caleb may be of help in this plan because..." Tharen prompted.

"Because his senior thesis was titled 'The Other-World Element in Legends of Old and Modern Culture'. He focused some on supernatural pathways to elsewhere."

"Yep, that'll do it," Tharen said. "What are you going to tell him though? He will likely want a reason for your inquiries."

Jaea shrugged her shoulders. "Undecided, though I have two ideas. One is to keep the conversation firmly in the theoretical. A just for kicks, how to find a gate brainstorm. The only other option I have come up with is to tell him I intend to try locating and using a gate and would like his help in composing a plan for doing so."

The truck sped past a sign proclaiming the assortment of seaside shops and dining choices available at the next exit. "I love that sign! It means we are almost there!" Jaea exclaimed as she dug a couple protein bars and some cookies out of the bag at her feet and offered some to Tharen. They made short work of the snacks as Tharen turned onto High Street. By the time they

20

had driven through town, they were in the process of polishing off a bottled water.

"The usual?" Tharen asked. "Free fall, practice, food, last round?"

"Sounds good. You wearing your seaweed?"

Tharen pulled the collar of his shirt down, revealing the dark green of the sleeveless wetsuit Jaea had made for him.

Jaea nodded her approval, then began untying her shoes. She had found she could make cloth of sorts from small amounts of natural materials. Items made from such cloth, like their swimsuits, would stay with them while Shaping. Needless to say, it was preferable to have clothes on when returning to one's human form. "You Shaping from the start or you want a ride to the cliff?"

Tharen pulled into a parking spot a ways down the beach. "Up to you. Care to give me a lift?"

"I'll run you up there. I could use the practice carrying a passenger anyway. Just let me run a circle or two real fast first."

They climbed out of the truck and surveyed the coastline. Seeing that it was completely empty, Jaea let out a cheer and started shrugging out of her outer layer of clothing until she stood in the parking lot in a dark green, one-piece swimsuit. She shivered once as the light rain hit her skin. She shot Tharen a quick grin before darting down the beach, bare feet kicking up wet sand as she ran.

Jaea sprinted down the shore, reveling in the feeling of freedom. She wanted to thunder across the sandy expanse like she had seen horses do in movies. So that is exactly what she did. She thought of hooves kicking up turf and of a mane and tail flowing behind her racing form. *Four powerful legs. Four strong hooves. Arching neck. Glistening black coat. Mane the color of midnight.* She felt herself drop to all fours and her face change. The violet vines that marked her upper right arm in human form shifted to fit the

21

right foreleg of the horse she had Shaped into. Today she let her marking stay completely visible instead of dimming its color. It was not a day for hiding she decided. She felt the wind play through her mane and tail. She saw the plumes of air she breathed out her nose turn foggy. Jaea turned abruptly and reared on her hind legs. She whinnied a joyful call to the cloud laden sky then dropped back to all fours and raced toward Tharen. She came to a halt a few inches from him, sending sand skittering across his bare feet.

Tharen smiled at her as he shook his feet out of the sand. "Black today, huh?"

Jaea pranced in place a bit to show how pretty a horse she was.

"And boldly Shaper, too," he said as he ran his hand down the bright purple vines.

Jaea arched her neck and bobbed her head once. She bumped her head against Tharen's chest and stamped one of her front hooves twice.

Tharen nodded. "I'm ready."

Jaea folded her legs under her to make it easier for Tharen to climb on her back. Once he was settled, he patted her neck, and she rose up again shaking her head. Tharen wound his hands into her mane and tightened his grip with his knees.

"Okay," Tharen said.

Jaea took a few steps at a walk to get used to the feel of Tharen's weight, then broke into a run. She ran through the surf for a while, making Tharen laugh as she chased waves randomly. A few minutes later, they left the water and made their way closer to the rocky cliffs farther down the beach. Jaea slowed as the shore began to rise and walked the path to the top.

Tharen slid to the ground and strolled toward the jagged line where the ground abruptly met open air. He stood looking out over the water as Jaea shaped back into her usual form.

"Gorgeous isn't it?" Jaea asked as she moved to stand beside him.

Tharen nodded. "All those clouds and the churning water. I can feel it pulling me like a fish on a line, reeling me toward it."

"I think I will fly with you a bit today if you don't mind the company."

"Of course I don't mind. I don't have many opportunities to fly with others, you know. What shape are you taking?"

Jaea grinned. "Same as yours. Too hard to keep up if I shape into anything smaller. Well, that and I can still only take that form when I am around you."

"Just using me for the wing span. I see how it is," Tharen joked. "Best to get a running start I imagine," he said as he turned away from the view.

"Well, you use me for my legs so I guess we are even," Jaea replied as she followed him away from the cliff face. She laughed. "You know, saying that to anyone else would be awkward."

Tharen shook his head. "It's still a little awkward. I feel like I need to be on the look out for your Dad trying to snipe me just for the wording."

"What was that?" Jaea asked. She saw a strange flickering light out of the corner of her eye.

"I said if your Dad heard that comment I'd be in trouble," Tharen repeated.

"Not that, I heard you. I thought I saw something, well, glow," Jaea mused.

"Something glowing? Like lightning in a cloud?" Tharen asked sarcastically, pointing up at the brewing storm.

"No, on the ground over there." Jaea pointed. She moved to get a closer look. "Like something reflecting light." Jaea got down on all fours and began sweeping the area with her hands. She found what she thought may be an old silver brooch lodged in the ground. Jaea gave a tug with a triumphant shout. She looked up at Tharen from her seat on the ground and held up her find.

"What is it?" Tharen asked. He offered Jaea his hand and pulled her to her feet.

"It's a key." Jaea dusted it off. Two graceful silver spirals curved around an empty circle to form most of its head. This then flowed down into a smaller oval flanked by more spirals. "An odd key. It almost glows. What's up with that?" She handed it to Tharen.

"Hmm. It does sort of glow. Weird. It looks familiar for some reason, like I have seen a picture of a similar one somewhere. It was just stuck in the ground here?" Tharen handed the key back to Jaea and knelt to look at the place she had pulled the key from.

"It does seem familiar now that you mention it." Jaea turned it over in her hand. She held it up for a moment admiring the juxtaposition of the key and the looming storm clouds. Then it flashed. "Tharen." She looked closer and sure enough, the key was pulsing light. "Tharen! Something is not right with this key!"

Tharen returned to her side just as the key's flashing increased. "Uh oh, that can't be good."

Lightning shot through the clouds behind them unseen. The resulting crack of thunder made them both jump. They instinctively moved to stand back to back, an old habit from years of facing bullies together. Jaea closed one hand over the key and reached behind her to make sure Tharen was okay with the other. Tharen clasped Jaea's hand as she extended it back to find his.

That was how the Keeper saw them as he walked over the rise. "Some said you were a doomed pair," he declared. "But I always knew you had greatness in you."

CHAPTER THREE

Tharen shifted to stand at Jaea's side and face the odd character that had just come out of nowhere. He thought the short fellow looked something between an old renegade sea captain and St. Nick. The red sash around his waist holding a massive key ring and a number of jangling keys said "pirate" as much as the strange tattoo twined around one forearm. The bulging bag he dropped at his feet when he got closer screamed "Santa."

"Who are you, and how do you know us?" Jaea demanded.

"Well, I know I have not seen you in a few years, but what is time like that to you and I? Don't you recognize your old friend Ransley? How did you come to be here though? I never thought you for a key thief, Nirah."

Jaea seemed too taken aback to correct him about her name and simply stared at the stranger.

"And how would you happen to know Nirah?" Tharen demanded.

"Nirah and I have been friends since long before your kind arrived in Caeldighn, little Shaper," Ransley said stiffly. "A fact you well know, and one that I grow tired of repeating." He sent Tharen a grudging look, as if remembering past conflicts with the man before him.

"Enough!" Jaea yelled. "Please sir, step closer and better

observe your companions. Then kindly tell me how you know of Caeldighn, my stone enclosed friend Nirah, and the people known as Shapers."

Ransley picked up his bag and closed the distance between himself and the two confused Shapers. As he came closer, he began to look just as confused and wary as Jaea and Tharen. "Hmm, not Nirah." When he was a foot or two from them, he dropped his bag to the ground again. "Maya?" he asked, leaning toward Jaea a little. "No, not Maya. Who are you girl? And why do you have my key?" Ransley demanded.

Tharen glanced at Jaea long enough to see that while the first mention of Maya had drained the color from her face, fury at this stranger's tone was quickly returning it. Tharen smirked at Ransley and crossed his arms over his chest. He had seen this side of Jaea before. Soon there would be answers, or else Jaea would have Ransley's head on a platter.

Ransley chuckled. "No wonder I mistook you for Nirah. Well, my dear unknown Shaper girl, I am the Gatekeeper who made Caeldighn's first key. That key." He nodded toward Jaea's hand where the glowing light showing through her clenched fist was slowly fading. "Nirah is of that land. That is a fairly long story in itself, and I don't think you've the patience for it just now. I know of Shapers because less than one hundred years after Caeldighn came to exist, Shapers took refuge there. Another story there, again for later. We can discuss as much or little of all this as you like, once you answer me two things. First, please turn your arm toward me so that I can see your mark more clearly. Then I need to know how you came by that key."

Jaea looked at Tharen. When he only shrugged, Jaea nodded. "I found the key stuck in the ground here a few minutes before you showed up." She turned her arm to show the purple vine that wrapped around it.

Ransley stepped nearer to inspect her arm. He looked up

sharply, meeting Jaea's eyes. "Jaea?" he whispered.

"How do you know my name!"

"By all the known keys in the universe, it is you! I need to sit, I think." And so he did sit, a mite harder than he had planned.

Tharen thought that sitting would probably be best for Jaea, too. She looked as though she may faint at any moment. He knew her well enough to know that suggesting so would earn him a shiny new bruise. So he kept his mouth shut, merely putting one arm around her and gesturing to the ground with his free hand. Jaea nodded and allowed him to help her sit without the jarring impact Ransley received.

"I don't suppose you have anything to drink in that bag?" Tharen asked Ransley.

"Drink?" Ransley nodded his head uncertainly. "I hope so. Some tea? That or a nice whiskey," he muttered as he began to rummage through the bag's contents. In a matter of moments, he had placed a camp stove, a teapot, three blue camp mugs, and a rounded box clearly marked 'Tea' on the ground in front of him. After another moment of mumbling, he produced what looked like a toolbox with a triumphant "Aha!"

"Ransley, have you ever heard of Santa Claus?" Jaea asked.

Ransley paused in preparing the tea to let loose a loud laugh. "I have. And no, I am not him."

"Just checking. You can start in on how you know my name any time," Jaea prompted.

"Right." Ransley pulled a large bottle of water out of the toolbox and set the kettle on the now lit camp stove. "Rusty hinges. It's still a bit of a shock is all. Seeing you all grown up and here of all places."

Jaea arched an eyebrow at Ransley.

"Answers. Right." Ransley rubbed his hands together as he gathered his thoughts.

Tharen smiled to see that his friend had not lost her ability to encourage others to talk.

"Everyone in contact with Caeldighn knows the name Jaea McClanahan," Ransley began. "I, at first, mistook you for Nirah, because you look so much like her, especially from a distance. Though, come to think of it, I'm not sure Nirah can leave Caeldighn. I don't know Maya well, or I imagine I would have noticed your resemblance to her more quickly. Nirah and I are quite close. She isn't always encased in stone. I have seldom seen her in such a way. And you, boy. You I mistook for a ghost. Unlikely though it seems, it would not have been the first time I saw Nirah's husband in spirit form. Aye, she was married, pick your jaw back up, dear."

"She never mentioned..." Jaea sputtered. "Did she have children?"

Ransley smiled. "She did. But let's skip ahead in the story here. Do you remember how you came to be on Earth?"

"Not really. I remember talking to a rabbit and sitting under a big sycamore tree to catch my breath a bit. And then I met Mom and Dad." Jaea shrugged.

"Your parents?" Ransley asked incredulously.

"Adoptive parents," Tharen told him a bit defensively. "Jaea wandered into their yard one day, and they took her in. They are the best people you can hope for as parents. Even after they learned she was different."

Jaea put her hand on Tharen's arm. "I don't think he meant anything by it. Did you know my real parents then?"

Ransley nodded solemnly. "I did, though mostly by reputation. How did you know they were gone? You were so young when you were taken, I wasn't sure you really understood."

"I knew they were deceased. When I first met mom, I apparently told her that my parents had gone to the stars. I remembered that I had lost Maya, my sister, and was trying to find her. Mom finally assumed I was talking about an imaginary friend when I spoke of her. And after a while I believed it too."

Steam shooting out its spout, the kettle began to whistle. Ransley quickly turned off the stove. After popping the lid off the kettle, he dropped a large tea bag into it. Shaking his head, he looked back at Jaea. "Maya is definitely not imaginary. She lays flowers on your stone every year on your shared birthday. Not that she ever allows anyone to see her do so." Seeing Jaea's head tilt down at the mention of the stone, he quickly added, "It's not a grave marker. Maya refused to let anyone place one on your parents' plot for you. Just a stone in the garden with your name and your Shaper mark on it." He pointed at the purple vine spiraling down Jaea's arm. "She has a stone as well, your parents put them in. Honey in your tea?"

Jaea and Tharen both nodded.

Ransley spooned a generous dollop of honey into each cup before filling them with tea. He handed the Shapers their mugs as he continued his tale. "You and Maya were in a caravan en route to your aunts'. Your parents had named them your guardians. But the caravan was attacked, and you were thought to be kidnapped. By your memory, though, I would say you escaped your attackers, and thank the powers that be you did. They were a nasty lot, working for those that wish to see someone from a previous ruler's line take back Caeldighn's throne. Some of the same group managed a shot at the queen of the time that day. She was dead by the time your sister arrived at the castle."

Tharen saw his own confusion reflected back at him on Jaea's face. The furrow in his brow deepening, he looked back at Ransley. "Uh huh."

Ransley tapped his pinky against his mug and sighed. "After the attack on the caravan, the remaining escorts took Maya to the capital, fearing your aunts' home had been compromised.

Your aunts are Chiefs, you see, and the guard overseeing your move couldn't be certain that the rebels hadn't targeted your Aunt Adrielle before coming to attack you. So he took Maya and your things to your Aunt Jayla at the castle. Which turned out to be for the best as I hear it. Maya and the queen's daughter, Kaylee, were able to console each other in their grief. A child's heartache is often difficult for those who are not children themselves to understand. They struck up a friendship and have been near inseparable since. Aurora, she was Queen Sarai's sister-in-law, has been acting ruler since the queen passed; she can't get anyone else to do the job. I'll not even try to explain the politics right now. That is an entirely different conversation. Caeldighn has not been the most peaceful land in your absence. You should know that before you return. You will be a target once the rebels realize who you are. They attacked your caravan to eliminate the threat you posed, and you and Maya certainly posed a threat. You come from very old Caeldighn lineage and arguably had legitimate claim to the throne. They will think you aim to take the throne yourself."

"How do you know she means to ever go back?" Tharen asked. "She is doing quite well here, you know. Why should she go back to a people that never bothered to look for her, to get herself shot at?"

Jaea held up a hand. "What do you mean? Legitimate claim to the throne? I just want to find my sister!"

Ransley smiled sympathetically at Jaea. "The key came to you. Tricky things, keys off their rings. I do not believe it would have if you did not intend to return. Besides, I am a superstitious sort. I heard a riddle once about a lost key and a missing sister. I could take you to Caeldighn now if you liked," he offered.

"I can't! I haven't even told my family I am leaving yet," Jaea said panicked.

"That's fine. Better even, to leave when you are ready,"

Ransley assured her.

"But I don't know how," Jaea protested. "I have barely the slightest idea how to get back. Tharen and I have been mulling this over and haven't come to much conclusion. We plan to meet with a friend of mine who has researched folklore dealing with gateways to other places. Beyond that, all I can think to do is search the woods I came through for the millionth time in hopes of stumbling upon the door to Caeldighn."

Ransley laughed. "That's a better plan than you realize. Keep with it. Say your goodbyes and gather what you can for supplies. Then go the woods again, but this time with that key." He pointed to the key lying at Jaea's feet. "I will give you a string for it, so it will shape with you and not stray to someplace else. My advice, leave for Caeldighn in the next two weeks if possible. The Council meets early next month, and unrecognized travelers will be the norm across the country with folks coming out of the woodwork to head toward the meeting. For now though, drink your tea, and let's see if there is anything helpful I can tell you."

"How about where the gate is?" Tharen asked dryly.

"I gave you the key!" Ransley exclaimed. "What else do you want, a three dimensional pop-up map?"

"Well, yes actually," Tharen said. "That would be great."

"Sorry, kid," Ransley said. "Some things you have to do yourselves. There are rules. You understand?"

Jaea nodded and took another sip of her tea. Deciding it was too cold to just sit around in a swimsuit, she put one hand to the grass to make a covering out of it." What is she like? My sister?" As she talked a green cloth of sorts knitted its way across her shoulders. "Is she happy? Does she even want to see me again after all this time?" She put her hand on Tharen's shoulder for a moment, and the grass green material began creeping up his arm as well.

Ransley poured a little more tea in his mug. "I would be

honored to tell you of your sister. Though I fear my knowledge stems mostly from her reputation. I can tell you that she looks a bit like you, tall with black hair and green eyes. Maya is mostly happy, I'd say. She has a great knowledge of her country stemming from her deep love of its history, and that has made her is very grounded, focused. She is training to be a Chief like your aunts. So if you miss her at the Council, you may try the capital. That, my dear," he said pointing to the two green blankets that had appeared around his companions, "is very good work. I have seen few who could manage it so quickly. You may even be near Maya's skill there."

Tharen concluded right then that he liked Ransley. He had just made Jaea incredibly happy, revealing that she and her sister had even something so small as a skill in common.

"I think seeing you will be a bit of a shock for Maya," Ransley continued, "but she will be glad for it all the same. Oh, I need to get you that string." He dug around in his bag for a moment, his entire right arm disappearing into its depths. When he found what he was looking for, he tossed it to Jaea.

Jaea caught the small bobbin of string and began to thread it through the key, tying it off when she had unraveled enough to wear around her neck. The string above the knot instantly frayed and separated itself from the rest. She looked at Tharen, a question on her face as plain as day. Tharen gave her an encouraging nod, silently agreeing and prompting her to lead.

"Ransley, how do we know we can trust you?" said Jaea.

Ransley looked at Jaea and Tharen in turn, straight in the eyes. "You are Shapers, yet you are not trying to shape into something big and mean to rip me apart. Instead, we are sitting to discuss what is a foreign land to you over a cup of tea. I realize that I did just essentially come out of nowhere and may have come off gruff at first. I can appreciate your wariness to trust me, but I suspect you have already determined that you could do so.

Am I correct in this assumption?"

Tharen shrugged. "For the most part, though I am not entirely certain why, and my general belief is to trust no one but Jaea completely. No offense meant, sir."

"None taken. And you?" Ransley asked Jaea.

"I find myself trusting you to a rare degree," Jaea admitted. "Just be warned that if you try to cause us harm, I will do everything in my power to ensure that our next meeting is not nearly so pleasant. I do not know if one of my abilities could challenge you, but I promise I would live long enough to make you regret crossing us."

"Yes, very understandable that I first mistook you for Nirah." Ransley chuckled. "I hope we have chances to chat again. I find I enjoy your company." Ransley began to repack the bag beside him. "Rain coming in again. Give me a shout when you and the key are in the woods ready to set out. Unless something prevents it, I will escort you to Caeldighn's gate. If I'm busy and don't show, don't worry. That key will bring another Keeper to help you."

"It was nice to meet you, Ransley. I think." Tharen shook hands with the Keeper.

"This will shape with me? And stay on no matter where I go?" Jaea asked gesturing to the key around her neck. "It isn't going to suddenly start glowing again is it? That could be troublesome."

"It will hold, as sure as keys open locks, and no it won't glow again until you are at the gate," he said amused. "Until next time, Shapers." Ransley winked and disappeared, leaving as quickly as he had come. Jaea and Tharen looked at each other as the wind increased, slanting the curtains of rain that had begun to fall the instant Ransley vanished.

"Well, that was interesting," Tharen stated.

Jaea nodded. "I could use some air. You still up for a bit of Shaping while we are here?"

"Absolutely," he answered with a grin.

The two threw the green blankets from their shoulders and ran toward the ledge. As the Shapers changed form and leaped into the air, the blankets were caught up on the breeze and tossed skyward briefly before they unraveled, leaving only a few blades of grass to fall to the ground.

CHAPTER FOUR

Caleb Stone walked carefully across the cafe, his goal being only that he not spill the three drinks he carried. A lock of his sandy blonde hair fell across his forehead. When he reached the table, he triumphantly set an iced tea in front of each of his companions. He brushed his hair out of his hazel eyes and smiled at Jaca. "I figured we should stick to a classic. Besides, I know it's your beverage of choice." He sat down and turned to Tharen. "I have heard Jaea talk of you so often I feel as though we met years ago. I am glad to have the chance to actually meet you."

Tharen sipped his tea and laughed. "I am glad to have the chance to meet you as well, especially after Jaea told me where your academic focus is usually centered. I have studied similar topics, with the exception of portals to other, well, places."

A grin stole across Caleb's face. "I could talk your ears off with my opinions on gateways, but I want to ensure I see these Ireland photos I have heard tell of before I launch into that and lose all track of time. May I?" he asked, pointing at the album on the table.

Jaea poked Tharen. "Told you he would want to see them."

Tharen pushed the book toward Caleb and flipped it open to the page Jaea requested.

The talk continued as Caleb admired Tharen's work with a camera. As the subject turned to gates and those who may have used them, Jaea suggested they walk while they talked. The conversation was studded with Jaea or Caleb pointing to things that had changed about campus since Tharen had transferred abroad. Eventually they settled under one of the large trees shading the commons.

"So we agree then that there is a possibility that such openings into other worlds may actually exist?" Jaea asked.

"I think it is beyond a shadow of a doubt," Caleb said. "There are too many strange happenings that seem to stem strictly from relation to a location to honestly believe otherwise. Of course, I would never say something so bold in print or in uncertain company for fear of finding myself in one of those fancy coats that make you hug yourself all day."

"But how would a person go about finding and then utilizing such a gate?" Tharen asked.

"Well, I am under the impression that you two have already found one, but I promise I won't press for details. I would hate for you fine individuals to clam up on me now." Caleb noticed that Jaea and Tharen paled slightly, but pretended not to. "You see, I have little desire to actually use a gate myself," he explained. "I would much prefer to stay where I am and hear back from such travelers occasionally. So I will simply take this time to hint that I greatly enjoy postcards." He winked at Jaea.

A look crossed Tharen's face that made Caleb suspect Tharen saw right through his plan for a quiet life on Earth. He wondered again just what Jaea had told her friend about him. Maybe Tharen was simply trying to warn him away from Jaea? That was more likely, Caleb decided.

"Anyway." Caleb coughed. "Finding a gate? Hopefully to begin, you are seeking a known gate. You know, one that has a bit of a record to follow. If that is the case, try to search the area where the gate is believed to have been, or still be, for clues or markers. It would be best to be there around the time the gate was supposedly open before. In most cases, there is something physical to indicate the gate's location. But, since you are picking my brain on the matter, I am going to go out on a limb and say you have your hearts set on a more unknown gate." He raised his eyebrows in question.

Jaea fiddled with her necklace and offered no answer. Tharen seemed to have taken an interest in something on the horizon and likewise ignored Caleb's question.

"Right. Well, in that case the tactics differ. Generally, individuals seeking unknown gates are actually seeking particular places: somewhere that they claim to have been before and now can't find or a place they visited in a dream or vision. Keeping the thought of that place in mind as the goal helped in some of the stories I read. Look for something extraordinarily ordinary. Something that your eye wants to pass over unless you are focused on seeing it." He paused a moment, thinking. "Watch the animals, they will sense the difference before you will. And above all, trust your instincts. In some tales, there is a test to pass or a secret code for passage. So if you feel suddenly like knocking on the trunk of a tree or throwing a penny into a puddle, I suggest you give it a go."

"You have given me a lot to ponder, Caleb, as usual," Jaea said. She was still twirling whatever hung on the necklace.

"A lot to ponder," Tharen agreed. "Like what should I do if I find myself on the other side of a gate and there aren't postcards to be found?"

Caleb laughed heartily. "I suppose a regular old fashioned letter would suffice."

Silence settled over the little group, and Caleb's brain lurched into overdrive. A handful of details connected and began to form a much different picture of the people he sat beside. Finally, Caleb could take the curiosity no more. "What is that?" he asked, pointing to Jaea's necklace.

"Oh, just some key I found," Jaea said.

"May I see it?" Caleb asked.

Jaea hesitated. "I don't see why not." She shrugged. "I have been wearing it since I found it. Sort of a good luck charm, I guess." She held the key out for Caleb to see.

Caleb felt his heart stop. This was certainly unexpected. "It looks pretty old," Caleb commented. "Such a unique design. It is a beautiful good luck charm."

"Thank you." Jaea smiled as she let the key fall back against her shirt.

Caleb's gaze was drawn to the purple vine decorating Jaea's arm when she tucked a flyaway strand of hair back in place. He had never given it much thought before and just assumed it was a tattoo. How had he never noticed it was a Shaper mark?

"I don't think I've ever see your whole tattoo before," Caleb told Jaea.

"Really?" Jaea asked. "Well, I guess I don't wear tank tops all that often."

"It's impressive," Caleb said.

"Thanks." Jaea smiled. "I like it."

The big campus clock loudly chimed the hour and made the group realize how time had passed.

"We should probably head back to Opal's," Tharen said.

"I should be getting home, too." Caleb offered Tharen a hand. "It was good to finally meet the infamous Tharen McKenna I have heard so much about."

Tharen shook Caleb's hand. "I enjoyed meeting you as well, Caleb Stone."

"Jaea," Caleb said. "Always a pleasure. I guess I'll see you around."

Jaea grinned. "Look for my postcard."

"Will do." Caleb smiled back.

As Caleb walked home, he mentally reviewed the information

that had just fallen in his lap. "She is a definitely a Shaper," he said to himself, remembering the violet markings he had seen on Jaea's arm. "And not just any Shaper." For that matter, Tharen was no more human than Caleb was a bird. "Father will know what to do." Caleb found himself regretting having befriended the girl, though Jaea had been a good friend, and those were hard to come by. He shook his head to dispel such thoughts, he of all people knew family duty must take precedence over personal life. He had to tell his father. Jaea had the key to Caeldighn. She was one of the enemy, or at the very least on her way to becoming the enemy. Hadn't she stolen the key from his father? There was no other explanation for her having it. He noticed absently that he had reached his front door.

"The Stone line must be restored to Caeldighn's throne." Caleb nodded decisively. Mind made up, he strode through the door, set straight for his father's study, and knocked.

"Enter," Mr. Stone called in response.

His father was standing at the window, looking out into the garden, when Caleb came in. "I have news of the key."

"Let's have it," Mr. Stone said curtly. It was a tone Caleb was used to, having rarely ever heard his father speak more kindly.

"It is on a string around Jaea Harbour's neck. She and her friend Tharen seem to know the location of the gate. I know her, Father, she will leave within a few days now that her mind is made up."

"Not much chance to retrieve it then?"

"Not likely," Caleb agreed. "And there is more."

"Spit it out," Mr. Stone said gruffly. "Your first revelation requires a great deal of attention."

"Jaea is the lost twin. I saw her Shaper mark today."

"You are certain?" Mr. Stone asked. His eyes lit with a greedy calculation that Caleb couldn't quite write off as mere ambition or excitement.

"Absolutely," Caleb confirmed.

"This is extraordinary news, son! Not only of the key, but of the movements of our greatest enemy. The missing twin," Mr. Stone said happily. "We will have to move our plan forward. I will contact the family, and we'll leave Sunday morning. If she goes through Caeldighn's gate with the key it will only be open for two days." Mr. Stone clapped Caleb on the back. "We have work to do. Send Sam in on your way out."

Stamping down the feeling that he had just betrayed a friend, Caleb nodded to his father and turned to do as he had been bid.

C820

Late Friday afternoon, Jaea stood in her now empty room looking at the space that had so perfectly suited her over the last few years. Tharen had helped load all her boxes into the truck that morning. The space was clean even to Opal's standards. Jaea had put fresh flowers in the vase on the bookshelf, but the desk looked huge without her books scattered across it. The bed looked lonely and bare jutting out from the wall. Jaea sighed, feeling empty herself and dreading saying her goodbyes. But she had to try to find her sister. Nothing outweighed that duty. She turned, walked downstairs and out of the house, locking the door behind her. Opal had left to do some grocery shopping and would be leaving for Mom's in the morning.

Tharen was leaning against the truck bed when she came outside. "Ready?" he asked.

"As I'll ever be," Jaea said as she opened the driver's side door. "Mom is expecting us for dinner."

"You okay?" Tharen asked as he climbed into the passenger seat.

"Undecided." Jaea gave Tharen a small smile. "I'll be fine."

The sun was beginning to set when they drove through their

small hometown. A few minutes later, the truck's tires turned off the paved county road to crunch down the gravel driveway to the house Jaea had grown up in. Her parents, Ben and Maggie Harbour, jumped up from their seats on the porch to welcome their daughter home again. Their excitement extended to Tharen as well. So many hugs were passed around the small group that an outsider would have thought it had been years since they were together instead of just a few days. Ben took Jaea's duffel bag when Tharen pulled it out of the back of the truck.

"If you have all you need for the night in this bag, we can move your truck into the carport and get the rest out in the morning," Ben suggested.

"Yep, I just need that one for now," Jaea said. "Unless there is a monsoon coming in tonight, the tarp will keep everything good and dry till we get to it tomorrow."

"By we, she means you and I," Ben told Tharen as he slung the bag over his shoulder. "My wife will likely kidnap Jaea tomorrow so they can get caught up on all their girly talk."

Blue eyes full of mischief, Maggie put her arm around Jaea. "He's right, you know, my girl. I do intend to keep you all for myself till I feel caught up. We will just let those strong men folk haul in that load. It's good for them. Keeps them out of trouble."

"I am not opposed to this plan." Jaea smiled.

Saturday's party kicked off when Maggie and Opal had the table set to their standards, completely loaded down with way too much food. Everyone filled plates and headed out to scatter across the back porch. When everyone had eaten their fill, Ben declared it time for presents and everyone went to get their gifts for the graduate.

"Be right back." Ben grinned at Jaea.

"You just stay right there," Opal told Jaea as she headed

inside. "You move from that spot and I'll eat your share of the cake, little miss."

When they all gathered on the porch again, Doc insisted on going first and handed Jaea a box wrapped with brown package paper and twine. Jaea opened it to find a canteen with a horse decorating the face. She ran her fingers over the flowers around the edge. "Doc, I love it!"

"Well, there is more in the box, you goose," he said.

Jaea returned to the box and pulled out a small wooden circular object that easily fit in her palm. It bore the same floral pattern and horse emblem. She was surprised to see a compass inside when she opened the lid. She skipped over to Doc and kissed him on the cheek. "They are beautiful. Thank you."

"Recognize the flowers?" Doc asked her with one eyebrow raised.

"Derby, Belmont, and Preakness," Jaea answered, laughing as she hugged him. She had been watching the Triple Crown races with Doc since she was a little girl. Every year they huddled around the small television in his veterinarian clinic hoping to see one beautiful thoroughbred make history by winning all three races. It was their own little tradition.

"My turn!" Ben said. "I want a kiss too!"

Jaea felt like the most loved person in the world as she looked over all the gifts she had opened. They knew her and loved her so well. That message came through loud and clear in both the gifts and the faces of those who gave them. She had a necklace from her father, an amethyst violet on a gold chain. He had clasped it around her neck as soon as she opened it. There was a leather bound sketchbook and some new drawing pencils from Opal. Her mother had presented her with a charming bracelet that matched the violet necklace, as well as a fashionable clutch style purse. From Tharen, a travel size picture album so she could easily carry pictures of those she loved wherever she went.

She had no idea how to tell them all she was leaving, and the knowledge that she would soon have to do exactly that weighed on her heart.

Someone produced a deck of cards, and Tharen went to get the pitcher of lemonade to top off everyone's glass before the game started. Maggie patted the seat next to her. "Sit here next to me, my girl." Small talk circled the table while the group fell into the pattern of the card game. A couple hands in Maggie nudged Jaea with her elbow. "I think perhaps you should tell me where you are going now, so I can be used to the idea before I have to start dinner. Fire and sharp objects and all that. You don't want me distracted then, do you?"

"How did you know I plan to go somewhere?" Jaea asked.

Ben laughed from the other side of the table. "Sweetheart, you haven't unpacked a thing yet, and you have been dodging questions about your post graduation plans. Give us some credit, little one."

"And here I thought I had done so well!" Jaea shook her head. "I was trying to figure out when to tell you. I knew it should be today while we are all together. Just harder to bring up than I thought. I didn't want to just drop it on you and yell surprise."

"Best to just fill us in," Maggie encouraged.

"Alright then." Jaea sipped her lemonade, suddenly nervous. "Do you remember me talking about Maya?"

"Hard to forget," Maggie answered. "She is almost all you talked about for years."

"Do you remember me telling you about Nirah?" When her parents had both nodded, Jaea continued. "I dreamt of her again on my birthday. She told me that she had figured out our two biggest questions. One being why I go there so often in dreams, the other being why I was looking for Maya there the first few times." Jaea took a deep breath and quickly told them the rest. "I am from a place called Caeldighn. Maya is my sister, my twin in

43

fact. She lives there, in Caeldighn. That's where I came from when I stumbled through your woods and into your yard that day. So I am going back to find my sister. It could be dangerous but I can't pass up this chance to learn about people like me and find my family." She glanced around the table to try to gauge their reactions.

Doc was the first to speak. "Well, we knew you had to be from somewhere and that it wasn't likely to be anywhere we knew of. People don't simply turn up suddenly out of thin air, with no traces of a past to be found, especially not ones with your particular abilities."

"Is Tharen going with you? To find your sister?" Maggie asked, her voice quieter than usual.

Jaea and Tharen nodded.

"Is Tharen from there too?" Doc asked.

Tharen shrugged. "Not that I am aware of. But if it is a place where people like us live, then they might know something about my family as well. We are something of a rare breed here," he answered with a small smile.

Jaea looked at Ben and then Opal. Neither had spoken yet. Ben was rubbing his chin with one hand.

"How?" Ben asked. "How do you get there?"

"A gateway of some kind, back in the woods," Jaea explained. "I walked through it once to get here. It must have been closed since, but now I know how to open it."

"When do you set out?" Ben asked.

"As soon as possible," Jaea said apologetically. "There is apparently a meeting among their government officials soon, and we wouldn't be seen as unusual since there will be so many people traveling to attend it. It will give us time to understand the situation before drawing too much attention to ourselves."

"You should leave early on Tuesday then," Opal said. "Wednesday night is supposed to bring a lot of rain so you want to give yourselves plenty of time to find and get through your gate before then."

Jaea looked at Tharen. "Work for you?"

"Sounds good to me," Tharen answered.

"Tuesday it is then." Jaea let out a deep breath. "To think, I've been a wreck wondering how to tell you all this."

Maggie put her arm around Jaea's shoulders. "It isn't easy letting you go, but we always knew we only had you on loan, sweet girl." She sighed. "Do you think you will be able to come back?"

Jaea leaned her head on her mother's shoulder. "I found my way here once, so I have to believe I can do it again. I love you people too much to leave forever."

"Alright ladies, hold the waterworks till Tuesday," Ben warned. "I intend on living in denial on this whole matter until Monday night if at all possible. Right now we have cards to play!" He grabbed the cards and dealt out another hand as laughter floated around the table.

CHAPTER FIVE

Tuesday morning saw a sad gathering in the Harbour living room. Opal had brought a pack chock full of provisions and made Jaea promise to share the cookies with Tharen. Doc gave Jaea one of his vet books and Tharen a tin with matches, a pocket knife, and the unmistakable bright blue spare key to his house. Opal and Doc said their goodbyes to Jaea, then pulled Tharen into the kitchen with them to let Ben and Maggie talk with Jaea alone.

"Back to being Jaea McClanahan, huh?" Ben asked, tweaking Jaea's nose.

Jaea stuck her tongue out at her dad. "You adopted me, so you're stuck with me for good, and I get to keep your name."

"Of course you are still a Harbour, goof," Maggie chided. "But you are also still a McClanahan." She put her hands on Jaea's shoulders, giving them a quick reassuring squeeze. "It's your birth name, honey. Take pride in that and get to know your birth family. It won't make you any less a part of this family."

Jaea's eyes welled with tears despite her best attempts to keep them in check. She suddenly threw her arms around her parents, desperate not to leave. "I promise," Jaea said fiercely. "I promise if there is a way back I will find it."

"You had better," Maggie told her, reluctantly stepping back with Ben. "Otherwise I may just have to find a way into

Caeldighn. Come on, we'll walk you out."

At the door, Jaea and Tharen hugged everyone one last time. They hoisted their packs and were on their way. At the tree line, Jaea and Tharen looked back to wave before stepping into the shaded woods.

"Well, the hard part is over," Jaea said with false enthusiasm. "Now we just have to find a gate to another world and navigate said world to locate my long lost twin." She wiped a tear from her cheek, hoping Tharen wouldn't notice. She pulled the key out from under her shirt and patted the pocket holding the compass Doc had given her.

"Piece of cake," Tharen agreed cheerily. "So, what exactly is our plan for the gate finding bit? Because Caleb's input didn't really clear that up for me."

"He said in stories there are two types of gates: those clearly marked and those not. I would guess ours is of the not marked variety since we haven't noticed it in all the years we have been playing out here. Meaning, according to Caleb's research, that we pretty much just have to follow our instincts, even if they seem silly. Thankfully, we also have the key, which I am hoping will guide us somehow and tip Ransley off to our presence. Then he opens the gate and ta-da! Caeldighn."

Tharen nodded. "So we wander aimlessly, and I eat all of Opal's cookies."

Jaea bumped his arm with her elbow. "No, we go to the big sycamore back this way to start because that's where I stopped to catch my breath coming from, wherever, before I wandered into mom and dad's yard. Then we will see where instinct, the key, and our limited knowledge of gateways to other worlds leads us."

A short time later found them at the sycamore Jaea remembered. Tharen suggested they keep going south, and so they did. After a hour or so, it was unanimously decided that the whole plan was crazy. The key apparently did not feel like doing its bizarre glowing trick or anything really other than hanging from Jaea's neck. Tharen had begun to knock on tree trunks at random, hoping one would reveal its true nature as a magical gate. Jaea had eaten a large amount of spiderwebs inadvertently while investigating an arch made by two trees' drooping branches. This reminded Tharen that they had not yet eaten lunch so he pulled two sandwiches out of the pack from Opal, while Jaea finished pulling spider web and leaves from her face and hair. On then the pair walked another couple hours. They stopped next to a stream bed that only ever ran with water after a good rain. Tharen sat on the bank and set to locating the cookies Opal had sent. Jaea paced the currently dry waterway, occasionally kicking at or picking up rocks to send them clattering further down the bed.

"I do not understand. I thought for sure the key would have tipped us off, or given us a clue by now. We have walked all over these woods and circled that sycamore, what, three times?" Jaea asked annoyed.

Tharen pulled the cookies out with a triumphant shout. "Here. Food for thought. Always a sure-fire solution to get the gears grinding again."

Jaea slumped next to Tharen and took the offered cookie. "Mmm. I love Opal. Think she would make us more of these if we completely fail to find the gate?"

"Probably, but knowing her she would just send us back out to try again. 'Right thing to do, find your roots' mumbo jumbo."

"Probably," Jaea agreed smiling.

They ate a few cookies in silence and then forced themselves to put the others away in order to conserve resources a bit. Jaea drew hearts in the dirt while Tharen took a turn chucking rocks. An idea hit her, and she leapt to her feet, startling the robin that had been watching her.

"Tharen! Where does the creek end that way?" Jaea asked

excitedly.

"East? I have no idea. We never went past here when we played. We usually went west back toward Doc's woods so we could visit with his patients before we had to go home," Tharen answered.

"Why did we never go that way?"

"Well, Jaea, because, well, I'm not sure." Tharen scanned the eastern path of the creek skeptically. "Shall we?"

"Yes! Best lead we have had all day!"

Glad to have a plan again, Jaea and Tharen hoisted their packs and resumed the search. They had only walked a few minutes before they stopped to collect a few choice rocks. Jaea called them back to their mission, and they set off determinedly. But they were having an unusually difficult time focusing on the task at hand. It was as though some unseen force was purposefully distracting them to prevent the pair from proceeding further east. The friends fell in step together out of habit and wasted a chunk of time trying to throw each other out of step. Tharen's comment about finding Maya pulled their search back into focus. Then a low hanging branch caused them to reminisce their childhood adventures, playing in these woods all those years. They started up a competition to see who could throw a stone the farthest, which soon had them stopped again to argue who won. When the breeze began to pick up and surround them with the smell of rain they knew they needed to get a move on it. Apparently, the rain wasn't going to wait for its scheduled arrival time on Wednesday afternoon.

"I can't believe we have only come this far!" Tharen exclaimed looking back over the ground they had traveled.

"It does seem strange. We have to cover some more ground today. Let's keep going. First rumble of thunder, we stop and pitch camp. Deal?"

"Sure. Are we certain this is the right way?" Tharen asked.

49

"Tharen, we have yet to be certain of anything, but I am determined to try it. Come on!" Jaea said impatiently.

"I am coming. I am coming," Tharen grumbled.

As they continued, Jaea began to walk closer and closer to the right side of the creek bed while Tharen veered farther and farther left. Then for no reason at all they joined back up in the middle a few feet later. Jaea stopped abruptly.

"What's up?" Tharen asked looking from her to the seeming empty western woods, trying to figure out what had stalled her.

"Why did we do that?" Jaea asked, studying the area in front of her.

"What did I do?"

"We hugged the banks like we were walking around something."

"Weird, we did." Tharen bent to pick up one of the small stones in the stream bed.

"Why?" Jaea demanded, hands on hips.

Tharen threw the rock. It sailed straight down the middle of the bed, then suddenly veered right and landed on the bank.

"The gate! It has to be!" Jaea yelled jumping up and down. "Right?"

"Dunno. It's something for certain," Tharen answered.

They walked around both sides, looking for all the world like mimes with their hands trailing along something invisible. It was completely solid all the way around. There were no openings of any sort. No visible change since discovery. And nothing at all resembling a key hole. Jaea walked all the way around it again with the key in her hand, but neither it nor the solid block of air showed any reaction. She even tried calling for Ransley. When thunder began to roll in the distance, Tharen pointed out a good spot for the tent that was well within view of area in question.

"We can take shifts tonight. See if there is any change," Tharen suggested.

"Yeah," Jaea replied dismayed. She was certain this was the gate, which only made it more frustrating that she couldn't figure it out. "Let's not unpack any more than absolutely necessary though okay? I want to be able to bolt through that thing if it opens."

Tharen had finally convinced Jaea to get some sleep, promising at least fifteen times to wake her if anything even remotely small appeared to change. He checked the perimeter of their campsite to reassure himself they would likely stay dry in the tent, and that said tent was far enough from the stream bed as to not find itself afloat. He sat down under a tree and stared into the dark as the rain began to fall. Occasionally he rose to shine his flashlight onto the creek just to keep tabs on the amount of water gathering there. He made sure to shine the light toward the gate as well, in case it had decided to cooperate. He was supposed to wake Jaea for her watch in a couple hours, but planned on letting her sleep. He could tell by her eyes that she hadn't been sleeping the last few days, and so intended to let her get what rest she could. She would probably yell at him when she did wake up, but it would be worth it if some of the shadows left her face. Three hours later he had gone over what was passing as their plan, made a flower chain out of some nearby clover, tried to estimate the amount of rainfall the creek was swelling with, cursed the rain a few times, and eaten four cookies. Boredom threatened to swamp him, so Tharen began to mentally recite one of the songs he had learned in Ireland to further commit it to memory. He had no idea that he was humming it. And he could not have told you when he began to quietly sing. Tharen was certain though, that for the rest of his days he would be able to recall with perfect clarity the moment he stopped singing that night.

The hair stood up on the back of Tharen's neck as the air

filled with a strange scent. Then time seemed to stand still as everything around him was thrown into high relief, like an enormous flashbulb camera had just captured an image: Jaea running toward him with her hand gripping the key, the open tent door, the tree sparking where lightning connected with it, and the ghostly outline of Caeldighn's gate reflected on the water of the rapidly filling creek. An ear splitting crack of thunder, the click of the camera's shutters, and time rapidly began again as if making up for that lost minute. Tharen stood dumbstruck, his hand pointing to where his eyes claimed to have seen the impossible.

"Tharen! Are you alright?" Jaea shook him trying to get his attention. "Tharen!"

Tharen closed his mouth, which had apparently dropped open in surprise. His arm fell back to his side as he turned to look at Jaea. "I think I saw the gate. Or Caeldighn. Maybe both."

"Tharen! Are you okay?"

"Yes." Tharen blinked hard and rubbed his hands over his eyes. "Yes, you?" Suddenly concerned, he looked Jaea over for injuries.

"I'm fine. The key briefly went crazy, but it stopped as soon as the lightning's flash did."

"Did you see it? The gate?"

Jaea shook her head. "All my attention was on the key trying to Houdini away and then whether or not a tree was falling on you. I don't see it now, though, either," she said, shining Tharen's flashlight in the gate's direction.

"No, the flashlight doesn't show it." Tharen looked at Jaea inquiringly. "Is this whole trip going to be weird?"

"That would be my guess, yes. However, right now you're going to take a trip to bed. You were supposed to wake me hours ago."

"Not sure I could sleep. Sit with ya for a while?"

"No, to bed with you, sir." Jaea pointed at the tent. "I will wake you at first light."

"Right. Sleep. Good night." Tharen kissed Jaea on the cheek and walked toward the tent.

Tharen woke on his own just as Jaea was rising to get him. "Hungry," he grumbled in response to Jaea's questioning look. Tharen glanced at the creek. It showed no sign of the gate's presence in the gray-pink light of morning.

"No change as of yet," Jaea said.

They ate breakfast in silence as the sky slowly grew brighter. Tharen ducked his head to keep the sun out of his eyes. When light continued to shine in his face, he shaded his eyes and looked around, trying to locate what seemed intent on blinding him.

"Jaea?" Tharen said deliberately.

"Hmm?" Jaea was looking up at a little red bird hopping about the tree branches.

"Jaea," Tharen said urgently. "The key is glowing again."

Jaea quickly looked down and grabbed the key. "The gate?" she asked hopefully.

Tharen shrugged. "One way to find out."

Jaea followed Tharen to the creek and studied the place they suspected held the gateway. They viewed the area from different angles as they paced their side of the creek and still saw no change, though the key continued to glow brighter.

"Maybe we have to stand in the creek? Look straight at its front? Or back?" Jaea suggested.

"What I saw last night looked like the gate's silhouette almost, when the lightning flashed. In that instant it also reflected a clear image of the gate on the surface of the creek." Tharen turned eastward and glanced toward the ever brightening horizon. "The flashlight showed us nothing, but lightning, arguably natural lighting, did. Maybe we just need a little more natural light yet."

Jaea cocked her head. "The key has only reacted during lightning and now with the sunrise. Speaking of the key."

Tharen turned back to Jaea. The key was pulsing with a bright light and straining against the string that kept it around Jaea's neck. It stuck straight out away from her in the direction of the gate, like a compass pointing north. Jaea gasped and pointed at the water. Tharen looked just in time to see the ghostly image beginning to form. It continued to develop until a crystal clear picture of what must be Caeldighn showed on the creek's surface and a shimmering door, featuring the same ornate pattern as the key, stood in the center of the creek.

"Wow," Jaea whispered, stepping toward it.

"Packs!" Tharen exclaimed, quickly returning to their camp. What few items laid about found themselves unceremoniously stuffed back into bags. He hoisted their belongings and ran back to Jaea, who had taken the key from around her neck and wadded into the creek.

"I vote we abandon the tent," Tharen told her as he swung his pack onto his shoulders then carried Jaea's into the stream to stand beside her. His feet and calves did not appreciate the cold water, but he was too excited about the gate to think much about wet feet. "Brought your stuff." Tharen slid the bundle onto Jaea's shoulders as she passed the key between her hands to put her arms through the straps. Then he fastened Jaea's walking stick to her bag like he had already done to his own.

"Thanks," Jaea said.

"Yep. Now what?"

"Umm. Ransley?" Jaea called. "Ransley the Gatekeeper? I would love a word if you do not mind."

Nothing happened. The gate continued to shimmer in the air before them and the image of Caeldighn continued to reflect in the creek around their feet. She looked at Tharen. He nodded.

"Ransley!" They shouted together.

A form appeared on the creek bank opposite their camp; a short, thin man who sneered down at them. He wore a sash around his waist like Ransley's, but with a smaller ring of keys.

"Ransley is currently needed elsewhere. So I've been sent to see if I can assist you," the Keeper told them. He sounded as though someone had filled his morning coffee with sand, and his demeanor was nearly hostile.

"And you would be, who exactly?" Jaea asked as she settled the key back around her neck.

"I would be Morgan, exactly." Morgan stepped down the bank and fumbled with his keys. "Here's the deal, kiddos," he sneered. "I open the door with this key." He inserted one of his keys into the gate and turned it. He took his key out of the door and gave it a small push. The shimmering form swung open to reveal the image they had seen reflected on the creek. "Then you give me Ransley's key and mosey away on into Caeldighn, thus allowing me to return to my breakfast."

"Why?" Jaea asked. With the gate open, the key no longer strained toward it but fell back against Jaea, still glowing.

"Why what, Shaper brat?" Morgan retorted.

"Why would she give you Ransley's key, Morgan?" Tharen demanded.

Morgan stood as tall as his small frame allowed. "Because I am a Keeper. You two are not. Keys belong in the hands of Keepers. I will return it to its proper holder."

"Morgan, my dear, I find I just do not believe you. I thank you for aiding our entrance to my birth land, but I will not be releasing Ransley's key into your custody. Good day." Jaea nodded to Morgan and began to walk through the gate.

"Stop right there, you!" Morgan yelled. "I have gone out on a limb here to retrieve that key. I must insist you hand it over."

Jaea looked down at the Keeper, her green eyes steely. "I dislike repeating myself. Ransley can reclaim his key when next I see him. I do not trust you in the least. Goodbye."

"Best not to test her. She has not had any caffeine yet this morning. So long," Tharen said, smiling as he followed Jaea through the gate.

Neither Jaea nor Tharen had noticed the one legged mocking bird that flew over the top of the gate as they passed through. Morgan did however, and the sight made him beat a hasty retreat. If he guessed correctly, that bird was one of Stone's men, which meant he could be in bigger trouble than he first thought.

As Jaea moved past the ornate door, both it and the key ceased to shine. When Tharen was beside her again, they waded through the Caeldighn side of the creek until they saw an easy place to climb out.

Back on dry land, they took stock of their surroundings. They were standing at the edge of a small group of trees that clustered around the stream, with a large field spread out in front of them.

"It looks a lot like Maine," Tharen said. "Well, more flat that way. And warmer."

Jaea arched an eyebrow at Tharen.

"Okay, maybe not Maine." Tharen laughed. "At least it resembles places we have been on Earth."

Jaea smiled. "We're in Caeldighn."

"Yep. Kale deen." Tharen sounded out. "Now what?"

Jaea glanced at her compass. "Well, if the compass is correct, this way is North."

"North is good," Tharen said. He eyed the fat gray and white clouds above them. "I hope these clouds keep the rain to themselves, though. I'd like to dry out a bit before getting drenched again."

"North it is then." Jaea put the compass back in her pocket and started forward. "Here goes nothing."

Tharen fell in step beside her. "Jaea?"

"Yeah?"

"Welcome home."

"Thanks." Jaea grinned. She pointed at something in the distance. "Race you to that road!"

"What road?" Tharen yelled, running after her.

CHAPTER SIX

Caleb Stone had grown up knowing that gateways to other worlds existed. His father frequently talked of their ancestor who had been king in one such land. Caleb himself had been born in Caeldighn. He and his family had lived there, happily, until they had been forced to flee. However, this did nothing to diminish his awe of the Caeldighn gate. Right in front of him, in the middle of the woods, was a portal to another world. Caleb's father came to stand beside him.

"Beautiful isn't it?" Mr. Stone asked. "That is our family's heritage, waiting to be reclaimed. My man tells me Morgan opened the gate for Jaea this morning. I sent some of our people through right off to get things ready for us and to alert our people in Caeldighn to the twin's presence. Thanks to your having found her I was able to give them a description of the brat and her companion." He clapped his son on the back. "I would have recommended killing them both before they have a chance to cause us trouble, but that worthless Morgan failed to retrieve the key. With luck they will both be in custody by tomorrow evening."

"Is it possible that she simply wishes to be reunited with her sister and not take the throne?" Caleb asked. "If she has been on Earth all this time she may not be aware of the Riddles' predictions."

"Doubtful. They cannot be trusted, the McClanahans. Don't worry, my son, the twins will be taken care of. Soon our family will sit on Caeldighn's throne once more. Now come, we've much to do." Caleb's father walked through the gate, never doubting that his son would follow and that his men would bring their belongings as ordered.

For a moment, Caleb entertained the idea of simply running away. Then he squared his shoulders and stepped boldly through the gate to the land of his ancestors.

಩಩

Jaea and Tharen noticed the buildings at the same time. Tall grasses and clumps of trees had blocked the houses from sight before.

"Let's try there shall we?" Tharen asked hopefully.

"Sure. At the very least we may be able to get a better idea of where we are going."

Jaea found she was both incredibly excited and incredibly nervous at the idea of meeting people in her native land. It was a feeling she had experienced at least once a day since Nirah confirmed Maya's existence. She took a deep breath and tucked the renegade emotions away, to examine later when she was alone and could process them.

"Don't forget that you aren't going by Jaea yet," Tharen reminded her. "If Ransley was right, I would prefer to not become targets for assassination by an angry rebel group."

"Of course. Janna Harbour forgets nothing. Except for the things we need to find out, like where in Caeldighn are we and which way is this Council thing if it has not already happened."

A short time later they discovered the houses were part of a small town apparently called Shannen, as that was the name scrawled across its few businesses. Shannen boasted an inn, a pub, and a general store advertising a sale on stationary in one of its front windows. As Jaea and Tharen made their way toward the inn, a horse and rider drew to a stop in front of its door. The rider slid off the chestnut horse and pulled a pack down from the horse's back.

"Thought my spine was going to spear clean through my skull!" the lanky rider complained to the horse. "Your gait is terrible!"

No sooner had the bag's straps brushed across its back than the horse reared. Before Jaea could really react, the horse had quickly Shaped into human form.

"Tell you what, friend. You learn to Shape into something that can keep up with a horse, and I will work on my stride," retorted the other Shaper. "Until then, I suggest you limit your conversation to thanking me for covering so much ground."

There were few others walking the road and the evening was quite still, so Jaea and Tharen caught most of the pair's continued banter. When the two Shaper men disappeared into the inn, Jaea looked at Tharen, and they both broke into laughter.

"That answers that. Shapers are definitely not uncommon here," Jaea said amused.

"It is going to take getting used to, though. More than I thought it would," Tharen admitted.

Jaea nodded in agreement. She realized with a start that was the first Shaper, other than Tharen, she had ever seen Shape. She shrugged off the feeling that Caeldighn had many surprises in store for her. "Well, no time like the present. Let's go meet some Caeldighnians."

As they came to the inn, a group of people was leaving. One of the men in the party plucked a flower from a nearby planter and offered it to Jaea with a wink before rushing to catch up with his friends.

"He gave me a flower," Jaea said, smiling as she tucked it behind her left ear.

Tharen opened the door and tried to usher Jaea inside.

Jaea was secretly amused by Tharen's frown." A flower," she repeated happily as she stepped inside.

"I saw," Tharen muttered, following her in.

Jaea barely had time to take in their surroundings when a large man rose from his seat at the front desk.

"Welcome to the Shannen Inn. I am Graeme, the owner of this establishment," Graeme said with a small flourish. "Can I help you folks?"

"We were hoping to board here for the evening if you have space available," Jaea said politely as Tharen moved to her side.

"Ah, you are in luck. We've one room left this evening," Graeme told them. "Meals are included in the fee. Shelia can help you rustle up some chow once you've settled your belongings. Shall we put you fine people in the books?"

"That sounds lovely, sir. I don't suppose you would let us wash dishes or something to settle our tab?" Tharen asked hopefully.

"No money, eh?" Graeme asked skeptically. "Where are you bound in such a hurry that you forgot to bring coin?"

"We are going to the Council meeting if we make it in time. The capital if not," Jaea told him. "I recently learned I have family that way. It was quite a shock actually, as I thought I was alone in the world save my friend here."

"Well," Graeme said, sounding surprised. He tugged on his beard as he studied Jaea thoughtfully. "I find that I believe you. You had truth in that tale somewhere. And my son is fond of you, I see." He pointed to Jaea's flower in explanation. "Dish washing won't do though, I'm afraid. However, if one of you can carry a tune and will play bard for a few hours I will gladly give you the room."

"Done!" Tharen exclaimed shaking Graeme's hand.

"Splendid! If I had to listen to Benton the Bard of Bloomdale again I may have gone mad. Man just can't sing. Have you ever heard a man who can't sing try to sing in the old Irish?" Graeme shuddered. "Now then Mister..."

"Tharen McKenna," Tharen filled in. "Do you mean Benton sang in Irish Gaelic?" he asked intrigued.

"Yes, supposedly, he studied at the Dragon University for a year to learn. He is human, you see, and language doesn't come as easily for him as it does some of his fellow bards. Still, man should have stayed longer if you ask me. Now then, Tharen, if you could just sign in here. And Miss..."

"Janna Harbour," Jaea said, offering her hand. She hoped she sounded convincing. Most of the name was true.

"Janna Harbour," Graeme repeated, somewhat disappointed. "Settles that I suppose. Thought for a moment you were someone I met a good many years ago. She didn't go by that name, though." The innkeeper shrugged dismissively. "Well Miss Janna, if you could sign here. Thank you. Now then, let's show you to your room."

An urgent knocking brought Jaea quickly awake around dawn. Tharen was standing to one side of the door, a knife in hand. He nodded to Jaea and gestured for her to stand at the opposite side of the door. She scrambled out of bed, wondering why things always had to be complicated with Tharen. She grabbed her walking stick en route to her post. The knocking began again. Tharen held up three fingers. Jaea nodded, tightening one hand around her makeshift weapon. Tharen counted to three and quietly slid the chair out from under the door handle. Jaea jerked the door open, causing the innkeeper's son to stumble into the room.

"Shut the door!" he whispered frantically.

Jaea moved to do as their unexpected guest requested. She

glanced around the hall before she closed the door and dropped the latch into place.

Tharen pointed to the chair. "Sit," he ordered calmly. "Explain. Now."

"My name is Jakes. We met briefly last evening," Jakes began hurriedly. He moved to sit down. "Two men rode in about an hour ago, claiming to be looking for a couple of friends. Thing is, you two match the descriptions of the folk these fellas are after. Father sent me up here to warn you and help you get out of here while he stalls them with breakfast."

"Why would your father want to warn us about these men?" Tharen asked.

"And how did they have a description of us?" Jaea demanded. She felt a chill shoot down her spine. Ransley had warned her of this.

"They are known Stone supporters," Jakes answered as if that explained everything.

"Stone?" Jaea asked, looking at Tharen in surprise.

Jakes nodded. "The Rebels. They side with the Stone family. My family remains loyal to the crown, even in its current state. It's a pretty good bet that whatever Stones want, we would prefer to prevent."

Jaea had a feeling the innkeeper and his son knew more than they were letting on. She bent down to look Jakes in the eye. "Spit it out, Jakes. What's going on?"

Jakes smiled sheepishly. "My father thinks that you are the lost twin. Maya McClanahan's sister."

Jaea straightened abruptly. "What makes him think that?"

"Father knew the family well, years ago. Says you look like Maya's mother when she was young," Jakes said shrugging.

Jaea glanced at Tharen, then walked to her bed and began to pull on her socks and boots. They needed to leave quickly, but she wasn't sure where they would be safe if she was so easily recognizable.

"Already with the hit men?" Tharen sighed. He folded his pocket knife and glared at Jakes. "How do we know we can trust you?"

"I told you, we are loyal to the crown. Besides, I'd sooner take a roll in dragonfire than cross the McClanahans. You're really her, aren't you?" Jakes asked, looking at Jaea in awe. "You are Maya's lost twin. Jaea McClanahan?"

Jaea paused in tying her hair back. "I've not gone by that name in a long time. I have been Jaea Harbour in most of my memory. But yes, I am Maya's twin. I think we should be on our way, Tharen." Jaea zipped up her bag and started to make the beds as Tharen tugged a shirt over his head and crammed his boots on.

"Why are you making the bed?" Jakes asked as he rose to help Jaea.

"If they don't look slept in it may be easier for your father to deny having offered us shelter," Jaea explained. "Soon the other guests will be wandering down for breakfast. If those men are after us, they will question the guests and put the pieces together, pretty quickly I imagine since Bard Tharen was so popular last night. They may start searching the inn."

"Have you encountered these fellas before then?"

"Nope, but that is what I would do," Jaea told him.

"I would wait till after breakfast personally," Tharen said wistfully. "Don't suppose our Stone admirers will let us eat before pursuing us to kingdom come though."

"Father has some provisions set at the back door for you," Jakes said. "If you are ready, I will lead you out."

"Jakes, my friend, lead on to the food and escape," Tharen said.

Jaea followed Jakes, Tharen right behind her. Jakes had them pause in the hall while he made sure they could cross the open space before them without being spotted by Stone's men. He pointed the men out to Jaea and Tharen from the kitchen doorway.

"Hopefully you can get to the capital without further trouble and never see these two again. The big one is pretty dense. The smaller fellow is meaner than a feral cat and twice as tricky. Now that you've seen them, you can steer clear of 'em." Jakes ushered them outside through a small mudroom off the kitchen. He hoisted a bag from its hiding spot behind a rain barrel and handed it to Tharen with a smile. "Breakfast is served."

"Not right now." Jaea smacked Tharen's hand and retied the bag. "In a bit of a hurry here, remember."

"Right." Tharen nodded. "Sorry."

Jaea turned to Jakes, intending to shake his hand in thanks. Jakes surprised her by dropping a kiss on the back of her hand instead. "It's been an honor to meet you, Jaea McClanahan Harbour." He handed her a small coin bag. "Father said this should get you a ways down the road. If you are able, I suggest you Shape into horses and run for all your worth. Good luck, and God bless!"

With that, Jakes disappeared back into the house, before Jaea even had a chance to thank him. She looked at Tharen and shrugged. "Care for a ride?"

"Sure," Tharen said nonchalantly as he took Jaea's pack.

Jaea kicked off her boots and tossed them toward Tharen. She briefly debated shimmying out of her jeans before deciding against it. Good jeans were hard to come by, but better to lose a pair of pants than strip out in the open like this.

"It's a beautiful morning to flee for our lives, don't you think," Tharen quipped stuffing her boots into her bag.

Jaea, who had already Shaped into a horse, stamped a hoof

near Tharen's foot.

"Yeah, yeah. I know," Tharen complained. He looped their packs together and settled them on Jaea's back before swinging up behind them.

Jaea shot off at a gallop the moment Tharen was astride. She ran as long as she could. She was forced to slow to a walk a couple times to catch her breath, and once or twice for a drink or a quick bite to eat. Since she was anxious to put more distance between them and the inn, she refused to stop for long. Thankfully, she was easily able to follow the directions she had received the night before. The sun was beginning to set when Jaea spied a grove the mapmaker had mentioned. She stopped to let Tharen down and bobbed her head at the trees.

"I'm going to go out on a limb here and guess that you'd like some clothes?" Tharen teased.

"Hurry or I'll just take your shirt," Jaea said impatiently.

Tharen laughed when she huffed and began to tug at the hem of his t-shirt. "I wonder if I will hear other Shapers the way I hear you when you are Shaped?" he mused.

"I imagine we'll find out soon enough. Clothes please, I'm tired of hooves."

"It's just that it still intrigues me," Tharen explained as he dug into her pack. "The whole, not quite English, but not really animal and still somehow in your voice, way of speaking when Shaped. Like right now, I hear you speaking, and I also hear a horse. I understand the horse part of your speech, just as I would any other horse, and I understand you just as I would when you aren't Shaped."

Jaea whinnied loudly in Tharen's ear.

"Ah!" Tharen winced. "What was that for?"

"If you can hear me talking, you should have heard me ask you to hurry up," Jaea said pointedly.

Tharen pulled out one of her pre-bundled outfits. "Well, here then. You can find a different set later, when you have hands again, if you don't like these."

"Thank you." Jaea gripped the small bundle in her teeth and trotted to hide behind the largest tree to Shape back into a human.

"Why I didn't wear Shaping clothes to begin with I will never know," Jaea said. She tied her hair back with a leather strip while walking back to Tharen and their packs. "Ugh, I think I could sleep for a week."

"You may need to," Tharen said. "You could have taken a break, and I could have carried you for a while. And don't say you were afraid we would be spotted. We've barely seen anyone on the road since it forked, hours ago."

Jaea glared at Tharen. "We don't know the range of forms Shapers take here, what is normal and what isn't. We couldn't take the risk, and you know it. So quit grumbling. I'm going to go sit before I fall over. You fire build, and I will fill you in on what I learned last night." She shouldered her bag and walked away.

Tharen caught up with her as she sat down beside a fire pit. Jaea pointed tiredly at a stack of firewood beneath an oiled cloth nearby. He set to the task Jaea had given him and arched an eyebrow at her.

Jaea took the hint. "While you entertained the masses, I spoke with a mapmaker. According to him, the inn is about two and a half days travel from the capital. Travelers often use this camp, and he asked that we replenish the firewood if we were able. The reason we have seen so few people is because the Assembly, as he called it, began this morning."

"So we missed it," Tharen said, adding sticks to the flame he had coaxed to life.

"Yep, most attendees are already there and any late comers would have been somewhere down the road that forked off this one earlier today. Maya would likely have been long gone by the

67

time we got there, if she even attended at all."

"Lame. Where do we head now then?"

"The capital. This road leads us straight there. We should get there by dinner tomorrow if we don't run into any problems," Jaea said cheerily.

"Remind me why the capital is our Plan B?"

"Two reasons." Jaea tried and failed to cover a yawn. "First, because Ransley said to try there since Maya was training for some official position. Where better to inquire about an official than the governing city? Secondly." She paused to yawn again. "Secondly, because it's likely the largest city, thus the most people to ask about Maya. Also, because we couldn't come up with a better idea."

"Right. Unless you want to eat the rolls I left for you, get some rest now. I'll stand watch."

"Okay," Jaea said laying her head on her pack. "Wake me up, well, sometime."

CHAPTER SEVEN

Tharen woke abruptly the next morning, startled by the sounds of conversation nearby and the smell of cooking food. Angry with himself for falling asleep, he took a wary inventory of the situation. Seeing that Jaea was no longer lying where she had so quickly fallen asleep the evening before, he wrapped one hand around his walking stick before jumping to his feet to confront whoever had overtaken their camp.

Jaea and Ransley, the Gatekeeper, looked up at him from their seats by the fire.

"Good morning, sunshine." Jaea laughed. "Care for some breakfast? Ransley makes some mean eggs and toast."

Tharen rubbed a hand over his face. "Hello again, Ransley," he said as he sat beside Jaea.

"Hello again, Tharen Shaper." Ransley grinned and handed him an empty plate and mug. "Tea in the kettle if you'd like a bit."

"Of course there is." Tharen filled his plate while Jaea took his mug and filled it with tea.

"So?" Tharen asked around a mouthful of toast. He took a quick sip of tea. "To what do we owe the pleasure, Ransley?"

"I sensed that my key was again in Caeldighn," Ransley replied. "I came to offer what assistance I can to get you to your destination. As I have already told Jaea, I truly had meant to be there to open the gate for you. A task came up that required my immediate attention though, and I was sadly unable to do as I had intended. Since I was not permitted the chance to grant you entrance, I thought I could make it up to you by seeing you safely to Maya."

Tharen motioned to Jaea. "She already told you about your slimy coworker?"

"Morgan? Yes, he and I will have to have a chat about how he treats travelers," Ransley said ominously. "Not to mention his interest in my key. Jaea was right to keep it. By our laws, since I gave the key into her keeping it is considered her property until I ask for its return. Never mind that now though, let's get to the matter at hand. I hear you have already had some trouble with Stone's men. Jaea asked earlier if I knew the reason she's a target. We decided to wait until you awoke before delving into that can of worms, so that the tale need only be told once. It's a ways to the capital, however, and if you do not object I would prefer telling it on the way." He looked at Jaea for confirmation.

"Works for me," Jaea said getting to her feet. "I want to find Maya as soon as possible. But I would prefer to know a little more before someone else has a chance to gawk at me the way Jakes did."

"Splendid! I do so love a good walk." Ransley snapped his fingers, and his supplies busied themselves with jumping back into his bag.

Tharen tore his eyes away from the astonishing sight as Ransley's words registered. "Walk? Can't I Shape here? I had hoped to give Jaea a chance to rest some."

"You have a lot to learn yet about this land. It has been a great many years since a Shaper of your ability was last seen. And he is not remembered fondly by many here. It would be wise to hold off Shaping if you can. Jaea can take any of her other forms, but that one I would not recommend either of you take just yet." Ransley shouldered his bag as Jaea and Tharen stepped onto the road beside him. "Oh! Keep your Shaper marks covered for now; probably best not to draw attention until we find Maya."

Jaea shrugged at Tharen's inquiring look. They followed Ransley down the road toward the capital.

"All right. Stop being so cryptic. Who was the guy, and why was he so disliked?" Tharen asked.

"Well, he was the Stone that took the throne by force. The primary reason behind the unrest here is the Stone family's effort to reclaim the throne. The movement was already underway when the Riddle at the time predicted peace would come to Caeldighn when a missing person returned from another world to reunite with their family here."

"Like me?" Jaea asked surprised.

"Not like you. Most loyal to the crown believe it to be you specifically. You and your sister had already been marked by Riddle, you see. A previous Riddle had foretold a pair of powerful twins born to the First Queen's line. That is why your caravan was attacked. The Stone family was afraid of what you might accomplish. When you disappeared, those against the Stones began to think peace centered on your return. The Stones, of course, interpreted the riddle differently, saying it was evidence for the need of a Stone ruler once again."

"Hang on. What in the world is this riddle thing you keep talking about?" Tharen asked.

"First Queen!" Jaea yelled. "Ransley you could have mentioned the bit about my family being royalty sooner, don't you think?"

"You aren't royalty. Not really. The Caeldighn political system is not your typical monarchy. I thought I mentioned it before. You are descended from a very old Caeldighn family that has often provided Caeldighn with a ruler, though that doesn't mean you can inherit the throne any more than Tharen can. Anyone of age can try for the throne and, if approved, rule. The crown does often pass down through the approved person's family but not always," Ransley tried to explain. "I am certain someone at the capital will be able to enlighten you more on the matter if you would like."

"I'm not sure I followed that. So, not a princess or anything? Just from a noteworthy family that has been in Caeldighn a long time, apparently since the First Queen? Did I get that right?" Jaea asked confusedly.

"Yes, that is correct, and the Stone supporters are after you because they think you know about the riddles and intend to try for the throne," Ransley added.

"Uh huh. Well, that is still pretty out there, but not nearly so terrifying as having a long lost royal family," Jaea said with obvious relief.

"Okay. Time out." Tharen got in front of Jaea and Ransley and made a "T" with his hands. "What is, or who is, riddle? And why do we, let alone all of Caeldighn, care what he, she, it, has to say about anything?"

"Ah," Ransley said. "Riddle, capital R, is the head of the Readers, or those that stand at Nirah's monument. She is well known and highly respected throughout Caeldighn, and her words are not to be taken lightly. Readers interpret the smoke within the stone and keep very detailed records. Some are gifted as seers. Their predictions are sometimes called riddles, little r. From what I remember, Riddle is in charge of making sure that Caeldighn's citizens are aware of the those predictions. Again, that is something to ask someone else about. I don't usually see Nirah in her stone, and the whole thing sometimes confuses me."

Tharen narrowed his eyes at Ransley. "I feel as though every time you speak I have more questions to ask you."

"No kidding," Jaea said.

"Most of what I know of Caeldighn comes from what Nirah has told me. I have observed some of this land's history, but I do have other responsibilities you know. Maya filled me in some when I spoke with her, though the only reason I met Maya is because she demanded an audience with me a few years back to see if I could tell her anything about the Stone king," Ransley said defensively.

"People can demand to speak with a Gatekeeper?" Jaea asked.

"Not everyone. In certain situations, or if the individual in question has enough influence, it is possible," Ransley said with a shrug. "Do you suppose you two could pause your interrogation until we stop to eat? You are beginning to give me a headache, which would decidedly ruin the scenery."

Jaea smiled. "Fair enough."

Tharen nodded. "Just let me recap to see if I am up to speed so far," he said sarcastically. "Some long dead Riddle reader ladies predicted Jaea's birth, as well as her subsequent return to Caeldighn and thus reunion with her twin sister, would bring about peace. Her sister, mind you, who is scarily influential enough to demand an audience with a Keeper. You know all of this because the lady stuck in a rock, except when speaking with you apparently, told you so. Jaea isn't a princess, but she is of age to try for the throne, of the land she hasn't lived in since she was almost killed by some crazy family that has a bad Shaper guy for an ancestor. Which is why I can't Shape yet, and people are trying to kill my best friend. But our questions are tiring you, so instead of trying to figure out how to not get dead, we are going to quietly observe the Caeldighn countryside, which currently looks remarkably like the American Midwest, until we stop to partake in a picnic around lunch time."

Ransley had stopped walking during Tharen's rant. He blinked, then cleared his throat. "Umm, yes," he answered uncertainly.

"Joy," Tharen said miserably, throwing his hands in the air in exasperation. He shook his head and continued down the road ahead of Jaea and Ransley.

Jaea admired the Caeldighn landscape as they walked. It amused her that it was so ordinary, so very like Earth. There weren't two suns or orange grass or strange glowing plants. Yet, she amended. She hadn't come across strange glowing plants yet.

"Within the hour we will be in Maeshowe, Caeldighn's capital," Ransley announced suddenly, interrupting Jaea's thoughts. "Within the half hour we will be walking through part of what is called the 'First Queen's forest.' We will pass a number of impressive trees, and then suddenly the city will come into view. It is a marvelous city. There is nothing quite like it in all the worlds."

"I saw a number of impressive places on Earth, Ransley. What makes this one so special?" Tharen asked skeptically.

"Wait and see, Shaper," Ransley said smiling.

"Ransley," Jaea said. "So far this world is remarkably usual, are all worlds like Earth or just Caeldighn? And do things have the same names here? Is an oak tree an oak in Caeldighn's language?"

"There are many similarities, yes," Ransley agreed. "The Creator made all worlds unique, though some more noticeably than others. In regards to language, the Shaper language is dominant here I suppose. It is actually more or less English. Originally, it was a hodgepodge of Gaelic languages and Latin. Very persistent language English. You would be surprised how many worlds it appears on." He shrugged. "But it hardly matters what language is used since you two are Shapers. I would imagine you have discovered your gifts in that area?"

"Told you it had to be a Shaper thing!" Jaea exclaimed triumphantly, pointing at Tharen. "Language has always been a breeze for us. Even if we haven't encountered it before we can understand what is being said within a minute or two, and not long after are able to speak it fluently. Annoyed and baffled all of our teachers," she told Ransley.

Ransley laughed. "I bet you pretended that written language was more difficult, just to placate them."

"Absolutely," Tharen agreed. "It kept the peace and made us slightly less odd."

"Odd," Ransley repeated. "That reminds me. You should know that the some of native species here are quite different than those you are accustomed to. Not too many griffins, unicorns, pegasi, centaurs, or even dragons left on Earth. There are no waya on Earth at all. And very few Shapers, as you know."

"All those creatures live here?" Jaea asked. "With Shapers. What do they all eat? Is there an abundance of deer here or something?"

"Are the dragons hard to find?" Tharen asked excitedly.

Ransley held up his hands. "You two ask more questions than anyone I have met to this day!" He looked at Jaea. "Yes. They all live here, quite happily, and they eat all sorts of things." He turned to look at Tharen. "No, they are not difficult to find. Although I would be willing to bet that they find you first."

"What do you mean by that?" Tharen asked cautiously.

Ransley shook his head. "That, my new friends, concludes today's bout of completely random questions about one of the many keys I tend. While I am very attached to Caeldighn, I do not, in fact, live here. When the occasion arises, I promise I will point you to someone who can answer all the thousands of questions still bubbling around those little brains of yours. But those men there are part of the Forest Guard." He nodded toward two men standing guard a ways ahead of them. "Their men will lead us through the wood to the city. They generally request that you stay quiet, so that they can listen for attackers."

"Attackers?" Jaea and Tharen asked together.

"If we are lucky, no. Come along."

Jaea sighed. "I knew things were going too smoothly." She followed Ransley toward the guards, her sense of unease growing. When the trio neared the treeline, two men stepped out of a small cabin at the side of the road and moved to block their path.

"Halt. State your business," said the guard on Tharen's right.

"Passage through the First Queen's Forest. We make for the castle," Ransley answered.

The guard on the left signaled behind him. As two more guards walked toward them he asked, "Do all present in your party know the laws associated with passage through the First Queen's Forest?"

"They do not," Ransley replied.

The left hand guard nodded and launched into a well rehearsed speech. "These men will see you through the forest along designated roads and pathways. They are with you to help discourage would be bandits from robbing you, as well as to ensure that you do not partake in any unauthorized planting or removal of plant or animal life. This area is protected under the laws set forth by the First Queen. Shaping is discouraged while you are in the company of your escorts, as it could be seen as disregarding the law or an attack against the Crown's Forest Guard. Any actions against the regulations explained to you will result in an investigation and sentencing of all members of your party."

"If you do not agree to these terms," the right hand guard continued, "an alternate route to Maeshowe will be outlined to you and a physical map drawn if requested. Do all those in your party agree to these terms?"

"Yes," Ransley answered.

The guards looked at Jaea and Tharen expectantly.

"Oh! Yes," Jaea said realizing they each had to answer. She nudged Tharen who had been frowning more as the guards laid out rules.

"Must be some important trees," Tharen said. "But yes, I agree," he added quickly when Jaea glared at him.

"Then the Forest Guard grants you passage," the right guard answered.

"Good!" One of their escorts waved them on. "If you folks would follow me, we can have you safe and sound in Maeshowe in time for dinner at Rosie's. Leastwise that is the establishment where I intend to seek dinner this evening. Welcome to the First Queen's Forest."

Ransley winked back at Jaea and fell in step with the forward guard.

Jaea hesitated for just a second, which was apparently enough to concern the rear guard. She sent a quick smile at the serious face beside her, grabbed Tharen by the arm and towed him after the Keeper.

The guards kept them at a steady pace, and the road was well worn and easy to follow. Freed from having to pay much attention to her feet, Jaea's mind drifted among the vast green canopy above her. There are some impressive trees here. She had heard about about redwood trees in California that were big enough to drive cars through. Certainly, some of these trees were on that scale. Jaea was relieved to learn that bandits weren't common along the Forest Road. According to one of their guides, the Crown went to some effort to ensure that remained the case. The Guards' job was more often to protect the forest from tourists trying to collect memorabilia.

"The tree spirits would not take kindly to some fool carving names into their bark. I would almost pity the individual that tried, almost," Christopher, the more talkative guide, told them.

Jaea, head still spinning from the few questions Ransley had answered, only half paid attention. Memories were surfacing from the dusty archives of her mind. An aunt had introduced Jaea to some griffins once, she was sure of it. And roses were special, but she couldn't quite remember why. She felt as though more memories were prepped for launch if the right word or place triggered them. She was so lost in thought, wondering what flood of memories or emotions awaited her when she saw Maya again, that she didn't hear Ransley's question. The group had stopped walking and seemed to be waiting for her answer.

At Jaea's blank look Ransley rephrased and tried again. "This is the point of no return, girl. If you wish, I could take you back through the gate to your parent's home. It is possible that Maya would seek you out there. However, you should be aware that if you continue around that bend, your life will be changed completely and irrevocably, for better or worse. It is your choice, Jaea Harbour McClanahan."

The Guards looked at Jaea in shock. Christopher reached over to close his companion's mouth.

Jaea blushed slightly, uncomfortable with the attention. She looked questioningly at Tharen who merely nodded to indicate he would go where she went, either way. She squared her shoulders. "Maya, or someone who can lead me to her, is that way. There is no other way for me to go. We go to Maeshowe."

Ransley smiled. "After you my friends."

The trio fell in step again between the Guards and followed the road as it curved right. As they rounded the turn, the forest stopped abruptly. The trees at their back cast long shadows across a wide road before them, pointing them toward a large sprawling city. The widest part of the road continued straight in front of them while slightly smaller roads branched left and right of the main one.

"Wow," Tharen said in awe.

"I told you there was nothing like it, Shaper." Ransley

chuckled. "What do you think Jaea?"

"I think that in our biggest Shapes, Tharen and I could very comfortably walk side by side down these roads. And even then, there would be room for others to do the same. Are those all homes? How many people live here? How am going to find Maya here? It's like New York City with elbow room!"

Ransley put his hand on Jaea's shoulders and turned her to face the road on their right. "To find Maya, we walk this road until we reach the castle."

"Okay." Jaea nodded calmly. "I can do that."

"The big road," Ransley said pointing. "That is the South Road, until it crosses with East Road and West Road anyway. It is wide enough to accommodate four dragons walking abreast and is patterned after roads in the dragon city, Silverhaven. I do not know how many citizens reside in Maeshowe. There are many homes, shops, churches, and all the things you normally find in cities. Most relevant currently, are the eating houses." Ransley looked back at Christopher. "You mentioned somewhere to eat, did you not?"

"Yes!" Christopher said excitedly. "Rosie's is just up here on King's, so it is even on your way to the castle." He paused as he passed Jaea. "Don't worry. We'll keep your name under wraps, ma'am." He shot her a grin and began to lead the group to the pub.

Jaea's mind briefly registered that Ransley had said Caeldighn had churches, filing that interesting tidbit away for a time when she could give it her full attention. She wondered if there would ever come a time when speaking with Ransley didn't leave her with more questions than she started with.

"Is every male here going to flirt with you?" Tharen grumbled, stepping to Jaea's side.

"You've nothing to worry about from Chris there. He is completely smitten, head over heels, for Rosie," the quieter guard said, surprising Jaea as he moved to walk at her other side. "But I imagine most in Caeldighn would like a relationship with the returned twin. Guard your heart, miss. Not all pretty faces have pretty souls behind them." With that, he opened the door to Rosie's, where Christopher was already getting the group a table.

Jaea tried to eat. It had seemed like such a brilliant idea when she followed the group into the Rosie's. Stop and refuel before walking yet farther to the castle in hopes of reuniting with Maya. After the first few bites had settled into her stomach like lead, she focused instead on drinking her tea. She pushed the food on her plate around a little as the others ate contentedly. When the table was cleared the guards insisted on paying the group's tab. Jaea only agreed after Christopher argued he could probably write it off in their books and be reimbursed later.

Outside, the air had grown cooler and the stars were just beginning to peek through the sky's dark curtain. The guards bid Jaea and her group adieu and ambled back toward the First Queen's Forest. Jaea stared numbly down King's Street and tried in vain to convince her feet to propel her body forward.

"Ready?" Ransley asked.

"Yes," Jaea said resolutely.

"We just follow this road to the castle door. Someone else will take the matter from there." Ransley smiled. "Lead on, my dear."

Jaea nodded decisively and strode forward. I can do this, she told herself. No big deal. Nonetheless, she was glad when Tharen offered her his arm.

It didn't seem to take long to reach the castle, and once they did Jaea stopped and stared in awe for a moment before Ransley nudged her toward the gate. The darkening night sky hid the finer details and some of the outline from her view, but what she could see impressed her. Large lamps chased shadows from the stone structure, closer together and more decorative than those that had lined the road from Rosie's. A tall stone wall encircled the place, and taller rounded peaks showed over the top of it. When they came to the gate, Jaea was dismayed to see that it was closed. She mentally kicked herself for not thinking of this possibility sooner. When had she ever heard of castles granting any old passerby entrance after dark? Two guards frowned at Jaea and Tharen from the other side of the iron gate.

"No entry until morning," one guard said gruffly. He put a hand over his bearded face to cover a yawn. "Everyone knows that."

"Clearly not everyone," the other said. "What business have you here?" he asked suspiciously.

"I brought them to see Maya McClanahan," Ransley said as he stepped closer. "I would really prefer it be sooner rather than later, and you asked me not to materialize in the keep unless strictly necessary."

"Ransley!" the clean shaven man laughed. "I imagine coming to the gate at night is preferable to popping into existence and scaring our men half to death. I'll have to get the captain to let you in. Who can I say is with you?"

Ransley smiled wide. "Jaea Harbour McClanahan and friend Tharen McKenna."

The young man's eyes bulged as his gaze jerked back to Jaea. "Jaea McClanahan, by all the stars," he said reverently. "Back in a moment, ma'am." He dashed off to notify his captain while his bearded coworker sat down heavily, looking shocked. In no time at all, Jaea, Tharen, and Ransley were welcomed into the grand building and ushered into some sort of receiving parlor called the Fairy Room. Jaea half heard the page call their attention to the beautiful tapestries and elegant woodwork the room boasted. She barely noticed the room's furnishings beyond recognizing that the room was indeed furnished. The friendly young man had invited them to take a seat before rushing off to notify Maya of her visitors.

Jaea didn't much feel like sitting and had only managed to remain seated for about a minute before abandoning the attempt. Back and forth, back and forth she walked, her footfalls muffled by the midnight blue rug covering most of the room's floor.

Tharen tried, twice, to convince her to sit down again. Finally, he gave up and perched on the arm of a sofa, resigned to watching Jaea pace.

"How can you just sit there so calm!" Jaea demanded of Ransley.

She didn't wait for his answer, merely resumed walking. What if Maya hated her? What if Maya didn't believe Jaea about her identity? Ugh. For all she knew Maya wasn't even here. Out of the corner of her eye, Jaea saw Ransley shrug at Tharen. Tharen started to laugh, but abruptly turned it into a cough when Jaea shot him a glare.

After what seemed an eternity, Tharen moved to intercept her path again. "Jaea," Tharen said kindly. He glanced toward the door.

Jaea followed his gaze and saw the door had opened to admit two young women. One, a redhead, waved to Ransley. The other, a dark haired woman, watched in a kind of stupor as Jaea crossed the room again. She wasn't identical to Jaea, the dark haired newcomer, but any fool could guess they were related. "Maya?" she asked quietly.

The dark haired lady nodded in response. "Hello, sister."

"Maya!" Jaea rushed forward to embrace her twin. "Hello." She felt a tear streak down her face. "I hope it is okay to hug you, because I'm going to keep hugging you for a minute anyway."

"Hugging is perfectly acceptable," Maya said as she hugged back. "Welcome to Maeshowe, Jaea McClanahan."

CHAPTER EIGHT

Tharen mentally reviewed the events of the last couple weeks as he walked the streets of Maeshowe. He felt as though he had traveled through time. Not back in time, but sideways somehow. The whole place had an antiquated feel to it, except that there were centaurs scattered throughout the crowds milling about and the occasional pegasus or griffin perched somewhere like a misplaced statue. Shapers would Shape for seemingly no reason, a fact his brain still refused to process as normal. The word "dragon" popping up so often was also taking getting used to: dragonfire in the streetlamps, dragon crafted items for sale, snippets of conversations about dragons or the dragon university in Silverhaven. Talk of dragons tended to make him wary.

A display in one of the shop windows caught his eye, and he decided to take a closer look. Not quite what he was looking for though. He moved on, keeping an eye out for the shop one of the castle cooks praised at breakfast. He patted his pocket to make sure he had remembered to bring the funds Maya had allotted him. She had dubbed Tharen an Ambassador-in-training the day before, when he asked if there was something he could do while the twins caught up. Tharen had begun to feel in the way. Jaea was pretty busy learning about Caeldighn and her family here. As an Ambassador, he had a weekly allowance, room and board in the castle, access to the Maeshowe library and a sort of legitimate task to occupy his time. Plus, he got to wear a cool badge that made shopkeepers lower their prices for him and encouraged random people to strike up conversations with him. Tharen could have kissed Maya. He hadn't, of course. He wasn't the kind of guy that just went around kissing people, at least he tried not be. A pleasant ding from a bell on a shop door saved him from that train of thought. He made his way toward it after spying the sign above it.

"Welcome to Teresa's Trinkets!" a pixie of a girl said excitedly from a seat by the counter.

"Why thank you, ma'am," Tharen replied with a bow, making the girl laugh.

"I am a miss, not a ma'am!" She stood up from her chair giggling. "See? I'm little." She hopped back onto her perch. "Mama said I need to sit here and stay out of trouble. If you tell me what you are looking for I can point where it would be. And my name is Terra. You can call me Terra instead of miss if you want, so you won't get confused and call me a ma'am," she whispered loudly.

"Deal," Tharen told her with a grin. "And you can call me Tharen. I wouldn't like to be called ma'am either."

Terra succumbed to the giggles again. "I like you, Ambassador Tharen," Terra said, pointing to his badge. "You are funny. Are you here to learn about our trade? If so, you'd have to wait to talk with Mama about that, but I can keep you company while she helps that lady over there."

"I wouldn't mind learning about your trade sometime. Today, though, I came to buy a necklace for my friend," Tharen confided. "Maybe you could recommend one or two?"

"Yes!" Terra exclaimed. "There are some that are all put together over there. My favorites are the pendants, over there." She pointed to two different displays, one on a counter along the wall and the other a large stand more in the room's middle. "We have a few chains that will Shape Stay, too. Mama can get those for you, if you want."

"Which pendants do you like best?"

"The one that looks like a tree from the First Queen's Garden," Terra said immediately. "I also really like the horse one. And the little bird."

"Thank you very much, Terra. I will be sure to let you know which one I pick."

Tharen easily found the pendants Terra had mentioned. Most of the pendants were made of glass, though a number of them incorporated wood as well. They were all beautiful, but he liked the three Terra singled out the most. He decided to go with the one fashioned like a tree and made his way back to the counter, just as the lady Terra had pointed to concluded her business.

"Can I help you, sir?" the woman behind the counter asked.

"Teresa?" Tharen asked. When the woman nodded, he continued. "A reliable source told me I could purchase necklaces here that would Shape Stay. I was hoping to buy one for this pendant."

"Psst! Tharen! Which one did you pick?" Terra whispered, her freckled face peeking around the counter.

"The tree. Which chain should I get to go with it?" Tharen whispered back.

"The leather cord with the pretty silver leaf clasp."

Tharen looked back at Teresa. "I'll have the cord with the pretty silver leaf clasp, and this tree pendant, please."

"You have a very good source in that one. She knows all my pieces as well as I do. If you like, I can wrap this for you as well, Ambassador," Teresa told him.

Tharen glanced over at Terra, who nodded emphatically. "Yes, please," Tharen said to Teresa.

"Do you want to come to my tea party?" Terra blurted. She was standing on her chair now to see Tharen over the counter.

"You don't have to. But if you want to, I think it would be fun. And I can tell you all about Caeldighn, and you can tell me about where you are from! So do you want to come?"

"Terra! Don't hound the Ambassador! And sit down!" Teresa admonished. "I'm so sorry, sir," she said to Tharen. "Her friend canceled on her yesterday, and she has been trying to find someone else to attend since."

Tharen grinned. "I accept your invitation gladly, Terra. I would love to come to your tea party. Do I need to bring anything?"

Terra shook her head no. "Your friend can come, too. If she wants. It will be at two o'clock, here in mama's shop, on Monday," she said excitedly.

"I look forward to it. See you then."

"Alright! Bye, Tharen!"

Tharen waved and pulled the door closed behind him. He laughed to himself and started walking back toward the castle. He found he was glad for the chance to get to know that little imp better, and hoped Jaea would be able to come with him for Terra's tea party. With any luck, he'd be able to talk to Jaea alone for a while after dinner, to hear how her day had gone and give her the necklace. Odds were that Maya had another round of Q and A lined up for them, though. The first couple evenings in Caeldighn, he and Jaea had brought Maya up to speed on their lives and what they knew of Shapers. Maya noticed the significant gaps in their knowledge and set out to educate them on what she saw as Shaper heritage. So far they had learned of the wide range of Shaping abilities, none of which included Tharen's Shaped form. They also learned that divorce was nearly unheard of, and that Shapers generally lived two to five hundred years. It had been a relief to learn that a normal Shaper life expectancy was at least that of a human, but five hundred years seemed a tad excessive. Yesterday, Maya had suggested they bring her friend and fellow Chief, Kaylee Buchanan, in on the sessions, to help answer their questions and set up a less scattered learning structure. Perhaps he should find Jaea before dinner.

Jaea sat in one of the more secluded gardens behind the castle trying in vain to still her mind for a few moments. Her head was reeling with everything she had been told since she walked through the gate. She wished she could talk to her mom or dad about it. Ransley had hinted that he could take her home again if ever she wanted to return, but Jaea couldn't even think about leaving yet. How could she explain that to Maggie and Ben? They would tell her to march her butt back to Caeldighn and get to know her birth family. A family, Jaea thought with a groan, that remained one of the most respected and honored families in Caeldighn since Shapers first settled here. Older than the Stone claim to the throne by far, Maya had said. The thought of the Stone Rebellion just furthered Jaea's headache. It couldn't be a coincidence that her best friend from college had the last name Stone and was interested in other worlds. Innocent until proven guilty, part of her argued. Caleb may not be connected. And he's your friend, hopefully.

She heard someone approaching and looked up to see Tharen striding toward her. "Hey there, stranger."

"Right back at you," Tharen said. "Mind if I join you?"

"Please do. Distract me for a moment from the insanity that has befallen my life," Jaea said, patting the seat next to her.

Tharen gave her what she thought of as his spill-the-beans-already face. "Whatcha thinking about?" he asked, settling down in the offered seat.

"Family," Jaea told him with a shrug. "Adoptive family. Birth family. The whole, get to know your sister that you have next to nothing in common with thing." She sighed. "And Caleb. Caleb

Stone."

"Ah," Tharen said sympathetically. "I have been trying to think of a way to tactfully bring him up since we learned that the big bad rebels here support the Stone family. Do you think he is involved?"

"I want to say no, of course my friend from school, on Earth, isn't in league with Team Rebellion, plotting to destroy the land of my birth. I just keep thinking how odd he was when he saw the key," Jaea admitted.

"He definitely knew more than he was letting on," Tharen agreed.

"Ugh. Not another word on this unless he shows up here as a heavily armed villain. Deal?" Jaea pleaded.

"Works for me." Tharen reached into his pocket and pulled out the prettily wrapped little box from Teresa's Trinkets. "Now for something fun and happy and not at all connected to glum thoughts," he said cheerfully as he handed it to Jaea.

"What is this for?" Jaea asked.

"To open. Duh."

Jaea made a face at him and opened the small package to reveal a charming necklace. "Tharen! It is beautiful. Thank you." She pulled it out and immediately put it on. "I love it." She smiled at him.

Tharen shrugged. "You have seemed a little lost without a necklace since you gave Ransley his key back. The lady I bought it from says it will Shape Stay. I thought if you liked this you may be able to ask her to make a chain for the violet your dad gave you."

Jaea leaned over to hug him. "You are such a wonderful friend. I don't know what I would do without you. Oh! I can wear this to the party!"

"Party?" Tharen asked confused. "I haven't told you about the tea party yet."

"Right. I haven't filled you in on that bit yet," Jaea said apologetically. "Wait, tea party?"

"Yeah. I was invited to tea, Monday at two. You wanna go?"

"How cool! I can't though. I have already agreed to try to learn as many family members names as possible before the big welcome thing. So I will be staring at photos and trying to memorize random information while you relax over tea." She clapped him on the back. "That reminds me! They can do photos here. More old timey, and slightly different than the darkrooms you are used to. Maya said you can ask around at a shop called Image, in town, if you want to learn more about it."

"Really? I will be sure to stop in there tomorrow," Tharen said. "Now, what is the party you mentioned?"

"The Crown wants to host a formal welcome for me, the Friday after next, July 5, as long as stuff falls together just so and certain individuals can attend at that time," Jaea said with false excitement. "Dual purpose gathering to confirm that the McClanahan twin has indeed returned and to introduce me to society. I haven't decided if I am honored or insulted that I am to be thrust into Caeldighn's social elite. I half expect Maya to introduce me to some man that my birth parents arranged to have me marry. I think I like the idea of meeting lots of Caeldighnians in one go, though."

"Arranged marriage, huh? It could save you a hundred years of trying to find your one true love," Tharen joked.

Jaea's heart twisted a little when Tharen said love, but she expertly covered it up. "You are within hitting range Tharen James McKenna," she warned.

Tharen laughed. "Come on. Let's grab some grub before Shaper History 101 starts up again."

"Do you think they will start in the beginning this time? All the hopping around is making me crazy," Jaea said as she followed him inside.

"We can only hope," Tharen said sincerely.

Later that evening, Jaea and Tharen followed a page down the castle's many halls to the library. As soon as they stepped through the door Kaylee waved from one of the room's large tables, calling them over. Jaea smiled at Kaylee's excitement. She still felt she didn't quite understand the redhead, but she very much liked her. As far as Jaea could tell, Kaylee was equal parts flamboyant and steel, like a fun cocktail that packed a hard punch.

"Good evening, ma'am," Tharen said when they neared the table.

"Psh. None of that." Kaylee laughed. "I'm off duty. Besides, I've decided to make you two my friends, and friends shouldn't stand on formality unless absolutely necessary."

"In that case," Jaea said, taking a seat. "Good evening, friend. Fancy seeing you here."

"Being friends with Maya guarantees hours in libraries," Kaylee chuckled. "As you are about to discover."

"Where is Maya? Is she not joining us tonight?" Tharen asked.

"Currently wrapping up a last minute meeting. She should be arriving shortly," Kaylee said. "In the meantime, Maya has told me some of the types of questions you both have and what you have covered. I believe the best approach right now would be to give you a better idea of Shaper beginnings and then skip ahead to what is currently taking place in Caeldighn." She pointed to the variety of books and maps spread across the table. "Having this basic background knowledge should make it easier for you to delve into topics more to your interests later, as you will not need to have every answer given to you explained as you do now."

Jaea saw Kaylee glance at the door and turned to see Maya hurrying across the room.

"Does Kaylee's plan suit you?" Maya asked Jaea and Tharen.

She popped the last bite of a turnover in her mouth and took a seat beside Kaylee.

"Absolutely," Jaea said. "I feel like I am trying do a puzzle without having all of the pieces right now. This, big picture then zoom in if you want to, plan sounds pretty good."

Maya and Kaylee looked at Jaea confusedly.

"That would be a yes." Tharen laughed. "That approach would be met with resounding approval. From both of us."

Kaylee smiled. "I caught the yes in there," she told them. "It was the "zoom puzzle" bit that threw me off for a moment. It has been some time since I've spoken to someone who is new to Caeldighn. Even our current Ambassadors, with the exception of Tharen, have been so since I was a child."

"The more we speak, the easier it will be to understand each other," Maya said reassuringly. "Slang, odd speech patterns, and words for things you have not encountered take the longest to translate. However, even those reach the point where it is understood immediately. It is part of our heritage, which Kaylee and I are going to explain right now."

"Right!" Kaylee said. She pulled a book from the top of the stack and placed it before Jaea and Tharen. "This is one of the most popular volumes on Shaper history. Due, in large part, to the illustrations."

Jaea and Tharen leaned forward to examine the picture in front of them. It was beautiful. Dragons lounged around what appeared to be a human celebration. One dragon had a child gleefully sliding down its tail while another seemed deep in conversation with two young men.

"I know these are not the usual manner in which dragon human relationships are portrayed on Earth. I can assure you though, this is a more accurate representation," Kaylee said. "Shapers are descended from dragons. Well, the children of dragons. Dragons have the ability to take on a human appearance. They often mingled amongst the humans on Earth, sometimes acting as bards. They made friends with many humans, and some even fell in love and married humans. Usually the human knew of their lover's true identity, although there were cases this was not so, and they remained ignorant until a child came of the union. The child of a human and a dragon in their human form is a Shaper." Kaylee paused. "Are you still with me?"

Jaea glanced at Tharen. They both nodded uncertainly.

Kaylee continued her explanation. "This is where we get the ability to understand any language we encounter. It is a trait that dragons possess which was passed on to their human offspring. The dragon shaping trait also impacted these children and allowed them to shape-shift as well, hence the term Shapers. Most found they could Shape into one or a range of animals. A few could Shape into dragons, but usually could not do everything a regular dragon could, such as breathe fire. Only one other type of Shaper is known to have existed since the first of our kind, and that is a Shaper who received a different gift from their dragon parentage. These more rare individuals have the gift of magic instead of Shaping."

Maya picked up where Kaylee stopped. "Those that can Shape into a range of animals are appropriately called Range Shapers. Some of these individuals are able to Shape into different animals that all have something in common, such as four legs or a common habitat, like the sea. Shapers with the ability to take the form of single animal are generally known as Type Shapers and are often specified by noting the particular animal. A Cat Shaper, for example, is a Type Shaper who can take the form of multiple types of cats. Then there are the All Shapes Shapers who, as one can imagine, are able take nearly any animal form. The rare Dragon Shapers may or may not have the ability to take other forms depending on the Shaper. No amount of practice can make one category of Shaper into another. Shapers are born with a set number of forms just as they are born with a certain eye or hair color."

"Answers at last," Jaea said. *Except, what does that make Tharen?*

"Uh huh," Tharen said. "So I have a human parent and a dragon parent?"

"Not necessarily," Kaylee corrected. "Odds are you have two Shaper parents. Or a dragon and a Shaper. Very rare nowadays for a human and a dragon to be together. Not since our kind was chased off Earth. Not all humans were friends with dragons. Eventually Shapers became seen as bad omens, or just plain evil."

"That is when Ariel led the Shapers through a gate from Scotland, Earth to Caeldighn, Avalon. Later she would become Caeldighn's First Queen," Maya added. "Ransley pointed her to the gate as well," she told Jaea.

"Avalon?" Tharen asked.

"The name of the planet on which Caeldighn resides with two other continents," Maya clarified.

"No kidding. How about that."

Jaea just nodded when Tharen looked at her. Yes, yes. Avalon, very cool. Planet name noted, on to more pressing matters. "Our parents were both Shapers, right?" she asked Maya.

"Yes," Maya answered.

"And Shapers were originally from Earth? So Tharen and I were not really aliens so much as misplaced in the old world somehow?" She pulled one of the books on the table closer and began to flip through it.

"Yes?" Maya agreed reluctantly. "I think. Although I do not know Tharen's lineage as I do ours. Shapers live on a number of worlds now."

"Were the dragons originally from Earth as well then?" Tharen asked.

"Yes and no," Kaylee told him. "All life originated on Earth. Not just humans, Shapers, and dragons, but everything from the smallest insect to the largest sea dweller. Over time some creatures found their way to other worlds by traveling through gates. Dragons, being prone to wanderlust and having a desire to learn, were especially quick to spread out among the worlds. There was one world in particular that drew dragons after a library was established there to record what they had learned. The planet quickly became one big town as those who came to visit decided to stay. It was very crowded, a dragon metropolis from the tales. Dragons were constantly in human form so there would be room for them all. Finally, a handful of dragon families left that world to return to Earth in hopes that their children would, literally, be able to stretch their wings and lead happy lives in a world with room to spare. Most Shapers descend from those dragon families."

"Interesting," Tharen mused. "These tales? Are they recorded in volumes like this one? Do you have them in this library?"

"They have been recorded, though you would need to go to Silverhaven to learn more. The dragons have an extensive library that dwarfs ours. And dragons are almost always willing to tell you the stories themselves. They prize knowledge and can recount a great deal to any who ask," Maya said. "Your Ambassador badge will help get you an audience with someone there as well."

Tharen looked at the badge pinned to his shirt. "I love this thing!"

Maya and Kaylee laughed but then almost immediately looked somber.

"What is it?" Jaea asked concerned.

Maya shook her head. "It is just that we have not seen such enthusiasm in an Ambassador in some time. The current situation here in Caeldighn, with no official leader, has strained our relationship with a number of worlds."

"An issue we can discuss tomorrow evening!" Kaylee exclaimed. "For now, are there any pressing concerns or questions before we wrap up for the night?"

"Actually, yes," Jaea said uncertainly. "When Ransley brought us to Maeshowe, he mentioned that the city has churches..."

"That would be correct. Did you have a question about them or merely wish their existence confirmed?" Maya asked.

Jaea squirmed in her seat, she wanted to get the words right. "I was wondering what they are like, compared to those on Earth."

"Well, they are the same, of course." Kaylee laughed.

"Similar at least," Maya amended. "Shapers brought their religion with them through the gate. Even had they not, those here still followed our Father the Creator. The dragons, waya, unicorns, centaurs, griffins, and pegasi that preceded Shapers in settling Caeldighn have been aware of and worshiping the Creator since their oldest ancestor first drew breath on the newly formed Earth."

"So, you guys don't like, worship Nirah or anything?" Tharen ventured.

Jaea's eyes widened at Tharen's lack of tact. She looked at Maya and Kaylee anxiously, hoping they hadn't crossed the line with their inquiries.

"No," Kaylee said firmly. She shook her head wearily at Maya. "Where do off-worlders get these insane ideas?"

Maya patted Kaylee's arm sympathetically. "Nirah, like all else in creation, was fashioned by the same hands that made you and I, our ancestors, and the ground beneath our feet."

"So the churches here?" Jaea asked again.

"Nowadays they are predominantly Christian," Maya confirmed. "Before the arrival of Shapers, the other races often identified as simply Created. It is a common term throughout the

95

worlds for one who follows the Creator. Other religions do have followings as Caeldighn does have a great deal of traffic from other worlds, especially in times of peace. Overall though, the country is Christian."

"Huh. Cool," Tharen said.

"Can we attend service?" Jaea wanted to know. "You know, can anybody go?"

"Absolutely." Maya smiled. "You can come with me Sunday if you like. I go to the morning service in the castle chapel."

"Or you can go later with me, if you want," Kaylee offered. "I go in the afternoon, when I'm more likely to be fully awake."

"I'd like that." Jaea smiled.

"As would I," Tharen said. "Could we meet you somewhere and follow you to this chapel? I've definitely not seen it in my wanderings."

"That would be fine. We can discuss it further tomorrow." Maya yawned.

"Back on track here," Kaylee motioned to the books stacked on the table. "Maya dug these out for you, in case you wished to dive further into Shaper history or lore. You may bring as many or few as you like back to your quarters or read them here as you please."

Jaea grinned at Maya. "Thank you! That was very thoughtful," she said gratefully.

Maya shrugged. "I like books. I knew where these all were. It was no trouble."

"Still," Tharen said. "Thanks."

Maya nodded. "I am off to bed. I will see you both tomorrow."

"Good night," Kaylee said cheerily as she also made to leave the library.

"Good night," Jaea and Tharen chimed back. They spent a few minutes shuffling through the books, deciding which ones to bring back to their rooms.

"Maybe after your big welcome festivities we could try to visit Silverhaven," Tharen suggested.

"I would like that," Jaea said. "It sounds fascinating. Plus, it seems that if anyone here would have knowledge of your ancestry, they would be in Silverhaven."

"Perhaps. Everyone comes from somewhere, but I had pretty well given up on finding my roots until you asked me to come here. It feels good to have a lead again," Tharen admitted.

"You can share my roots. I apparently have a lot of them here." Jaea laughed. "It's still a little strange. Maya says our family is practically chomping at the bit to come see me. She asked them to keep their distance for now though so that I wouldn't feel overwhelmed. Family has a way of asking all the questions you can't answer according to Maya, and it would likely be easier to decide my course of action first."

"Course of action?" Tharen asked. "So, whether or not you are going to stay?"

"Yeah," Jaea said. "No pressure, right? I think she is trying to look out for all of us. She is worried that I will leave, and also worried about how things will change if I stay. That's the vibe I get anyway. I'm still trying to figure her out."

"I wouldn't worry about it too much. I bet she is just as uncertain what to make of you." Tharen looked up from the book he was holding. "What is our plan from here? Ransley seemed to be willing to return us to your parents at anytime if we want."

"Plan? Hmm." Jaea had decided on three of the books, which she now shifted to cradle in one arm. "My plan is to reconnect with my family, Maya especially, and to learn as much as I can about Caeldighn and then make a bigger plan."

"Uh huh," Tharen said picking up his choice of books. "Live, laugh, love, and make a plan in a few months?"

"Yep. Maya has already told me that we are both welcome to stay here in the castle or in one of my family's homes while we decide," Jaea told him.

"I like this plan. And you know what? I like your sister too." Tharen held the library door open for Jaea.

"So do I." Jaea smiled.

CHAPTER NINE

Caleb Stone made his way through the house full of his father's associates. He had to stop a number of times as people introduced themselves. Apparently being Mr. Stone's son had weight in this world as well, although he knew these were not the simple introductions they looked like. Caleb was being measured by each individual. Was he as loyal to the cause as they? Did he understand his role? Would he sit the throne if tragedy befell their other candidate? They did not ask such questions outright. That would be disrespectful to Mr. Stone. Still, in each handshake, smile, and clap on the back, the questions came through easily enough. He stepped out the front door and took a moment to enjoy the sun soaked view and the relative quiet. He spied a number of people coming down the road on horseback. They were too far yet to hear the soft clopping of hooves on the beaten dirt path.

Taking a small notebook and pen from his pocket, Caleb jotted down a quick note in blue ink. *I could use a bit of a walk, if you don't mind another in your company on the way back.* The ink had barely dried when a response scrawled in black formed below it. *Please do. Mother and I have both been looking forward to seeing you again. I shall be relieved to put these messenger pens away for a time, as I will soon once again have the pleasure of speaking with my scrawny brother in person!* Caleb smiled and began walking toward the riders.

As he walked, Caleb thought about the last time he had seen his older brother. It was more than a decade ago, when his family had been living in a small town in southeast Caeldighn. They had never been overly popular among the other residents and just knowing they bore the Stone name made many uneasy around them. Most of their extended family lived in neighboring towns, and none were their age. Caleb and Jakob had been close friends, often only because there was no one else to fill the role. After the McClanahan caravan was attacked, some of the villagers retaliated against his family even though there was no proof that they were involved. The last Caleb had seen of Jakob, he was running with their mother as Caleb ran the opposite way with their father, fleeing for their lives. Their parents had taken them through separate gates in hopes of keeping them safe until they could all return and live again as a family in Caeldighn. The brothers had only been able to keep in touch through the message pens they had received as gifts from their grandmother earlier that day.

Caleb looked up and was startled to see how far he had come. It had taken less time than he had estimated to reach the group. He stopped a few feet away and waved a hand in greeting. The riders came to a halt so he could approach. A broad shouldered young man quickly dismounted to embrace Caleb.

"Hello, brother!" Caleb laughed, clapping Jakob on the back. "How have you and Mother fared traveling?"

"Good! We've hardly had any trouble finding you here. Father did not underestimate our supporters. Two of our company came through the gate with Mother and I from Tinalt. The other four we met on the Caeldighn side of the gate, and they have been graciously leading us in your direction," Jakob told him. He turned to fall into step with Caleb and return to the others. "Do you know that we still have cousins here, brother? Distant cousins, but all the same. I met them just last evening.

Can you imagine?"

"I am afraid I can. We have two at the house Father secured for us. I sincerely hope those you met were happier souls." Caleb looked up at the woman whose horse he and his brother had stopped beside. "You look lovelier than ever, Mother."

"You only say that because you know you inherited my good looks," she teased. Her eyes became bright, filling with joyful tears, as she clasped hands with Caleb. "You have grown into yourself since last I saw you," she said proudly.

"Feel free to tell Father as much. He is still waiting for my frame to fill out like his and Jakob's. But at least no one can say I am scrawny now," Caleb said, making his mother laugh.

"I beg to differ. You will always be my scrawny little brother to me, even if you wake up nine feet tall and five feet wide some morning," Jakob said affectionately. "Mother, would you mind if I walked with Caleb? Surely we would not arrive far behind you."

"Take your time. I will let your father know you are together." She pointed at two of the men in their party. "You two will accompany my sons and ensure no ill befalls them." Looking back at Caleb and Jakob she said, "Stay out of trouble. I will see you soon." With that, she and the riders she had not singled out rode toward the house.

"Do we not always stay out of trouble, Caleb?" Jakob asked, grinning.

"No." Caleb laughed. "Generally when together, we stay in it!"

CRBO

Tharen muttered a greeting around a mouthful of toast as Jaea sat down beside him at the tall work table in the kitchen. It had been part of their routine to eat breakfast together there since their first morning in the castle, when they had missed the morning meal served in the dining hall and begged the cooks to take pity on newcomers. The head cook had decided she liked their company and invited them to break fast with the kitchen crew any morning they wished. One of the cooks filled a mug of tea and passed it to Jaea, earning a grateful smile from his sleepy friend.

"Thanks, George," Jaea said. She spooned honey into the mug. "How are you always so chipper in the morning?" Jaea asked Tharen, cautiously sipping the hot tea.

"Habit?" Tharen shrugged. "What has you so tired today? You look less awake than usual."

Jaea tried to cover a yawn. "I stayed up reading longer than I should have."

"Ah. That will do it. Are you free for a while after this?"

"I am. What's up?" Jaea asked as she filled her plate from the spread of food that filled the table's center.

"Well, this fine young lady," Tharen said pointing to a plump older woman who oversaw castle desserts, "has informed me that it is custom to bring a small present for the host when attending a tea party. I had hoped you would help me shop for something suitable."

The woman he mentioned reached over and swatted his arm teasingly. "I have not been a young lady since your pappy was in swaddling! I've always cut this striking figure, though." She laughed, causing the others in the kitchen to join her.

Jaea's eyes crinkled in mirth over the brim of her mug. She set it down to answer Tharen. "Sure. I'm not meeting Maya until lunch, and I have been meaning to poke around the shops a bit more."

"Great!" Tharen said rising from the bench seat. "I have to go turn in my report to Maya. I'll meet you at the courtyard fountain when you are ready?"

"Sure," Jaea agreed absently. "You write reports?"

"Yeah, every couple days as part of my Ambassador gig. My impressions, what I've learned or done. Where I am spending my allowance, yada yada." He paused to kiss the head cook's cheek on his way out. "Thank you for another fine meal, Gwena."

"You are welcome at my table anytime, you charmer. We cooks do so enjoy compliments!" Gwena replied happily.

Tharen waved to the whole group from the door and hurried off to turn in his report.

After wandering town for a few hours, Tharen walked Jaea to Maya's rooms for lunch. Maya had extended him an invitation when he turned in his report that morning. Jaea knocked, and the door was opened almost immediately by a friendly looking woman Tharen recognized as Maya's maid. The woman ushered them into welcoming living quarters and sat them at a small table situated near one of the windows.

"Maya is concluding a meeting in her office," the maid informed them politely, gesturing toward a door off to the left of the room. "She asked me to assure you that she would not be long and requests that you make yourselves comfortable." With that, the woman returned to her post beside Maya's office door.

Mere seconds later a striking blonde woman stormed out of Maya's office. Tharen thought she would have been rather pretty if her face weren't set so angrily. The friendly maid hurried to open the door and see her out quietly, but the woman turned in the open doorway to shout, "You are no Chief yet, Maya McClanahan! Your aunt still holds that title, and it is she I will see resolves this matter!" She pulled the door closed loudly behind her, making the maid scowl.

Maya smiled apologetically at her maid and moved to greet her guests.

"Jaea. Tharen," Maya began. "I apologize for my tardiness and the display you witnessed just now." She motioned to her maid, whose frown had vanished. "I believe you both already know my friend, Emily Connor. She does her best to keep me on time and in order, no easy task I can tell you."

"You need an occasional push out the door is all." Emily laughed as she uncovered the serving dishes already arranged prettily on the table.

"What was the scary lady screeching about?" Tharen asked.

Maya rolled her eyes. "That woman, the bane of my existence these last few months, is Elaine Ryan. She is convinced that every single detail of every single matter in Caeldighn should be done exactly as she and her family dictate. They are the wealthiest family in the country currently and have been, on occasion, a great aid to the crown since Queen Sarai's death. Unfortunately, they try to use their money as a bargaining chip. Though to hear it from them, they have saved our people ten times over and asked for nothing in return." Maya ran her hands over her face. "Sorry, that was rude of me. I had not meant to rant and portray her in an ill light."

"I thought it was brilliant," Tharen said earnestly. "I haven't heard you speak so frankly before. Wasn't sure you had it in you," he teased, making his lunch companions smile.

"You are a Chief though aren't you?" Jaea asked. "Every time I am with you, someone comes to ask you a question or get your approval or relay information on everything under the sun."

"Ah. Technically, I am still only an apprentice, although I do the bulk of the job now. The position can only be granted by someone sitting the throne, which you may have noticed Caeldighn lacks of late. So Aunt Jayla is still the actual Chief of State, as she was the last one named," Maya explained. "Meaning that Aunt Jal and Aunt Adi are trying desperately to retire, but typically end up with the same headaches as Kaylee and I at the end of most days."

"Enough gloom," Emily said. "Tell them about the party!"

"Right. That is the reason I asked Tharen to join us today, Jaea. The welcome we have been planning is coming together. Most of the Council members will be able to attend on the date we had previously mentioned. I know that you both have been wearing the clothes you brought with you from Earth since you arrived, but I was hoping I could convince you to allow me to commission more formal clothing, in the Caeldighn style, for the party. It will be something of a fancy affair, and you may feel more comfortable in dress similar to those around you. Also, it could not hurt their opinion of you, were you to be clad in garments of local make for the occasion."

"Will I still be able to wear the necklace Tharen got me?" Jaea asked.

"Absolutely," Maya answered. "You can even ask Mrs. Lind, the seamstress, to fashion something to match it if you like. I'm certain she would be pleased to do so."

"Alright then. When do we meet with her?" Tharen asked. "I've no objection to fitting in a bit more around here."

"Splendid!" Maya said happily. "She keeps a small shop here in the castle near the royal wing. Mrs. Lind is visiting her daughter this weekend, but I can take you there Monday evening after dinner if you have no objections."

"Works for me," Jaea said.

Tharen nodded. "Me as well."

"Oh, you'll love her shop!" Emily gushed. "So many beautiful materials and designs! You will have to hire servants to help you carry all your treasures back!"

"That reminds me," Maya said cautiously.

Alarm bells went off in Tharen's brain. That was Maya's sneaky voice. He had discovered that people, himself included, often found themselves involuntarily volunteering for tasks when

Maya broke out the sneaky voice.

"I've been meaning to suggest you each do just that, hire on someone," Maya explained. "Especially if you decide to stay on here in Caeldighn permanently. Even if you only stay a couple months as you have hinted before, I am sure you would find the assistance invaluable."

"I don't know Maya," Jaea said doubtfully. "A servant?"

Tharen knit his brow. "How could we even pay them, if we did take one on?"

"You are an Ambassador. The crown provides the service of one servant to aid you in learning the customs of our world, such as proper manners and appropriate dress. We had a number of interesting Ambassadors before this became the common practice, in hopes of avoiding embarrassing situations," Maya replied. "And Jaea has funds, left to her by our parents. I have kept her accounts in order in hopes she would find her way back to us one day, which she did." She smiled at her sister.

"I have accounts?" Jaea asked surprised. She shook her head. "Still, what would she do?"

Emily laughed. "A servant in your employ would be just that, a servant. The terms of service would be discussed and agreed on by both parties. Laundry, mending, shopping, correspondence, or merely someone to talk with to save you from boredom. You seem to fear we are mistreated in some way. We are citizens of Caeldighn who happen to be in search of employment. We have all the rights anyone else does under the crown," she said reassuringly.

Tharen still felt uneasy at the prospect of having a servant. A quick glance at Jaea confirmed she wasn't certain she like the notion either.

"You would also be easing the burden of the general castle staff that has been seeing to some of the duties Emily mentioned," Maya added.

She's good, Tharen thought in admiration. *She knew that would get us on board so she saved it for last.* "Well, okay then," he relented.

"I suppose it wouldn't kill me," Jaea agreed. "How do we proceed in hiring a servant?"

"I will notify the castle housekeepers. One of them will meet with you to determine the qualities or skills required for someone in your employ, and they will send you an applicant or two based on what they learned about you in said meeting. If you would prefer not to hire the suggested person others will be sent your way until a suitable match is made." Maya frowned. "I feel as though I am constantly explaining some dull matter or another of late. I hope I am not boring you."

"No! Not at all," Jaea assured her.

Boring? Tharen thought. *Not in the slightest. Filling my head with so much information I fear my brain will burst, yes.*

"Still," Maya said as she selected another dainty sandwich from the platter. "Perhaps we could take a break from the lecturing, or at least from the castle, and get out of Maeshowe for a time. See a little more of Caeldighn. Due to a rescheduled meeting, I have all of next Saturday free. I know that you came through the First Queen's Forest on your way here, but it is a beautiful place that merits multiple visits. Would you two be interested in seeing some more of it Saturday?"

"Oh, yes please!" Jaea said happily.

"Sounds like a plan," Tharen agreed. "And on that joyful note, I must part from your lovely company, ladies. I am due for an appointment at Image, Fine Art and Photography. Thank you for the meal," he said, rising from his seat. "See you both for dinner?"

"Yes," Maya answered. "Kaylee has requested we all dine together this evening. She feels she has not had sufficient chance to converse with you outside of what you call Shaper 101."

Tharen laughed. "I bet it was closer to a demand than a

request."

"I can escort you out, Mr. McKenna," Emily said. "I will notify the head of staff of your and Jaea's plans so they can prepare. I have no desire to study McClanahan family history this afternoon after helping Maya make flashcards this morning." She grinned.

"Have fun!" Jaea called to Tharen as he left.

"I'll tell you all about it later," Tharen promised, closing the door behind him.

Jaea felt a little awkward with the crowd reduced to only herself and Maya. When she wasn't with her sister, she could think of dozens of questions to ask her. As soon as Jaea actually had a moment to ask them, they all fled her mind. "Flashcards, huh?" Jaea managed.

"I may have gone overboard, a tiny bit, preparing for our meeting today." Maya chuckled. She shrugged. "Better to be over prepared than under. Let's get settled in more comfortable chairs before we launch into our family tree further." She crossed the room to a cozy seating area comprised of a few well stuffed armchairs arranged near the fireplace.

Jaea settled in one of the chairs as Maya lifted a kettle from the top of a glass box that appeared to be holding fire captive somehow. She filled a blue teapot from the kettle's steaming water. After she had done so and returned it to its place on the glass box, she pushed a small wheeled table to rest between Jaea's chair and her own.

"Since Tharen mentioned his plans to attend a tea party, I have wanted to have one as well," Maya admitted.

"I like your tea set," Jaea said, running a finger along the rim of the small blue cup in front of her. "It looks familiar for some reason. Unlike that box. What is that?"

Maya turned so she could see the object in question.

"Dragonfire," she answered. "It is amazing stuff. The dragons make all sorts of things with it. That particular box is made of a glass the dragons designed to hold their fire. It burns like that only when there is water above it to heat. Otherwise its flames are dimmer and a purple color."

"That is so cool! I have got to get to Silverhaven."

Maya smiled at her, but quickly turned pensive. Jaea wondered if there had ever been a time when her sister's smile was not haunted as it often was now.

Maya looked at Jaea carefully. "Have you been remembering more of your life here since you returned?"

"Bits and pieces. Mostly impressions and blurry memories. Why do you ask?"

"Partly just out of curiosity. You said this set looked familiar?"

"Yes," Jaea replied warily.

"It was our mother's," Maya told her. "It seemed fitting to use it today, as I tell you about our family."

"This was our mother's?" Jaea repeated, cradling the cup in her hand. "That's even better than dragonfire." She set the cup back on the table and wiped her eyes. "It's so weird, this two sets of parents thing. All I remembered about our parents was that they were gone. I love Ben and Maggie, and I will always be grateful for them. I just... Was it easier to bear the loss here? Growing up with people who could tell you about Mom and Dad?"

Maya frowned. "Easier to grow up an orphan in a kingdom perpetually falling into war?"

"Not that part obviously," Jaea conceded. "But you have always known your heritage. You have the McClanahan family to tell you stories about our father when he was younger. People reminding you of your mother's eye color or how she laughed."

Maya shook her head. "I don't know that either way is better. I was aware of just how much was missing, what had been taken from me. Other people can only understand one's grief to an extent. I lost my parents, my sister, and my home in such a short time. I grew up in the shadow of memories. You grew up lost, but blissfully unaware of the troubles here."

"I didn't mean to leave and have such a drastically different life," Jaea tried to joke.

Maya waved her hand in dismissal and managed a small chuckle. "I didn't intend to be nearly killed as a child and raised in a political mess. I think we've done quite well for ourselves, considering."

Jaea did laugh this time. "Absolutely. Just look how adjusted we are, blubbering over tea cups." She swiped at the few tears that trickled down her cheeks.

Maya smiled and wiped her eyes. "You sounded like Aunt Adi just now."

"Okay. Catch me up on our family tree and be as silly as you can before we digress and burst into tears."

Maya nodded and poured tea in each of their cups. "Did you know that Grandmother McClanahan could only Shape into water animals, but that in human form she couldn't swim to save her life? Or that when our Great Aunt Mildred was a child, she Shaped into a green cat once on accident?"

"How did she make herself green," Jaea asked, amazed.

"To this day, no one has a clue." Maya shrugged.

CHAPTER TEN

Monday evening saw Tharen rushing back to the castle. He would never have guessed that tea parties could be so entertaining, or enlightening. He had become so caught up in conversation with Terra and her mother that they invited him to stay for dinner. Well, Teresa had politely invited him. Terra had pleaded, saying she had to hear just one more story about Earth. Terra made him promise to come by for tea again soon since he couldn't stay for dinner that evening. Tharen went over everything Terra and Teresa had told him as he hurried to meet Jaea and Maya. While he had learned a few fun and interesting things regarding Teresa's craft, he had also learned more about the effects of Caeldighn's political situation on its less wealthy citizens. Some of it troubled him, and some of it just downright angered him. Maybe Maya and Kaylee would explain the matters to him in better detail.

Tharen tried not to scowl as he nodded to the guards on watch at the main gate. He took the side path through the courtyard that pages used to run messages to people in the dining hall. Hopefully he could catch them before they left the hall. If not, he figured one of his kitchen friends could tell him how to find them. Those people knew shortcuts like you wouldn't believe. He stopped between the open doors of the dining hall to look for Jaea. He spotted her quickly and made his way toward her. A ring of men surrounded her, hanging on her every word. Apparently, Tharen wasn't the only one seeking her company.

"No, it's not like a stage." Jaea laughed as she tried to explain. "It's a box, that plugs into the wall. You can watch shows and movies and stuff on its screen."

"Fascinating!" One of the men exclaimed, moving closer to Jaea and putting his arm around her shoulders. "However, I still have no idea why you would watch a box."

Tharen watched in disbelief as Jaea laughed again and elbowed the man playfully. Was Jaea flirting? Jaea never flirted. She didn't want to get close to someone who might leave her when they found out she wasn't a normal human. Except no one in Caeldighn would be shocked by her Shaping, Tharen realized with a jolt. All these hooligans putting the moves on his girl were Shapers too! Friend, he reminded himself firmly. Jaea was his friend, not his girl, not anymore. Tharen took a breath to calm himself and tried to get Jaea's attention.

"Hey there! I see what you are doing Clint," the man to Jaea's left teased. "Trying to win her over before she has a chance to get to know us charming, more handsome fellows."

"Oh, you poor thing," Jaea joked, patting his cheek. "Are you feeling left out of the conversation again?"

Tharen cleared his throat. The two men that had been standing beside him, took one look at his face and decided they had better places to be just then. Jaea looked at Tharen reproachfully.

"There was no need to scare them off, Tharen. We were just talking."

Tharen eyed Clint and the guy on Jaea's left. It seemed they were made of sterner stuff than the others. "We have plans, do we not?" Tharen asked.

"That we do. Now that you are finally here. Maya was called

away earlier, so we are to meet her at her quarters." Jaea rose from her seat. "Thank you for keeping me company, gentlemen. Perhaps I'll see you at dinner tomorrow."

Tharen offered Jaea his arm and led her toward the huge wooden doors at the end of the dining hall.

"Rude much?" Jaea asked when they were out of earshot.

"Maybe I was just taken aback by the forwardness of your crowd of admirers," Tharen said.

"If someone wants to flirt with me, they can," Jaea retorted. "I am allowed to flirt, you know. I can date even. There is actually a chance that I could live a normal life here, without having to hide the real me."

"I thought you hadn't decided to stay yet?" Tharen felt a bubble of panic in his chest.

"I haven't. I've thought about it, though. Haven't you?" Jaea asked.

"Well, yeah, but I go where you go. You know that."

Jaea shook her head sadly, making Tharen wonder if she knew something he didn't.

"Friendship only goes so far," Jaea said quietly. "I've seen the women practically throwing themselves at you, Tharen. You may change your mind." She rose her hand to knock on Maya's door and nearly knocked on Emily's nose.

"Oh! Good timing," Emily said cheerfully. "I was just on my way out."

"Is Maya in?" Tharen asked.

"Mm 'ere!" Maya said around a mouthful. She came around the corner with a roll in hand. "I'm ready. Let's go, before something else needs attention. Good night, Emily!"

"Good evening, Maya." Emily waved.

"Right. This way." Maya took another bite of her roll and led them down the hall. "Gwena is having some food put back for you, Tharen, since you missed dinner. How was your tea party?"

"It was more fun than I expected," Tharen said honestly. "Although our conversation raised a number of questions I would like to run by you, or anyone with expertise in Caeldighn politics and economy."

"You? Questions? Why am I not at all surprised," Maya teased. "I believe I could arrange for someone to meet with you and discuss such matters. Are you curious about the political and economic structure of Caeldighn in general, or their current standing?"

"Both. All of it. Everything," Tharen answered.

"I would like to attend these meetings as well, if that is alright," Jaea added.

Maya looked at her companions seriously. "I knew you were both interested in this world, but something has changed. What happened?"

Jaea shrugged. "My people are here. I need to know that they are okay. Even if we do go back to Earth, I want to know my homeland is thriving. The longer we are here the more it becomes obvious that Caeldighn is not."

Maya looked expectantly at Tharen.

"Her people are my people," Tharen said. "That's how it was on Earth, and how I see it here. I just like to know what I am dealing with."

Maya's stare made Tharen feel like he had been sent to the principal's office. It made him anxious. "Have we done something wrong?" he asked.

"No," Maya said quickly. "I had not realized you felt this way is all. I will see to the arrangements first thing tomorrow." She resumed leading them down corridors toward the royal wing. A few minutes later, they arrived at the tailor's. "Here we are. Our fashions are somewhat different than those of your world, but I hope you find them pleasing."

Jaea thought that finding Caeldighn formal wear would be like shopping for a vintage prom dress. Some old fashion designs, a few unknown materials with odd patterns, one hideous thing barely classifiable as a dress, and a handful of selections that she could make work. That is not what she found when she followed Maya into the shop. Everyday clothes like those she had seen most Caeldighnians wearing filled the first portion of the shop, but the materials here were finer and the colors more vibrant. The displayed styles grew more formal the farther into the store they explored. Bits of lace, feathers, and beading integrated themselves into fabrics patterned after tree barks and flower petals. One whole wall was overrun with bolts of material and bins full of odds and ends. Jaea was reverently tracing the tiny stitches that decorated the bodice of one of the gowns when a cheerful bell sounded, pulling her out of her reverie. She looked up just in time to see Maya speaking with a petite woman while she signed them in. Jaea went to stand by Tharen, who had his hands in his jeans pockets and was looking at everything with distrust.

"Aren't these fabrics beautiful!" Jaea said excitedly. "I can't make anything like these. Oh! That one looks like it's covered in frost. How did they do that?"

"No idea," Tharen said, clearly not very interested. "Do you think that is the formal stuff then?" He nodded toward a back corner of the room.

"Of course not! Those are semi formal. Formal wear is this way." The woman Maya had been speaking with came out from behind the counter and started through a doorway Jaea hadn't even noticed. "Well, come on then," she called when she saw that they weren't behind her.

"After you," Maya said waving Jaea and Tharen forward.

As she entered the adjoining room Jaea couldn't help but gasp. Even Tharen let out an appreciative whistle. An abundance of styles leapt out at them, everything from simple elegance to over-the-top grandeur. Bold, vibrant colors nearly overwhelmed Jaea as her eyes adjusted. The magnificent skill and attention to detail in each of the pieces demanded admiration.

"Why, thank you," their guide said, amusement adding wrinkles to her face. "I made most of these myself, although my apprentice aided me with a number of them."

"Mrs. Lind, may I introduce my sister Jaea McClanahan," Maya said politely. "As well as our newest Ambassador, Tharen McKenna."

"Pleased to meet you," Mrs. Lind said. "I'm told you are seeking garments to wear to Jaea's homecoming celebration."

Jaea and Tharen nodded.

"As you can see, I have a quite a few selections here that can be tailored to you. I can also make you an entirely new piece if you prefer. I will walk you through the designs and fabrics I have so I can learn more about your tastes and help you find something you will be both comfortable and fashionable wearing. Any suggestions or questions before we begin?" she asked.

"Please don't make me wear something like that," Tharen begged, pointing out a tunic that seemed to be fashioned out of peacock feathers.

Mrs. Lind grinned. "Noted. And you dear?" she asked Jaea.

Jaea handed Mrs. Lind the necklace Tharen had given her. "I would like something that would pair well with this."

"Ah. Beautiful. One of Teresa's?"

"It is," Tharen answered when Jaea looked at him uncertainly.

"I thought so. Such wonderful craftsmanship," Mrs. Lind said. "Now then. Who first?"

"Me, please!" Jaea exclaimed.

Tharen laughed. "No complaints here."

"Alright. Tharen, if you like you can browse the men's fashions, just over there, while Jaea and I play. Jaea, come with me!"

"Have fun," Tharen told Jaea with a wink before he set off as ordered.

Mrs. Lind steered Jaea closer to a set of three gowns. "Now I think the simpler styles would suit you best," she said. "You don't strike me as the gaudy type."

"I couldn't agree more," Jaea said.

"Since this ball is serving as both a homecoming and a coming out party, I would suggest that you stick to off whites or pastel colors. It isn't saying that you want a husband, but it would give the men pause enough to wonder if you may."

"I knew you were trying to marry me off!" Jaea joked, poking Maya in the arm.

"Not a chance," Maya told her. "I just got my sister back. I am not yet prepared to share you with a husband."

"From what I hear, there are a number of men that would happily take either of you for a bride," Mrs. Lind said matter of factly. She took advantage of the stunned silence to get the conversation back on track. "Truly though, you would be splendid in an ivory or dusty lilac. Nearly any shade of pink."

"Her Shaper mark is violet." Maya offered. She looked at Jaea. "Would you be comfortable showing your mark? It is kind of a tradition for coming out events."

"Absolutely!" Jaea answered. "I've often had to hide it. It would be nice to be seen for all that I am for once."

"How much more of your arm is covered by your mark?" Mrs. Lind asked Jaea.

Jaea rolled up the right sleeve of her t-shirt to show the purple vine twisting from bicep to shoulder blade.

"We should have no problem there, especially with more

117

traditional sleeves like these," Mrs. Lind said, pointing at the gown on her left. "There are a number of options for slits in the fabric, making little windows of a sort, so the mark would be clearly visible. Completely bare shoulders and arms is seen as distasteful, but we can do a corset style top with sleeve like tails coming off the shoulder, or even give it straps like a halter style. Or perhaps you would prefer a one shoulder piece so that the arm with your mark is bare but the other is covered?"

"More of a corset style," Jaea said definitely. "I like the one shoulder sleeve idea a bit. And pink, I think."

"I have just the thing! I heard you admiring the frost effect earlier," Mrs. Lind admitted. "You look through this, and I will be right back." She handed Jaea a large book and scurried off.

"Oh, these are just wonderful," Jaea breathed. She showed Maya the page. "Wow! And these are loud!" The page she held up for her sister pictured two boldly colored and styled dresses that reminded Jaea of a parrot.

"Those are fashioned after some of the birds that live on the islands," Maya told her. "Mrs. Lind tried to get me to wear something similar to the Queen's Festival last year."

"What are you wearing to this ball thing?" Jaea asked as she continued to flip through the book.

"Red, always red. That one there, actually." Maya smiled and pointed to a wine colored creation on a nearby stand. It had a collar that dipped into a v-shaped neckline partly filled with lacing. Gauzy material spilled from where the short dressy sleeves gathered, and a good amount of embroidery was stitched from one bottom corner all the way to the opposite thigh leading the eyes back to the prettily belted waist.

"Oh, Maya! It is stunning! I love those little flyaways coming off the sleeves."

"Mrs. Lind fashioned it after one of the roses from our father's garden. They are my favorites, his roses."

"Dad grew roses?"

"The only thing he could grow according to Aunt Jal. The man was rubbish with every other plant. She says he only learned to grow roses so he could bring them to our mother," Maya told her. "That reminds me. Jayla and Adrielle have requested the honor of introducing you at the ball. They are hoping you will take tea with them tomorrow, so they can ask you themselves."

"I get to meet my aunts tomorrow? How cool is that!" Jaea said excitedly. Then her shoulders slumped. *At age twenty-two, I am going to meet my aunts.* "I barely remember them. What if they don't like me?"

"They will adore you," Maya assured her.

Easy for you to say, Jaea thought. *You've known them your whole life.*

Mays bumped Jaea with her elbow. "I think you are growing on me as well," she teased. "Although I am a tad envious of your willowy frame and devoted man."

Jaea laughed. "Willowy is a romanticized word that sounds too graceful to apply to me. The girls at school made it clear that I have the curves of a bean pole. I'll trade you any day, Ms. I-look-gorgeous-in-anything."

"Do I get Tharen if we trade bodies?" Maya grinned.

"He isn't mine!" Jaea felt a blush creep into her cheeks. "He made that clear some time ago," she said quietly.

"Sister of mine, you are blind to how he looks at you. It's not like a brother. More like a jealous suitor or a someone with claim to a gold mine. He does not want anyone else near you."

Jaea shook her head. "I once thought so, too. But Tharen is just my friend."

Maya shrugged. "Perhaps I am mistaken. You know him better than I do."

"Found it!" Mrs. Lind said excitedly as she hung the dress up in one of the fitting rooms. She poked her graying head around the corner. "Well, come see!"

Jaea and Maya obediently hurried over.

"Now this isn't the frost technique, but a similar one I call sun kissed. I thought you may like the warmer tone, as it would complement your complexion very well. And lucky for us, the wrap is already on the left arm. So if you wish to wear it, I need only do a quick fitting. What do you think?" Mrs. Lind practically bounced in place.

"It is more than I could have imagined!" Jaea said happily as she reached out to touch the rosy pink dress. Her fingers traced the stitched flowers that belted the waist and trailed down the left side of the dress. Matching stitching adorned the gossamer wrap that flowed down to form a left sleeve. "Sun kissed," Jaea mused, spying the golden tints that shot through the material. "How did you do that!"

"I pulled some of the threads through a tool one of the fire smiths at Silverhaven made me," Mrs. Lind told her. "Do you like it then?"

"I love it!" Jaea exclaimed. "Can I try it on now?"

"That is why you are here, dear." Mrs. Lind grinned. "Maya, would you mind checking on our young man, while I help Jaea into this? I will call you both over when we are done."

"Yes, ma'am," Maya said. "I'll go make sure he hasn't dozed off."

Tharen did a quick experimental spin in the kilt he had donned. The sheer joy on his face was soon replaced with mild embarrassment when he realized Maya had seen him twirling in circles.

He smiled and shrugged. "I love kilts. Can I please keep this kilt? That book says this is an Ambassador's plaid." He patted the black material and pointed to the thin gray and blue lines that checkered it. "I always wanted a kilt, but I don't know anything about my ancestry or what colors I could wear. I am an Ambassador! Ambassador plaid. Please?"

Maya pressed her hands to her mouth to stifle her laughter. "I am sure Mrs. Lind will allow that when she assures it fits you properly. It is appropriate wear for the ball, or anywhere really. Kilts are quite popular still among Shapers, a carry over from our time on Earth, I suppose. You certainly would not be the only dashing gentleman in a kilt vying for a dance with Jaea."

"Best news I've had all day!" Tharen said. "Wait a minute. Who will be trying to dance with Jaea?"

"Likely every male in Caeldighn when they see her in that dress."

"I see. Am I allowed to carry a sword or club or frying pan to this shindig?" Tharen asked hopefully.

"Not particularly," Maya told him. "Why? Afraid someone will sweep her off her feet?"

"No. Not exactly," Tharen said reluctantly. "I want her to be happy. I'm just afraid that means I'll lose her."

"Uh huh."

"Friend! She is my friend. I don't want to lose her friendship because some dandy in a peacock shirt decides to woo her," Tharen said.

"Alright you two! Come admire my new favorite customer," Mrs. Lind called.

"Should I change back into my jeans?" Tharen asked Maya.

"Absolutely not. Come along, Ambassador McKenna."

Mrs. Lind laughed when Tharen and Maya came back into view. "I see you found the kilts."

"Yes ma'am," Tharen said.

"Looks like it was made for you. Would you like to wear it to the ball or were you just trying it on?"

"I'd hoped to wear it to the ball," Tharen answered. "Well, everywhere possible really."

"Ah. A kilt man. I like you even more, McKenna. We will get you set up momentarily. First though, I should like to introduce the lovely Jaea McClanahan. Come on out, dear!"

Jaea stepped around the corner from the dressing area, beaming like a child at Christmas, a vision in pale pink. "I feel like a fairy princess. I think I've spent the last five minutes swaying and spinning just to watch the dress swish back and forth. So, what do you think? Will it do?" she asked.

"You look heartbreakingly beautiful," Tharen told her. He kissed her on the cheek.

Jaea smiled a little sadly.

"You look splendid," Maya told her.

"Of course she does!" Mrs. Lind cried. "We are all agreed then? This is the dress for her coming out?"

Everyone nodded. "Good. On to the gentleman in a moment then. Just let me help Miss Jaea out of this so she doesn't stick herself with any of the pins. And don't you worry, sweet, it will take me barely any time at all to bring the seams in a touch. It will fit you perfectly next time you have it on," she assured Jaea as she ushered her back into the fitting room.

Within no time at all, Mrs. Lind had outfitted Tharen with a light blue shirt to match the blue on the plaid of his kilt and a collared black vest with obsidian buttons. Maya and Mrs. Lind seemed a little suspicious when Tharen emphatically dismissed the notion of showing his Shaper mark at the ball. However, they knew that some Shapers disliked strangers seeing their mark so they did not pursue the matter further. With Tharen's measurements taken, Mrs. Lind led them to a wall of footwear and pointed out boots that Tharen could choose from before selecting a pair of slippers for both Jaea and Maya to try on.

"Since you will be on your feet all night, I recommend flats? I think these will go best with your dresses, and they are some of the more comfortable shoes I've seen. They look plain now, but I

122

intend to remake them a tad with materials that match your gowns," Mrs. Lind told the girls.

As the girls busied themselves following orders and trying on the selected slippers, Mrs. Lind turned back to Tharen who was hopelessly staring at the two different boots he was wearing.

"They are both comfortable and handsome things. Please just tell me which one to wear," Tharen pleaded.

"The left. They suit you more," Mrs. Lind said decisively.

"Thank you," Tharen said.

"These will be perfect," Maya told Mrs. Lind as she and Jaea set their shoes down.

"Good," Mrs. Lind said. She walked them to the store's entrance. "I believe that is all we need do for now. I will send word when I have them all ready. Though you need not wait to come visit me or shop around some more." She smiled.

"Thank you again for seeing us on such short notice," Maya said.

"Nonsense. I am thrilled to have you. Business has been rather slow since Queen Sarai went to the stars. It is nice to feel a bit of the hectic bustle and rush again. Goodnight, dears."

"Goodnight," the three answered.

Maya yawned. "We had best get to bed. Big day tomorrow."

"Really?" Tharen asked.

"My aunts are here!" Jaea said joyfully.

"Yes," Maya said. "And they have business with all of us. They wish to spend time getting reacquainted with Jaea. They have a few small mountains of papers and reports to see to with Kaylee and I. And they are going to interview you, Tharen, like we discussed."

"Interview?" Jaea asked.

"To make me more officially an Ambassador," Tharen explained. "Technically there is no ruler to approve it since Aurora is only a Regent, not the full Queen. So I'm getting approved by the Chiefs and Aurora. I meet with Aurora tomorrow afternoon."

"With Jayla and Adrielle as well," Maya told him. "Hopefully by nightfall you will be as official as can be had."

"No pressure," Tharen said sarcastically.

"You will be fine," Maya said. "Both of you," she added, putting her arm around Jaea's shoulders. "Now hurry it up, or I may fall asleep here in the hall."

CHAPTER ELEVEN

Jaea fussed with her tree necklace while Maya knocked on the door to their aunts' quarters at one of Maeshowe's inns. Apparently whenever their aunts stepped foot in the castle they were quickly bombarded by people, so Jayla and Adrielle stayed elsewhere if at all possible.

"You look fine," Maya told her. "And they will love you. Stop worrying."

Jaea just nodded and took a deep breath, trying to keep from fidgeting. Then the door opened, and there was neither time nor reason to worry when she was pulled into a tight hug.

"You're alive! You're safe! And you are home!" Jaea's hugger cried thankfully, rocking her back and forth. "You cannot imagine the sleepless nights I have had wondering how you were faring all these years."

"Adrielle, you could let the girl in and introduce yourself," a woman called from just inside the door. "At this rate, you will suffocate our niece before she gets to say hello."

"Goodness! Yes," Adrielle said, releasing her hold on Jaea. "Sorry. Got ahead of myself there." She wiped her eyes and smiled at Maya and Jaea. "Come in, please."

Maya kissed Adrielle's cheek then walked in to greet her other aunt. Adrielle closed the door after Jaea followed her sister into the room.

"Aunt Jayla, Aunt Adrielle," Maya began. "My sister Jaea, recently returned from Earth."

Not quite certain what to do, Jaea smiled and waved at her aunts. Both were shorter than their nieces, but Adrielle was shorter than Jayla as well. Both women had dark brown hair and brown eyes, so Jaea guessed hers and Maya's green must have come from their mother's side.

"Oh! Can I hug you again now?" Adrielle asked impatiently.

"I am not opposed to hugs," Jaea said, and found herself instantly back in Adrielle's embrace.

"I am just so happy to see you. I can't help it," Adrielle explained. "I refuse to be held accountable for being ridiculously sentimental."

"What if I want to hug her? She is my long lost niece too," Jayla said.

Adrielle sighed dramatically and let loose of Jaea. "I suppose I can share. Besides, I have not yet received a hug from my Maya-girl. Switch!" Adrielle nudged Jaea toward Jayla and pulled Maya into a hug.

Jayla wrapped her arms around her niece. "Welcome back, my dear."

"Thank you, Aunt Jayla," Jaea replied.

Jayla laughed. "When we can escape formality, all of our friends and family worth their salt call me Jal and her Adi. Now before I forget, we have something for you."

"But I didn't get you anything," Jaea protested as Jayla led her to the sitting room area in their quarters. Adrielle and Maya followed, settling into seats opposite the others.

"This was delivered to my house last week. I believe the post officers must have mistook it for a misspelling of my name. As you can see, it is in fact addressed to you." Jayla handed Jaea a thick envelope.

"It's from my Mom!" Jaea exclaimed, nearly leaping from her

seat when she recognized Maggie's handwriting. "My adoptive mother," she explained to the group.

"Would you like us to leave you to your letter for a time?" Jayla asked.

Jaea debated for a moment. "No. Doubtless it is for Tharen as well. I will wait until we can both read it," she decided, tucking the letter reverently into her pocket.

"Great! Because I have a present too!" Adrielle said. "Well, actually part of it is from Ransley." She handed Jaea a small notebook and a pen.

"From Ransley?" Jaea asked.

"Yes. He said if you intend to have contacts in multiple worlds you should have a better way of contacting them than relying on him as a mailman," Jayla told her.

"We ran into him at the monument on our way here. Now open your book!" Adrielle added.

Still confused as to why she had been given pen and paper and wondering if she was meant to be taking notes throughout this meeting with her aunts, Jaea tentatively lifted the front cover. She laughed aloud when she saw her father's handwriting scrawled across the top of the page. It read, *Hello, brat. This thing working? Some jolly pirate dropped it off. He said it was like your world's version of a telegram. So write back. Quick like. Love you. -Dad*

"It's called a messenger pen. Very handy things," Adrielle explained when confusion returned to Jaea's face. "Anything you write with that pen will show up on whatever paper your Earth parents place it on and vice versa."

"I don't know what to say," Jaea said stunned. "This is the best present I have ever received! Thank you!"

"Well, like I said, the pens are from Ransley. I know from experience, that using them is easier when you have somewhere to keep all the back and forth messages together. Hence the notebook. You can use any paper, if you would prefer to use something else." Adrielle shrugged.

"No. It's wonderful," Jaea said, tracing the design on the leather cover. "And incredibly thoughtful."

"Alright you lot. Some of us have work to do," Maya quipped. "I should likely get back to it."

"So long as you return here in time for dinner tonight," Jayla said. "I would like to push the reports back until tomorrow though, if you and Kaylee don't mind."

"Gladly," Maya answered. "On both counts. I will let Kaylee know."

"Invite her to dine with us tonight while you are at it," Adrielle requested. "And Jaea's young man, if he is available."

Jaea threw her hands in the air. "He isn't my man!"

Maya just laughed and waved on her way out.

"Oh! I sense a story," Adrielle said happily. "Lucky for you, we have tea and cookies. Essential storytelling aids in my opinion." She kissed Jaea's brow as she walked past her to gather said tea and cookies together.

"You do not have to tell us if you would rather not," Jayla told her. "I imagine this is all still a little overwhelming for you. We would love to hear anything you feel comfortable telling us. We do have a couple of decades to catch up on after all. And you are more than welcome to ask questions of us, all morning if you like." Jayla took Jaea's hand. "Truly, we are just happy to see you alive and well."

Adrielle sat back down across from Jaea after setting a tray on a nearby table. "Aw, do we not get the dirt on the fella?"

Jaea laughed. "I suppose Tharen is as good a place to start as any." Jaea nodded her head when Adrielle motioned to the honey and spooned some into her tea. "Where to start?" she mused.

"Typically the beginning works best, but starting in the middle is perfectly acceptable as well," Adrielle teased as she handed

Jaea a cup and saucer with a large, precariously balanced, cookie.

"How did you meet?" Jayla asked as she fixed her own tea.

"Well, we met in school, at recess. I was in first grade, about six years old, and he was a year ahead of me, in second grade. The other kids thought I was weird, so they didn't exactly seek my company. Tharen was sitting on a picnic table, just kind of glaring at the world. A bully by the name of Jason and his cronies started picking on him. You know, taunting him and making fun of him. It made me mad. I had heard Jason was mean, but I had never actually witnessed it until then. So I went over and sat down next to Tharen on the table and asked Jason how his cat was doing." Jaea laughed.

"His cat?" Jayla asked. She dunked a cookie into her tea before she took a bite. "I don't think I am quite following."

"My neighbor is a vet, and I had seen Jason over there when he and his parents dropped off Jason's cat. That cat was probably Jason's only redeeming quality," Jaea explained. "He seemed really wary when I sat down next to Tharen to begin with. Then I went and asked him about his beloved pet. He blushed and informed me that Muffin was fine and had just had kittens the day before. Then he quickly walked away, and his confused buddies followed him. I just sat and talked to Tharen the rest of recess that day. And the next, and the next. Until he finally asked me why I was there."

"What did you tell him?" Adrielle gushed.

Jaea smiled, remembering. "I told him that I was in need of a best friend and so was he, and that obviously meant that we should be each others' best friends. First grade logic, what can I say? But it worked. At first he only shrugged and seemed to just accept that I wasn't going to leave. And then he seemed to decide overnight that I really was his best friend." Jaea sipped her tea. "After that we were inseparable. He was at my house more than he was at his foster home growing up. We told each other everything, including the whole more than just human bit after I Shaped in front of him on accident. We watched each other's backs, both with keeping our secret and keeping away from bullies. We got into a number of scraps with people who thought the two odd kids would be easy prey. He moved in next door with Doc when he got emancipated at sixteen. Even after he graduated and went to college a town over, we talked all the time and went to the coast or somewhere to Shape whenever possible."

"I think I will like this Tharen chap," Adrielle said. "Though I find myself wondering, what happened between the end of your story and today?"

"Adi, stop pushing!" Jayla admonished.

"What do you mean?" Jaea asked.

"It seems to me that there is more to the tale of Jaea and Tharen to date. As in to this point in time, date. Not romantic dinner, date," Adrielle clarified.

"Oh," Jaea said around a mouthful of cookie. "Well, we dated for a while. But-"

"Aha!" Adrielle grinned.

No aha! We dated once and now we aren't. Nothing else to discuss, Jaea thought, pushing down a flare of panic. She shrugged, hoping it looked like she was indifferent about the topic. "It was a long time ago. We ended it before he went abroad for school. Tharen loved it over there. So he stayed. Finished his Bachelors, got a Masters. Spent a lot of time at different digs. He studied archaeology," Jaea explained at her aunts' confused looks. "It's a way of learning about the past, literally digging up a physical record. We lost touch more the longer he was gone, but we are still friends. He came home to surprise me on my birthday, woke me up from a Nirah dream. Not long after that we met Ransley and came here."

Jayla looked at Jaea thoughtfully. "Nirah dream?" she asked.

"Yeah. Since I was a kid, I've always had dreams where I visited a monument and talked to a lady named Nirah who was stuck inside it somehow. Maya told me that it's an actual place here, but I haven't had the chance to see it yet."

"Hmm. Interesting. Makes sense I suppose. Your mother descends from Nirah's line," Jayla said.

Jaea nodded. "Maya has been showing me stuff about our family history. My biological father was your brother, and that branch of the family goes all the way back to the first queen, right?"

"Correct," Adrielle answered. "Bowen, your father, was our parents' middle child. I am the youngest and my dear older brother helped spoil me rotten according to my elders. He simply adored his big sister, Jayla. He even named you after her."

"Really!" Jaea said happily. "How cool is that? Our names are quite similar," she said pointing half a cookie at Jayla. "He was a good brother then? My Dad?"

Jayla grinned. "I am not certain it is possible for someone without a brother to completely understand the situation of having a brother. We often drove each other crazy, but we were siblings, and we loved each other."

"It must have been wonderful. Growing up here, all of you together," Jaea said a little wistfully.

"It was!" Adrielle laughed but quickly fell somber. "We lost too many of our family, much too soon." She shook her head. "But the sadness of that loss cannot discount the joy their lives infused into the lives of those around them. Even with the war and this mess that has followed it since, I don't think I would have traded it for all the worlds."

Jayla smiled at Adrielle. "It is certainly a blessing, to have friends and family like ours." She looked at Jaea. "Were you lonely? On Earth?"

Jaea shrugged. "I suppose I was sometimes, everyone gets a little lonely now and again. It can be difficult living among humans, knowing you aren't quite one of them. It was only really when I wondered how far the differences went that I became lonely. I was really lucky, though. I have wonderful adoptive parents. Our neighbor and his sister claim me as family. And I always had Tharen, well almost always."

"I am so deeply sorry that you were robbed of the chance to grow up here with Maya, knowing about your people," Jayla told her sincerely. She hung her head. "I should have been there. We tried to find you, for years. I think even to this day everyone in Caeldighn and the worlds we trade with would recognize your Shaper mark."

Jaea knelt beside her aunt's chair and pulled her into a hug. "My disappearance was not your fault Aunt Jal. Or yours Aunt Adi," she added when she saw Adrielle start to tear up. "Neither of you could have predicted or prevented it, my walking through that gate. And I've not had a bad life! I have grown up in a loving home, accepted despite my difference. And I am here now."

"You are here now." Jayla nodded, pulling out of the hug and wiping her eyes. "Please know that wherever I am, you are welcome. Even if you decide to return to Earth. You have family here too. And we love you." Jayla stood up and started collecting the empty tea things. "I'll just get these out of our way and be back in a moment."

Jaea looked at Adrielle questioningly as she settled back in her chair.

Adrielle was looking at Jaea in shock but quickly recovered when Jaea glanced in her direction. She managed a small smile. "Sorry. Jayla is not usually prone to tidal waves of emotion like the rest of the living. It took me aback," she explained. "Still, I can hardly believe that Jal let you through her defensive walls, let alone so quickly."

Jaea rubbed her hands over her face. "It goes both ways. I can't believe I have just opened up like a book to you two. Must be getting easier with practice. I have been telling Maya much of my life as well."

Adrielle clapped her hands loudly as Jayla came back into the room. "Well, there is only one thing to be done now as I see it."

"What?" Jaea asked.

Adrielle rubbed her hands together. "Shopping."

"What?" Jaea asked again, laughing.

"Fresh air, walking, buying of baubles!" Adrielle exclaimed. "Just the thing for dispelling any remaining gloom and prompting further cheerier conversation. Come along!" she called as she opened the door.

Jayla put her arm around Jaca and led her out the open door after Adrielle. "She won't give either of us any peace if we don't catch up to her soon. You up for an outing?" Jayla asked.

"Always. And it just so happens that I am free until dinner," Jaea responded.

Jayla chuckled. "I had heard something to that extent."

All morning Jaea had been waiting for an opportunity to ask her Jayla about the necklace she wore. She decided to bring it up now while they walked out to meet Adrielle. "Aunt Jal, what sort of claw is that? On your necklace?"

"I saw you trying to puzzle that out earlier," Jayla said with a smile. "It is a waya claw, from my friend Tsagi. He gave it to me when I was made part an honorary part of the pack, to help keep track of my location. Plus, as long as I wear it, I can hear the pack songs. I never go without it."

"Now that sounds like a story," Jaea said appreciatively. "Tell me about the waya?"

"If Adi lets us get a word in edgewise, I shall do just that,"

Jayla said as they walked outside. She nodded toward Adrielle standing just a few feet away.

"Now," Adrielle said as she linked arms with her sister and niece when they rejoined her outside the inn. "Jal and I have until around three. Then we have to get ready to interview your Tharen. I propose we wander that way and see what strikes our fancy."

"Sounds good to me," Jaea said.

Jayla nodded.

"Splendid! If either of you sees a yellow cloak or coat, let me know. I am in the market for a new one," Adrielle confided conspiratorially.

CHAPTER TWELVE

Tharen walked into the meeting room feeling more self conscious than ever before in his life. Well, maybe not quite as self conscious as he had felt during one particular conversation with Ben Harbour. Tharen quickly squashed his panic as best he could when he remembered how that day had gone so incredibly different than he had hoped. He took a deep breath and told himself firmly that everything would work out. Besides, Jaea had a letter from Maggie to share with him later, no matter how the interview played out.

"Good afternoon. I take it you are Tharen?" An aristocratic woman asked from her place at a large table.

"Yes ma'am."

The woman nodded, the movement highlighting the silver threads in her chocolate colored hair. "My name is Aurora Buchanan. As you may be aware, I serve Caeldighn as Queen Regent. Basically meaning I have all the life threatening work of a Queen without the pay and fancy stamp." She waved her hands toward the women seated at either side of her. "Jayla Campbell and Adrielle McClanahan, Caeldighn's Chiefs."

"Trying to retire," Adrielle quipped. "Feel free to badger the citizens you meet into trying for the throne."

"Tharen McKenna," Jayla said politely. "It is good to put a face to the name. Jaea and Maya speak highly of you."

"I am pleased to hear that I remain in their good graces," Tharen said.

Adrielle smiled slyly. "I think you would have to try hard indeed to fall from Jaea's good graces. She seems very fond of you."

Tharen shifted his stance, uncomfortable with his relationship with Jaea being addressed.

"Take a seat, McKenna," Aurora invited. "Let us get this interview in motion shall we?"

"Absolutely," Tharen said. He settled into a chair across the table from the women. "So, what would you like to know?"

"Well, that is an interesting question," Jayla said. "We are Chiefs, and so it is our job to ensure that Ambassadors and other people from different worlds are not a threat to our land and our citizens. However, as you are aware, we also are Jaea's family. I find myself torn between my duties as Chief to help appoint new Ambassadors and my duties as an aunt, who is concerned as to whether certain individuals have my niece's best interests at heart."

Tharen met Jayla's warning look with one of his own. "Jaea is my best friend and has been for most of my life. There is no one else, on any world, that I care about more. Now, I will gladly answer your questions in regards to the Ambassador position. But I will not be sharing anything beyond that with you today."

"May I ask why?" Adrielle inquired, intrigued.

"You may, though, I doubt you will care for the answer," Tharen told her honestly. "I do not know either of you, and I am not yet convinced that you have her best interests at heart. Regardless, I will not play spy for you so that you can learn more about Jaea. You can learn of her life by speaking with her."

"Told you so." Aurora laughed, poking Jayla's arm.

Jayla gave Tharen a wry smile. "I am glad she has you, my niece."

"She always will. So long as I have breath," Tharen promised. He saw an odd look cross Adrielle's face as she studied him. He had the distinct feeling that his well being hinged on her opinion. He was relieved when Aurora saved him from pursuing that worrisome train of thought by continuing his interview.

"Tharen, to begin, could you please tell us why you wish to become an Ambassador for Earth in Caeldighn," Aurora requested.

"A number of reasons I suppose," Tharen began. "Although it really boils down to the fact that I would like to get to know more about this world and its inhabitants. I have traveled a fair bit on Earth and believe that I could secure trade for Caeldighn if Jaea and I return to live on Earth. If we choose to remain here, it seems to be the best way to get involved and acclimated to life in Caeldighn." He shrugged. "Besides, Jaea has been busy getting back to her roots, and I am in dire need of something to occupy my time. I would need a job anyway if we stayed, and frankly this one sounds awesome."

"So you would like this job in order to relieve yourself of boredom?" Aurora asked dryly.

"No!" Tharen answered quickly. "Well, if I am being honest, that does factor into it. That just isn't the main reason. It came out all wrong." Tharen sighed. "I can help here. Jaea and I can. We don't have to hide half of ourselves and try to keep from getting too close to anyone or place. Admittedly, I am not yet ready to Shape in broad daylight in the middle of town like Jaea and Maya did the other day. But people, here and on Earth, decided a long time ago that I am someone to talk to. I've heard the life stories of old men and the desperate wishes for puppies or ponies by small children." He paused trying to get the words right. "In Caeldighn, though, I feel like I can live the life I wanted to on Earth. I can become close to people. I may be able to get answers as to who I am, and what happened to my family.

I think I could really do good here. I want to stay and help make Caeldighn what it once was."

The three women looked at him approvingly.

When Tharen realized what he had said he clapped a hand over his mouth.

Adrielle laughed." What is wrong?"

"I didn't mean to say that bit about wanting to stay," Tharen said, a note of panic in his voice. "I didn't know that I wanted to stay. Please don't tell Jaea!"

"Why?" Jayla demanded, no longer amused. "I will not keep secrets from my niece."

"It isn't a secret," Tharen said. "I will tell her, if she asks. But Jaea needs to make the decision to stay or go for herself. No matter how much I may wish to remain here, I will go where Jaea goes. Her people are my people and whatever place she decides to call home, so will I. That's just the way it is, ever since she informed me at recess so many years ago that I was to be her best friend." Tharen laughed. "Jaea is probably the reason people are forever talking my ears off."

"Hmm. Alright," Jayla told him reluctantly. "I will keep your desire to remain in Caeldighn to myself."

"I like him," Adrielle said. "Despite the feeling that we are missing a piece of his story. I vote he gets the position."

"You want to put him in a position that would encourage our people to trust him and tell him everything about our world, and themselves I might add, when even you, with your so-called good judgment of character, believe he is withholding information?" Aurora asked Adrielle seriously.

"Yes," Adrielle answered defensively. "Whatever he is hiding, it is not a threat to us or our people. My informants bring me nothing but good things to say about him. He is very loyal to Jaea, and if we are lucky, he will extend that loyalty to Caeldighn when we have earned it. And my skills of assessment have not let me down as of yet."

"Informants?" Tharen asked in disbelief. "Why are you so convinced I am hiding something?"

Adrielle smiled sheepishly. "Sorry. I am the Chief of Military. Two Shapers from Earth, the last known hideout of some of the Stone rebels, show up in Maeshowe with murmurs of Stone pursuit from an inn en route to the capital? You have to admit it looked suspicious. Jayla's little birdies have been keeping tabs as well."

Jayla nodded, but offered no apology.

"Okay. But hiding?" Tharen repeated.

"Aren't you?" Aurora asked. "Can you honestly tell me that you have left nothing out? That there are no more pieces to your puzzle than what I have been presented with?"

Tharen avoided her gaze and inspected his fingernails.

"Most of what I know about you has come from the mouth of another," Aurora continued. "You have confirmed what information I have garnered, both when asked and simply through your actions. Who are you Tharen McKenna? I have no knowledge of your Shaping abilities, or even your Shaper mark. No knowledge of your family or history."

Tharen looked up. "I am Tharen McKenna. I am a Shaper, but that is all I can tell you on that matter. You now know as much about my family and history as I do. Does it really matter what Shape I can take? You have Ambassadors that are humans, mermaids, and selkies. I am willing to work to aid Caeldighn if I can. What more must you really know?"

Aurora looked at Jayla.

"I agree with Adi," Jayla said, half surprised. "He would hardly be in a position to cause great harm to Caeldighn just because we make him Ambassador. A discount rate in shops and a working knowledge of our libraries? Not exactly threatening. Besides, with the exception of the men seeking Jaea's company, everyone seems to like the man. The cooks, servants, shop owners, even the guards have taken a shine to him. Among children he is the talk of the town. Some folk are uneasy not knowing his Shape, but I am not overly concerned. Though there is quite the bet running on that matter. I believe blue whale is the leading guess currently."

"Blue whale?" Tharen muttered.

"Yes." Jayla laughed. "You apparently said something to a couple children about swimming."

"Tharen," Aurora said abruptly. "Do you understand the role of Ambassador and agree to adhere to the regulations and requirements afforded the office?"

"Yes," Tharen responded, confused by the sudden change in the conversation.

"You are aware that you would be a Junior Ambassador until Caeldighn is again graced with a King or Queen, as only a King or Queen can raise you to the full position of Ambassador?" Aurora asked.

"Yes."

"Then I congratulate you on your new title and occupation, Ambassador McKenna." Aurora stood and offered Tharen her hand.

"Thank you!" Tharen said as he shook hands happily with Aurora and then Jayla and Adrielle.

Aurora smiled. "Please continue to report to Maya. You and she may work out the details on how often you need report. Maya can get you any supplies and allowances you may need as well."

Uncertain he had been dismissed, Tharen stood awkwardly beside the table.

"Go!" Adrielle laughed. "I can practically hear Jaea's impatience for your news from here."

"Thanks!" Tharen made for the door, trying to keep his walk

just under a sprint as he hurried through the castle halls to Jaea's quarters. He slowed his pace as he neared Jaea's rooms. Tharen knocked on Jaea's door, a grim expression fixed on his face. It was difficult to keep it there when Jaea opened the door looking thrilled to see him. "It's official," Tharen told her dejectedly.

Jaea ushered him in with a sympathetic smile.

"I'm an Ambassador!" Tharen shouted. "I will likely be wearing kilts of the Ambassador variety everywhere from now on!" He lifted her off the floor and spun a quick circle.

He kept his arms around her a moment too long after he put her down. He forced himself to step back before he was further tempted to kiss her. He saw the faintest flash of disappointment dim Jaea eyes when he did so and instantly regretted the movement. But he knew now was not the time for that conversation, not with so much else going on.

"So," Tharen said. "Did you give up waiting for me?"

"What?" Jaea asked.

She looks flustered. Tharen thought. *Is she blushing?* He felt his spirit soar a little higher. Maybe things between them stood better than he feared.

"The letter? From home?" Tharen clarified.

"Ah. Right," Jaea said. She crossed the room to retrieve the swollen envelope. "I waited. How should we do this? Take turns reading aloud?" She took a seat at the little table her quarters boasted.

Tharen cleared the books from another chair and pushed it as close to Jaea's as he could. "I figured we would just huddle over it. Because let's be real, there is no way you are going to let go of that paper until you've read the whole thing. And I would like to see Maggie's hand writing, if only to assure myself it is really from her." He sat down, resting one arm on the back of Jaea's chair. "Though I won't complain if you read it aloud as well."

Jaea grinned. "Sometimes I wonder if you know me too well."

She excitedly opened the envelope and pulled out the folded pages. She quickly pressed them flat then scooted closer so Tharen could see the pages as well.

"I feel like we should be in a blanket fort, reading by flashlight." Tharen chuckled.

"Shh! I'm reading," Jaea said, bumping Tharen with her elbow.

"I thought you were going to read it out loud?" Tharen complained, bending to look over Jaea's shoulder. "Now I am behind!"

Jaea turned her head and nearly collided with Tharen. She yelped and motioned for him to back up.

"Sorry." Tharen reluctantly leaned back to give Jaea more space.

"I think it will prove safest to read it aloud." Jaea laughed. "It is Mom's writing," she said as she moved back in the chair trying to get comfortable.

Tharen let his arm fall around Jaea, inviting her to lean against him. He thought Jaea scooted just a hair closer than was strictly necessary, but he may have imagined it. Maybe there was still something there. He grinned as Jaea began to relay the letter's message. It wasn't about anything in particular and was mostly just Maggie relaying bits of news from the area. Even so, it was good to see her handwriting march neat lines across the pages. A reminder of their ties to Earth couldn't have come at a better time. He silently thanked Maggie as he saw Jaea relax in the presence of this piece of home.

Early the next morning, Tharen was surprised to see Jaea already in the kitchen when he arrived. Usually he would be working on his second cup of caffeine when she stumbled in sleepily. He raised his eyebrows at one of the cooks, who shrugged and passed Tharen the tea pot.

"She has been in here scribbling away in that book for about an hour now," George said as he passed.

"What's up, Jaea?" Tharen asked.

"Mom and Dad saw that we wrote them last night with this messenger pen thing," Jaea answered. "I learned this morning that the end of this one lights up when the other one is used. All its blinking woke me up. Wanna say hi?" she asked, offering Tharen the pen.

"Sure." Tharen took the pen and scratched good morning across the page. He was trying to decide if he should sign his name or something after it when the end of the pen glowed orange and neat black letters began to appear underneath his.

Hello Tharen! Good morning! I am so glad you and Jaea are doing well! Love, Maggie.

And me! I say hello too! -Ben

Tharen laughed and went back to eating his breakfast while Jaea resumed writing to her parents. "So what are your plans for the day?"

"Nothing," Jaea said cheerfully, looking up from her notebook. "Maya and Kaylee have Chief business with Aunt Jal and Adi, possibly all day. So I currently have not a single thing planned. It is fantastic!"

"You have been rather busy since we got here. Not like the good old days when all I had to pry you away from was studying." Tharen sighed dramatically. "I suppose sister trumps best friend."

Jaea threw a roll at Tharen, who caught it and promptly began to drown it in jam.

"Do you intend to leave any jam for the rest of us?" Gwena asked as she bustled past.

"If I must," Tharen said. He grinned at Gwena and pushed the jam jar back toward the center of the table.

"I was thinking I would go exploring today," Jaea said.

"Supposedly there's a pond around this place somewhere. And there are a few shops in town I wouldn't mind visiting. Since you are feeling so neglected, perhaps you would like to join me?"

Unable to speak with half a roll in his mouth, Tharen nodded and gave Jaea a thumbs up.

"Great. I am going to stash this back in my quarters. Meet you in the library when you're finished here?"

Tharen gulped down the remainder of his tea. "I'm good. I'll walk with you." He grabbed another roll as he rose. He clapped George on the back as he passed and paused briefly to kiss Gwena's cheek. "So what should we explore first?" he asked Jaea as he followed her out of the kitchen.

CHAPTER THIRTEEN

Jaea and Tharen walked through some of the gardens and stumbled across the rumored pond. She led Tharen to a bench where they could sit for a moment to watch the ducks. Jaea knew that humans enjoyed watching ducks as well, but she felt bad that they missed out on the conversations. The sudden dives and feather ruffles were much more entertaining with the commentary.

"I miss home," Jaea admitted suddenly.

Tharen nodded. "I miss Opal's cookies. And our coast trips."

Jaea gave Tharen a sympathetic look. "I have had so much fun Shaping here that I forget you haven't yet. Do you think you will soon?"

"I hope so. I am going crazing, confined as a wingless two-legger," Tharen answered. "I need to know that it is safe to do so first. I do not want to jeopardize your time with Maya by unveiling a less than beloved facet of ourselves. Even if you refrain from that Shape forever, being friends with me could reflect poorly on you." He shook his head. "Your friendship with me has put you in enough trouble over the years. I refuse to mess up this chance for you to live among your own kind."

"They are your kind too!" Jaea protested.

"Maybe," Tharen agreed. "We don't have any evidence for that yet. And we have been here, what, a month?"

Jaea frowned. "We need to get to Silverhaven. From what I can gather, the dragons keep records that would make the most meticulous archivist green with envy."

"It will be a while before we have a chance, though. Best to wait until after your ball."

"It just doesn't seem fair," Jaea said.

"I'll live." Tharen shrugged. "So where to next?"

"Ballroom?" Jaea suggested. "I want to see the place before the party. Hoping the event will be slightly less intimidating if I am familiar with the room."

"Aren't you getting dancing instruction between now and the ball?"

"Yes, but not in the ballroom. There hasn't been a ball in decades, so there is a lot to be done to get the room ready apparently. The instructor says it would be distracting," Jaea told him.

"Ah." Tharen arched an eyebrow. "Don't suppose you know where this fabulous room is located?"

"Yes. Mostly. Vaguely. Shut up."

"I wasn't going to say anything," Tharen said innocently. "Lead on, my knowledgeable guide. I humbly propose we head toward the formal courtyard, as the cooks assure me it is how the good people of Caeldighn enter the castle for such occasions."

"Smartypants. Come on. If we hurry we can head into the city for lunch afterward."

The paths became more and more crowded as Jaea and Tharen made their way to the large courtyard. The pair quickly lost track of the number of times they stopped to offer their help, only to be politely refused as people hurried on their way. Servants, couriers, decorators, carpenters, and pages bustled to and fro. A small army of gardeners was filling large urns with plants and placing greenery and blooms seemingly everywhere. The lush gardens that framed the area were beautiful without extra additions. With them it was clear they would be magnificent.

"Let's make sure we won't be in the way if we pop into the ballroom," Jaea said. She linked arms with Tharen and made her way toward a tall, dark skinned, man standing at the center of the courtyard. He was frantically scribbling notes on a clipboard and pointing people different directions. Jaea and Tharen reached him as the man finished speaking with three young pages who dashed off repeating their instructions to themselves.

"Yes?" the man asked without looking up from his notes.

"Hi," Jaea said. "I was hoping to get a look at the ballroom today, to familiarize myself with the area before the ball. I hadn't expected it to be so busy already, though. I just wanted to make sure we wouldn't be interfering with the work by venturing in."

"We are trying to keep non-essential persons at bay as much as possible, ma'am. For the safety of the visitor as well as the workers. So much is being done at the moment that it would be easy to get lost or injured in the jumble." The man looked up to smile apologetically. His amber eyes widened when he saw who he was speaking to. "Forgive me, Miss McClanahan. I hadn't realized it was you I was talking with. Of course you may view the ballroom. I only ask that you take care as you proceed through the entrance and watch your head in the ballroom itself. There were a couple of scaffolds checking on the chandeliers last I heard."

Jaea quickly subdued a flash of annoyance. She thought she may have preferred the man simply leaving the answer at no instead of so drastically changing his tune when he realized she was a McClanahan. It was becoming a theme in Jaea's life, the instant attitude changes caused by being known as a member of one of Caeldighn's oldest families.

"If we are going to risk being in the way, is there at least

147

something we can do to help?" Jaea asked

"Not really," the man said carefully. "I assume you have business to attend to and are not merely seeking to relieve boredom by causing trouble?"

"You assume correctly, Mr. ?"

"No Mister required, ma'am. Please, call me Wren."

"Wren." Jaea smiled. "Are you sure there isn't anything we can do? Like carry something in with us?"

"I'm certain, though I thank you for your offer. We have everything under control here. Besides, Rebekah will murder me if I muck up her system," Wren said.

Jaea nodded politely. "Okay. We'll just walk through real quick and then get out of your way."

"As you wish, ma'am," Wren said. "Just remember to mind the scaffolding."

Jaea and Tharen turned to follow the slow stream of people heading into the ballroom.

"Jaea!" Wren called. "It was nice to make your acquaintance. I look forward to seeing you again at the event."

"I'll save you a dance!" Jaea called back, making Wren laugh as he turned his attention back to his clipboard. They followed a couple of men carrying crates through a set of huge oak doors and down a wide hall, swerving to avoid collision with the occasional page. Jaea and Tharen stopped just inside the ballroom's main doors, where the men they followed in were depositing their cargo. The crates had barely touched the floor, with the carriers quickly out the door to bring in the others, when a towering blonde strode over.

"Not there! These go to the reception hall! How many times must I say such for it to be understood?" the blonde woman demanded, her icy blue eyes boring into Jaea and Tharen. "Well? Get a move on it! What are you staring at?"

"A viking?" Tharen guessed. He looked at Jaea for

confirmation.

"Quite possibly." Jaea nodded.

The blonde relaxed a fraction as a smile tugged at the corner of her mouth. "What?" she asked.

"You look like a viking. Well, you look how I imagine vikings looked," Tharen clarified.

"We would be happy to relocate these boxes for you, if you tell us where they should go," Jaea offered.

"Are you two incredibly difficult to intimidate, or have I completely lost my touch?" The woman laughed. "Who are you?"

"I'm Tharen. This is my friend Jaea," Tharen told her. "And you are?"

"Rebekah," the woman answered. "Jaea. As in the Jaea? McClanahan?"

"Guilty," Jaca admitted. "Now where can we put these crates for you?"

"Nowhere. Don't worry about it. My men will see to it," Rebekah said politely. She hurriedly scribbled a note in the binder she held. A moment later, the end of her messenger pen glowed pink, and she nodded at the response. "There. Taken care of. Wren is reminding them where these particular crates were assigned. Now, what can I do for you, Miss McClanahan?"

Jaea again stamped down the now familiar stab of annoyance. She managed a thin smile at Rebekah.

"I'm only here to take a look at the space. I thought the ball may seem less intimidating if I at least recognized the room. We tried to get Wren to give us a job, but he said you had a very good system in place, and it was best we not interfere."

"Smart man, that Wren," Rebekah said. She looked at Jaea oddly. "You aren't used to the royal treatment yet I take it?"

"Not so much," Jaea said.

"For your sake, I hope you can adjust to it quickly. As the lost twin, the attention isn't likely to wean anytime soon."

"That's what I'm afraid of," Jaea said.

"Well, I have a great deal of work to see to," Rebekah said, her pen blinking rapidly. "If you need further assistance, please come find me. I should be in here the rest of the day."

Jaea looked at Tharen as Rebekah left. "Does it show that much?" Jaea asked. "My being annoyed?"

"Perhaps a bit." Tharen shrugged. "Come on. Let's do a once around and get out of here."

After walking the perimeter of the ballroom, Jaea and Tharen decided to take a peek into the reception hall while they were in the area. As soon as they walked in, they saw Gwena and George unpacking a catering cart.

"Hello, friends!" Tharen said happily.

"Oh! Hello!" Gwena replied. "What brings you two here today?"

"Trouble," Jaea grumbled.

"Is that so?" George asked.

"Not on purpose," Jaea explained. She paused a moment wondering if she should save her questions to ask Maya later. If she could keep her frustration bottled up long enough to find Maya without losing her mind and biting someone's head off. Safer to ask Gwena now, she decided. "It's just most people I meet here in Caeldighn start out treating me like any other person, and then they see my mark or learn my name-"

"And suddenly it's Miss this, Ma'am that, please just sit here and look pretty," Gwena finished.

"Exactly!" Jaea exclaimed. "I go from an interesting conversation partner to dumber than a box of rocks and fragile as glass snob. In the blink of an eye!"

"Well, that is easy enough to fix," George said.

"How?" Jaea asked hopefully.

"Don't blink," George teased.

Jaea threw her hands in the air. "I walked right into that one."

"Only a little," Tharen said consolingly. "Anyway, I've decided that cooks are the only sensible people in this world. None of you have ever treated either Jaea or I differently than the average passerby."

"Yes we do," Gwena contradicted. "I wouldn't give the time of day to most upper society folk like Jaea. Ambassadors are often just as meddlesome, so most of the castle staff are polite but try to keep their distance. And off-worlders? In my kitchen for breakfast every morning? Not likely."

"Then why do you treat us differently?" Tharen asked.

"That first morning we let you eat in the kitchen as a favor to Maya," George admitted. "She is a nice lass and has always looked after our best interests. You two earned your seats at our table after that. You treated us just like everyone else, when many folk turn their nose up at the company of servants and cooks."

"In other words," Gwena continued. "We like you two, and we are keeping you."

"Brilliant," Jaea said discouraged. "We are oddities in this world also. If we are assigned servants, the poor things will probably high tail it out of dodge after a day or two in our company."

"Oh! My niece is one of your choices," Gwena said. "Her name is Lily. I told her I would put in a good word on her behalf. She is a sweet thing, but isn't afraid to speak her mind once she gets to know you."

"Perfect. She's hired." Jaea laughed. "Do you know when they are sending her to meet me?"

"If you walk with us back to the kitchens to refill this tray, odds are you will run into her. She planned to take midday with us before setting out to find you," Gwena said.

"Hey. What about me? You have a nephew?" Tharen asked.

Gwena patted his cheek. "Sorry, dear, I'm fresh out of nephews."

"Not to worry," George assured Tharen. "I know a couple of the lads suggested for the position. They are good fellows, and you would get along well with any of them."

"Come along then, my trouble makers. Help me with this cart, and I promise to sneak you a couple of stuffed rolls on the way out." Gwena turned to George. "You fine to keep setting this batch out? We are bound to have a hungry crew descend in here soon."

"I can see to this just fine," George said. "Go on."

Jaea waved back at George as she followed Tharen and Gwena. The head cook led them through a maze of hallways, and it seemed like ages before Jaea recognized where they were. When they came to large open area, she realized they were in one of the more commonly used castle entries. It was the one she had first entered the castle through. Lately there had been an increased number of guards at this entrance, making Jaea wonder if the castle guard was expecting trouble or if there was simply more traffic into the castle this time of year.

The door to the Fairy Room was open to welcome guests to come admire its delicate decor. A young woman in a moss green dress with a pale pink shawl came bounding toward them happily. For a second, Jaea had to wonder if the girl was a fairy escaped from one of the artworks in the room behind her.

"Aunt Gwena!" the woman called.

"Lily, my dear girl!" Gwena cried. She abandoned the cart momentarily to embrace her niece. "How are you child?"

"Anxious," Lily confessed. "I want to meet Miss McClanahan as quick as can be so she can decide if she wants me as her maid or no. The not knowing is driving me mad, Aunt."

"Well, the wait will soon be over," Gwena told Lily. She turned to Jaea and Tharen. "Come here you two and meet my beautiful niece."

"I love to meet beautiful women, especially when they are related to wonderful cooks!" Tharen quipped.

"Oh, you." Gwena laughed, swatting Tharen's arm. "Lily Marshall, may I introduce Ambassador Tharen McKenna. And--"

"Good day, sir!" Lily beamed. "I have heard good things about you."

"And I of you," Tharen replied.

"Yes, yes. We are in a hurry here. I've to bring the rest of midday to the other end of the castle if you recall," Gwena said. She pulled Jaea to her side. "This is Jaea McClanahan. Now off you two go. I will see you shortly. Tharen, come make yourself useful."

"Yes, ma'am," Tharen said. He hurried to open the door to the kitchens for Gwena.

"Hi," Jaea said. She waved awkwardly to Lily.

Lily bobbed a quick curtsy. "Pleased to meet you, ma'am. Please forgive my rambling just now, I did not notice my Aunt Gwena's company at first."

Jaea shook her head. "No more curtsying at me. No more 'ma'am'. I'm just Jaea to my friends."

"Yes, ma'am. I mean Jaea." Lily smiled. "Would you like to sit in the Fairy Room to interview me, or do you prefer to walk whilst discussing things?"

"Walking is good, if it suits you? We could stroll toward my quarters and then head back to the kitchen to enjoy midday with your aunt?"

"That sounds sensible. I can get a feel for the workload while you decide if you would like to hire me." Lily nodded and followed Jaea as she started down one of the corridors that led past the Fairy Room.

"I hired you about half an hour ago." Jaea laughed. "So it is

153

up to you now, if you'd like to be my maid or not. I thought you may like to see the servant's room attached to mine in case you wanted to move in there. You will have to guide me on this business of what your duties would be, though. I know very little on the matter."

"How did you hire me without having met me?" Lily asked.

"Gwena said you are sweet but capable of speaking your mind. I like people like that. I hired you. Granted it was mostly in jest, but now I have met you. I like you, and Gwena says you're good. Thus, hired," Jaea explained.

"Has anyone ever told you that you are odd?" Lily asked.

"All my life." Jaea grinned. "So what do you say?"

"Well, I would like to say yes. However, I think it wise we conclude the duties of the position first," Lily answered uncertainly.

"Right. That makes sense. Well, here we are. These are my quarters." Jaea unlocked the door and waved Lily in.

Jaea stood nervously as Lily surveyed the scene. She had always thought herself to be fairly tidy, but as she tried to see the room from a maid's perspective, Jaea feared it wasn't quite up to par. A layer of dust was beginning to show in places. Books and papers were stacked everywhere in the living space. Jaea hadn't bothered to straighten the sapphire quilt on her bed, and the cream colored sheets poked out from underneath it. A rumpled towel hung on a hook in the wash closet. Jaea frowned at the overflowing basket of laundry tucked beside the wardrobe. She had forgotten to bring it to the laundry yesterday. Her quarters were rather void of personal touches, since she wasn't certain how long she intended to stay. She wondered what Lily would think of that.

"My younger cousin tells me that you are prone to giving children sweets when you wander the castle or city." Lily smiled when she spied a large box of candy on the little table by the door.

Jaea shrugged, a little embarrassed. "I share when I can. Candy is such a small thing, and it makes them so happy." Looking for a quick change of topic, Jaea's eyes alighted on the attached servant's quarters. "I am told that these two rooms are typically for a maid or butler," she said. "As I mentioned earlier you are welcome to move into them, as much or as little as you wish. What duties would you like?"

Lily laughed. "What do you need assistance with? Laundry, mending, errands, cleaning, shopping?"

"Oh. Maybe an hand with cleaning?" Jaea suggested. "I have been rather busy lately, and I fear the room has not been shown the care it deserves. The laundry here at the castle does my washing so long as I don't try to help, that is, when I manage to bring it to them. I would not be opposed to your company while shopping, but I would rather not have you do it for me. I enjoy my time meandering Maeshowe's shops and meeting more of Caeldighn's people. Though, come to think of it, I still get lost if I try to find new shops sometimes." She fidgeted with the hemline of her shirt. "Okay, maybe I do need help. It's just hard to admit that I can't do it all on my own, I guess."

Lily smiled encouragingly. "Needing help is nothing to be ashamed of. There's none of us can make it through life all alone."

Jaea was grateful that Lily hadn't laughed at her, and it pushed her to say what was most on her mind. "Really, I need someone who can be trusted and can be frank. I am still learning about Caeldighn's culture and customs and would appreciate a friend to assist in navigating them."

Lily nodded. "You are certain you want me to be blunt? We did just meet. I would hate for you to think me scandalous for speaking my mind."

"Absolutely," Jaea said heartily.

"The usual wages I assume?" Lily asked.

"No, I don't think I want a typical servant so yours will be more, if you approve. There is a weekly sum listed on the contract the head of staff has drawn up for us. If you do not agree with the number there, just write in one that suits you between what is listed and the typical amount," Jaea said. "And I won't require it of you, but we can decide on a uniform if you wish to wear one. I would rather just give you coin for clothing you like."

Lily studied Jaea for a moment, her brown eyes thoughtful. "I'm not sure I've quite got your measure, miss. It's a very unusual feeling for me."

"I promise to do my best to show you who I am and to not let my family standing go to my head, if you would be so kind as to help me through the maze of society," Jaea said solemnly.

"Then I would be pleased to accept the job, ma'am," Lily said happily. She held up a hand. "Though I do hope you will allow me to take on further duties as time passes. I guarantee you will be far busier after you've been introduced completely to society at the ball. And please understand that it is proper for me to address you as ma'am or Miss McClanahan, so there will be times that I must do so. I will certainly do my best to call you Jaea in other situations."

Jaea laughed. "I suppose I have to get used to the 'ma'am' stuff anyway. What do you say we head back to the kitchen and beg some lunch from your aunt?"

"Oh yes, please. I am starving now that my nerves have settled," Lily admitted.

Jaea locked the door behind them as they left. "I will have to get you a key," she realized.

"That would be helpful if I am to move into the rooms attached to your quarters," Lily agreed.

"You are moving in then? Hurray! Be warned though that I

have very little experience with roommates."

"If you snore too loudly, I will simply throw pillows at you until stop," Lily promised.

Jaea looked at her new maid approvingly. "You know, I think that you are just silly enough that you and I are going to get along fabulously."

As they came to the corner by the Fairy Room, they saw Tharen sitting just outside its door speaking with a middle aged man. Tharen waved a quick hello and returned to his conversation.

"That is Charles O'Shea," Lily said. "He must be Mr. McKenna's new butler. Oh! That reminds me. Would you mind terribly if I did have a uniform, for formal occasions if nothing else?"

"If you would like to have a uniform then I have no objections," Jaea said puzzled.

"It is just that I would so love to see Amelia's face if I could strut past her in McClanahan colors," Lily said wickedly.

"Ah. Well, then we must see what we can do," Jaea said conspiratorially. "But who is Amelia?"

"My archenemy." Lily sighed. "Always the best at everything and makes you feel like a bug under her boot. She also works for the Ryan family and likes to brag about her good fortune to snag such a wealthy and powerful employer."

"I see," Jaea said. "So you want to show off the fact that you are working for one of Caeldighn's oldest families. While, as a general rule, I try not to encourage bragging or petty behavior, perhaps a tiny bit can be excused in this instance."

Lily stifled a laugh. "That was very well done, miss. I actually feel slightly rebuked."

Jaea laughed heartily. "You wicked little mite!"

Lily smiled angelically. "Are we waiting for Mr. McKenna or should we continue on to the kitchen?"

"Let's go to the kitchen. Tharen has seen us and knows where we are headed. What are the McClanahan colors by the way?"

"Oh! I forgot that you are still rather new here. They are a lovely-"

"Jaea McClanahan! Just the person I wished to see." A tall blonde strode over. "We haven't been properly introduced. My name is-"

"Elaine Ryan, I believe," Jaea said icily. Jaea had first encountered Elaine when she had made a loud and rude exit from Maya's office. Her opinion of the woman had only gone down from there.

"How delightful!" Elaine cried. "Does my reputation precede me? I'm told I am one of the most charming companions, though I must say some of my admirers are likely only after my father's money. I wonder if you would take midday meal with me today? We can have one of the servants bring something out to the gardens for a little picnic of sorts."

Jaea noticed that Lily had moved a few feet to her right to stand meekly out of the way. Elaine hadn't acknowledged Lily at all, let alone apologized for interrupting her. The blonde snob also seemed to think she was above the protocol Maya had been drilling her on, which clearly demanded that members of high society not try to gain advantage by buttering up those preparing to come out into society. And Elaine stood there oozing false friendship and charm when just days ago she had publicly ridiculed Jaea at dinner for having played Shaper tag with some children. Jaea hadn't forgotten Elaine throwing herself at Tharen either. She took a breath to try to calm herself and overlook the negatives. "I can't today. Though I thank you for the invitation. Besides, all the servants are otherwise occupied with preparation for the ball, their regular chores, or enjoying their own meal. They are much too busy to change their plans for us."

Elaine faltered a moment, but she quickly pasted a

patronizing smirk on her face. "You are new here, dear Jaea. No servant is ever too busy to see that the needs of Caeldighn's most important citizens are attended to."

Jaea felt something inside her snap. She was done with this woman and all people like her. Suddenly she no longer needed to worry that fiery language and shouts would escape her lips to call Elaine out on her false facade. She had ice water running through her veins. Jaea sensed Tharen start toward her from the Fairy Room. She saw Elaine slowly take two steps back from her cold glare.

"I think, perhaps, that you and I have differing opinions on the word important, Miss Ryan," Jaea said calmly. "And the servants really are too busy today to hop around trying to fulfill your every whim. However, you are at least correct in that your reputation has preceded you, though I fear you have been tragically misinformed about its nature."

"You dare insult me!" Elaine shouted, striding forward to stand face to face with Jaea.

Tharen and Lily both started to cut in. The few other people standing about the large entry hall were all now looking in their direction.

Jaea waved her friends back. "Oh, I dare do much more," she retorted. "If you can so flippantly ignore proper manners, I promise I have no qualms in following suit. I suggest you apologize to my maid for so rudely interrupting our conversation and then be on your way, dear. Unless you would like me to blacken one of those charming eyes of yours."

"You will pay for this, McClanahan!" Elaine sneered. "You will find no friends among the Ryans after today!" She spun on her heel and stormed out of the castle.

Lily stood fixed in place, staring at Jaea.

"What?" Jaea said shortly. She shook her head and tried to rein in her anger. "Sorry, Lily," Jaea said more calmly. "What is it?"

"You would have made her apologize to me, a servant you just met?" Lily asked. "Miss Ryan is of the most wealthy and powerful family in Caeldighn. And in defense of my feelings, you asked her to apologize to me, your maid?"

Jaea's eyes blazed and her whole body radiated with a powerful temper held tight in check, but her voice betrayed none of her anger when she spoke. "Wealth and power are pitiful credentials for the measure of a person," Jaea said. "That awful girl was rude to Maya. She was also mean to the kids I play tag with some mornings. Besides, you are a servant in my employ. You are fast becoming my friend. Even were you not these things, you would still be a living creature with thoughts and feelings. Yes?"

"Yes?" Lily answered uncertainly.

"Then I will gladly defend you if necessary." Jaea resumed her path to the kitchen, leaving everyone in the entry hall to go about their business. A single burst of applause caused her to pause briefly and look back. A tall red haired man bowed when he caught her eye. Jaea merely nodded in return and quickened her pace to the kitchen in hopes of finding quiet and hot tea.

Lily looked to Tharen for her answer as Jaea fled the room. "Why?" she asked of Jaea's friend.

Tharen draped an arm around Lily's shoulders and steered her after Jaea. "Because it is the right thing to do," he answered simply.

CHAPTER FOURTEEN

Tharen shifted a tray of muffins and cookies, trying not to crumple his report in the process, and knocked on Maya's door.

"I come bearing gifts," Tharen said happily when Maya opened her door.

Maya look confusedly at Tharen and the plate of muffins he held out.

"Am I too early?" Tharen asked. "I can come back later if you prefer."

"No. Come in. Time just got away from me," Maya said, ushering him in. "Besides, those muffins look ten times better than the stale biscuit that has passed as breakfast so far this morning."

"Well, I will remember to bring food if I ever need to bribe you." Tharen winked. He flopped down in his usual chair after passing the plate to Maya. "I've this week's report right here." He set a couple of papers on the table beside him. "When you are ready."

Maya frowned at her empty teacup. She refilled it from the kettle kept hot on its dragonfire stand and poured Tharen one while she was at it.

"Thank you," Tharen said around a bite of muffin.

Maya nodded and chose a muffin for herself. "We can get to the report here in a second. Before I forget though, the meeting you asked about has been set. I have put together something of a panel for you and Jaea. Kaylee, and or myself, will be in attendance to lend the experience some familiarity. I have a historian from Silverhaven for questions regarding Caeldighn's past, one of my best economists, a prominent merchant, a judge, and one of Kaylee's military officers. Sound acceptable?"

"Sounds fantastic. When do we meet?"

"Ah. There is the downside. The earliest I could get them all together for your purpose is the Monday after the ball."

"That is fine. Jaea and I know everyone is pretty busy right now," Tharen said.

"Good. If you or Jaea have any pressing concerns in the mean time, I hope you feel comfortable bringing them to me. I will do my best to get you an answer. Although I must admit I am still uncertain why these matters are so important to individuals that don't intend to remain in Caeldighn for long," Maya prodded.

"Maya, I feel like I belong here more than I ever did on Earth. But it is up to Jaea." Tharen shrugged. "Either way, I'd prefer knowing more about Caeldighn's current situation. Call it curiosity. Studying other cultures is sort of what I do."

"Surely if she knew how you felt she would give staying in Caeldighn more consideration," Maya protested. "You are her best friend. She must have given you a clue to her plans."

Tharen shook his head. "I was hoping she was confiding in her sister. She is being even more closed mouthed than usual. I think it is because there is so much at stake. If we stay, how often, if ever, will we get to see her family on Earth? How much of her life will they miss out on? If we go, we leave all of this and her birth family. Heartbreak no matter how the cookie crumbles."

Maya slumped in her chair. "I cannot guarantee anything. Caeldighn is too unstable for me to make her promises. And if I understand the pair of you correctly, you have become aware of the precarious peace in this country. Who would wish to stay in such an environment?" She rubbed her hands over her face. "Ugh. I'm far too gloomy this morning. I'd say it's half this blasted weather and half my disdain for not knowing the variables. I wish it would just storm already or that Jaea would tell me she is staying. Or both."

"Have you asked her anymore about it?"

"No. Like you, I don't want my desires to sway her. It should be her own choice. I'm determined not to mention it to her until after the panel we set up," Maya said resolutely. "Maybe knowing more about our land will encourage her to decide."

"Here now. Eat another one of these delicious things Gwena made and cheer up," Tharen decreed, tossing her another muffin.

Maya laughed. "Yes, Ambassador McKenna. Then I need to get to work if our little group is to escape Maeshowe for a time tomorrow."

"Point taken. I'll be off and out of your way then, friend," Tharen said. "What?" he asked when Maya looked at him strangely.

"You called me friend," Maya said hesitantly.

"Yep. Because we are friends." Tharen laughed.

"So we are." Maya grinned. "Now, go try and keep my twin out of trouble for a day."

Tharen pointed at Maya from the doorway. "No promises, but I'll try."

Jaea turned when she heard Maya shout happily from across the yard. She waited for her sister to catch up with her and they linked arms to continue to the stables together.

"Sister dear," Maya said. "I can barely contain my gladness to be headed to the forest today. It is one of my favorite places in all Caeldighn. Oh look! We practically match!" She exclaimed

163

pointing at Jaea's outfit.

Jaea laughed to see that they wore the same type of pants and shoes, as well as the same style shirt. "The seamstress did tell me this was a popular cut for a shirt. I'm just glad she did it up in this violet color. You couldn't be unhappy in a color like this."

"Exactly how I feel about my rose red," Maya agreed. "Oh good. It looks like everyone else is already here," she said as they walked through the stable's wide double doors.

Maya went to check in with the stable master, leaving Jaea with Tharen and Kaylee. They heard her thank the stout man for readying the horses and cheerfully greet the two guards that were to accompany the small party. Jaea noticed with a start that one of their guards was the red haired man who had witnessed her argument with Elaine the Snob. She turned quickly to avoid his gaze and gave all her attention to the golden filly assigned to her for the outing. Maya strolled past her, leading a large smoky gelding.

"Alright folks!" Maya said when she made it to the front of the group. "I only have today off, and I had quite the time making it understood that I was not to be reached for anything short of Maeshowe being under siege. So if you lot don't mind, I would like to get to the forest as quickly as possible before some poor page is sent to ask 'just one more question' before we depart." A chuckle went through the group. "Michael, with me please. Neilan and Kaylee, take charge of the pack horses and bring up the rear. Jaea and Tharen, stay between us until we are safely lost in the forest."

"Good morning, Spitfire," Michael said as he moved past Jaea on a gelding as red as his hair.

"Good morning to you, Red," Jaea countered, making Michael chuckle.

"Who is your new friend?" Tharen asked.

"Michael, apparently." Jaea shrugged nonchalantly. "I haven't actually met him yet. Just seen him around the castle."

"Uh huh," Tharen said as he mounted up.

In what seemed no time at all, the party had traveled down King's Way and was at the foot of the First Queen's Forest. Maya handed a badge of some sort and a small parcel of papers to the guard on duty, and the group was waved on into the woods without the speech Jaea and Tharen had received on their last visit. Jaea almost couldn't believe their luck. Maya was so often stopped by people on their other outings together that Jaea had grown used to the stop and go manner of travel required when walking anywhere with her sister. A few feet into the forest, Maya led them down a smaller and less used path. It was still well trodden and wide enough to ride two abreast, but green things grew in patches down its middle. Jaea saw Maya lean toward Michael to tell him something. Michael sighed dramatically, making Maya laugh, and held up a closed fist to signal back to the others to halt.

Maya turned in the saddle. "If you don't mind, I would like for Tharen and Jaea to ride beside Kaylee or myself at intervals today. That way we can point out some of the more interesting flora and fauna, and answer any questions you have on them. Jaea, you expressed an interest in herbs a few nights ago. This area is popular for gathering plants for medicinal and therapeutic purposes."

"Oh, come now. I just got Neilan here to start talking," Kaylee objected. "Besides, Michael would be better suited to discuss herbs and such, with his mother being a healer. You lot switch partners for now, and I'll take second shift with the Ambassador's never ending curiosity."

Maya glanced at Michael who nodded. "Works for us. Tharen? Jaea?"

Jaea and Tharen shrugged.

Maya waved Tharen forward. "Alright. We will be riding for

another hour or so. When we get to Fae Hollow we will give the horses a rest."

"Hello again, Spitfire," Michael said cheerily as he took Tharen's place beside Jaea.

Tharen muttered something about flirts and gave Michael a warning glance before he rode forward.

Jaea shot Michael a sidelong look. "Why do you keep calling me that?"

"Well, that's how I thought of you during your battle with the Ryan woman," Michael explained as the group resumed their course. "I just haven't been able to remember to call you Jaea instead, since I thought of you as Spitfire first."

"I was so embarrassed when I saw you were to come with us today," Jaea admitted. "I try to refrain from losing my temper as I did that day."

"Nah. That girl had it coming," Michael said.

Jaea laughed heartily, feeling she was in good company. "Kaylee said your mother is a healer?"

"Yes," Michael confirmed. "She does house calls occasionally. Primarily though, she runs a shop called the Sunshine Cup. Sells teas and tonics and a range of medicinals. Knows about every plant in Caeldighn, my mother."

"I have heard of the Sunshine Cup!" Jaea said happily. "Gwena keeps some of her teas in stock at the castle. I have heard good things from others about her shop as well. Please send your mother my regards."

"I shall pass them along gladly." Michael grinned. "Now, Maya tells me you've an interest in Caeldighn plant life. I confess I do not know everything on the subject, but I have soaked up a fair bit over the years. Do you have any specific questions or is it more of a general fascination?"

"I would like to know what I am looking at. I especially like to know if it can be a helpful thing or if it would give me a fearsome rash. Caeldighn's plants call to me much more than those on Earth did, though I liked green things at home as well." Jaea shrugged. "Maybe it's because the flora is the only thing here not expecting something of me." She arched an eyebrow at Michael. "That was an odd thing to tell a stranger."

"Stranger?" Michael said playfully. "Not I. Didn't you know, our souls have already decided to be friends. Lieutenant Michael Black, at your service."

"Are you trying to flirt with me?" Jaea asked suspiciously.

"Now, would I flirt with a strange beautiful woman?"

"It would appear so." Jaea laughed.

"Then allow me to put your mind at ease, for I'm already keen on someone. You have naught but friendship to fear from me." Michael promised.

"Well then, Michael Black, it's good I'm still 'keen' on another too, or I may have been offended."

"Hmm. I smell gossip brewing," Michael said ominously. "Best not mention that last bit to the ladies unless you are prepared to bare your secrets."

"Noted," Jaea said. "Back to the matter of plants?"

"Right. It may be connected to your heritage from Nirah," Michael suggested. "The plants calling to you," he explained. "It is said some of her descendants inherited sparks of green magic from The Lady."

"Green magic?" Jaea asked skeptically.

"Well, talent," Michael amended. "Called magic mostly for the romance it implies. Good many green thumbs along your family tree though, sweetheart."

"Sweetheart?" Jaea asked, eyebrow arched.

"I'm working my way closer to Jaea! Help a fellow out. I'll get it by the end of the day," Michael promised.

"Stars grant me patience." Jaea laughed. "Oh! That is gorgeous! What is that?" she asked excitedly, pointing to several large clusters of bright blue and violet blooms.

"Cobalt Stars, sometimes called Ground Stars," Michael answered. "Prized among dye makers, painters, and flower enthusiasts. They are luminescent in the early dawn hours and guarded by a number of dryads. They will be knee high or taller in a month. In two months time, the aforementioned folks will flock here in hopes of receiving their seeds to plant elsewhere or use as a pigment."

"Dryads," Jaea repeated. "As in tree spirits? Guard flowers?"

"Correct. Ground Stars are a favorite of theirs as they are not only beautiful, but also good for the soil around them. It is as unwise to cross dryads as it is to cross dragons. They can get quite creative in maintaining justice."

Michael continued to tell Jaea about the different plants they passed, always including a bit of a tale with the description. Jaea found she sincerely enjoyed the redhead's company and was a little sorry to lose sole claim to it as the party came to Fae Hollow.

"You'll like this," Michael told her. "Maya may be able to coax her friends out for a visit."

"Who lives here?" Jaea asked.

Michael just raised his eyebrows as Tharen returned to Jaea's side. Then he sauntered off to talk to Maya.

"I really like him," Jaea told Tharen. "And he says he will introduce me to his mother. Then I can set up a day to follow her around and soak up some knowledge."

"Ride together for an hour, and you have set a date to meet his mother?" Tharen asked.

Jaea punched Tharen lightly in the arm. "Oh, knock it off. You're living proof I can be just friends with a man, Tharen. And as I recall that was your choice, so I'll thank you to drop the jealous act."

"I'm not jealous!" Tharen objected. "I don't want to lose best friend status is all."

"Never," Jaea assured him. "Never ever. You are irreplaceable. Now come on before we lose the others."

Maya tossed a handful of colorful glass beads into a small moss encircled pool as Jaea and Tharen caught up. "I've brought someone I think you would like to meet," Maya called. "Do not be shy, now. Come see my sister."

Two pale green figures peeked out at the group from behind a pair of beech trees. They stepped forward hesitantly and settled beside the pool, dipping their slender feet into the water. Jaea, eyes wide and grinning like a child on Christmas, moved closer unknowingly. The green ladies smiled in return. Then much to Jaea's astonishment, the beads Maya had tossed into the water gathered together and moved toward outstretched green hands. The water rippled, and part of it became more solid. Masses of dark blue curls emerged from the water followed by a pale blue woman in a pearly dress. She filled the green ladies hands with the beads. The green women emptied the treasure into their laps before clasping hands with their blue friend and hoisting her up to sit between them.

"Well met, Maya-Shaper. Who did you have to shoot for a day off this time?" the blue woman asked, eyes twinkling with mirth.

"You are never going to let me live that down are you?" Maya laughed. "It only happened once, and I did warn him."

Michael coughed and held up two fingers. "General Rolfe," he reminded Maya.

"That doesn't count. I told him not to open that door," Maya objected.

"Hang on," Jaea said. "Who did you shoot?"

"Oh Lorie, you've done it now," Maya accused the blue lady. "Now I have to tell the story again."

"I like that story." Lorie shrugged and turned her attention to the beads her friends were sorting through.

"Well, come on then," Tharen prompted.

"It was years ago," Maya explained.

"Four years ago, to be accurate," Kaylee added.

"Kaylee and I had only just been named Junior Chiefs," Maya continued. "There were a number of individuals determined to see if we would measure up to the title, so we were quite busy for a good long time. Then came the drought. It was awful. It didn't rain at all for months. We were pulled here and there for the next two years to sort out arguments over water rights, pasture rights, how food and supplies were to be portioned out, you name it."

"It was not what I would call fun," Kaylee said with a shudder.

Maya shot Kaylee a look.

"Fine, I'll be quiet," Kaylee said.

"I needed a break from civilization, and it was my birthday, perfect timing. It took me three hours to get out of the castle. At the door of the South entrance, I repeated for the fourth time that I would shoot the next person that further postponed my day off. Halfway to the stable, a man who worked in the treasury and oversaw the bookkeeping came striding angrily toward me demanding to know why I had allotted a farmer twenty crowns. I put an arrow to my bow and fired a shot over his head, but he just kept yelling and walking toward me, telling me that he refused to allow me to leave the castle until he had his answers." Maya looked down, embarrassed some having to rehash her actions. "So I shot him in the leg and informed a stable boy to send for a medic as I rode out of the yard."

"And she hasn't had to fight for a day off since." Lori laughed. "Which my cousins and I certainly appreciate. Maya always brings the most news and the best presents."

"There have been rumors that it is unwise to speak ill of Miss

Maya or her friends whilst traversing the Forest," one of the green women confided. "All unfounded. Aren't they, Matilda?"

"Of course, Magdalene," Matilda answered sweetly. "Some Shapers simply can't walk among trees without tripping. It isn't our fault some people are clumsy."

Jaea had no doubt that Matilda and Magdalene were at least partly behind whatever incidents had begun the mentioned rumors. She was glad there were people that had no qualms standing up for her sister. It was good to know that someone would look after Maya if Jaea left.

"You just shot him and left him in the stable yard?" Tharen asked amazed.

"I warned him," Maya said defensively. "Besides, it was hardly a serious injury."

"Didn't I hear something about food when we stopped?" Michael asked suddenly.

"Are you always hungry?" Maya laughed.

Michael thought for a moment. "Yes," he admitted ruefully.

Maya rolled her eyes. She nodded to Kaylee, who had walked to the pack horses moments before Michael asked about food. As their picnic was laid out, the group settled in happily, chit chatting with the nature spirits and laughing at Tharen's unending thirst for knowledge as he peppered the conversation with questions for the colorful women.

Jaea sat down back to back with Maya after filling a small bowl with snacks. "Church tomorrow at the castle chapel?"

"Same time every Sunday." Maya chuckled. "Meet you there?"

"Sounds like a plan." Jaea was quiet for a moment, enjoying the sounds of the forest. "Sister of mine, this was a fabulous idea."

"That it was, dear twin," Maya replied.

CHAPTER FIFTEEN

"I think I may faint," Jaea said. The reflection staring back at her from the mirror looked unfamiliar. The girl in the mirror was draped in an elegant gown, but her face held a note of panic around the eyes. The violet Shaper mark looked strangely vulnerable wrapping around her bare right arm. "Yep. Gonna faint."

"Don't you dare!" Lily exclaimed. She abandoned Jaea's laces for a moment and turned her missus away from the tall oval looking glass. "You muss up your hair or wrinkle your dress after I've worked so hard and there will be no breakfast for you for weeks," she threatened.

"I suppose I can fight it off, for the sake of Gwena's muffins," Jaea smiled weakly.

"Let's hope so," Lily retorted, hands on hips. "You really can't afford to miss meals. Too scrawny as it is."

"Hey!" Jaea cried indignantly.

Lily just smiled and spun her employer around to face the mirror again as her spunk returned in spades.

"I'm not scrawny," Jaea objected. "I'm slender."

"As a twig," Lily agreed cheerfully.

"Well, at least I won't look like one tonight. Mrs. Lind outdid herself with this dress," Jaea conceded.

"She really did." Lily sighed appreciatively. She fastened the tree pendant around Jaea's neck. With that finishing touch, she stepped aside to admire her charge. "Oh my, Miss. You are such a vision."

"Quit calling me Miss, or I'll start calling you Miss!" Jaea threatened for the thousandth time that week. "You really think I look alright?" She nervously brushed her hand over her Shaper mark.

"I think you will have at least five marriage proposals by the end of the night. No doubt, that Michael Black will claim a number of your dances. Mr. McKenna will be beside himself trying to keep you from the other young men." Lily smiled and handed Jaea her shoes.

Jaea shook her head. She had given up trying to convince Lily of Tharen's disinterest. "I wouldn't mind dancing with Michael. He is just a friend though, so stop making that face. Besides, I think he is sweet on Maya." The gown's golden pink material whispered as Jaea sat to slip on the dainty slippers Mrs. Lind had fashioned for her. A knock at the door sent Lily scurrying to answer it, shrugging into the green waistcoat of her dress uniform on the way.

"I've come to see my two favorite girls," Gwena announced when Lily admitted her to Jaea's quarters. She set a basket on the small dining table. "Just in case you two dance so much this evening that you forget to eat. Now, let's finish getting Lily ready real quick. I want to see you both in all your glory before I head back to that crazy kitchen."

Jaea set Lily's things out across the small vanity while Lily did up the buttons of her waistcoat. Then Gwena shooed her to a chair and started gathering Lily's hair into a fashionable up-do. Jaea ignored her maid's protest and helped Lily into her shoes.

"Not so fast," Jaea said when Lily started to rise. She pulled an emerald and pearl comb out of its hiding place in the vanity drawer. "Tharen's friend Terra helped me pick this out from her mother's work. Teresa promised you could trade it in for something else after the ball if you'd rather a different style." She tucked the small comb into her speechless maid's hair.

"And these are from your mother and I," Gwena said, fastening a string of pearls around Lily's neck.

Lily shook her head at Jaea and Gwena. "For sure, you'll both spoil me. I've never had anything so fine."

"Come on then, stand together so I can admire our handiwork," Gwena ordered.

Jaea and Lily stood side by side, turning dutifully when Gwena twirled her finger.

"You'll do." Gwena grinned.

"Oh, I can't wait to see Amelia when I walk in wearing McClanahan emerald and cream!" Lily exclaimed.

The women gave themselves over to a fit of laughter at Lily's comment. Jaea was so caught up in the mirth that she nearly missed the knock on the door.

"Come on in!" Jaea called.

"Our colors suit you, Lily," Adrielle complimented from the doorway.

"Oh! Thank you, ma'am." Lily blushed.

"Hello, aunts." Jaea smiled. She moved forward to embrace Jayla and Adrielle.

"Hello, dear," Jayla replied. "Truly, you are both stunning," she told Jaea and Lily.

"Just beautiful," Adrielle gushed, dabbing her eyes with a handkerchief.

Jayla elbowed Adrielle. "None of that," she told her sister. "It is time we were on our way. They want us there before the crowd arrives. Are you ready?" Jayla asked her niece.

Jaea nodded.

"I should be off as well," Gwena said. She kissed both Lily and Jaea on the cheek. "You do Caeldighn proud. Have fun my beautiful girls." Then she ducked out the door, eyes over bright with tears held in check.

Jaea and Lily shared a smile over Gwena's praise.

"Are you coming with us, Lily?" Adrielle asked.

"Absolutely! I am sticking right by Missus until she walks out onto that platform," Lily said. "I'd not have a moment's peace otherwise fearing she had a loose thread or her hair came out of its pins." She picked up a small basket. "No employer of mine goes into a ball in less than perfect condition," she declared.

Jayla hid a smile behind her hand. "Come along then. If we are much later we may be subjected to the wrath of the event coordinator."

Adrielle shuddered. "No, thank you."

As she made to follow her aunts out the door, Jaea noticed the end of her messenger pen glow. She dashed over to it and quickly put it to paper. Her mother's handwriting sped across the page. *Have fun sweetie! Love you!* Bolder letters, her father's, appeared just under the first message. *No kissing boys. Love you, squirt.*

Jaea laughed, feeling much less nervous. Who cares what high society thinks, when you have such wonderful people who love you. She turned the key to lock her door and hurried down the corridor after her frantically waving maid.

An hour or so later, Jaea stood a few paces behind her aunts waiting for the herald to announce them.

The portly man let his staff strike the floor beside him. The resulting 'crack!' instantly quieted the room below. "Chief of State, Jayla Campbell. Chief of Military, Adrielle McClanahan." The herald paused to let Jayla and Adrielle step aside for Jaea. "Presenting to your company, and all of society, as we celebrate her return to Caeldighn, Miss Jaea McClanahan."

The room erupted in applause as Jaea moved forward to

stand between her aunts. Jayla and Adrielle led Jaea down the few stairs and across the ballroom floor toward a table reserved for Chiefs and guests of honor. Maya and Kaylee were already there, as were Tharen and Lily. Once Jayla and Adrielle had taken their positions at the foot of the royal dais, the herald called the crowd's attention again.

"The audience will genuflect for our beloved ruler," the herald's voice boomed.

The rustle of fabric swept through the room as everyone bowed or curtsied toward the woman walking slowly to the staircase opposite the one Jaea had used.

"The Queen Regent Aurora Buchanan." When Aurora stepped off the last stair the herald rose from a bow and announced, "All may rise." With this, the room again filled with conversation as guests milled about greeting old friends and meeting new ones.

Aurora smiled and waved to Jaea as she passed her table en route to the throne like chair at its head. Jaea waved back, smiling as she remembered Aurora bemoaning fancy dresses when she last took tea with her and Maya to discuss the ball. Jaea returned her attention to the party and suddenly felt lost trying to take in the whole scene. Then Tharen appeared at her side, and it all looked much less daunting. *I know a few of these people at least,* she thought.

"You look fantastic," Tharen said. "And you didn't trip on the way down the stairs, so I'd say the night is going well so far."

Jayla and Adrielle came to stand on Jaea's other side.

"You did very well." Jayla smiled.

"Soon you will be free to mingle and dance, I promise," Adrielle said. "For now, though, we would like to introduce you to the Council members and some of the individuals under my and Jayla's command."

"Likely some of Caeldighn's more prominent citizens will

come over to beg an audience as well," Jayla added. "Don't worry though, everyone knows to keep their conversation brief so you may greet everyone seeking to say hello."

"Right. No need to be overwhelmed," Jaea joked. "I'm only about to be introduced to half of Caeldighn in the next hour."

Jayla laughed. "Take heart, little one. At least meeting the Council means skipping outside for a moment."

"Can we meet them first?" Jaea asked hopefully. "I could use a little air," she admitted.

"Certainly. They are by the patio just through there." Jayla pointed.

"I will have a drink here for you on your return," Lily promised.

"You aren't coming with us?" Tharen asked.

Lily shook her head. "Neither are you."

Adrielle sighed at Tharen's look of confusion. "I forgot about this part. I'm sorry, McKenna. You cannot accompany us to this portion of the evening."

"Why not?" Tharen asked.

"For two reasons. One being simply that the Council is here to meet Jaea. Having anyone else there could prevent them from getting a true impression of her, and she of them."

"That almost makes sense," Tharen said. "Reason two?"

"You are a Shaper of unknown background and ability. For their safety, you are not allowed a private audience at this time," Adrielle said bluntly.

"What, you think I may be a Stone assassin?" Tharen demanded.

"Tharen," Jaea cautioned.

"For all we know, you both are," Jayla said sadly. "I don't think you understand the lengths the Stones have gone to in previous situations."

"Apparently not," Tharen agreed stiffly. "Just who was killed

177

by someone that pretended for twenty years to be a friend, all for the chance to get close enough to do murder?"

"My father," Kaylee answered simply as she joined the conversation. "King Liam. He was killed by a man that had been his friend since childhood, had served faithfully in Caeldighn's military, and had saved my father's life on two occasions.

"I'm so sorry," Tharen said sincerely. "I didn't mean any disrespect."

"I know." Kaylee smiled. "Neither do we."

Tharen nodded. He gave Jaea a slight nudge. "Go on. I will stay right here, very well behaved."

Jaea held Tharen's gaze for a moment, looking for signs of trouble. "Keep Lily company?"

"Yes, dear," Tharen said dutifully. "I will stay where Lily can keep an eye on me. If I promise not to talk to strangers will you go?"

"Smartypants," Jaea smirked.

"Smarty kilt." Tharen bowed.

Jaea linked arms with Jayla. They moved to catch up with Adrielle, who was already halfway to the door. "So tell me again about these Council people."

"For starters," Jayla began. "They are not people. Leastwise not in the humanoid sense."

"Walk faster ladies!" Adrielle urged once her sister and niece were in earshot. "I haven't seen Gale in ages!"

Jayla made a shooing motion with her hand. With a grin, Adrielle all but ran out the door.

"Gale?" Jaea asked as they walked out onto the patio.

"Griffin," Jayla answered, pointing to a large gold and black eagle head currently encircled by Adrielle's arms. A long lion like tail twitched about the pair madly while a loud rumbling purr filled the immediate area. "They have been best friends since

Adrielle could walk," she explained. "Come, I'll introduce you to the others while they catch up a bit."

Jayla led Jaea across the large patio and out into the grassy yard surrounding it. Tall dragonfire lamps lit the outside gathering places, though not as brightly as those that graced the ballroom. Giant urns overflowed with vibrant blooms, echoing the elaborate flower beds. The sturdy benches scattered about in clusters all sat empty, their would be occupants sent elsewhere to make room for the council. Jaea closed her eyes and took a deep breath, savoring the perfumed air and a moment away from the crowded ballroom. When she opened her eyes again, she was surprised to see a huge ruby colored creature dwarfing the scene before her.

"Did I startle you, Shaper?" A melodious chuckle sounded from somewhere above Jaea's head.

Jaea gazed upward, and then up some more to locate the animal's head. The lamplight flickered merrily across the many scales covering its long body. "Perhaps a bit," Jaea admitted with a laugh. "Mostly because I don't know how I didn't see you earlier. Hard to miss a dragon."

"Raja likes to try to play tricks on me," Jayla said. "She has been working on one which can make her completely unnoticeable until she wishes to be seen." She shot a wry look at the dragon. "It appears she has figured it out." Jayla put a hand against Raja's scaled hide. "Raja of the Silverhaven Dragons, may I present my niece, Miss Jaea McClanahan."

A delicate head dipped down to get a better look at Jaea. "I was most glad to hear of your return. However, I felt even more joy when I learned you were blessed with a good and loving home while you were away from your birth land. Well met, Jaea Harbour McClanahan of Caeldighn and Earth."

Jaea felt as though the dragon's dark eyes had seen into her heart. Having her adoptive parents recognized by such a majestic being, on their first meeting nonetheless, was a balm to Jaea's pride. She hadn't realized how much it bothered her to be introduced without the name she had grown up with until she was standing between her aunts in the ballroom being announced as solely a McClanahan. The growing bubble of discontent subsided as Jaea grinned up at Raja. "Well met, Raja of Silverhaven, most gracious of dragons."

"Oh no," an airy male voice cautioned from behind her. "Never inflate the ego of a dragon. Their heads are big enough as it is."

Raja snorted and Jayla hid a smile behind her hand as Jaea turned to face the speaker.

"A pegasus!" Jaea said, surprised.

"Jaea Harbour McClanahan meet Dayun of Canary Islands," Jayla said.

Dayun, a dun colored horse with snowy white wings dipped in a graceful bow at the introduction. "The pleasure is mine. Welcome home, my dear."

"Thank you. It is good to be among kin again," Jaea said. "Not to mention the fantastic company I find myself in now," she complimented.

"Great! So you are staying then right?" Adrielle cheered as she and Gale joined the group. "I know, I know," Adrielle added quickly. "Undecided as yet." She draped an arm across Jaea's shoulders. "Niece, I should like to introduce you to an old friend of mine. This is Gale, of the Sea Cliffs Griffins."

Gale dipped his head. "It is an honor to meet you Shaper. I also wish you welcome home."

"Thank you Gale. It is a pleasure to meet a friend of my aunt," Jaea replied politely. Before Jaea could reign in her thoughts enough to say anything further, Gale looked at someone behind her.

"Good evening, Zorya," Gale greeted.

"Good evening, friend. Is it yet my turn to bid the girl hello?" an amused voice asked from beside Raja. "It seems I am always last to these meetings. I do so apologize for my tardiness."

Jaea felt the day's tension leave her as the newest voice continued. She was certain the flower blooms nearest the group had doubled in size and their fragrance washed over her as she turned to find the voice's source. Jaea was completely enchanted in a way she had never been before, nor ever would be again, for standing before her was the most beautiful thing she had ever seen. A mare, the color of moonlight with a mane and tail of palest silk and a single golden horn extending from its forehead. "Are you real?" she whispered.

The unicorn bobbed her head and walked up to Jaea to rest her head on Jaea's shoulder. "My name is Zorya. I should have guessed you had not seen one of my kind before. One's second encounter with a unicorn usually causes the system less shock. But you did so well with the others I thought my presence may not affect you so strongly."

Jaea hugged Zorya's neck. A single tear slid down Jaea's face to land on the milky coat. "I should feel silly, but I don't care. Unicorns are real."

Zorya chuckled along with the other Council members gathered around them. "Quite. And there is no need to feel silly. All descendents of Adam and Eve react in the exact same manner when they first see one of my kin. There are many theories why this is so, though they are all too lengthy to get into just now."

Jaea stepped back from Zorya with a smile and returned to stand between her aunts. "Are these all the Council members then? Or is someone else going to sneak up behind me while I speak with those who are in sight?"

"There are two other members who were unable to attend tonight. You will meet them at a later date," Jayla answered.

Jaea nodded. "It is a great honor to meet each one of you. I cannot thank you enough for taking the time to meet me."

"I like her," Raja said bluntly to her fellow Council members, startling a laugh out of Jaea. "When can I see her again?"

Jayla and Adrielle looked at Jaea.

"Oh!" Jaea exclaimed when she realized the answer was up to her. "Whenever you like. I have no objections to getting to know you better. The same goes for the rest of you."

"You shall be hearing from us soon then, young Shaper," Zorya said happily.

A murmur of agreement rippled through the gathering.

"For now though," Jayla said. "Since the initial introductions are past, we should get her back to the ball."

"Yes indeed!" Dayun exclaimed. "There are many others yet waiting to meet this charming woman."

"Until next time, Miss McClanahan," Gale said in farewell.

Jaea waved back at the odd mix of beings from the patio stairs. "To think I have to return to talk with Shapers and regular humans now," Jaea mused. "Did I do okay?" she asked her aunts suddenly. "Do you think they like me?"

"You were marvelous," Adrielle reassured her as they stepped inside. "They loved you."

The crowd seemed to notice Jaea's return instantly. Something of a line began to form, starting near the seat she had abandoned in favor of a few moments outside. Maya and Kaylee kept them a few feet away from the table with an occasional stern look.

"Ready?" Jayla asked as the trio took their places to form a receiving line with Tharen and Aurora.

"As I will ever be," Jaea said wryly.

Jaea lost track of how many greetings she had smiled through. The names of those she had met were one long blur in her memory, although she was certain she had met at least a dozen McClanahans. One of few individuals that stuck out from the haze of faces and names was her Aunt Jayla's husband, Alaric, who had come to stand by Jayla after she threatened bodily harm to a man refusing to let go of her hand. Jaea was happy to notice that the nearness of her towering uncle helped keep the many introductions brief. Half way through, her face was starting to hurt from keeping a polite smile pasted on it. On the bright side, she had only had to speak with a single member of the Ryan family. She could feel that clan's collective glare trying to burrow a hole through her from across the ballroom where they were grouped together. She was thankful that she hadn't needed to talk to more of Elaine's family. When the last of the well wishers finally dispersed, Jaea collapsed into her chair and thirstily downed the glass of water Lily set before her.

Tharen sat down to Jaea's left while Maya and Kaylee settled on her right. Kaylee was instantly in conversation with Adrielle, asking after the Council members.

"That was fairly insane." Tharen laughed. "And I am not even the popular one."

Maya smiled sympathetically. "I know it is a lot to take in, but you are both doing splendidly. After the initial dance, you will both be free to do as you choose for the remainder of the ball. Be it continued dancing, conversing, eating, or merely standing against the wall and observing. Kaylee and I will be roaming around the room, as will Aunt Jayla and Adrielle. Please do not hesitate to seek us out if you are in need of an answer or introduction."

"Who am I to dance with for the formal first dance thing?" Tharen inquired.

"You shall be my partner. Jaea will be partnered with the eldest male McClanahan in attendance, which I believe is our fourth Great Uncle Bartholomew," Maya explained. She chuckled. "He is nearly three hundred years old but is still a fine dancer. Uncle Bart will tell you the secret is to remain young at heart."

"When does the first dance begin?" Jaea asked. No sooner had she spoke than a lively tune burst forth from the musicians' balcony. The music had its intended effect, everyone in the ballroom quickly hushed and looked toward the sound.

"It would appear to be starting now," Maya answered, rising from her chair.

At the top of the decorative staircase leading to the musicians' box, a short man waved the band to a halt. "If the good people could be so kind, we ask that you retreat from the center of the dance floor. Give our guest of honor space to claim her place among both kin and country in the opening dance. Would the eldest male McClanahan present please make your way to the dance floor to lead the Miss Jaea McClanahan."

A tall fellow with broad shoulders, slightly slouched with age, met Jaea in the center of the cleared space. He bowed to Jaea then spoke loudly to address both her and the assembled crowd. "It is with abundant joy that I stand here beside my great-great-great-great-niece this evening. Being the eldest of our family in attendance I, Bartholomew James Matthew McClanahan, beg the honor of escorting Jaea Marie McClanahan through the opening dance of this ball admitting her to society."

Jaea felt all instruction on how to respond leave her head. So she simply nodded and prayed that sufficed. It must have, for Bartholomew took Jaea's hand in his, and the band started up a tune. Jaea followed her uncle's lead through something like a waltz and found she could easily keep up. She suddenly felt grateful to the waspish fellow who had been tutoring her in Caeldighn's dances. Bartholomew's emerald green tunic made a pretty contrast to Jaea's pale pink dress, just as her sleek dark hair contrasted his white mustache and balding crown. After a

184

few moments, she noticed others joining the dance. Tharen expertly led Maya through the steps. Aunt Jayla and Uncle Alaric looked exceedingly happy moving around the floor. Kaylee was joined by Michael, a fellow redhead. Jaea thought he looked very nice in his uniform. When she missed a step and faltered Jaea decided to keep her attention on following her uncle. The band brought the tune to a close, and Bartholomew bowed over Jaea's hand, eyes twinkling under bushy white brows.

"Thank you for the dance, my dear," Bartholomew said. "I am always glad to dance, but especially when facing so beautiful a partner."

Jaea returned his grin as she dropped into a curtsey. "Thank you, Uncle. Without your aid I would have certainly fallen on my face."

Bartholomew laughed loudly. "Thank the heavens, our newest member may have a sense of humor! Though you should know that you danced wonderfully. May blessings rain upon you," he said sincerely.

Michael came to stand at Jaea's side in hopes of claiming her next dance. Bartholomew clapped him on the back. "She is all yours, young sir," he told Michael. He winked at Jaea as he turned to go. "Look me up if you tire of tea, and we will share a good strong cup of coffee."

Michael held a hand out to her. "Would you honor me with a dance, Miss McClanahan?"

"I'd love to, Lieutenant Black." Jaea smiled and placed her hand in his as the music began again. She recognized the dance within a few steps and relaxed as she followed Michael's lead. "So, I noticed the other day that you and my sister make quite the pair," Jaea baited.

"You have my permission to tell her so." Michael smirked. "Frequently and at length."

Jaea threw back her head and laughed. Michael spun her in three quick circles perfectly in time with the dancers around them.

"Sshh," Michael whispered when they faced each other again. "I can feel McKenna's glare enough as it is. He is convinced I am trying to sweep you off your feet and whisk you away from him."

"Let him glare," Jaea said defiantly. "I certainly wouldn't mind being swept off my feet."

"Ah," Michael said knowingly. "Have you told the man in question that you care for him?"

"He knows, or at least he did know. Just as I've known for a good long while that he doesn't want me." Jaea shrugged. "Perhaps one day my efforts to get over him will stick. Until then, I fear my heart is his whether he wants it or not."

Michael shook his head. "Oh, how well I know your predicament. If only hearts listened to minds, maybe I could convince myself there is no point in my loving your sister."

"Listen to us. What a sorry lot." Jaea poked Michael in the chest. "How do you always get me to tell you such absurd truths?"

Michael just grinned and sent her spinning through another set of circles. "The same way you pull the truth out of me, I suppose. Kind recognizes kind."

"Must be. Well, enough of such gloom. Tell me something cheerful."

"Mother is all a tither readying her shop for the day you said you would visit next week."

"Her shop was already spotless when you brought me by the other day!" Jaea exclaimed.

Michael nodded, a smile crinkling his eyes. "It always is. Now though, she is especially convinced there is a speck of dust somewhere or that some of her supplies are recklessly low. She

186

has had my brothers and I scouring for plants and supplies all over. Da told me this morning that he hasn't seen her in such a tizzy since his parents came over for dinner a month after he wed my mother."

"Oh no! I hadn't meant to for her to go to any trouble!"

"Nonsense. Mother is in her element. The woman thrives in hectic situations," Michael assured her. He spun Jaea in two slow circles then a quick one. The dance had ended. "You have quite a group of admirers forming." Michael told Jaea, inclining his head toward a group of young men at the edge of the dance floor.

Jaea saw Tharen step forward from the group with a scowl at those beside him. "Oh drat," she muttered.

"I don't know about you, but I find I am terribly thirsty," Michael said with a wink.

"Wouldn't you know, I am feeling particularly parched." Jaea grinned. She turned toward Tharen and mimed getting a drink. Then, much to the dismay of the pack of young men, Miss McClanahan took Michael's offered arm and walked away.

CHAPTER SIXTEEN

Tharen navigated around as many people as he could, especially clumps of women. He was learning that Shaper women could be awfully determined when it came to trapping someone they wanted to meet. It seemed as soon as he decided to join up with Jaea and Michael for refreshments, small groups of females began to close ranks between him and the door. He soon gave up trying to get to the room across the hall and returned to the dance floor with a lady named Sabrina. Even distracted as he was, Tharen could hardly help being impressed by his current dance partner. There was something different about her. She couldn't be an ordinary Shaper. Sabrina certainly looked splendid in her black gown. The collar of it fanned out and up at her shoulders, reminding him of the Maleficent character in that cartoon Jaea made him watch years ago.

"I hear you are interested in visiting Silverhaven," Sabrina inquired.

"I am interested in visiting every last corner of Caeldighn," Tharen replied politely. "But yes, Silverhaven does have a unique appeal for me."

"May I be so bold as to ask why?"

"Knowledge," Tharen answered simply. "I hope to find some answers about my family. I am told that nothing can top the archives in a dragon library."

"Ah," Sabrina said, impressed.

"What is that grin for?" Tharen laughed. "Did I just pass some test?"

"I am always happy to see an individual with a yearning for knowledge. I teach courses occasionally on how to navigate the archives, both at the castle here and at the Dragon University."

"Really," Tharen said excitedly. He dutifully exchanged Sabrina for the woman on his left and tried to wait patiently for the caller to tell the dancers to return to their previous partners. Thankfully, he didn't have to wait long. Sabrina curtsied as the other women dancing did. Her eyes danced with mirth. Tharen bowed with the men and dropped a kiss on Sabrina's outstretched hand.

"I hope you seek me out when you are in Silverhaven. I would be happy to assist you in your venture," Sabrina told Tharen. "My office is just to the side of the library's main door."

"I cannot thank you enough for your generous offer," Tharen said sincerely. "I look forward to seeing you again in Silverhaven." Spotting Jaea and Michael as they returned to the long table near Aurora, he excused himself from the dance floor and made his way toward them. It proved a much easier task than trying to leave the room.

"How did you fare with the dragon?" Michael teased.

"Dragon?" Tharen asked confusedly.

"Sabrina, the woman you were just dancing with. She is a dragon," Michael told him.

"A Dragon Shaper?" Jaea asked excitedly.

"No. A dragon dragon. Good old fashioned, fire breathing, winged lizardy creature capable of taking human form. Dragon," Michael clarified. "You didn't know?"

"No," Tharen admitted, dumbfounded. "Huh."

"I brought you back one of Gwena's turnovers," Jaea told Tharen. "Well, I brought back a stack of turnovers with the

189

intent of letting you have one or two," she corrected.

"Thank you!" Tharen said heartily. "I tried to get to the refreshments earlier, but I didn't have your fancy soldier escort. It's more difficult than I expected, leaving a ballroom," he said wryly.

Michael clapped Tharen on the shoulder. "You are the new man in town. What did you expect?"

"A chance to dance with my best friend," Tharen retorted. He held a hand out to Jaea. "What do you say, gorgeous?"

"I imagine I could tolerate one dance with my best friend," Jaea said as she took Tharen's hand. "Probably only the one, though. I have a reputation as a single woman to uphold." She grinned wickedly.

"Yes, of course," Tharen said loftily. "We couldn't have people suspect we are an item." He stood smiling at Jaea, an idea forming.

"You realize, I'm sure, that the dance floor is over there," Jaea said warily.

Tharen nodded solemnly. "It's possible you are aware that I am gaining a reputation as your loyal and somewhat ridiculous companion. I would hate for people to lose faith in my dedication to you when they note that we dance but one set this evening." With a wink at Michael, Tharen quickly lifted Jaea off the floor. One of her shoes fell off in the process, and Michael was kind enough to return it to Jaea's foot. Jaea tried to thank Michael but couldn't stop laughing long enough to say the words.

"Much obliged, Sir. I'll have her back by midnight!" Tharen told Michael, carrying Jaea toward the dance area. He cheerfully greeted everyone they passed on the way.

"Are you ever going to put me down?" Jaea asked.

"I haven't decided yet," Tharen answered.

While the reactions of those they passed by en route to the

dancing area varied between amusement and shock, the musicians simply took it as cue. No sooner had Jaea's feet alighted on the floor than the band abandoned the slow song they had been playing to strike up a more lively tune. Tharen knew the song immediately and waved his appreciation to the director. He pulled Jaea through the fast paced steps, and following the pattern, weaved them in and out of line. This particular dance was full of flourishes and was all about showing off your female partner. Tharen spun, dipped, and lifted Jaea by turn. By the second round of flourishes, many of the men were competing to see who could lift their partner highest. Tharen raised his eyebrows at Jaea and when the part came again she jumped as he lifted her. They spun a circle with Jaea held aloft and sent the competition into overdrive. The band must have found it all hilarious because they began to play faster and faster to see who could keep up. There were only three other couples on the floor when the song came to a close. Tharen bowed to Jaea, who curtsied in reply. Then they turned with the other dancers to bow or curtsy to the musicians as much of the crowd broke into applause.

"I don't know about you, but I need a drink," Tharen whispered in Jaea's ear.

"Yes, please!" Jaea sighed.

When they made it back to their table, they were delighted to see that Maya and Kaylee were there as well. Jaea and Tharen sank gratefully into their seats and thirstily reached for their wine glasses.

"You two appear to be enjoying yourselves," Maya commented happily.

"They certainly do." Kaylee laughed. "That was quite the show over there."

Tharen smiled. "Dancing is almost always fun." He shrugged. "The rest? I was simply reminding everyone that I had the prettiest partner."

Jaea snickered. "And by that he really means he has a competitive streak. Mom and I have had many an entertaining evening watching Dad and Tharen try to outdo the other in some task or game."

Tharen was glad to see the brilliant smile the memory called to Jaea's face and was confused when it suddenly dimmed. A glance at Maya's cold look cleared it up for him.

"We should make the rounds again, Kaylee," Maya said abruptly. "I will take the outside this time." She strode off toward the open patio doors without waiting for Kaylee's response.

Kaylee put her hand on Jaea's shoulder. "She will get used to it eventually, your other family. Give her time." She turned to speak to Adrielle. At Adrielle's nod, Kaylee set off opposite the direction Maya had gone.

"You okay?" Tharen asked sympathetically.

"Come now, Tharen, you know me," Jaea said stoically. "I am always okay." She picked up the last apple turnover on the plate between her and Tharen. "I spotted Wren over there earlier, frantically doing Rebekah's bidding. I think I will try to bribe her with a turnover to lend him to me for that dance I promised him." Jaea wrapped the gift safely in a napkin and began her way across the room.

Rebekah laughed heartily when Jaea proposed trading the turnover for a dance with Wren.

"I hardly need bribing! That looks delicious, though, so I'll agree to take it off your hands." Rebekah grinned. "Wren made me promise to let him dance with you tonight. All evening he has been afraid you forgot and has been trying to work up the gumption to go ask you."

"Poor guy," Jaea said. "I didn't forget. I just haven't had the chance to find him until now."

Rebekah held the turnover in her teeth and quickly penned a note on her clipboard. "He should be here in just a minute," she told Jaea.

Wren appeared at her side a moment later with an armful of flowers and dirt speckled across his rust colored shirt. "Yes?" he asked Rebekah.

Rebekah nodded to Jaea.

"Miss Jaea!" Wren nearly dropped his flowers. "Hello again."

"Hello, Wren." Jaea smiled. "I've come to beg you for a dance, but it looks as though you're a bit busy."

"Oh!" Wren exclaimed looking down at the flowers piled in his arms. "I was just bringing these to the reception hall. One of the urns in there was knocked over. The urn survived unscathed, but the blossoms were rather crushed. I've the mess cleaned up and was headed there to replace the flowers."

"I see. I can wait here until you're finished if you like?" Jaea asked.

"Nonsense," Rebekah said. She waved someone over. "Jonah here can take care of the flowers. Go have your dance. Go on," she urged. "Out of my hair so I can get back to work."

Wren gladly handed the flowers over to Jonah and took a minute to brush the dirt from his shirtfront. He gallantly held a hand out to Jaea and led her into the midst of the other dancers.

Jaea stayed on the dance floor for some time after her waltz with Wren. She saw Tharen watching from their table with his 'we need to talk' expression on, which she avoided as she had no desire to talk. When she finally returned to her seat it was only to take a drink before heading to the patio.

"Mind if I tag along?" Tharen asked.

Jaea only shrugged and left Tharen to interpret an answer as he wished. She wasn't surprised when he took it as a yes and followed her outdoors. They stood quietly at the delicate rail that separated the patio from the gardens beyond it. Jaea felt tension building between them as the minutes of silence dragged by.

"So are you going to tell me what's wrong?" Tharen asked.

"No, I do not believe I will." Jaea sighed. "Besides, it is just a number of little things piled up."

"Like what, per say?"

"Like nothing I wish to get into tonight," Jaea snapped. "So drop it, please."

"Right. Change of subject," Tharen said. "How is Wren?"

"He is well," Jaea answered. "Busy, though. He reminds me of Dad some, just younger," she said. "He has the same quirkiness about him."

"Your dad is kind of goofy sometimes." Tharen laughed. "Hello Maya," he called, his laugh ending abruptly. "You come to check up on our girl too?"

"I came to try to apologize," Maya answered. "I should not have stormed off like that earlier."

"Why did you?" Jaea asked without turning around.

"I haven't quite figured that out," Maya admitted. "I suppose it is difficult for me to understand your loyalty to Ben and Maggie when you are here in Caeldighn among your real kin and other Shapers."

Jaea whirled around. "Ben and Maggie are my real kin. Blood doesn't make family in my experience." She shook her head sorrowfully. "I am trying to get to know you. I am trying to fit in here while I learn about my heritage. But I am sick to death of people pretending I don't have important ties to Earth. They are my parents, Maya! You cannot get to know me without accepting that."

"They are not your parents!" Maya yelled. "Our parents were Shapers named Clara and Bowen McClanahan. They worked tirelessly for the crown and the good of our country. The only thing they loved more was us. And then they were killed. Our parents no longer draw breath, Jaea."

"Ours don't, but mine do!" Jaea yelled back. "They are the only parents I have really known. The only family I have known. Stop trying to write them off! They are important to me, okay. I didn't get to grow up here knowing all about Shapers and being free to Shape whenever I wanted. I just had Ben and Maggie helping me accept that I wasn't like everyone else. And Tharen," she added. "But we only have one Shape in common, so I couldn't be sure that we were even the same type of nonhuman."

"So you will choose them over your own people," Maya concluded bitterly. "Just as you have been doing since you arrived. At least you are being honest about it now."

"Whoa, hang on!" Tharen said cutting off Maya's exit. "Jaea has always been upfront with you. And you know she is trying to adjust to this life."

"Can it, Tharen," Jaea growled. "You do not speak for me. She will think what she likes about me anyway."

"I was just trying to help," Tharen said stiffly.

"Well stop," Jaea ordered. "You have no right to interfere in this conversation. This is between my supposed sister and myself."

"Jaea!" Tharen admonished. "What is the matter with you lately? You aren't acting yourself."

"How do you know how I act!" Jaea demanded. "You've barely spoken with me the last three years. You broke up with me and put an entire ocean between us. Not long after I told you I loved you, if memory serves me," she said sadly. "You think you can just pick up our old friendship again without so much as an explanation? Just ignoring that pesky year we were a couple? And then you think that you are somehow justified in trying to scare every man in a mile radius away from me. Well, that is not how it works. Either I am yours, or I am not. Since you placed yourself firmly in the friend column, you don't get a say on who I spend time with."

"Jaea," Tharen began. "It's not like that."

"Don't," Jaea told Maya and Tharen when it looked like they were going to say more. "I am going to sit out here and gather myself together, and then I am going back to my quarters. Please make my excuses to Aunt Jal and Adi and just leave me alone for a little while."

"I don't think you should be alone right now," Tharen said.

"I agree," Maya added.

"Leave. Now please," Jaea said firmly. "It shouldn't be difficult. You left me once before," she reminded Tharen. "And you never came to find me," she accused Maya. Tears streaming down her face, Jaea fled.

Tharen felt Kaylee grip his arm when he tried to follow Jaea into the garden. She had come outside sometime during the argument. He was about to protest her interference when he saw Michael appear with Lily and Charles in tow.

"What is going on?" Lily demanded of Maya and Tharen. "Michael said something was wrong with Jaea."

"Yeah," Tharen said. "Us."

Lily looked back and forth between Tharen and Maya. Hands on hips she sent them each her sternest look. "What has happened?"

"Maybe one of us should go after her," Maya said to Tharen.

"Absolutely not," Kaylee intervened. "You are the last people on all the worlds she wants to see right now. Lily, Charles?" she asked. "Would you be so kind as to escort Mr. McKenna back to my quarters? And put on the kettle please, I think we will be needing it."

"Will I be getting answers there?" Lily asked Kaylee.

"I believe we will," Kaylee said determinedly. "Maya and I

will meet you there shortly after we let our aunts know we are retiring. The ball is wrapping up anyway, so I don't think they will mind."

"I can't just leave her there alone," Tharen protested.

"I can make sure she gets back to her room safely," Michael volunteered.

Tharen was less than thrilled with that idea, but could think of no alternative. At least Jaea wouldn't be alone. He nodded and turned to follow Charles.

Maya stopped him. "I tried to find her," she pleaded.

"I tried to propose." Tharen laughed bitterly. "Her father said no."

Tharen avoided Michael's gaze as he walked passed. "She is likely near a tree if there are any out here. She always goes to the trees when she is upset."

"I'll find her," Michael promised.

Jaea found an unoccupied bench nestled under a weeping willow. She dropped down on it and gave into the tears. What a terrible thing to do, yelling at her friends! And crying! Jaea thought she heard footsteps and quickly tried to dry her eyes.

"You alright there, Spitfire?" Michael asked cautiously.

Jaea was immensely relieved to realize her visitor wasn't Tharen or Maya. Much to her horror, the initial relief only brought on even more waterworks. "No!" Jaea answered loudly. "I lost my temper, and now I am crying! I hate crying. I hate it even more than I hate losing my temper. Alright isn't the word I'd use, Michael."

"Now, now. Take a breath, sweetheart," Michael comforted. He sat down next to Jaea and pulled her into his arms. "It'll all work out, you'll see. In fact, it is probably good that you finally got all that off your chest. Now Maya and Tharen know the burden your heart has been carrying around. It will help them understand you a bit more."

"Oh nooooo!" Jaea sobbed. "You heard all that?"

"Just the dramatic ending," Michael offered lightheartedly. "Don't worry about it. I was rather glad to see you and Maya acting like real siblings."

"What are you talking about! Real siblings don't try to tear each other's heads off!" Jaea argued.

"Oh yes, they do," Michael assured her. "And I should know, I have a lot of them. Siblings often get along just fine and dandy. There always comes a point, though, when siblings just need to have it out with each other. Then they get over it and go back to being just dandy. It's a crazy cycle."

Jaea tried again to wipe her tears away. "Really? You don't think she will hate me?"

"Really. I know she doesn't hate you," Michael promised.

"How come you are so good at this?"

"I have a younger sister."

Jaea laughed weakly. "There is one poor girl with all you boys?"

"Yep. The lass will be lucky to ever get a date. We can be an intimidating lot." Michael shrugged. "She takes turns favoriting one of us depending on what her current problem is. I seem to be her go to when she is blue. Boys are frequently the root of it, as I understand."

"Oh, what am I going to do about Tharen?" Jaea muttered.

"Well, it is up to you. Most folks would tell you to find him and talk it out, or apologize for shouting at him. But," Michael said. "Seems to me, it should be him to do something. In my opinion, he needs to clarify once and for all if he wants you or not. He should have done so before now, judging by your speech back there. How else does he expect you to be able to move on? That's just my two cents."

Jaea nodded. "You sure you are stuck on Maya? I'd marry

you," she offered.

Michael chuckled. "Were I not 'stuck' on your sister, and you not in love with McKenna, I'd happily elope with you right now."

"Sounds about right," Jaea said. "Good to know I am appreciated by someone. Maybe you can set me up with one of your brothers, once I'm over McKenna a little better."

"Mother would be overjoyed."

Jaea threw back her head and laughed in earnest. "I'm so glad we are friends, Red."

"Me too, Jaea," Michael agreed. "Now, what say we get you to your room. A good night's sleep and you'll feel right as rain."

"Okay. As long as you know a route that keeps me from having to see any other people."

"Done," Michael said pulling Jaea to her feet.

True to his word, Michael got Jaea to her quarters without them running into anyone else. They followed the gardens around to a door well away from the ballroom and any activity still there. He stole her a small box of tea and a little jar of honey from the kitchen as they passed.

"I left Gwena a note," Michael assured Jaea when he rejoined her in the hall.

"Good," Jaea said, placated. "I don't want Gwena thinking she erred in her inventory. I can have her deduct it from my kitchen funds tomorrow."

"Kitchen funds? Maya has you set up as a proper guest then huh?"

"Yeah. Gwena and George are convinced I'm not eating enough since there is still so much credit on my account. They keep sending food to my room to fatten me up."

Michael laughed. "Those two seem quite taken with you. I haven't seen them take a shine to many other guests that way.

And Gwena recommending Lily to you, well it speaks highly of you."

Jaea ducked her head, not sure how to respond. "Well, this one is me," she said. She pulled her key out of the small pocket Mrs. Lind had sewn into her dress just for that item. "Oh! What is this?" she exclaimed when her foot hit a vase sitting before her door. A giggle escaped her as she read the card tucked in its fragrant blossoms.

"What is so funny about flowers?" Michael wanted to know.

"Rebekah sent them. She says Wren told her my favorites." Jaea giggled again. "Poor man's arms were overflowing with flowers when I found him for a dance."

"Rebekah?" Michael asked. "Tall, fierce, imposing Rebekah, the ball coordinator, sent you flowers?"

"She's not so bad once you talk to her," Jaea said amused. "She's just, you know, terrifying until you do." She turned her key in the lock and pushed the door open enough to set the flowers, tea and honey on a small table just inside the room.

Michael shook his head. "I am increasingly more impressed by you. Both in your interactions with others and their response to you. My countrymen adore you, Jaea." He shuffled his feet. "It isn't my place to say, I suppose. I know that you have loved ones on Earth, but I hope you decide to stay on here in Caeldighn. Please do not let your heartache tonight send you fleeing tomorrow."

Jaea kissed Michael on the cheek. "I promise to take it under advisement. Thank you for walking me back."

"Anytime." Michael smiled. "Goodnight, Jaea."

"Goodnight." Jaea slipped into her room and quietly closed the door. There was moonlight aplenty flooding the space, so Jaea had no trouble finding the latch and re-locking her door. She doubted Lily would be back anytime soon. Jaea remembered Lily telling her she planned to help the kitchen staff once Jaea left the party, that way Lily could be sure Gwena got to bed at a decent hour. Not bothering to cover a yawn, Jaea turned up the dragonfire lamp nearest her. Spying the tea Michael got her, she decided to brew up a cup. *Or ten,* she amended, certain sleep was a long way off yet. She had just lifted the box off the table when a hand covered her mouth as another snaked around her waist. The tea box dropped to the ground.

"Don't scream," a man's voice cautioned. "I just need to talk to you."

CHAPTER SEVENTEEN

And here she was thinking the night couldn't get any worse. *I just wanted to sit and have a quiet cup of tea! Is that so much to ask?* Hoping her attacker hadn't brought along any pals, Jaea bit down hard on the hand covering her mouth. She jabbed backward with her elbow and was rewarded with the sound of air whooshing out of the man that tried to contain her. Free from his grasp, she quickly spun and grabbed the staff she kept behind her door. She whipped it behind the man's knees and sent him sprawling to the floor. The tip of her walking staff was at his throat before he had a chance to retaliate.

"How is it that in the four years I have known you, you failed to mention you were some kind of ninja?" the man on the floor asked.

Recognition flooded her memory as she placed the voice. Jaea leaned forward to confirm his identity in the dim light. "Caleb!" she exclaimed. "What the hell are you doing here?"

"Kindly remove the weapon from my windpipe, and I'd be happy to explain," Caleb informed her.

Jaea narrowed her eyes at him and weighed her options. "Don't do anything stupid," she warned, stepping back.

"I sincerely hope I have used up my quota of stupid for the night," Caleb grumbled as he rose.

Jaea barked out a laugh. "We'll see. Sit down," she ordered, pointing to a chair at the dining table. She figured that seat afforded him less advantages than one near the door or fireplace. "Do not move. I have had a very bad evening, and am not above cracking your skull if you again prevent me from making a cup of tea."

Keeping an eye on her unexpected guest, Jaea filled her kettle from the water jug and set it to boil on its dragonfire stand. The small violet flames changed color as they grew and rapidly filled the glass stand with brilliant orange light, heating the tea pot. She retrieved the fallen tea container and grabbed the honey from the table by the door. She measured out enough tea to steep a full kettle and set two mugs and spoons on the serving tray.

"Am I allowed to talk yet?" Caleb asked hesitantly.

"I haven't decided," Jaea retorted. She rubbed a hand over her face. "I was really, really hoping that you wouldn't turn up here in Caeldighn. Because then I would be forced to admit that someone I knew and thought of as a friend was part of an organization that has been actively plotting the destruction of my family. If you know where to start this conversation, by all means do so."

"Really, McClanahan? You're the one that stole the key and set this all in motion again," Caleb protested. "I didn't even know you were a Shaper, let alone the lost freaking McClanahan until I saw the key around your neck at the school cafe. So maybe try not putting all the blame on my head."

"What are you talking about, stealing the key?" Jaea asked. "I found it sticking outta the ground when Tharen and I went to the coast to Shape. Then Ransley showed up, actually out of nowhere, and scared a decade off my life."

"Right, you just happened to find the key to Caeldighn days after my father received it from a Keeper. Who is Ransley?"

"Ransley. The Keeper who made Caeldighn's first key. It was

his key," Jaea answered slowly.

"No, it belonged to a fellow named Morgan," Caleb argued.

"Definitely not," Jaea said emphatically. "I met the ill mannered Morgan. He opened the gate for us with his key and then tried to demand I give him Ransley's."

Jaea and Caleb stared at each other, perplexed. The kettle's whistling brought them back to the situation. Jaea removed it from the heat and dropped the tea bag in before she settled it on the tray with the mugs. She added the honey jar and a sugar bowl to the tray and turned to glare at Caleb. "Out of respect for our previous friendship, I will join you at the table and share my tea with you while we sort this mess out. If you are anything less than a polite house guest, I will Shape into something large with sharp teeth and make you regret it. Understood?"

"You have a deal."

"Good." Jaea placed the tray's contents on the dining table and pushed Gwena's basket of treats toward the table's center. "Let's try this again, shall we. If you would be so kind as to explain why you were hiding in my quarters and tried to attack me?"

"First off, I wasn't trying to attack you," Caleb said. "I just wanted to make sure you didn't scream and bring half the castle through the door. Secondly, as I mentioned earlier, I need to talk to you."

Jaea motioned for him to continue while she spooned a generous amount of honey into her tea.

"I hadn't quite figured out what to say when I snuck in here," Caleb admitted. "I managed to convince my father not to have you killed on the way to the ball tonight, partly with the argument that you may not be an enemy, so he should give me the chance to find out."

"Your father was going to have me killed?" Jaea repeated incredulously.

"Yeah. Sorry." Caleb shrugged. "He did finally listen to reason and agreed to give your old classmate a chance to speak with you."

"So, I'm not dead right now because your dad didn't want to off one of your school chums?"

"Well, more because I convinced him that killing you at this time was a strategically bad move. He only agreed after I argued that Caeldighn needed to see the returned lost twin, or else its citizens would forever be waiting for her to come back. Which would lessen my brother's reign and undermine his authority over the people," Caleb amended. "This is off to a bad start again."

"Hard to put a good spin on assassination," Jaea quipped angrily.

"It's not like that. You don't understand. The Stone family has been trying to regain the throne for generations. It rightfully belongs to a member of our family. Caeldighn's crown was taken from my ancestor by force and every generation since has felt the sting of carrying the name Stone. My brother and I were separated and chased out of the land of our birth simply for being part of the same family tree as the old king. We just want the crown back, Jaea. Promise me you don't have a problem with that, and I can go back to my father and secure your safety," Caleb urged.

"I would love to tell you that I take no issue with a Stone king," Jaea began. "However, I'm afraid there are quite a few holes in your theory. Your people have been going about this all wrong, and it has brought only death, tension, and poverty to Caeldighn's people. I know I am new here, but I've been doing a lot of reading. Your ancestor, whom you seem to think so gallantly ruled here, took the crown by force against the wishes of Council. And Nirah said no, too. Still don't quite get that part, but it is a big deal apparently."

"The royalty were corrupt," Caleb countered. "He tried to save Caeldighn and could have if it hadn't been for the Council. Besides, he was a Dragon Shaper. This country had been ruled by Dragon Shapers for centuries prior but wasn't so when Quint Stone took over. The Caeldighn throne should be ruled by someone who shares the vision and abilities of Caeldighn's first king and queen."

Jaea held up a hand. "Is your brother a Dragon Shaper?"

"No," Caleb said reluctantly.

"Uh huh. So your whole argument rests on the basis that your ancestor was justified in sending Caeldighn into war because he was a Dragon Shaper like the First Queen. The resulting ongoing war that has taken the lives of many of Caeldighn's people, including my parents, is also justified because your ancestor hundreds of years ago shared a Shape in common with the First Queen." Jaea paused, rubbing her temples. "But the candidate your family intends to thrust on the throne, presumably after yet more war and destruction, is not a Dragon Shaper."

"There aren't Dragon Shapers anymore. Everyone knows that," Caleb responded simply. "And there is no need for further bloodshed if those in power step down. We have the most legitimate claim to the crown. Jakob will make a fine king. He has been prepped for it all of his life. It seems Aurora and your aunts have a pretty shaky hold on things at best anyway."

"You smug idiot. Do you even realize you aren't making sense?" Jaea demanded. "The Caleb I knew on Earth wasn't so dense! Can you honestly tell me you think your brother is the best thing for this country? Even at the expense of the war it will most likely bring?"

"There is a good chance this will end the warring, not make more," Caleb tried to explain. "There are many in this land who support our cause. How do you think I got in here undetected?"

"Trying not to think about that honestly," Jaea admitted. "Caleb, I have only been here a couple months, and even I have picked up on the tension. I hear whispers of Stone attacks every week. Too many adults here have a haunted look about them. The children I play tag with are missing parents and grandparents thanks to the incessant skirmishes and foul play of the Stone regime. They hate that name. One boy told me recently that he wants to be a soldier when he grows up so that he can help defeat the Stones. How can you sit here and tell me this Jakob guy can sweep in and fix it?"

"What do you want me to say, Jaea?" Caleb asked. "I am a Stone. I must be loyal to my heritage. I didn't get a break from this mess like you did. This war is all I've ever known."

"I would have you tell me the truth and listen to reason," Jaea said angrily. "Like you say, I haven't been witness to most of the power struggles. So, tell me the Stone side. Then I will find someone to tell you the, well, the other side."

Caleb looked at Jaea doubtfully. "You are just going to sit here and unbiasedly listen?"

"And drink tea," Jaea said innocently.

"Uh huh. Then, what, organize a secret meeting between me and your sister? I'll not agree to that Jaea. She'd kill me."

"Hmm. Okay, not Maya. I'll find someone, though," Jaea said. She had a potentially brilliant idea. "Do you have any problem with accepting the word of servants?"

"Servants will lie for their master nine times out of ten," Caleb said matter of factly.

"Fine. Let me worry about that part. Start talking, kid. This may be your one and only chance to tell a McClanahan your version."

Caleb refilled his mug. "Right. So, from the beginning then?"

"You're stalling."

"Confirming," Caleb argued. "Beginning it is."

Jaea listened to Caleb narrate his ancestor's arrival in Caeldighn and the objectionable state the country was in then. She had already drained a mug of tea, and she didn't think they were anywhere near the end of the tale. Thinking about the hours ahead with more of the same made her already long day look endless. She covered a yawn and refilled her mug.

"You sure you need me to go through the whole story?" Caleb asked. "It's long. I don't mind telling it, but it's long."

"I suppose you can abridge it some," Jaea conceded.

Caleb paused, looking puzzled, presumably trying to decide where to pick up the tale. "Let's jump ahead a mite to the all out war across Caeldighn. It went fairly quickly once it really got going, due in large to the dragons lined up on the Stone side of things. Stone won and took the throne. Quint and Morgana lived happily ever after. Did a pretty decent job of ruling."

"Hang on," Jaea demanded. "They ruled Caeldighn for the rest of their lives?"

"Pretty much. Crown passed to their son Bastian about five years before Quint passed away," Caleb answered. "Things were trucking along just fine until some McClanahan got a in a tizzy over taxes and riled up what remained of those who supported the war's losing side."

"Uh huh. Blaming my ancestors now for the last few hundred years of war and strife?"

"No. Well, actually yes," Caleb said. He ignored Jaea's indignant look. "Though it took them a good deal of time to get any real plan into action. Bastian's son, Leonidas Stone, inherited the throne in 1700 after his father was assassinated. Unfortunately, his father's death rather signaled the beginning of the end for his heritage. The dragons were not wholly committed to the Stone cause after Quint left the throne, and their support quickly dwindled to nothing during Bastian's reign. Leonidas ruled for a good sixty years. He fathered a number of children before becoming King. They were all daughters, and most of them illegitimate. His sister, Minerva, nearly married. She refused to marry her fiance, even though she was pregnant, because her brother still hadn't produced a son, and she was determined that the name Stone could continue through her. Luckily, she did have a son who could carry on the family. Drove Leonidas crazy that his sister had a son when he did not. He did finally manage sons, twins, in 1660. Most Stones in Caeldighn today are descended from those three boys. My father was the only son of an eldest son and so on, going all the way back to the eldest twin of Leonidas. Jakob is my father's eldest son, and thus in our eyes he has the closest claim to inherit kingship. And ta da! You are up to date."

Jaea contemplated the man across from her. "I feel as though there is still something you aren't telling me."

Caleb shrugged. "We abridged it. War and bloodshed and lots of boring trivia. Can you see our side of it now at least? Can I tell father you are not opposed to Jakob's rule?"

Jaea scoffed. "How can they ask me to do that? Support some fool that hasn't even the nerve to come speak to me in person!"

A knock sounded at the door, abruptly cutting off Caleb's intended reply. Jaea shrugged and silently warned Caleb to keep quiet.

"Who is it?" Jaea called.

"It's Lily."

"I thought you were going to stay with Gwena tonight," Jaea said. She sent a panicked look about the room trying to think of a quick way to dispose of Caleb.

"I heard about your night. Thought it would be best if I kept you company instead," Lily explained.

"Uh. I think I'd rather be alone for a time." Jaea pulled Caleb out of his chair. She quietly opened the window nearest the table. "You should head on back to Gwena's. I don't want my poor evening to turn yours rotten." She shooed Caleb toward the open window.

"Nice try, Miss," Lily said wryly. "Open up or I'll just use my key to get in," she warned.

Caleb perched in the window sill and starred unhappily at the bushes beneath him.

"Don't you dare!" Jaea exclaimed. "I'll let you in momentarily. Give me a few minutes to compose myself please."

"Compose yourself? Did that McKenna send you to tears?" Lily turned her key in the lock.

"Lily! Two minutes!"

"Oh fine," Lily relented, locking the door back. "I'll go in through my rooms. Knock on our connecting door when you are ready to be seen."

Jaea listened to her maid walk the few steps to her own door, grumbling all the while. She ran to close their connecting door when she heard Lily step into her room. Hurrying back to the window, she snatched up Caleb's mug and remaining half cookie.

Caleb looked at her questioningly, but she shoved the cookie into his mouth and pressed the mug into his hands before he could ask what she was doing.

"Lily would notice the two place settings," Jaea explained as she tossed his saucer out the window. "Sorry in advance." She pushed Caleb off the sill.

Caleb landed feet first and up to his knees in greenery. He turned to glare at Jaea. "Thanks for that."

"When can we meet next?" Jaea asked, ignoring both glare and sarcasm. "You aren't getting out of our bargain."

Caleb thought for a second. "Monday! Dawn in the stable loft. We should both be able to get there without trouble."

"You better come alone. No funny business. I'll bring just someone to talk with you about the Stone opposition. Maybe you'll see reason after that," Jaea said hopefully.

"Or you will," Caleb countered. "But yes, I will come alone. Till Monday then." He set the teacup upended on the shrubbery and walked off into the night.

Jaea looked the room over once. She straightened things here and there that had been disrupted during her tussle with Caleb. She took a deep breath and opened the door to Lily's room.

"I take it I may be permitted to enter now," Lily said politely.

"Yes. Please," Jaea beckoned. "I'm sorry to have kept you waiting. I just needed a minute to reign in my thoughts is all."

"I suppose I understand," Lily said kindly. "Do you wanna talk about it?"

"No. Absolutely not," Jaea said. "Maybe tomorrow. How much do you know?"

"Enough." Lily shrugged. She held up a large silver flask. "George sends this with his love. He raided the castle whiskey in case you wished to drown your sorrows. And he assures me you will sleep well indeed after a touch of this."

Jaea shook her head. "Does all of Caeldighn know I had an argument with my sister and my friend?" She flopped into her chair at the table and resumed drinking her tea.

"Not at all," Lily assured her. "Just most of the castle staff."

Jaea grimaced.

"Oh, it's not so bad. Just be advised that you are likely to have several suitors before the week is out. News travels fast. And there are many young gentlemen that will try to make up for Tharen's absence, should there be one," Lily said.

"Should there be one?" Jaea echoed. "An absence of Tharen in my days?"

"I imagine only you and he can decide that." Lily set the flask in front of Jaea. "Some swear alcohol helps a mind come to a decision. Never quite understood that myself. Although, an occasional drop of whiskey is a wonderful addition to a nice cup of tea."

"No, thanks." Jaea chuckled. "I think I may have had too much wine tonight as it is, but feel free to help yourself."

Lily shook her head. "I need no help to sleep. I'm usually out before my head hits the pillow." She covered a yawn. "Speaking of, we should both have been in bed some time ago. Do you need any help with your laces or letting your hair down?"

Jaea yawned in answer. "I hadn't realized how tired I was. Some help wouldn't go amiss I suppose." She pushed herself out of her chair and started toward her dressing area.

Lily loosened Jaea's gown and helped her slip out of it. She draped it over the dressing screen before turning to the laces of Jaea's corset. That done she moved to stand just outside the screen and handed Jaea's nightdress over the top when it was requested.

"Let's get those pins out of your hair so you don't go poking your eyes out on one tonight," Lily said, steering Jaea into a chair.

Jaea turned to look at her maid, only now noticing she wasn't in her uniform. "When did you change?"

"Right after the ball came to a close." Lily turned Jaea's head to face front and began to free the long black hair from the many pins she had put there hours before. "I wasn't going to take a chance at mussing up my new clothes. Switched to these just before helping Aunt Gwena."

"What would I do without you, Lily?" Jaea asked as she watched her maid add another pin to the growing pile on the vanity desk before her.

"Just be a mess I guess." Lily smiled. "There. Last one. Now into bed with you, Miss."

"Yes, ma'am," Jaea said obediently.

Lily just raised an eyebrow and shooed Jaea toward her bed.

"I'm going." Jaea laughed.

"I intend to make sure," Lily informed her. She shut the window and turned down the lamps as Jaea crawled into bed.

"Goodnight," Jaea yawned.

"Goodnight," Lily answered as she stepped back into her room.

Jaea turned down the dragonfire lamp beside her bed and was asleep before its light completely faded, her last thought being that tomorrow was going to seriously stink.

CHAPTER EIGHTEEN

Jaea knew she should speak with Maya. She had been mulling it over all morning, trying to douse the feeling of guilt eating at her. Seeing Maya would certainly be easier than talking to Tharen after...well, after all of that mess. Jaea pushed away the scone she had been picking at.

"I'm going to go find Maya," Jaea announced.

"I think that is a good idea, starting with Maya," Lily said. "I doubt you or McKenna quite know what to say to each other yet." She set all their dishes to soak in a wash pan. "Do you know where our other cup and saucer got to?"

Jaea smiled sheepishly. She leaned out the window and snatched the missing items from where they had landed the previous evening. "Sorry."

"Whatever were they doing outside?" Lily asked, bewildered.

"Uh, I may have sorta thrown them through the window last night," Jaea said uneasily.

Lily merely shook her head and added the dishes to the wash water. "Go see your sister before I try to ask anymore questions." She went about straightening the room, adding the occasional spoon to the sudsy water. "I still say out of the two of you, McKenna should have to make the next move. At least let him sweat for a day."

"I won't see Tharen yet," Jaea assured her. "Don't think I'm at all ready for that. Wish me luck."

"Luck and blessings!" Lily called as Jaea closed the door.

Jaea must have stood outside Maya's door for a full five minutes before she finally gathered her gumption and knocked. Even then, she wanted to bolt down the hall before someone answered. Emily opened the door a crack. Seeing it was Jaea, she slipped into the hall and quietly shut the door behind her.

"I'll not have you causing Miss Maya more heartbreak," Emily informed her curtly. "You have no idea what my mistress has gone through these last years. I thought you had more sense and heart than to attack her the way you did. If you have come to yell at her some more, you are out of luck. You may just turn around now and go." She crossed her arms over her chest and managed to look rather intimidating.

"Miss Maya has no idea what I have gone through either. But I came here to apologize," Jaea responded coolly. "That is, if you will allow me to see my sister to do so."

"Good. Door is unlocked. I'm off to find some coffee." Emily turned on her heel and headed down the hall toward the kitchens. "And wallop George," she vowed grimly.

Jaea quickly turned the door handle before she could lose her nerve. "Maya?"

"Ssshhh!" Kaylee whispered from the table.

Jaea looked over at Kaylee and felt every ounce of her carefully gathered gumption fall right through the floor. Maya, Kaylee, Michael, Charles, and Tharen sat around the table in what appeared to be varying degrees of hungover. Everyone, except Michael, was resting their head on the table or cradling it in their hands. When Michael saw her, he waved hello and pointed at Maya. Jaea nodded. Michael pointed at Tharen. Jaea shook her head and took a shaky step backwards. Michael nodded and held up a hand, motioning her to wait. A second later, Michael shot her a smile and gave her a thumbs up before pointing at Maya's office. Jaea nodded and made her way as quickly and quietly as she could to the adjoining room, which proved to be locked. Jaea sent Michael a panicked glance. He shrugged and pointed to the door to Emily's rooms at the opposite side of Maya's quarters. Jaea shook her fist at him and darted across the room to try Emily's door. It was open! Jaea slid into the next room with a sigh of relief.

Jaea peeked out the door and saw Michael inch back from his place at the table. Moving quiet as a cat to Maya's side, he scooped her out of her chair and started toward Emily's door. When Maya looked like she was going to say something Michael bent his head to whisper in her ear. Maya pointed a finger at him and opened her mouth to say something. Michael shook his head and sped through the door Jaea was holding open for them. Once safely in the connecting room, Michael released Maya and set her on her feet.

"Just what was that about!" Maya demanded.

"You were gonna wake up the others if you spoke. Your sister only wanted to talk to you," Michael said simply.

"Jaea?" Maya asked hopefully. She moved sideways so she could see around Michael.

"No. Your other long lost twin." Michael chuckled.

"You hush," Maya said icily. "I'm not through with you."

"I should hope not," Michael said with a grin.

Maya gave Michael a small push to the side and crossed the room to Jaea.

"I'm sorry!" Jaea and Maya blurted at the same time.

Jaea laughed. "Oh, just hug me and tell me you still love me." She pulled her twin into her embrace.

"Of course I do, you goose," Maya said wiping a tear off her cheek. "Do you still love me and want me as a sister?"

"You bet," Jaea told her. "Hard to get another twin at this

stage in life."

Both girls laughed, though doing so made Maya grimace and put a hand to her aching head.

Tharen heard Jaea's laugh nearby. He quickly sat up and turned around trying to locate her as she laughed again. "Jaea!" he shouted jumping up from his chair only to fall back into it holding his head.

"SSShhhhh!" Kaylee hissed, glaring at Tharen from across the table.

"Jaea," Tharen whispered, pointing at the door.

"No," Kaylee ordered. She sat up and rubbed her hands over her face. "You wait here." She stood up and stumbled toward Emily's door. "Maya? Jaea?" she called through the door.

Tharen heaved himself out of his chair to follow Kaylee.

"We are in here." Maya opened the door a crack to answer.

Tharen tried to peek around Kaylee to see Jaea. Kaylee elbowed Tharen causing him to mutter impolitely and back up. "Is Jaea wanting to speak with Tharen?" she asked.

Maya glanced at her sister for the answer. "No, it seems."

"Jaea, please!" Tharen tried, and failed, to move past Kaylee to the door.

Kaylee yanked the door shut and spun around to glare at Tharen. "I am sleep deprived, mildly hungover, and armed. Kindly back away. Immediately."

Tharen threw his hands in the air. "Kaylee," he pleaded. "I have to tell her. She needs to know why I left."

"No, she doesn't," Kaylee said flatly. "And if it were so important that she know? Well, you've had plenty of time to right that wrong. You'll not be springing it on her now of all times."

Tharen nodded dejectedly. "You're right. Can I at least apologize for upsetting her?"

217

"Hmph. I suppose," Kaylee relented. "From this side of the door," she warned.

Tharen drew an X over his heart. He stepped up to the door as Kaylee made room and knocked lightly. "Jaea? Can you hear me?"

"I'm here," Jaea answered.

"I never meant to hurt you, Jaea," Tharen told her. "Never."

"I know," Jaea said through the door. "I'm sorry I yelled at you like that. It was wrong of me."

"No." Tharen laughed weakly. "It was a long time coming, and I deserved it. Still friends though?"

"Always, knucklehead. It will just take some time to get back to usual with you. It hurts to see you right now, Tharen."

"I know. I'm so sorry, Jaea," Tharen said, leaning his head against the door. "I'll keep my distance. You know how to find me."

At that moment, Emily returned bearing food and coffee. She frowned at the scene before her. "What has happened now?"

"Nothing," Tharen answered. He straightened up and, taking the serving cart from Emily, made his way back to the table.

"Hmph." Emily handed Kaylee a folded piece of paper. "A page was rather frantically searching for you."

Kaylee broke the letter's seal and skimmed its contents while she knocked on the door. "Maya. Emily is back with the coffee. Oh! And I have to go. I'm needed in the Fairy Room."

"Wait!" Jaea called through the door. "I'll walk with you."

"Are you sure?" Maya asked.

"Yeah. I'll go out this way, through Emily's door to the hall. You go get some coffee."

"Alright," Maya said reluctantly. "Could I come dine with you and Lily this evening?"

"In a hurry here folks," Kaylee reminded them.

"Dinner at my place it is," Jaea said. "Kaylee, I will meet you in the hallway."

Kaylee joined Jaea a minute later, and they walked a few feet before either of them spoke.

"So," Kaylee said to break the silence.

"I need a favor," Jaea admitted.

"Ah."

"I am meeting someone early Monday morning, and I hoped you would go with me."

"Who?" Kaylee asked.

"A guy." Jaea shrugged. "I don't want him to get the wrong impression. Normally I would ask Tharen along..."

"Sure. I'll come play chaperone," Kaylee agreed. "How early?"

"Dawn." Jaea smiled apologetically.

"Sheesh. Should have asked that before I said yes." Kaylee laughed. "Well, this is me." She pointed to the Fairy Room.

"Thanks! And please don't tell Maya. She'll think I'm eloping or something."

"You aren't though, are you?" Kaylee asked suddenly concerned.

"No!" Jaea laughed. "Definitely not."

"Okay. I'll meet you here a half hour before dawn Monday?"

"Perfect," Jaea agreed. She parted company with Kaylee and headed back to her own quarters. *Oh, I hope she doesn't kill me*, Jaea thought.

Jaea did her best not to make any noise Monday morning. She thought she was doing quite well. She had even remembered to step over the squeaky spot by the table.

"And just where are you going at this hour?" Lily demanded.

Jaea's shoulders slumped. She finished opening the door and turned to look at her maid. "I have a meeting," Jaea said

219

innocently. "I was just trying not to wake you."

"A meeting. Before the sun is even properly awake?"

"Yes," Jaea confirmed. She finished pulling her shoes on. "Kaylee is going, too," she added.

Lily eyed her suspiciously. "I'm not certain that reassures me. Will you be back for breakfast?"

"Should be."

Lily yawned. "Tell Kaylee she may join us if she likes."

"Will do. Thanks, Lily!" Jaea hurried out the door. She managed to restrain her pace to a walk, but just barely. Kaylee was already sitting outside the Fairy Room when Jaea turned the corner. "Sorry I'm late."

"Nonsense. You are right on time," Kaylee replied as she stood to stretch. "I'm only here already because I've been here most of the night."

"What on earth for?" Jaea asked.

Kaylee laughed. "Don't know. Never been to Earth."

"Oh, you know what I meant," Jaea said.

"Yes. Just part of my job. Preventing war," Kaylee said humorlessly. "In this case preventing what nearly became a family feud. The thought of mother-in-laws like that nearly squelch my desire for a family. No worries though, all is well." She rubbed her hands together. "So, where am I chaperoning you to this fine, incredibly early hour?"

"The stables," Jaea answered.

"The main stable?"

"Does it have a loft?"

"Yes," Kaylee said. "Most of them do."

"Hmm. Surely he meant the main stables if there are more than one?" Jaea wondered aloud.

"Didn't either of you think to specify your meeting details?"

"Well, it was decided rather quickly. Main stable is this way right?" Jaea asked, walking off to hopefully avoid answering any more questions.

"I don't think I like this, girly," Kaylee said, falling in step beside Jaea.

"I know," Jaea apologized. "But I can't tell you more yet."

They walked in easy silence the rest of the way. It was too early for unnecessary small talk, and Jaea was too nervous about the upcoming meeting to try it.

"Stairs to the loft are just on the left here," Kaylee directed. She looked around suspiciously. "It is much too quiet here, Jaea. Something isn't right. Are you in some kind of trouble?"

"Remains to be seen," Jaea muttered as she climbed the steps to the hayloft, Kaylee right on her heels. "Caleb?" she called. "You better be here, you twit."

"Hey now!" Caleb exclaimed. "No need for name calling. Over here, thought we could sit on the bales."

Jaea crossed over to where Caleb reclined against a bale of hay. Kaylee followed reluctantly.

"So who'd you find for storytelling at this hour?" Caleb asked.

"Kaylee, this is Caleb. Caleb, Kaylee," Jaea introduced as she drew Kaylee up beside her.

"Jaea! Are you crazy? She's the Chief of Military!" Caleb cried. He jumped behind the hay bale he had been sitting on.

"You look vaguely familiar," Kaylee said. "Do I know you?"

"I sincerely hope not," Caleb said earnestly.

"Caleb, get back out here," Jaea said. She turned to Kaylee. "My friend Caleb here is confused by Caeldighn history. I was hoping you could set him straight. And fill in some more blanks for me, as well."

Kaylee was obviously agitated. "At dawn, while suspiciously hiding in a stable loft? Is your friend here new to Caeldighn?"

"Newly returned," Caleb answered.

"I see," Kaylee said. "And how do you two know each other, may I ask?"

"We went to college together," Jaea offered.

"On Earth. A third Shaper from Earth. Why haven't I seen you before now?" Kaylee demanded of Caleb.

"I've been staying with family," Caleb said defensively.

"Jaea," Kaylee said deliberately. "Is this man before me Caleb Stone?"

"Yes. But-" Jaea's answer was cut off by an angry yell as Kaylee charged Caleb, knife in hand.

Caleb met Kaylee halfway and tried to wrench the knife from her grasp.

"Stop!" Jaea yelled. "Stop it right now!"

The two continued wrestling for control of the knife and paid no heed to Jaea's pleas. Not knowing what else to do, Jaea Shaped into the first animal with a loud voice that came to mind and prayed the floor held.

Caleb and Kaylee sprang apart and spun toward the roaring lioness now staring them down. Jaea circled the pair menacingly, making sure to display her many sharp teeth and large clawed paws. She stepped between them and sat down. She growled at each of them in turn, until they were seated as well. Happy with the distance now between Caleb and Kaylee, Jaea reverted back to human form, thankful her whole wardrobe was Shape Stay now.

"Now then," Jaea began. "The next one to move without my permission gets eaten. Are we understood?" She waited for them both to nod. "Good. Kaylee, would you please tell me the not Stone side's version of how Quint Stone came to reign, especially the very beginning, the death of a Riddle, and why a Stone should not be on the throne now."

"Are you serious?" Kaylee asked in disbelief.

"Completely," Jaea answered. "I sat and listened to his family's side of the matter on the agreement he would sit and listen to the other side."

Caleb shrugged at Kaylee's questioning look.

"Fine," Kaylee said. "I will play along. For now. First off, the name you are searching for is Royalist. The non-Stone side are Royalists, loyal to the Crown and our laws as opposed to a power hungry jerk."

"He was not!" Caleb cried. "And there were plenty of people in Caeldighn who loved him."

"I did not say he wasn't charismatic," Kaylee said politely. "I said he was an ass."

"Children," Jaea warned. "Play nice."

Kaylee huffed out a breath but continued the explanation. "The war began, well it was set in motion, when the dragons allied themselves with Quint and slaughtered King Patrick's soldiers when they were searching for his daughter, Morgana. The King and Queen believed Quint to be taking advantage of their young daughter's heart solely as a means of gaining power. When dragons, including the Shaped Quint, dropped the lifeless bodies of the King's men at the castle doors the fighting began in earnest. The Crown took that act as a declaration of war and began to organize to move against him."

"They returned the Shapers to the King that they may be properly buried," Caleb interjected.

"No," Kaylee disagreed. "They threw battered and bloodied Shapers at the Capital to incite fear of going against a Dragon Shaper. Quint wanted Shapers to see that the King could not keep them safe."

"Of course, it had to be a fear tactic. It couldn't possibly be out of respect for Shaper culture that he returned their dead," Caleb said sarcastically.

"Before you interrupt me again, please take into consideration the fact that my best friend, Maya, is a history nut. She has forced me to read more than I ever cared to on Caeldighn's past. Such reading included records from Silverhaven. I've read transcripts of Quint Stone's war strategy as well as excerpts from his personal diary. There was nothing respectful about what he did that day."

"Impossible," Caleb protested. "All of Quint's writings were seized and destroyed when Logan Walker took the castle."

"When have Shapers, let alone their dragon allies, ever destroyed information of any kind?" Kaylee demanded. "Never, that's when. Knowledge is too highly prized for such an occurrence. Even the insights of madmen can prove enlightening. Granted some of his things were damaged in the fire during that battle, but most of his documents are in the Silverhaven archives."

"And you have read them?" Caleb asked, surprised.

"Yes. Whenever there is the chance, know your enemy. Besides, it seemed like a good 'what not to do' guide," Kaylee said.

"Anyway!" Jaea interrupted when it looked as though Caleb and Kaylee were going to continue throwing snide remarks instead of getting to the matter at hand. "Moving on. What happened when Quint went to see Nirah?"

"I always hated pop quizzes in school," Kaylee grumbled. "Well, they killed a Riddle."

"And your people killed an innocent boy," Caleb spat.

"Hardly innocent. He had just murdered a woman," Kaylee countered. "And not just any woman, but the head of the order that stands with the Lady's stone. Only one of the most recognized and respected women in all Caeldighn!"

"Oi!" Jaea yelled. "You two play nice or I will crack your skulls together. Kaylee, what happened when Quint went to the monument?"

"Ignoring for the moment the fact that he didn't go through the proper channels to get to the point when he would be permitted to ask for her blessing," Kaylee began. "Nirah refused to give her blessing. The Lady said no." She shrugged. "It is rare, but it does happen. So the Riddle would have known what that looked like. By our laws, that means you cannot rule. Stone did not like that answer. So he accused Riddle of lying and threatened to tear down the monument. He said it was a ridiculous practice, asking a chunk of rock for permission. That 'men rule the land, it does not rule man,'" she quoted. "Riddle forbade Quint to come near the monument, which he really disliked. Quint ordered her death. Morgana's eager to please cousin jumped at the chance to show his loyalty to Morgana and her husband and killed Riddle."

"You read all of this in Quint's diary too, I suppose," Caleb said in clear disbelief.

"Yes. As a matter of fact, I did. And in other references as well," Kaylee retorted. "What else am I to outline to this fool?" she asked Jaea.

"I've had about enough of you," Caleb said angrily. "And enough of this distortion of the truth to slander my ancestor and paint me the bad guy."

"You are clearly lacking historical education." Kaylee laughed. "Just how much have the Stone's glossed over in this tale?"

"I've half a mind to let you two kill each other, your quarreling is getting on my nerves that much," Jaea said exasperated. "So why do Royalists want to keep Stones from the throne now? Sure, some guy hundreds of years ago messed up bad. What makes Royalists so certain a Stone ruler today would be awful?"

"Because," Kaylee emphasized, "they think they were completely in the right all those years ago and have been terrorizing this country since. Skirmishes, murders, arson, theft, poisoning, you name it. The Crown has been given no reason to believe that a Stone candidate would bring peace to Caeldighn.

Quint did not play by the rules and laws of our country. Nor do any of his followers or descendents seem to be interested in running Caeldighn the way it should be run. They just see power. Caeldighn would erupt into full blown civil war again. And on a personal note, because they killed my parents. They killed Maya's parents, your parents. The Stone regime is no good. Cunning, sometimes tactically intelligent, but brutal and evil."

Jaea sighed. "So, Caleb. You have heard the other side of the argument. Can you still tell me you think your brother, Jakob, would be a good king and bring peace back to Caeldighn?"

Kaylee's eyes bulged, but she kept quiet.

Caleb gave Jaea a pained look. "For all I know she just made all of that up. And it isn't as if the Royalist hands are clean either." He shook his head. "Jaea, if you cannot support my brother on the throne then you should leave Caeldighn. Get Tharen and go back home, now. I couldn't get my father to call it off. You are still a target here."

"Jaea!" Kaylee shouted. "You can't be seriously thinking of betraying your sister and Caeldighn! Tell me you aren't a Stone," she begged.

"I'm not a Stone," Jaea said while looking at Caleb. "So far I am not a Royalist either," she told Kaylee. "And I don't believe I will be leaving anytime soon," she said.

"Jaea, you have to get out of Caeldighn!" Caleb urged.

"Just what are you trying to accomplish?" Kaylee demanded. "Get her to abandon her sister again? Snuff out the hope blossoming in this country since the lost twin's return?"

Caleb ran a hand through his hair. "I'm trying to save my friend's life! If she stays here, she will die."

Jaea suspected that Kaylee wasn't going to stand for much more. A quick look at the woman to her right confirmed it. "Thank you for meeting me, Caleb. I promise to take what you

226

have told me into consideration. Now I think it is time you were going."

Caleb, picking up on the urgency in Jaea's voice, rose and quickly brushed a few pieces of hay from his pant legs. "I think you are right. Please go home though, Jaea. I can't guarantee we won't be enemies if we meet again in this world." He walked toward the stairs, but Kaylee moved to block his path.

"Afraid I can't let that happen, dearie," Kaylee said, almost apologetically. "I've learned more about your family's plans in the last twenty or so minutes than our spies have been able to uncover in a number of years. I'd be an idiot to let you, and all that information, just waltz out the door."

"I hope you don't think me so dull as to not have taken this scenario into account." Caleb shook his head. He began to slowly back away. "Why do you think we met in a stable loft? Near a nice big, open window."

When Kaylee started forward, Caleb turned and ran through the opening. He Shaped into a small bird at the last second, evading Kaylee's grasp only by a inch or two. Kaylee looked ready to jump out after him, so Jaea quickly wrapped her arms around Kaylee's middle and pulled her back from the window. Kaylee tore herself free, but knocked them both over in the process.

"What in the name of all that is good in the universe do you think you are doing!" Kaylee yelled at Jaea. "Do you realize this could be seen as treason?" she demanded. "He is a Stone!"

"And you are a Royalist! And I don't much give a damn either way!" Jaea shouted back. "Now please be still, and let me think for a minute."

Kaylee put her arms on Jaea's shoulders and gave her a gentle shake. "He is a Stone."

"Caleb is a good man," Jaea said. "I say he is a good man," she repeated when Kaylee tried to disagree. "And that's that."

She slipped an arm around Kaylee's waist and led her toward the stairs. "It is high time we had some breakfast. Lily will have something set out for us by now. Come back to my quarters with me and help me think, please."

"Think about what?"

"Do I stay and leave Maya through death? Or do I leave Caeldighn and risk Maya dying because I wasn't here to help? Which home should I give my allegiance?" Jaea asked bleakly.

"Good mercy." Kaylee sighed. "Yeah, let's get tea," she said stepping down the stairs with Jaea.

They walked past a groom leading a horse back to its stall. The look on his face when he saw them sent both girls into a fit of giggles. Jaea could only imagine what the poor man thought, seeing the Chief of Military and the lost twin with hair a mess, covered in bits of hay, walking arm in arm out of the stables at such an early hour.

CHAPTER NINETEEN

Well, she did ask Lily to be blunt with her. Jaea thought Lily may explode when she learned where Jaea had gone that morning. *Never in my life have I been so lectured or threatened so many times.* After a fair deal of arguing, Lily and Kaylee finally both agreed to keep the morning's occurrence under wraps. Not even Maya or Tharen were to know unless absolutely necessary.

Jaea let out a sigh as she came to the library doors. The panel Maya had assembled for Jaea and Tharen was meeting today. Hopefully it would be less exciting than her meeting with Caleb had been. She took a deep breath and pushed the door open. Tharen was already seated at one of the tables arranged in a horseshoe to her right.

"Good morning, Jaea," Tharen said hesitantly.

"Good morning, Tharen." Jaea smiled back. *Don't be awkward. Don't be awkward.* "This chair reserved?" she asked, pointing to the seat next to him.

"Not at all," Tharen replied. He jumped up to pull the chair out for her. "By all means, sit and admire the maps with me."

"Thanks," Jaea said. "Oh wow. That is a big map."

A large wooden frame before them held an equally large, detailed map of Caeldighn. Two smaller charts were similarly displayed to its sides. At the far side of the table, an older man and woman were deep in conversation, but the rest of the panel hadn't arrived yet.

"So," Jaea began. "You have any idea how this panel thing is going to go?"

"Nope," Tharen admitted. "Should be interesting, though."

Jaea nodded. "Here's hoping, anyway."

"Oh, before I forget. I have a favor to ask," Tharen said.

"Uh huh," Jaea said suspiciously.

"A small one. Itty bitty," Tharen promised. "Could I borrow your messenger pen for a bit? I haven't checked in with Doc in a while."

"Yeah. Sure. When?"

"As soon as is convenient?" Tharen shrugged. "I could walk you back to your quarters after this if you don't mind?"

"That would be fine," Jaea agreed.

"Alright. Thanks."

Silence stretched between the two. Jaea racked her brain for a topic only to come up empty handed. Thankfully, Kaylee plopped down into the chair at Tharen's left before they resorted to discussing the weather.

"Good morning, kids," Kaylee greeted before taking a sip from a large green mug.

"Good morning." Tharen laughed. "Does the huge mug mean you aren't quite awake yet?"

"Spot on." Kaylee grinned. "I've had too much tea already this morning. I'm sure there is at least as much tea as blood floating around in my veins." She barely covered a yawn. "That is what happens when you try to replace sleep with caffeine I suppose."

A girlish giggle called their attention to the library's entrance. A petite brunette woman and a lanky dark haired man came toward the table. A shorter man with a briefcase followed not far behind. Once all three were settled, Kaylee stood to call the meeting to order.

"Good morning. Thank you all for coming," Kaylee said. "As you are certainly aware, the purpose of this gathering is to bring Ambassador Tharen McKenna and Jaea McClanahan, one of our recently returned citizens, up to speed on Caeldighn's current state. Should we not conclude our business this morning, we will break for a midday meal provided by the castle kitchens before continuing with an afternoon session. I believe Maya sent you a rough outline to get the conversation going?" When all the panel members nodded, she continued, "To start, I think it best we introduce ourselves. I will begin, and we will go around the table to my right, ending with Mr. McKenna." She took a sip from her mug. "My name is Kaylee Buchanan. Occupation, Junior Chief of Military. I am a Range Shaper, meaning there is a range of Shapes I can take, but I am not an All Shapes Shaper," she reminded Jaea and Tharen. "I have lived in Caeldighn all of my twenty-seven years." She took a seat and held a hand out to the gruff looking man to her right.

"Sergeant Gary York, Range Shaper, of the Caeldighnian Army." A small smile tugged at the corners of his mouth. "I am a little bit older than my Commander, having lived in Caeldighn all of my one hundred and ninety-three years." He inclined his head to the woman next to him.

"I am Deborah Lapidoth, an Owl Shaper. I work for the Caeldighn legal system as a Judge. I'll not be telling you my age." She patted her silvery curls and winked at Jaea and Tharen. "Your turn, Fred."

Fred pushed his glasses back into their proper place. "As Mrs. Lapidoth introduced, I go by Fred. The whole mouthful is Frederick Fitzgerald Carter. Human, of Earth, merchant sailor. Accidental citizen. Those gates are tricky things, aren't they? One moment I was sailing the Atlantic in 1938, the next I crashed against something and was spat out in Caeldighn in the year 1981. I serve the Crown as a part time notary. Mostly though, I help oversee the merchant guilds. I've been here, oh, about fifteen years now. On to you, Miss."

With a smile about to split her face, the young brunette excitedly introduced herself. "Name is Millie Smith. Economist. So I'll be your number cruncher today. Thirty-four. Cat Shaper. If it's feline, it's a Shape of mine." She raised her eyebrows at the tall man she had walked in with.

Quite possibly the bluest eyes in existence caught and held Jaea's, making her blush and Tharen frown. "Emil," he said with a slow smile. "Two thousand year old historian. Another Caeldighn native. Oh, and a dragon. It passes to you, dear."

Jaea laughed and shook her head at the charming blue eyed man. "I've been warned about dragon egos, you big showoff."

"Guilty." Emil chuckled.

"Well," Jaea said, turning to the rest of the group. "My name is Jaea Harbour McClanahan. I spent most of my twenty-two years on Earth. I just returned to Caeldighn last month, with my friend Tharen. No occupation as of yet. Shaper."

"Tharen McKenna." Tharen waved when Jaea pointed at him. "Twenty-three. Shaper. From Earth. Recently appointed Ambassador."

"Alright then," Kaylee said. "Let us begin. Emil, I believe you are up first. Try to keep it brief, handsome. I know how carried away and tangent prone you are on the subject of history." She smiled and pointed at her mug. "I came prepared this time."

Emil chuckled. "I have bored Kaylee in the past with too long answers. I promise I will try to stay on topic. Rein me in if I start to wander." He winked at Jaea. "Many people will tell you that the root of all our unrest today in Caeldighn is Quint Stone. I disagree. He would not have had the success he did if the country were running perfectly on his arrival. So I will begin with the reign of Patrick and Maria Fraser, the monarchs on the throne when Quint came to this world."

Jaea listened as Emil spoke about the problems of Patrick's reign. She put every thing he said against what she had learned so far from Kaylee and Caleb, glad to have a third view. Patrick apparently started out quite fair and good. Then he and his wife grew a tad too fond of power and wealth. They began pushing aside the needs of Caeldighn's non-Shaper races. Eventually no one felt truly represented by the Crown, but Patrick ignored the people's concerns and hoped they would go away. The Council was planning a large summit meeting to intervene before it became more out of hand, when onto the scene waltzed Quint Stone.

Quint was very charismatic, and many were drawn in by his charm and the sense that he truly cared for them. Unfortunately, his exterior hid a darkened heart. *So far Kaylee and Caleb were both right*. Jaea thought. And then Emil revealed what her previous sources had left out. Quint brought knowledge of black magic with him through the gate, which he convinced one power hungry dragon to use on the rest of the dragonkind. Quint's greatest allies were won through a forbidden will-binding spell.

"Once Quint and Morgana had the throne," Emil explained, "Caeldighn seemed peaceful indeed. However, that was less because they were good and kind rulers, and more because Caeldighn had been so decimated in the war that there weren't the numbers to fight back, even if the courage to be had been present." He shrugged. "A theme that sets the pace for the next few hundred years I am afraid. Eventually the people rebelled, though not while Quint and Morgana sat the throne. Quint's grandson Leonidas ruled at the time of the next great war. The dragons were finally freed from the spell upon them, which had been fading since Quint's death. Leonidas was dethroned and hunted across Caeldighn. Cameron Ryan became King and married Ellie Cassidy a year later."

A light bulb of sudden understanding went off in Jaea's mind at the name Ryan. She wondered if that was why the Ryan family felt so entitled still today. It must have showed in her face, because Emil started to laugh.

"Yes, that is probably why that family thinks so highly of themselves to this day," Emil said. "Anyway, Ryan did a fair job of more or less reconstructing Caeldighn. He also sat the throne for a good hundred years, despite numerous attempts the Stones made to kill him. That pretty well brings us to today. Skirmishes aplenty since Leonidas was usurped, all the way through Jaea and Maya's caravan being attacked, to yesterday when a trade vessel bound off world was set afire and sank into the sea. Murder and assassination are scattered throughout the last couple hundred years. Council members, Kings, Queens, military leaders, spies, Ambassadors, shopkeepers, merchants, townspeople. All in the name of returning a Stone King to the throne. Liam Buchanan and Sarai, Kaylee's parents, fought hard to bring Caeldighn back to peace. After they were killed just as Liam's father had been, well, no one has been in a rush to try for the crown. So Aurora is stuck as royal steward until someone steps up."

Everyone turned to look at Kaylee when it seemed Emil was finished.

"Right," Kaylee said. "Millie and Fred, you two are up next. Tell us about trade and economy," she prompted.

"Well trade is at a near all time low. Both off world and with our neighboring countries," Fred began. "We are too risky a gamble with no official ruler and the continued unrest."

"Yeah, that pretty much sums it up," Millie said. "Do you want to go first?" she asked Fred. "I can fill in where you need me too, and then cover what you leave out."

"Fine by me," Fred said. He looked to Jaea and Tharen. "Would you like to start with on or off world trade?"

"I don't know much about Caeldighn's neighbors," Jaea

admitted.

"All I know about on world trade is that this planet is called Avalon," Tharen added.

Fred nodded. "On world it is. Caeldighn has two neighbors. Kigali to the far southeast and Raiatea more directly south. Our trade with them both has been more stable than that with our off world partners, but even it has waned compared to what it once was. We import numerous items from both countries. Kigali is a desert like country, slightly larger than Caeldighn, and the oldest landmass on this planet. Unlike Caeldighn and Raiatea though, it is native to Avalon." He chuckled at the look of confusion on Jaea and Tharen's faces. "Avalon's other two continents came here from somewhere else," he explained. "Anyway, Kigali is inhabited by a people called the Sandlost. From them we receive spices, salt, textiles, metalwork pieces, artworks, crafted items, cocoa, and sand primarily for glass making. Caeldighn similarly trades them produce and grains, straw, flour, crafted items such as dragonfire lamps, some textiles, seasonal fruits and flowers, occasionally fish. Are you with me so far?" he asked, concerned. "I know it is a lot of listing."

Jaea and Tharen nodded. Both were quite interested to learn about the other countries that made up the world they were visiting.

"Good." Fred smiled. "Raiatea is a collection of small islands. Think tropic. We send them a lot of the same products we export to Kigali. In return, Raiatea trades us sugar, more exotic plants and fruits, artworks, crafted items usually of wood or glass, coffee, nuts, and spirits. Raiatea is the newest country here, though even it arrived long ago. It was originally part of Earth, but was swept here during a great storm. Being from Earth, the population of Raiatea is primarily human. They are a people after my own heart, spending more time at sea than on land." He opened his briefcase and pulled out two packets. He handed

235

them to Deborah to pass around to Tharen and Jaea. "Don't laugh, I like lists and charts. These papers list our trade goods coming in and going out for the last hundred years or so. Off world and on world are separated to avoid confusion. There are several charts that span a greater period to give you an idea of just how greatly it has declined. I've included excerpts from books about our neighboring peoples and the book titles, should you wish to investigate the matter further. There are two maps of Caeldighn. One shows trade routes and roads for our country. The other tells you what each area and city is known to export or craft. A world map follows those two. And lastly, my contact information. I like company, especially from my home planet, and I would be more than happy to answer any questions that arise after today."

Two boys pushed a drink laden cart into the room and parked it beside Kaylee. "Sorry we are late, ma'am," the taller of the two told her.

"We got lost," the shorter boy said, discouraged.

"Not to worry. You came at the perfect time," Kaylee assured them. "Do you think you could serve beverages while we continue our meeting?"

The boys nodded emphatically and said as one, "We practiced."

"Splendid. I will leave you to it then. Thank you, boys. Tell Gwena I said you both deserve a healthy helping of cookies when you return to the kitchen." Both kids grinned hugely and set to pouring drinks for everyone. Kaylee nodded at Fred. "Off world trade?"

Fred frowned. "A mere trickle. It is not completely limited to Silverhaven, but nearly so. The goods being transferred are much the same, with the additional imports of varied written works as well as mined gems. Very few of our products our being shipped off world and those are, again, mainly from the

University or town of Silverhaven." Fred looked to Millie.

"The lack of Ambassadors has really damaged our trade with other worlds," Millie agreed. "But there will be no new Ambassadors to negotiate with until Caeldighn gets itself together and is under the rule of a King or Queen again." She shrugged. "In repercussion, a sincere lack of capital is coming into the country. We have also had a fairly large number of citizens pack up and leave for other worlds with a more stable economy. Few families or individuals have the extra money for even such luxuries as are imported from Raiatea or Kigali, let alone off world goods. Our neighbors to the south have had to trade more off world to make up for our not buying things. New structures aren't being built right now, as the Crown can't afford to commission them and pay the workers. Roads and buildings already in place are receiving only the most necessary repairs, something I'm sure your keen eyes have already noticed about the castle. Those farther from Maeshowe or other large towns suffer the most ill repair. Oh, thank you," she said, taking the cup of cider set before her.

Jaea didn't know that keen eyes were required to notice that the castle wasn't as well off as it once was. While the main entrances were nicely decorated and kept sparkling clean, she knew if one walked down the less used halls the floors were unpolished, bare and dusty. She herself had seen at least two places where faded tapestries had been relocated in hopes of hiding damaged walls. Beyond that, she had frequently heard Gwena wish for better knives and more spices. Mrs. Lind had leapt at the chance to help Jaea and Tharen add Shaper styles to their wardrobes, making Jaea suspect the woman hadn't had a lot of business lately.

"Terra told me some of this," Tharen said. "That there are much poorer parts of Caeldighn."

"Terra?" Sergeant York inquired.

237

"A girl in the city, friend of mine," Tharen answered.

"Girl as in child?" York asked resentfully.

"Yeah. She's a kid. Problem?"

"Children aren't what I would call a good source of information," York sneered.

"On the contrary," Tharen said as tactfully as he could. "I find them to be much more unbiased than adults. As an added benefit, children have a unique perspective. They see things adults miss or ignore, often because children too are ignored by adults. Children are less concerned by political tug-of-wars, but tend to notice the results quicker than their grown counterparts."

Jaea put a hand on Tharen's arm, a sign of agreement, as well as a plea for caution. Tharen gave her the smallest of nods.

"Anyway!" Millie said. "Aurora has a good system in place, the best that can be completed without a ruler. I can run through the outline, if you like?"

Jaea sent her a grateful smile. "If you wouldn't mind."

Millie quickly rattled off some of the measures Aurora had put in effect and figures pertaining to their success. When there were no questions for Millie, Kaylee had Deborah discuss Caeldighnian law. York chipped in occasionally in matters that pertained to military law or service. York briefly spoke about the chain of command, descending from Crown to Chief and through the ranks. It was an hour that dragged by in Jaea's opinion. She was certain she had never been happier at the prospect of a lunch break in her life.

"Let's call that a morning and break for lunch," Kaylee said. "I will be around for a little while, then Maya will be taking my place for the afternoon session. If you would all follow me, we are dining in one of the courtyards."

Jaea was glad to discover it was easier being around Tharen now that the initial shock had worn off. The afternoon session

238

was more informal, further putting Jaea at ease. She and Tharen asked questions occasionally, and Maya let the conversation drift where it would. The happy feeling didn't last long. An hour or so after it reconvened, the panel became heated. Jaea and Tharen were both having a hard time keeping calm as their questions were, rather poorly, answered. It was obvious that York and Tharen disliked each other. And Jaea, tired of playing peacemaker, was now openly glaring at York and having a hard time dimming her glare when speaking with the other panel members.

"Is there any particular reason you've been unable to give me a straight answer, York?" Tharen asked.

"Tharen!" Jaea admonished. "He has answered as he is able."

"Your friend seems smart," York said condescendingly. "You would be wise to listen to her."

"You should keep your idiot commentary to yourself," Jaea retorted. "This country has some real issues! Seriously big problems. And no one seems to be willing or able to take charge and fix it. We only asked if you could tell us why?"

"It is a touchy subject," Deborah apologized for York.

"It may have seemed like an attack on the military, ma'am. The way your question came out," Millie added when York was still too red faced to respond politely.

Tharen drew a deep breath. "Usually, this is when I would assure the group I am with that I meant no offense. However, in this particular case, that would be a lie. So, by all means, take offense. Get mad. Maybe then you will rack up the backbone needed to tell it to us straight."

Most of the panel was on its feet by this point. Maya abandoned her chair and moved to stand between York and Tharen, who had begun to inch toward each other from opposite sides of the table. Emil and Fred still reclined in their seats, but anyone could see they were prepared to move quickly.

Millie fluttered around York asking him to calm down, while Deborah stood at his side glaring him down.

"If everyone could please return to their places," Maya called over the noise. Her request went unheeded.

"How dare you judge my people!" York thundered. "You've been here all of five minutes!"

"I've been here a good deal longer than five minutes!" Tharen yelled back. "And, unlike you, I have been listening to your people since I got here. I am seeing your country through eyes unburdened and unbiased by the wars that have so divided Caeldighn that you can't seem to talk about it without wanting to fight somebody. I am just trying to help!"

"Help?" York scoffed. "Do you honestly think you could do a better job than we are managing under the circumstances!"

"Yes!" Tharen shouted.

The whole room fell silent for a second.

York shook his head in disbelief. "I suppose you will tell me next that you intend to try for the Crown?"

"Maybe," Jaea interjected.

Everyone looked at Jaea in shock.

Jaea shrugged. "I don't know how long I am staying here. Whether I stay or go, I know for certain I don't want a Stone in charge, and I want my birth country to be safe. I'm not saying that Tharen or I should take the throne. But maybe a fresh pair of eyes is what you need to help find the right candidate."

Tharen cleared his throat. "What she said."

"Is this your way of declaring your allegiance?" Fred asked, sitting forward.

Jaea shook her head and tried not to feel bad for the fallen look on Maya's face as she did so. "To a cause so full of holes that its followers have a hard time answering me truthfully? To a land I may have to leave at any moment to return to my Earth family? Without even discussing the situation with the only parents I can remember? I'm sorry, but I can't do that at this time."

"I like this girl." Emil grinned. "If you change your mind, I will back your efforts for the crown. Tharen's too, if you are on his side."

"You support this cowardly inability to commit?" York asked disgusted.

Fred laughed. "Look at them, Sergeant. Cowardice isn't what you are seeing in those steely glares. Caution perhaps. Intelligence for sure. I agree with Emil. Should you decide to stay in Caeldighn, and were you to step forward as a royal candidate, you have my support."

Deborah and Millie nodded their agreement.

"I think I would back nearly any candidate at this point," Deborah admitted dryly.

Maya, eyes wide in surprise, looked around the tables. "Well, it has certainly been an interesting afternoon. I think it is time to draw this meeting to a close. Thank you all for coming."

Dismissed, most of the group shuffled to the door. Maya gathered the notes she had kept on the meeting. Emil and Fred hung back to speak with Jaea and Tharen.

"Just out of curiosity, what is your Shape?" Emil asked Tharen. "I heard a number of theories on my way through town."

"A big one. With lots of teeth," Tharen warned.

Emil and Fred laughed. They shook hands with both Tharen and Jaea.

"Fair enough," Fred said.

"Until next time," Emil said with a wink at Jaea.

"Is every male in Caeldighn going to flirt with you?" Tharen grumbled.

"One could hope," Jaea said lightly.

Tharen's jaw dropped.

Jaea laughed heartily, glad her remark garnered the response she hoped it would. *See, we can still be friends*, she thought.

"What did I miss?" Maya asked as she joined them.

"Just that Tharen disapproves of flirting," Jaea joked. She nudged him with her elbow. "Come on. I will get you that pen. Just don't keep it too long. I promised to tell Mom about the meetings today."

As Jaea turned to leave, Maya caught her arm. "Two things before you go?"

Jaea nodded. "Sure."

"You previously expressed interest in visiting Nirah's monument," Maya said tentatively. "Kaylee and I are to meet Aunt Jal and Adi at an inn near there Saturday, to discuss Chief matters. If you would not mind traveling, visiting our aunts, and a degree of solitude while Kaylee and I are in meetings..."

Jaea was bouncing in place. "Yes!" She grinned. "Yes, please. Sign me up!"

"You truly wish to go?" Maya asked.

"Very much so," Jaea said.

"I can go too right?" Tharen asked. "I would like to see this rock lady I've been hearing about for a decade."

"Yes, you may come too." Maya laughed. " I would be honored to escort you both to the Heart of our land." She pointed at Tharen. "Before I forget, separate report on this. Bring it with your usual?"

"Yes, ma'am." Tharen smiled.

"You had another question," Jaea prompted her sister.

Worry replaced the smile on Maya's face. "I'd like to talk with you about what just happened here? Are you really considering the Crown?"

"I'm considering a lot of things lately. Nothing definite anywhere yet. Come by for dinner? Lily is eating with some friends in town."

Maya nodded. "Alright."

"Great." Jaea smiled. "I'll see you soon then."

"Come on, you," Tharen told Jaea. "Sooner I get the pen, sooner I can give it back."

Jaea rolled her eyes to make Maya laugh, then followed Tharen out of the library.

CHAPTER TWENTY

Jaea practically skipped to the courtyard she was so excited. It was a weekend, her sister didn't have office hours, and she was going to see Nirah. Life couldn't get much better. Jaea hoped she would be able to talk to her friend in person today. Well, as in person as you can be with a large monument made of glowing crystal. As she joined the group she would be traveling with, she was surprised to see a centaur and a huge white wolf with them.

The centaur was the first to notice Jaea. He bowed his head and put one black leg out in a courtly gesture. "Well met, Jaea Shaper," he said. "My name is Twil. I doubt you remember me. It has been some years since I saw you last."

"Twil?" Jaea mused " Did you happen to tell me once that to run like a horse I had to stop thinking like a two-legger?"

Twil smiled, his dark brown eyes crinkling at the corners. "I did indeed."

Before Jaea had time to think about the memory that had just resurfaced, the wolf sat down and began to lean on her. Jaea was still processing the sight of a five foot tall wolf when she thought she heard him say something. His broad head tipped back to nudge her.

"You had better hug me before I hug you, little McClanahan," the wolf said. "It is much easier that way. Though I have no problem leaning on you until you fall over so

I can lick your face, if you prefer."

Jaea laughed and hugged the wolf around the neck. "Hello. I'm sorry I don't know your name. Did you know that you are quite tall for a wolf?"

He licked Jaea's cheek before she straightened. "I am Tsagi. And I am not a wolf, exactly. I am a waya. My kin are distant cousins to the magic-less wolves. We have not had the pleasure of meeting before, but I am dear friends with your aunts, Jayla and Adrielle. I know how glad they are of your return, and so I am glad, too."

Maya saw Jaea and walked over to greet her. "I see you have met the remaining Council members, Twil and Tsagi.

"Yes." Jaea smiled, scratching behind Tsagi's ears. "Oh! They are the two I hadn't met yet?" she asked when her sister's statement sank in. "Are they going with us?

"I extended the invitation, but they have other business to attend," Maya answered

"We are on our way north now that we have passed our reports on to Maya," Twil told her.

"My mate wishes me to hurry," Tsagi said. "She says I am gone too often of late."

Tharen came to stand by Jaea, and she quickly introduced him to Twil and Tsagi. "I have been hoping to see a waya for some time now. I was told it is best not to go looking for them. It's nice to meet you," Tharen said.

"We have something of a reputation for fierceness," Tsagi said with a wolfish grin.

Tharen laughed. "I believe it. I'm told though, that you also have a reputation for beautiful Pack Songs. I would love to hear one someday."

"Perhaps you shall," Tsagi responded with a hint of warning, making it clear that he had not made up his mind about the Shaper before him.

Twil sought to diminish the threat in Tsagi's voice. "It is unwise to roam the forests where we reside in some Shapes," he explained. "Game animals run the risk of being mistaken for dinner. Shapes unusual to the area could be seen as a threat. The waya are careful and would not wish to harm a Shaper unintentionally, but there have been serious cases in the past."

Feeling the tension in those around her, Jaea decided to change the subject. "I thought most of us would get to the monument Shaped. Are we riding instead?

Maya smiled. "Yes. Not all of those in our party are so lucky as to be All Shapes Shapers," she teased Jaea.

"I can't do all Shapes, and you know it. Try as I may, I just can't be a fish. I'm practically useless in the water," Jaea said in mock dismay, coaxing a laugh from the group.

"I've been meaning to ask, how does that work? Domestic animals in a land of people who can turn into animals?" Tharen asked.

"Merciful stars. Tharen McKenna, don't you ever run out of questions?" Maya laughed.

"Now where would be the fun in that?" Tharen responded in kind.

"I'll try to explain on the road," Maya promised. "We should be going if Kaylee and I are to keep our meeting with my aunts."

"We should be on our way as well," Twil said. "Well met, Shaper friends. Good journey." He and Tsagi turned to follow the road leading north from the courtyard.

"Come," Maya said. "I will show you to your mounts."

Jaea and Tharen waved goodbye to their newest acquaintances, then followed Maya to join the rest of their party. Once mounted, they rode through the castle gates and into the city following the wide East Road. A handful of guards placed themselves throughout the group as they rode through Maeshowe toward Nirah. They were not inclined to conversation, and their rigid manner made Jaea uneasy. When she asked why they needed guards, Maya reminded her of recent Stone attacks. Trying not to dwell on the thought of an impending ambush, Jaea remembered that Maya had promised to tell them about Caeldighn's animals.

"I would guess that animals are treated well here in Caeldighn?" Jaea asked.

"Very," Maya said. She looked at Tharen and Kaylee riding behind them to make sure he could hear her. When Tharen nodded that he was paying attention she continued. "You will find nothing of the cruelty shown animals in some worlds here. We are too close to them to allow such, and it would be considered a severe crime. Yes, we raise animals for food or work, but they are tended kindly. To work with animals such as horses is a great honor in Caeldighn and requires years of training and tests before one is deemed a handler. Our ability to understand animals makes that job easier in some respects. Many domestic animals lose the ability to converse as their wild counterparts do. Even so, livestock is treated with respect and live with as much comfort as can be given them."

"Some from off world seem confused by this practice, thinking that since we can speak with animals we would all be vegetarians," Kaylee added with a shrug. "We are people and animals are animals. For all we respect their lives, they are not our kin. Even so, there are many Shapers who choose not to eat meat after having taken similar Shapes themselves."

"In regards to dragons, McKenna," Maya said, anticipating Tharen's question and making him grin. "There is a large farm near Silverhaven where sheep and cattle are raised primarily for the dragons. They also produce most of the realm's wool and leather. Does this satisfy your curiosity?"

"I believe so," Jaea said.

"It does for now," Tharen answered happily.

247

"Perhaps you could answer a question for me then?" Maya inquired.

"Of course," Jaea said.

Tharen and Kaylee rode forward until they were beside Maya. "Ask away. I will answer what I can," he promised.

"You two are still hiding something from me," Maya said. "At the very least, it is merely Tharen's Shaping abilities. What I want to know is why? Do you mistrust me?"

Tharen smiled sadly. "I trust you, Maya. More than I do most. But I have had little experience trusting people completely. One day, I will tell you, cross my heart. That day is just not likely to be today."

Maya frowned at him. "I would like to trust you completely. Both of you," she said looking at Jaea. "It is difficult to do so when I know you are not telling me the whole story." She was quiet for a moment, staring at the horizon instead of looking at Jaea or Tharen. "I have grown up in a time of betrayals, seeing those thought loyal to the crown for generations prove to have been traitors all along. It makes you a little paranoid. And I can guarantee the Rebels are plotting furiously now that the 'lost twin' has been reintroduced to Caeldighn. Especially after you declared interest in the throne to that panel Monday. The Rebels will not stop to ask which side you are on or if you really want the Crown. They will see you simply as a threat to be eliminated. I had hoped that by now I could believe, beyond the shadow of a doubt, that you would be on the same side I am should it come to battle. Make no mistake, sister. Eventually this rebellion will return our land to war."

Jaea laid a hand on Maya's arm. "I wish I could tell you that I would blindly back the Crown, if only because it is a cause you support. I'm sorry I cannot make that promise. I can tell you that I bear the Crown and Caeldighn no ill will."

"We are on your side, Maya," Tharen said. "We just haven't

been here long enough to extend the same courtesy to the empty throne in a land we barely know."

Kaylee let out a loud groan. "You people can be so serious and glum. It is downright depressing. Give them time to decide if they want to stay here, Maya. Then you can invite them to join our war." With that, she rode ahead to seek more lighthearted conversation.

Jaea, Maya, and Tharen looked at each other sheepishly.

Jaea coughed to break the awkward silence. "Tharen, did I tell you that my Great Aunt Mildred once accidentally Shaped into a green cat?"

Tharen laughed. "Green?"

Maya nodded, a smile spreading across her face. Just like that, the cloud lifted from the trio, and they returned to an easy banter as the road stretched on toward the land's heart.

When Nirah's monument became visible, it was all Jaea could do to refrain from Shaping into a bird and flying ahead of the group. To help curb her excitement, Maya started telling Jaea about the monument's history. It helped take her mind off the distance still to cover before reaching their destination. The slow pace became nearly unbearable after Maya was called away to talk with one of the officers. Then they were finally there! Their party had all dismounted, the horses had been seen to, but no one else seemed to be in a hurry to approach the obelisk. When Jaea could take it no longer, she tapped Maya on the shoulder and asked if it were alright to go on alone. Although Maya clearly would have preferred to go with her, she reluctantly nodded her approval as she was drawn away again by the man in charge of the horses.

Jaea grinned and went to find Tharen. She saw he was deep in conversation with Kaylee though, so she decided to go without him. She began to walk toward the monument, the picture of a respectful young lady. Maya had told her that it was considered incredibly rude to Shape at the monument, otherwise Jaea likely wouldn't have been able to contain her glee enough to keep to only one form. She paused for a moment admiring the graceful obelisk rising from the center of a small lake. From the book she had borrowed from the castle library she had learned that there was a waterfall where the lake connected to the river flowing by it. Legend said the deep pool was formed by Nirah's tears and that when the lake had filled, its water trickled west and formed the large river that cut north through Caeldighn's center. How many times had Jaea walked the circular bridge that surrounded the monument in her dreams? Hardly able to believe she would at last set foot there in person, she gave in to her joy and began to run the remaining distance between her and the glowing crystal she knew so well. That was when everything began to go terribly wrong.

Jaea had barely registered the two armed guards at the base of the bridge earlier, and she hadn't noticed the change in their stance as she walked closer. The moment she began to run, however, the guards shouted and began rushing toward her. Confused by their behavior, Jaea stopped, thinking she could explain that she was only happy to see Nirah. The men continued charging toward her, seemingly convinced she was a threat. Jaea heard someone come up beside her and wasn't surprised to see Tharen. They moved to stand back to back as two more guards came thundering across the bridge blocking their path. Jaea and Tharen found themselves loosely surrounded in the wide green clearing between the road and the monument. The four guards held spears, thankfully not yet pointed at them. A dark skinned woman stood beside Nirah's stone watching the scene unfold. The woman had an odd look on her face, like she had just been told a secret and didn't know what to think of it.

"Not a move, Rebels!" the head guard yelled at Jaea and Tharen.

"Attacking the Land's heart is low even for you scum," a guard added.

Jaea and Tharen bristled at the accusations. "I don't believe you quite understand the situation here, sirs," Tharen tried to reason.

"That is enough from you! Are there others in on your plot?" the leader demanded.

"You are mistaken, sir," Jaea began. "We-"

"I don't think you quite grasp the gravity of your situation," the leader growled. "I'm sure we will hear you sing a different tune when the Crown's soldiers haul you away," he added, nodding to the group led by Maya and Kaylee.

"Captain!" Maya called as she came within hearing range. "What is the meaning of this?"

"We caught these two preparing to attack the Heart, ma'am."

"Hardly," Maya said stiffly. "What you have done is threatened the well being of my sister. She is recently returned to Caeldighn from Earth and was unaware of the proper manner to approach the monument."

"Recently returned from a world known to have a Stone hold? Garners suspicion, ma'am, sister or no," the captain replied.

"How dare you!" Tharen yelled. He started to step toward the captain, but Jaea's hand on his arm stopped him.

"Please understand," Jaea said. "I have spoken with the Lady many times in my dreams. I was carried away by my excitement at seeing Nirah again. Truly. I just wish to see the monument in person."

"That is a creative story, I'll admit. But you will go nowhere near the Lady Nirah this day," the captain sneered.

"Nirah knows me! She knows I am no threat," Jaea insisted as she moved toward the captain trying to plead her case.

251

The guard nearest Jaea, thinking she intended to attack his captain, moved quickly to her side and grabbed her by the arm. Jaea turned to glare at the man. "Let go of me. Now."

"I do not take orders from the likes of you!" he spat. No sooner had the words left his mouth than he let go of her arm and stepped back, spear pointed at something behind Jaea.

Jaea turned around to see wisps of smoke curling away from Tharen's nose. He took a deep breath, and his body rapidly grew in size. He put one foot forward and before the other had moved to join it, there was a very large, very angry, sapphire dragon in his place. The jagged dark blue flames of Tharen's Shaper mark stretched across the dragon's left shoulder and part way down his left wing, clearly visible as he spread his wings to their full span.

"How do you feel about orders from the likes of me!" Tharen roared.

Jaea tried to calm the crowd, which had gone into a frenzy when Tharen had Shaped. Now even those that had ridden with them stood armed and ready. Jaea guessed that a few of the soldiers had Shaped in response, as there were now two leopards and a bear among them. Maya and Kaylee stood with swords drawn, waiting to see what happened next.

"Tharen is not a threat to you unless you first become one to him. He was only trying to protect me!" Jaea explained.

"Listen to the girl!" the woman on the bridge called.

"He is with the Stone rebels!" a guard cried.

"Dragon Shapers cannot be trusted!" another added.

Tharen turned to face his accuser. "I am done with this. Drop your weapons, or I'll make the lot of you an early dinner and use your spears as toothpicks!" he warned.

"No!" Jaea yelled, panicked as the soldiers began to move in on Tharen. "We are not with the rebellion!"

"He is a stranger to Caeldighn, and by his actions he has threatened our land!" argued one of the soldiers. He pulled back his arm to throw his spear.

It would be hard to say who was more surprised at first, Jaea or the soldier. Acting solely on the instinct to protect Tharen, Jaea had Shaped into her dragon form. She caught the spear in one large violet paw and snapped it in two.

"I am of Caeldighn!" she screamed as those around them fell back to regroup. "I was born of this land! I, Jaea Harbour McClanahan, am a Dragon Shaper, and I vouch for Tharen McKenna! What have you to say now?"

A single blinding flash of light erupted from the monument, briefly casting fearsome shadows before Jaea and Tharen. Most of the soldiers dropped their weapons and stared in awe at something behind the Dragon Shapers.

"Stop," a woman behind Jaea said simply. The familiar voice rang both in Jaea's ears and her mind.

Those who had been advancing on the dragons joined their companion in stillness. Those that had Shaped returned to their human form.

Jaea and Tharen had their backs to the stone and didn't dare turn to see why their adversaries seemed to be retreating. A smoky figure walked between them, a misty trail in her wake tying her to the monument. Jaea and Tharen, still dragons, cocked their heads at this new development.

The woman came to a stop in the space between the dragons and the larger group. "I am Nirah. You know who I am?" she asked.

Everyone in the group nodded yes. Jaea stretched her neck out trying to get a closer look.

"Yet you draw weapons here and dishonor my memory," Nirah admonished. "How dare you take up arms against someone, one of my daughters especially, because of the form she has Shaped into! Have you forgotten that you all descend from dragons? That your beloved First Queen was a Dragon

253

Shaper? Or that my husband, Jaea and Maya's ancestor, was a Dragon Shaper? Have Shapers become so shallow as to pass judgment on their fellows based solely on the mark they were born with?" She looked around at the now quite sheepish assembly before her. "Jaea, Tharen. Shape back into your human forms please?"

Jaea and Tharen returned to their human forms as quickly as they had Shaped into dragons. Jaea brushed a few wood splinters from her shirt. Tharen stood with his arms crossed and scowled at the soldiers.

"It is one's heart, not how they appear, that shows whether they are good or evil. Perhaps you find them less intimidating now, when they look just like you. Tell me, what is so different about the Shapers before you?" Nirah asked.

It must have been as obvious to the rest of the group as it was to Jaea that Nirah had asked a rhetorical question. No one offered an answer.

"Do you suppose it is within your abilities to finish settling this confrontation sensibly and without violence? If not, I can always open the ground at your feet and let the earth swallow you," Nirah said with a shrug. "I am not usually so dramatic. However, it is more unusual for my stone, or my friends, to fall under attack. I must say, I greatly dislike it."

"It shall be settled peaceably, Lady," Maya promised. "I will see to it."

Nirah smiled. "One of my own to oversee it, and one with such gifts. I would like to think it comes from my side of the family, though the dragons assure me this is not the case. And I am getting off course. Very well. Good day, Shapers." She turned back to her monument, stopping when she reached Jaea and Tharen. "Welcome home, Jaea! And welcome to you as well, Tharen McKenna, whom I have heard so much about."

Jaea grinned. "Hi, Nirah."

"Lady," Tharen said with a bow.

"Yes, I believe you two will do quite well here," Nirah said, giving them a conspiratorial look. Then she walked back to her monument and disappeared in the stone.

The dark skinned woman had remained on the bridge during all the commotion. She bowed to the crystal obelisk as it returned to its usual appearance, slightly glowing and filled with lazy foggy swirls. She then sat down and began to transcribe the event in a notebook.

Jaea realized the woman must be one of the Readers, the order of women that kept watch over Nirah's stone. She hoped she would have the chance to speak with her. That is if Maya didn't arrange to have Jaea and Tharen shipped out of Caeldighn through the nearest gate.

"Alright, now listen up!" Maya yelled suddenly, drawing everyone's attention. "All the soldiers who accompanied us out today are dismissed. You may return to the castle tonight or continue on to the inn as previously planned, whichever you prefer. Nirah's guards! You are to return to your posts. Jaea and Tharen, you will come with Kaylee and myself to the inn. Any questions?"

Most of the guards and soldiers shook their heads no, but one raised a hand tentatively.

"Yes?" Maya asked.

"What if you are attacked when returning to Maeshowe?"

Maya smiled politely and pointed to Jaea and Tharen. "I'm traveling with dragons. I will simply let Tharen sit on our attackers."

The soldier nodded vigorously and set to readying his men to return to the castle. Within a few moments, only Kaylee and Maya remained with Jaea and Tharen.

Maya punched Tharen lightly on the arm and laughed. "Not likely to tell me today. Seems you guessed wrong. I think we will have to postpone your visiting the monument, though. You rather terrified the guards."

"Is that why you have avoided Shaping?" Kaylee asked. "Did you fear a reception such as this?"

Tharen nodded. "So, you two aren't mad?"

"No," Maya answered without hesitation. "Suddenly I feel downright normal. It's a new feeling for me. I like it!"

"Care to explain?" Jaea asked.

Maya shrugged. "You have shown secrets today, so I will as well." She held up a hand for them to see. In the blink of an eye, thick brown fur covered her hand as her nails became claws and the pads of her hands more calloused. Then the claws changed to those of a large cat, the fur following suit, before her whole hand quickly morphed into eagle talons. She waved her hand, and it became her regular human hand again. "Dragon Shapers are not nearly so rare in our history as Partial Shapers. It is still nice to have some company in the 'unusual Shaping' category," she said.

"Neat." Jaea smiled. "But..."

Maya draped one arm across Jaea's and pointed in the direction of the inn. "Ask your question, sister. You too, McKenna. We've a way to walk yet."

They walked a few steps in silence while Jaea decided which question to ask first. Tharen and Kaylee walked beside them, Kaylee leading their horses. "Is that what Nirah meant?" Jaea asked. "About your gifts?"

Maya nodded.

"So Partial Shapers are rare but not unheard of," Tharen said uncertainly. "When was the last time there was a Partial Shaper?"

"The dragons at Silverhaven are still searching their records for that answer," Maya answered. "It further complicates the answer that I am not only a Partial Shaper but able to fully

Shape as well." When they had walked a few feet with neither of them saying anymore, Maya gasped. "Are you out of questions? I'm shocked!"

"I have one more, but it's unrelated," Tharen asked as they approached a small town. "Are we almost to this inn? Please say yes, and that they serve some beverage containing alcohol."

"Yes." Maya chuckled. "On both counts." She led them past a handful of buildings before opening the door to one on their right. "You two go on. Grab a table and order us some drinks. Kaylee and I will be in after we tend the horses."

CHAPTER TWENTY-ONE

Tharen patted his pocket for the thousandth time to assure himself the ring was still there. The day had not been going according to plan, but that was no reason the rest of it couldn't be awesome. Right? After the monument fiasco, he and Jaea had sat down for a quick meal with the four Chiefs, which is how he thought of Jayla, Adrielle, Maya, and Kaylee. Now the meal was winding down, and the Chiefs would soon be headed off to do their thing, going over reports and doing whatever they did. Then he would finally have a chance to talk to Jaea, alone. Nothing like a romantic evening walk as a backdrop for asking insanely huge, life altering questions.

Cue sudden downpour. Rain beat against the windows and drummed a rhythm on the roof.

Great. Tharen thought. *Anything else? Anything at all, that would also like its chance to dash all my hopes?*

The loud crack of thunder nearly hid the bang of the door as it flung open. Tharen wanted to beat his head on the table. Every person with half a brain knew better than to ask if a situation could get any worse, Movie Lessons 101.

The figure striding confidently through the door captured everyone's attention. She politely pushed the door closed and pulled back the hood of her cloak before walking to the middle of the inn's dining room. "I'm looking for the dragon," the petite woman stated.

Maya stood and waved the woman toward their table. "I'm Maya McClanahan, Junior Chief of State. I'm not sure what you are after, but perhaps we can help." She gestured to the rest of their group.

"The dragon," she repeated, ignoring the chair Maya offered. "The male dragon that was at Nirah's monument just hours ago." Her gaze drifted to Tharen like he wore a homing beacon for a hat.

"Um. I think that is me," Tharen said. He stood and extended a hand to the newcomer. "Tharen McKenna, Dragon Shaper."

The woman clasped his hand in hers, but looked at Tharen strangely. "No, you aren't."

"Really, he is," Jaea insisted. "I'm a Dragon Shaper, too. We were just at the monument. What do you want?"

"You could be a Dragon Shaper, yes," the woman agreed. "He is not a Shaper. He is a dragon."

Tharen paled and sank back into his seat. "What do you mean?"

"I think you should sit," Adrielle ordered.

"Please," Jayla added, though the word left no room disagreement. "Join us for a moment and explain."

"Very well, if I must," the cloaked woman huffed. She plopped into a chair. "I am Vasfee, a senior student at Silverhaven University. Master Caspar, head of the dragonkind in Caeldighn, sent me to retrieve him." Vasfee pointed at Tharen. "We were unaware of his presence until he Shaped, but he has broken protocol by not checking in at the University before wandering around Caeldighn."

"I would have liked to visit Silverhaven," Tharen said. "But I haven't had the chance yet. I've only been here about a month."

"So you are a month overdue to notify Silverhaven of your presence." Vasfee glared.

"That doesn't make any sense," Tharen objected. "Why would a Shaper need to register at Silverhaven to visit Maeshowe?"

Vasfee look at the questioning faces around her. "Surely it isn't possible that you don't know?"

"What are you talking about?" Jaea demanded. "Tharen is my best friend. He is a Shaper, from Earth, like me."

Vasfee shook her head sadly. "I'm sorry. That isn't possible. The man beside you is a dragon. Every dragon in Caeldighn was made aware of his presence when he assumed his true form, just hours ago. Usually we recognize our kind as soon as they come through a gate. For some reason his human form disguised his existence from us. You can understand our concern? An unidentified dragon, undetected until now. You must return to Silverhaven with me. Tonight," she told Tharen.

"I will do no such thing!" Tharen protested. "I am spending time with Jaea this evening. Come back tomorrow."

"I think you have to," Jayla said. "If you are a dragon, and Silverhaven suspects you are evading them..."

"It would not be good," Adrielle finished.

"Your friends are correct," Vasfee said. "I am under orders to bring you back, by force if necessary."

"How exactly does a little thing like you propose to do that?" Tharen asked angrily.

Vasfee reached across the table to wrap her hand around Tharen's wrist. "Simple," she bragged. "You see, I'm a dragon of the Verdi Region." She shifted her hand so that her fingernails grazed Tharen's skin. "In the Verdi, nearly everything is poisonous." She pulled her hand back and smiled sweetly at Tharen. "It would really be best if you cooperated."

Tharen stared at her wide eyed. He rubbed his arm and investigated for any puncture marks. "Jaea?" he asked. "What do you think?"

"You have been wanting to go to Silverhaven," Jaea said practically. "This isn't the visit we imagined, but it still gets you there. Where else are you likely to get answers about your family?"

"You think I'm not a Shaper?"

"I don't know. And neither do you," Jaea reminded Tharen. "How many conversations have we had over the years on just this subject?" She looked at Vasfee. "Can I come with you both?"

"I would love to extend such an invitation, especially if you are in fact a Dragon Shaper," Vasfee began. "Unfortunately, I do not have that privilege at this time. Besides, I would recommend letting your friend do this alone. Especially if he is as unknowledgeable about his heritage as he claims. Self discovery is just that, something that generally needs accomplished by one's self."

Tharen rubbed a hand over his face. *I officially have the worst luck in the universe.* "When would we need to leave?" he asked, resigned.

"Almost immediately," Vasfee answered. "We have already delayed longer than I would have liked. The more time that passes since I received orders to collect you, the more likely it is that Caspar will send other dragons to search for you as well."

"Of course," Tharen muttered. "And how long will I be gone?"

Vasfee shrugged. "It is likely up to you. Though many of our kind find they have no real wish to leave with so much to learn at Silverhaven."

"I have more reason to leave Silverhaven than I currently have to go to Silverhaven," Tharen said fiercely. "Can I at least have a few minutes to speak with Jaea?"

Vasfee exhaled a breath that was as much smoke as it was air. "If you hurry. Don't leave the room, or I will render you unconscious. I can carry you just as easily as fly beside you."

"Fair enough." Tharen pulled Jaea out of her chair and headed for an unoccupied corner of the dining room.

"Tharen, what is the matter?" Jaea asked concerned. "You are acting very strange. I thought you would be ecstatic to go speak with the dragons and search their library."

Tharen held Jaea's hands tightly in his own. "Any other day, I probably would," he admitted. "I had hoped to speak with you this evening. Alone. Just you and I. Like it was before we came through the gate and were surrounded by people all the time." He rested his forehead on hers. "Jaea, I..." He took a deep breath and tried again. "I..."

"What?" Jaea asked. "You are starting to scare me, Tharen."

"Just promise me you won't go and fall in love with Michael or somebody until I get back."

"What?" Jaea laughed.

"Wait for me," Tharen said quietly. "Just a little longer. Until I can explain. Please," he begged.

"Okay," Jaea agreed. She pulled him into a hug. "Okay."

Tharen nodded. "Thanks." He pulled out of her hug so he could see her face. "One more thing? Before I lose my nerve?"

Jaea nodded encouragingly.

"May I kiss you?"

Jaea's eyes widened in surprise. "Um. I. Uh. If you like?"

Tharen pulled her to him again and kissed her as he had wanted to for years. Then he stepped back and gave Jaea a shaky grin. "I'll be back as soon as I can." He hurried through the room and out the inn door, Vasfee on his heels.

For all the situation was less than ideal, Tharen was glad to be flying again. It seemed like decades had gone by since he had last felt his wings cutting through the sky. The summer storm had fizzled out as quickly as it had blown in, leaving only a misty rain in its wake. Nothing had gone to plan, and he had been essentially kidnapped by a scary little dragon lady, but he had kissed Jaea, and now he was flying. Not a total waste as far as days go.

Tharen tried to match the landscape below him to the maps of Caeldighn he had seen. The low light made it difficult to make out much of the unfamiliar land. By the time mountains loomed before him, Tharen was ready for a break. He didn't know if Vasfee could tell he was tiring, or if she needed to rest as well. They stopped next to a mountain stream, which Tharen drank from gratefully.

"Just how much farther is this place?" Tharen asked Vasfee.

"Farther than you are flying tonight," Vasfee answered. "You have already been traveling all day. If you are not opposed to the idea, I can carry you the remainder of the way."

"Is there another option?"

"Sleeping on the cold hard ground and hoping I don't accidentally set you on fire if I snore?" Vasfee offered.

"Riding sounds good," Tharen decided promptly. Then he remembered Vasfee's earlier threat. "Aren't you poisonous?"

"Not where you would be sitting," Vasfee assured him. "Just avoid my claws, tail and spikes."

"Gotcha." Tharen Shaped back into a human. "How ya wanna do this?"

"If you can clamber up those rocks, you should be high enough to slide onto my back."

A few minutes later Tharen was safely and nontoxically astride the bright green dragon. Vasfee was in flight again seconds after Tharen settled. When Tharen's eyelids grew increasingly heavy, he wondered if he had managed to avoid Vasfee's poison after all.

"It is safe to sleep," Vasfee called back to Tharen. "You are bound to be travel weary. I will not drop you."

Tharen tried to argue that he was fine. All that came out was a mumble, and soon he was slumped against Vasfee's scales, completely asleep.

It was mid-morning when Vasfee landed, waking Tharen. They were in some sort of enormous courtyard. A tall wall on one side boasted great archways that led to who knew where. The opposite half circle had no wall at all, simply open air. An incredibly tall fellow helped Tharen down. A woman hurried over with canteens for Vasfee and Tharen. Vasfee quickly Shaped into her petite human form and thirstily gulped the water. Fighting a foggy brain, Tharen drank more slowly.

"Ugh," Vasfee said as she stretched her arms above her head. "Been some time since I last carried someone. Forgot how much that little extra weight can wear you out!"

"Sorry." Tharen shrugged. He handed her his canteen in case she was still thirsty. "Next time you kidnap me I will try to be lighter." He smiled.

"Cheeky." Vasfee smiled back. She took the canteen and polished off what remained of its contents. "Thanks."

"Thank you, for the ride," Tharen responded. "I guess my wings aren't in as great of shape as I thought. Not a lot of chances to fly for hours at a time on Earth though."

Vasfee started to reply but changed her mind when she caught sight of the woman crossing the courtyard. She bowed her head in respect to the most beautiful woman Tharen had ever seen. Tharen, having never been to Persia, couldn't rightly say what a Persian princess looked like. Nonetheless, he was fairly certain the woman standing before him now was just that.

"Good morning. I am Raja, Council member for the Silverhaven Dragons. I am here to escort an unidentified dragon to Caspar?"

"Good morn, Raja. I am Vasfee. This is Tharen McKenna,"

Vasfee introduced. "He is whom you are seeking."

"Tharen McKenna? Jaea's McClanahan's friend?" Raja asked surprised.

"One and the same," Tharen said. "I believe you met Jaea at the ball. We had hoped to visit you together soon, but some guy named Caspar had different plans it seems."

Raja still stared at Tharen uncomprehendingly. "He is the dragon that Shaped at the Monument? You are a dragon?"

"I am a Tharen. And hungry. Beyond that, your guess is as good as mine."

"Yes," Vasfee answered quickly. "He is most certainly a dragon. Though there is admittedly something odd about him." Vasfee yawned. "If you do not mind though, ma'am, I would like to take a rest."

"Yes! Of course. Forgive me," Raja apologized. "Please come see Caspar and myself when you are up to it."

Vasfee nodded. "I will. So long, McKenna." She clapped him on the back as she passed.

"Well," Raja said decidedly. "If you would?" She pointed to the archway on the far left. "This way please. Let's try to sort this out, say, over some breakfast?"

"I find that plan incredibly agreeable," Tharen said happily.

Raja laughed. She led him through a couple of very wide corridors to a smaller hallway that held offices. "Here we are."

A brass plate on the open door read "Dragon Affairs". A sharp eyed, white haired old man sat at a table that could have once been the side of a small barn.

"Master Caspar," Raja said. "The dragon in question is here to join us for breakfast. He just arrived with Vasfee."

"Ah! Good, good," Caspar replied excitedly. "Come in, fill a plate. I have a good number of questions for you, young sir. But it is usually best to first break bread with new acquaintances." He passed Tharen and Raja plates and silverware. "Cups are there by the pitchers," he told them while he dished bacon and eggs onto his own plate. "Now then, as you have likely gathered, my name is Caspar. I head the Dragon Council and see to a great deal of our internal affairs. Your other dining partner is Raja, our elected Council member to the Crown. Might I ask your name?"

"Tharen McKenna, of Earth." Tharen offered Caspar his had. "Pleased to meet you. And thank you in advance for the meal. It smells delicious."

"It should be, as much as I pay the cook!" Caspar laughed. "McKenna of Earth, huh? Rings a bell. Haven't met before, have we?"

"No, sir."

"Hmm. And were you unaware that dragons are to register here before traversing Caeldighn?" Caspar inquired between bites of scrambled eggs.

"That is correct," Tharen said. "Although until recently I thought I was a Shaper, like Jaea."

"Jaea McClanahan," Raja clarified. "The recently returned twin of Maya McClanahan, Junior Chief of State. He came through the gate with her."

"You did not know you are a dragon?" Caspar asked shocked. "Is that even possible?" he asked Raja.

"I am not certain," Raja admitted. "I was hoping we could ask our young friend here to Shape for us after we eat. To confirm."

"I don't believe we need to confirm it. I can see the fire in him. Still, I would be interested in seeing him in dragon form if he were willing," Caspar said.

"I don't mind," Tharen answered when they both looked at him. "Well, so long as someone has a coat I can borrow. I hadn't planned on traveling to the mountains. It's a tad chillier here than in Maeshowe."

"Certainly. I will have something brought to the courtyard for you, the area you landed with Vasfee this morning. Will that be enough space for you to Shape?" Raja asked.

Tharen nodded. "That would be fine. What does seeing my dragon form tell you?"

Caspar shrugged. "Maybe something, maybe nothing. Our marks occasionally have clues to our histories. What can you tell me about your family?"

"Nothing. That is why Jaea and I were hoping to visit your archives at some point. I've been told you have extensive genealogy records." Tharen paused. "Do you really think I am a dragon? Not just a Dragon Shaper?"

"Yes," Caspar answered. "Without a doubt. Though you may not be just a dragon either." He pushed back from the table. "Alright, that is all my curiosity can stand. Let's head to the courtyard and see if your mark or Shape tells us anything. Then we will head to the libraries and find someone to pelt with questions."

Raja smiled at Tharen. "I'm surprised he lasted this long. Come on, he may implode if we dally."

"I heard that!" Caspar called from down the hall. "Old, not deaf!"

A few hallways later, Tharen found himself back in the courtyard Vasfee had landed them in. As requested, he Shaped before the small audience. Caspar and Raja Shaped as well after Tharen assured them it wouldn't scare him off. The handful of others present hung back by the wall in human form to give the three dragons room.

"So you are a sapphire. Not as many of those as there once were. No idea why," Caspar said to himself.

"What?" Tharen asked, intrigued.

The diamond colored dragon looked up from inspecting the mark on Tharen's shoulder and wing. "Oh. Dragons share colors primarily with gemstones. You are sapphire. Raja, as you can see, is ruby." Caspar explained. "It's not an exact science, what colors are common or why. There are other sapphires of course, but a great deal older than you. Haven't seen many young ones of this hue of late. There is a turquoise and an aquamarine of some sort enrolled here currently. Sorry, side tracked." He looked at Raja. "What do you make of him?"

"Obviously descended from some Western dragons. Not a water dragon. Although his mark confuses me," Raja said. "It is that of a dragon, but there is another element. It is too like that of a Shaper."

"Western?" Tharen asked.

"Yes," Raja answered. "As you may know, all life originated on Earth and spread from there to other worlds. So the dragon types known to Earth are still dominant throughout the universe. The lesser known dragons of Earth are more common on some planets now, but even they still fit the main categories. So, Western as in not Eastern and not Sea."

"Oh," Tharen said. "Okay. Maya and Kaylee mentioned something like that."

"Alright. That will do Tharen," Caspar said. "If you would, shrink back down to human. It is easier to navigate the library that way." He Shaped as he spoke.

Tharen and Raja followed suit and resumed human form as well. Caspar straightened the collar of his shirt and waved those at the wall, prompting a man and woman to rush forward, arms filled with an assortment of clothing. Caspar nodded at Tharen, and they hurried to stand beside the blue dragon. Tharen thanked them and chose a long brown coat from the mix. Then he and Raja both hurried after Caspar.

CHAPTER TWENTY-TWO

Tharen stood in awe, staring at a larger number of books than he previously believed to exist. He felt dwarfed by the orderly aisles of ceiling tall bookshelves that were packed to the gills with varied forms of written materials. "Library!" he laughed. "I have been to towns smaller than this."

"Meh." Caspar shrugged. "The other one is larger, but this one has all of the genealogy records."

"There is another library, a bigger library, here in Silverhaven?" Tharen asked in disbelief.

"Dragons like to read. And list. And research. And we are rather long lived," Raja said. "So the books stack up after a time."

Caspar led them to desk labeled "Genealogy" next to a giant blank wall. "Good morning," he greeted the man at the desk. "We need to learn about this young chap's history. He has nothing beyond his name, though. Are you free to assist us or able to call for someone who could?"

"I'm free," the man said excitedly. "My name is Kelv. I've been working in this department for about ten years. If we run into something beyond me, I can get someone more senior to aid you. For now, let's see what I can help you find."

"Good, good," Caspar said happily. "Kelv, meet Tharen McKenna. He is from Earth and is a sapphire colored dragon with an odd mark."

"Pleased to meet you. McKenna, huh?" Kelv asked. "Alright, how about we start at the wall? See what it tells us, and we will go from there."

"Sure," Tharen said doubtfully. "How is a blank wall going to help?"

"Trust me." Kelv grinned. He guided Tharen to the center of the space and pushed him right up next to the wall. "Kiss this spot," he instructed.

"Kiss the wall?" Tharen repeated uncertainly.

"Yep." When Tharen just arched an eyebrow Kelv tried again. "It is a newer take on 'blood calls to blood.' No finger pricking, no bleeding at all actually. The wall is spelled and holds almost all of our recorded names. So you touch your lips to it, here." He pointed again. "And in theory, your family tree sprouts out from it."

"If you say so." Tharen shook his head, but did as he was bid and kissed the wall.

Five surnames appeared on the surface. Tharen backed up to read them better.

"Hmm. Let us try this," Kelv said. He handed Tharen a pen. "Write your name."

With the addition of Tharen's name the inks swirled for a moment, painting the wall like some strange modern art piece. Two surnames formed out of the ink this time, one in blue, the other in red.

"Interesting," Kelv murmured.

"What is it?" Caspar asked.

Kelv pointed to the red name. "This name is human." He touched it and a small chart opened. The bottom name, the most recent, was a Kressie Ray McKenna. Kelv grabbed a pen and pad of paper from the desk. He clicked the pen twice, then scribbled down the search notes including the volume numbers next to Kressie's name. "Messenger pen," he said at Tharen's look. "I sent a request upstairs for help. I suspect you are an unusual case. Best to check the other name, too." When he touched the blue name, a much larger chart sprang open to cover much of the left side of the wall. "This name is a dragon family. Maybe McKenna pops up here as well?"

Tharen and the others eagerly searched the names listed. Tharen couldn't decide if he was excited or terrified to possibly be so close to learning what happened to his family. Sure enough, the bottom name had a note mentioning Kressie Ray McKenna, human.

"Oh dear," Kelv said quietly.

"What?" Tharen and Caspar asked at the same time.

Kelv jotted down some information from the second chart. "I don't think we are going to find a very happy story." He led them to one of the many tables in that area of the library. "You all just sit here for a moment, please. I will go pull these volumes from the archives." He looked down at his paper. "Merlin is on his way. Perhaps he can answer some of your questions while you wait."

Kelv hurried off, probably to avoid questions until he had more to go on.

"For a moment there I was really excited," Tharen told Caspar and Raja. "Now I just have a wrenching feeling in my gut."

Caspar nodded. "I have a bad feeling about this, too."

"Oh, knock it off," Raja ordered. "We are either about to learn your heritage, or we aren't. Either way you are probably closer than you have ever been to that goal."

"You're right," Tharen said hopefully. "Better to finally know."

"Ah! There you are!" A tall elderly man with a white beard cropped short came bustling toward them. "Came as fast as I could. Kelv not back yet?"

"No," Raja answered. "He just left."

"I know you," Tharen said pointing at the man.

"Well, I'll be!" the old man exclaimed. "Mr. McKenna, is it not?"

"I know you!" Tharen repeated. "From Earth."

Caspar looked back and forth between the two. "You've met?"

"Yes," the man answered, taking a seat. "We met in Ireland. It was my run in with you that sent me back this way for a time. I vacation here fairly frequently and help out in the library a bit. Read his palm," he explained to Raja and Caspar. "Threw me for a bit of a loop. Decided I was in need of a break."

"I didn't know you read palms, Merlin. What about his struck you?" Caspar asked.

"For a moment I thought he was Pendragon finally come back." Merlin laughed. "So I am here recouping and very seriously debating laying off palm reading in the future."

"Merlin," Tharen said. "Not, like, the Merlin?"

"Oh!" Merlin laughed again. "Heavens no. Just another, mostly immortal, magically inclined, friend of dragons from the Celtic lands." He scrunched his eyes in thought. "You know, some of those stories do sound rather like me. Don't think they confused us for the same fellow do you?" he asked Caspar.

"I couldn't say." Caspar laughed.

"This weekend has been too weird," Tharen muttered.

"Oh. Here is Kelv," Merlin said.

Kelv pushed a cart over to the table. "Alright, folks. I took the liberty of grabbing a few of what I suspect are relevant books. Here is the book that should combine the red and blue names we saw earlier."

"A red name?" Merlin asked. "Are you certain?"

Kelv nodded sadly. "Hence the extra issues." He opened the

volume and pointed to where McKenna was listed. "According to this, there was a dragon by the name of Eva. She was a rose quartz colored dragon who did an internship on Earth at Maeshowe, the one our capital here is named for, when she was four hundred years old. When we go to her pages," he said as he turned to a different section of the book, "we learn that while there, she met a man named Kressie, a human, from a small town in America. They fell in love and married just a few months after meeting. They traveled to Virginia, to meet his family. His family did not approve of the union, suspecting that there was more to Eva than met the eye. When Kressie's uncle learned his nephew's bride was not even human, but a dragon..." He shook his head.

"Oh no," Merlin said sadly.

Kelv continued. "They were chased from town under threat of death and Kressie was disowned. The couple traveled through a gate to Eva's home world, Islea, to seek haven with her family. By this time, Eva was with child. Eva's family, like many of our kind, frowned on female dragons having children with human or Shaper men, because the child of such a union would be more than just a Dragon Shaper. She was disowned by her family as well as by all dragons of Islea." He turned the book to show Tharen a stamp. "See this marking? It means her history as a dragon ends. So I brought this book, which documents like cases."

"Is she in there?" Tharen asked.

"She is. All it says is that she and her husband, Kressie, returned to Earth and settled in Maine."

"That's where I am from," Tharen said hopefully. "Is there anywhere else there may be record of them?"

"One." Caspar sighed. "Did you bring it?"

Kelv handed Caspar a black book.

Caspar searched the index and found Eva's name. "This is an

273

obituary record, Tharen. For those we cannot record in their proper place on family trees. Would you like me to read her entry?"

Tharen nodded dully. "Yes, please."

"Eva McKenna, wife of Kressie Ray McKenna, died at the age of four hundred and two. Cause thought to be poor health brought on by heartbreak. She was preceded in death by her husband less than a year earlier. Both were survived by baby boy, reportedly named Tharen McKenna. Location of child remains unknown." He pushed the book to Tharen so that the young man might read it with his own eyes.

"I don't understand," Raja said. "Why wasn't he found? Under the Harmony Act, his name should have been listed with other children of tragic circumstance. He should have been found."

"You're telling me," Tharen tried to joke. "That foster care thing needs some work."

"No, she is right," Merlin insisted. "You should have been found and raised at one of the dragon schools, like here in Silverhaven."

"They may have missed his name, since it is only listed in the obituaries," Caspar explained. "I doubt they even searched these types of records." He looked at Kelv. "I need you to bring all of our obituary records to the Searchers Department to ensure there aren't other instances such as this."

"Yes, sir," Kelv agreed. "Would you like me to get that underway immediately?"

"If you don't mind," Caspar said. "If there are any other children that have been forgotten, then I should like them to be remembered as soon as possible."

"Would you like more time with this volume?" Kelv asked Tharen.

"No," Tharen said immediately. "I agree with Caspar. Find

them." He handed the black bound book to Kelv. "Please."

Kelv nodded. "I will begin loading the carts with these. Sorry I had such grim findings to share with you, McKenna."

"No, don't be sorry," Tharen said earnestly. "You just answered twenty years worth of questions. I know my parents' names now. I-" He shook his head. "I can't explain how much that means to me. Thank you."

Kelv smiled. "I will make sure your name is added to the Searchers' found list. We can get started on reinstating you to your tree next time we meet."

"Wow," Tharen said. He looked at Caspar. "So, I'm a dragon? Not a Shaper?"

"Technically," Raja corrected. "You are a Dragon Shaper, I think."

"Is he?" Merlin asked. "Dragon mother, True Dragon?"

"You are both correct," Caspar told Raja and Merlin. "Tharen, you are a True Dragon Shaper descended of a human father and a dragon mother. You are completely dragon. And inherently human."

"This sorta makes my brain hurt." Tharen laughed. "So what does that mean for me? Abilities, responsibilities, lifespan?"

Caspar blew out a breath. "Right. You've a good deal to catch up on. The short answer is that you have the lifespan and abilities of a dragon. Though unlike dragons, you may have the ability to take additional Shapes that we cannot."

"That is quite a bit to take in all at once," Tharen murmured.

"Yes, I imagine so," Caspar agreed. "Are you fine to stay here for a little while?"

"As long as you let me send word to Jaea," Tharen answered.

"Done," Caspar said. "Come with me, McKenna. We will get you set up."

CHAPTER TWENTY-THREE

Jaea had never been happier to see a bed in her whole life. She was finally back in Maeshowe after that rather disastrous turn of events at the monument. The monument which she still hadn't gotten to see up close. She hadn't heard from Tharen since he kissed her silly and left her to explain it to their group. And she hadn't slept much the last few days on top of everything, because she was worried about Tharen at Silverhaven. She kicked her boots off and flopped down on her bed. *I'll just close my eyes for a minute.*

"Jaea! You're back!" Lily exclaimed. The door that connected their rooms shut with a bang. "How was the trip? Did something happen? The soldiers you left with came back earlier. There has been some talk, but nothing has been confirmed. Oh! And this came for you from Silverhaven." Lily held an envelope over Jaea's face. "Who do you know in Silverhaven?"

"Tharen! It had better be Tharen!" Jaea said, grabbing the letter out of Lily's hand. She tore it open and was relieved to see her friend's handwriting. Until she saw how short the letter was.

"Tharen? In Silverhaven? What's he say?" Lily said looking over Jaea's shoulder.

"Not much," Jaea grumbled. She scanned the contents and read it to Lily. "He is okay. He learned about his family! That's wonderful! Oh, but he has to stay for a while. And I am to remember my promise."

"Promise?"

"To not fall in love with Michael, or anyone else, and to wait for Tharen to explain... something," Jaea tried to explain. "I'm not really certain."

"If you didn't look so tired, I would drag the whole story out of you right now," Lily informed her. "Lucky for you, I'm feeling nice. So for now you just take a bit of a nap. I'll let Gwena know we will be having a late dinner."

"Lily," Jaea said with a smile. "You're the best."

"I know." Lily grinned back.

The next day Jaea felt much more herself after having slept like a coma patient until lunch. Sitting at the table she stared at the papers before her. So much had changed in just a few weeks.

"Lily," Jaea said suddenly. "I think I want to stay."

"Stay?"

"Here, in Caeldighn," Jaea clarified. "I haven't told anyone else yet. I haven't even wrote my parents about it. But if Tharen doesn't mind, I think I want to stay."

"Have you given thought to what you would do here?"

"Find Caeldighn a King or Queen?"

Lily laughed. "And if one were not forthcoming?"

"Take on the job myself."

Lily nodded. "I think that is a good plan, ma'am."

"Really?"

"Truly. Can I help at all?"

"Yeah. Do you know how the nomination process for the crown works?" Jaea asked.

"I do."

"Think we could go over it this evening? I want to write my parents first. Give them an overdue heads up. Oh, and please keep it to yourself for now. I have to talk with Tharen before I bring the matter to Maya."

"I can do that," Lily said happily. "I am glad you are looking to stay."

"Me too, I think." Jaea laughed. She picked up her pen and glared at the notebook. "Well, here goes."

Over the next two weeks, no one mentioned that Jaea was asking more questions than usual, or that her questions were more specific. At least, no one brought it up with Jaea. Neither did anyone ask Jaea about Tharen, but the castle was abuzz with rumors. Some said Michael had replaced Tharen in Jaea's affections. Why else would the pair be spending so much time together? Others were convinced Jaea's odd behavior was just her way of keeping busy while Tharen was gone to Silverhaven. Why the lad was still there was also a great topic of conversation. Only Lily knew the whole story and in a most un-maid like way, she wasn't saying. Then there was the Dragon Shaper news! All of Maeshowe was afire with the revelation of Tharen's Shape at long last, with the added gossip that Jaea was able to take dragon form as well. What a time it was to live near the capital!

Jaea collapsed onto a stool in Gwena's kitchen and rested her head on the table. "Gwena, the gossips are making me crazy." She looked up at her friend. "What do I do?"

Gwena laughed. "Don't know there is much you can do, dear. Other than what you've been doing, just minding your own business and going about your day."

"Answer their questions," George suggested. "Maybe they'll leave you be when there is enough fat to chew."

"Ha! Do you not understand women at all, George?" Gwena asked.

"I'm not so certain anyone does," George bantered back. "Tricky creatures, women."

"Men make no more sense," Jaea told George. "At least not many in my acquaintance."

"Have you heard from Tharen again?" Gwena asked sympathetically.

"Nope."

"Box his ears when he gets back," George said. "If you don't, I will. I've had more than my share of ill looks from a particular head cook, whom shall not be named." He pointed at Gwena. "Just for being male! I'm telling ya, girl. That man's got an ear boxing coming to him."

"Who is boxing whose ears?" Tharen asked from the doorway.

Jaea's laugh died abruptly.

"We," Gwena pointed at the three of them. "Are boxing yours." She threw a roll at him. "Mr. Leave-with-no-notice-and-stay-gone-without-saying-why."

"Hey now," Tharen argued. "I didn't have a choice in leaving. And I came back as soon as I could. Didn't Jaea tell you?" He took a bite of the roll Gwena had thrown at him.

"Oh yeah. That five line letter. Pshew." George laughed. "Very informative."

"When did you get back?" Jaea asked.

"Just now. Thought you may be in here since you weren't at your quarters," Tharen answered. "I have to check in with Maya in a few, but I wanted to see you first."

"Oh good! You two can take these baskets to Maya's rooms then. Save me a trip," Gwena said. She handed Tharen a large basket and Jaea a smaller one. "There you are. Off you go now." She shooed them out. "Work to do here. Dinner at the usual time. You both will be here if you know what's good for you."

"Yes, ma'am." Tharen laughed. He adjusted his hold on the basket and headed out the door.

Jaea turned to give Gwena a pointed look. Gwena and George

just smiled innocently and waved her on.

"So. How was Silverhaven?" Jaea asked, joining Tharen in the hall.

"Amazing! I have so much to tell you," Tharen said. "How have things been here?"

"Good," Jaea answered. "Quiet. Just been hanging out more with people we had already met. Trying to avoid gossipers. You'll be hounded too, now that your back. The Dragon Shaper thing has really upped the ante for how interesting we are apparently."

"Hmm. Hadn't thought of that."

They passed Michael coming from Maya's quarters. He sent Jaea a conspiratorial wink and began to whistle cheerfully as he continued down the hall.

"What was that all about?" Tharen asked suspiciously.

"Nothing much." Jaea giggled. "I'll tell you about it later. After you tell me about Silverhaven," she bartered.

"I suppose," Tharen agreed reluctantly.

Jaea knocked on Maya's door. "Hello, Emily," she said happily. "We come bearing gifts from Gwena." She held up her basket.

"Oh! Perfect timing." Emily smiled. "We were just sitting down for some tea. Come in, come in." She ushered them to the dining table. "Just put those here, and I will get them sorted. Maya!" she called. "Company!"

"Again?" Maya called from her office. "Who now? Is it important?"

"Not particularly," Tharen answered loudly.

"Tharen?" Maya asked coming to her office door. "It's about time you got back." She spotted Jaea. "Jaea! Thank the stars. I can break from all that mess for you two."

"Having fun with the festival planners still?" Jaea asked.

"No, I gave up on that for the day. Moved onto repair

requests," Maya said. "So." She pointed at Tharen. "You and I have a great deal to discuss."

"That's why I am here," Tharen said. "I know I am behind in my reports. I wasn't certain what all to include in those though, from the last few weeks."

"Probably best to just hash it out in person, pick up with the reports again next week?" Maya suggested. "I could meet later this evening if you-"

"No you can't, ma'am," Emily interrupted.

"That's right. Working dinner tonight," Maya remembered. "Michael is going to go over the new security and defense plans with me. And the castle and stable repair requests if we have time."

"Dinner with Michael, huh?" Jaea teased. "Wear your rose perfume. He likes that one."

"It's just work," Maya said. "He likes my perfume?"

Jaea nodded. "He said roses make him think of you now."

"Hmm," Maya mused. "Anyway. Not tonight. Tomorrow, lunch maybe?"

"Sure," Tharen agreed. "I am hoping to kidnap Jaea for the rest of today. Lunch tomorrow should work fine."

"I'm being kidnapped?" Jaea asked resentfully. "What if I have plans and don't want kidnapped?"

"Too bad," Maya said pushing her sister and Tharen out the door. "You two go fix..." She waved her hands at them. "This. Whatever it is."

Emily shoved the small basket Jaea had brought back into Jaea's hands. "Picnics are good settings for kidnapped conversation."

"Off you go now." Maya grinned and shut the door on them.

Jaea looked at Tharen confusedly. "This has been an odd day."

Tharen shrugged and took the basket from Jaea's hold. He

held an arm out to her. "Shall we picnic?"

"Apparently," Jaea said taking his arm. "Lead on, good sir."

Sitting against a large tree at the entrance to the First Queen's garden, Jaea tried to puzzle out the man beside her. Failing again to do so, she decided it may be best to just talk everything out. Once and for all. *Maybe after we eat,* Jaea thought. She nibbled on some cheese, while Tharen absently tore a roll to little pieces. *You're stalling,* her conscience informed her. Jaea defiantly finished a turnover, ignoring the little voice. Tharen still hadn't attempted conversation.

"You wanted to talk, if I recall correctly," Jaea prompted.

"Yes," Tharen said. "I just don't know where to start now. I learned some things in Silverhaven that may affect my previously planned speech."

"You had a planned speech?" Jaea laughed. "For me?"

"Oh yes." Tharen laughed. "A lengthy one."

"I have to hear this," Jaea declared. "Forget Silverhaven for now. It can't affect anything that greatly, surely."

"We'll see." Tharen sighed. "You're right, though. I'll start where I was going to start that evening after seeing Nirah."

Jaea made a show of settling in for a story. "Go on then."

Tharen nodded and squared his shoulders. "I didn't leave because you said you loved me." When Jaea tried to interrupt, he shook his head. "You need to know this. We should have talked it out a long time ago. Your loving me wasn't scary, Jaea. I didn't run from you. I did run to a jewelry store, but that rather failed. Not the point. Sorry." He took a deep breath and rushed through the next part. "I asked your father for your hand in marriage, and he said no because we were too young and he didn't think I had given you a chance to see if you really loved me, or if you just thought you loved me because I had always been there, preventing other guys from getting close to you. So

282

he said no. And it sucked. There was a lot of truth to what your dad said, so I didn't say anything to you about it, but I hung on to Doc's ring anyway. And I left. To give you space enough to get close to other people because I was afraid I was just taking up all your time. And I couldn't sit around and watch you pursue men other than me."

Jaea blinked. She wasn't sure she had absorbed any of that information. "What?"

"Hmm. Try again," Tharen muttered. He cleared his throat and knelt before Jaea. "I love you. I have since the second grade. Marry me?" He held a ring out to her.

"What!"

Tharen threw his arms up in the air. "I've been trying to propose to you for ages! Years! Why can't I spit this out right?" He put the ring in the palm of his right hand and held it out to her again. "Jaea, I love you. I always have, and I will continue to do so long after I'm dead. If I'm not too late, and haven't lost you, would you do me the honor of becoming my lawfully wedded wife? Marry me?"

Jaea gently lifted the ring and stared at it. "This has been a very strange day. And I feel like my brain hasn't quite caught up. So I am just gonna hold this, and let's go back to where we left my brain, okay? Why did you leave?"

"Fair enough," Tharen said. He shifted to sit cross legged. "So. Fall break of your freshman, my sophomore year, I asked your dad for his permission to ask you to marry me. We had been a couple for over a year, and I knew I wanted to be with you forever. I hoped to propose over Christmas break, before I left for that semester abroad. Your dad said no. He asked me to give you some space and let you grow into your own person. He made me promise to let you graduate college without a wedding band around your finger. Ben wanted me to take time to acknowledge that neither of us really knew who we were without having the other always there. No marriage would hold up if each party had to rely on the other for feet to stand on. So I took your Dad's advice and tried to see us how he did."

Jaea nodded to show that she was following the conversation this time around.

Tharen laughed. "And I hated it. It was awful. I knew he had a point, but I could hardly stand being around you without being able to tell you I loved you. Because if I had said it, I would have asked you to marry me in the next breath. Crazy perhaps, but that's the way of it. So instead of proposing over Christmas break, we had a much different talk and broke up. I don't know how many times, during that semester in Ireland, I almost said hell with it and thought about proposing via phone. I did write a letter once, but then promptly burned it when I realized that your last few letters had mentioned other guys. I was terrified that your dad had been right after all. Then my professor told me about a dig, and I stayed in Ireland a little longer. By the time I had to head home, I thought it may be best if I stayed in Ireland. I really liked the school and my professors, and I could focus my studies more. So I applied to transfer completely. When I got home to get everything together and finalized, I hoped to see where we stood. Except we didn't cross paths that often. And you seemed intent on remaining just friends."

Jaea remembered how different things were between them after her freshman fall semester. How they had seemed to drift further and further apart. She remembered being elated when Tharen came back from Ireland and feeling like there was something he had wanted to say. He never did, though. Somehow, it made her feel both relieved and annoyed to finally learn his side. She gave Tharen an incredulous look. "You are maddening. You know that?"

Tharen nodded and continued his story. "The last time I was

home for a visit, I thought there may still be something between us after all. Then you were graduating college, and I thought surely even your father couldn't say you didn't know who you were with that under your belt. So I decided to ask if you still had feelings for me while we had time together after graduation at Opal's. But then there was the stuff you learned from Nirah. I didn't want to complicate things further. Then we were here, learning about your family and about Shapers. Guys were hitting on you left and right, and you seemed interested in them back. Then there was the ball! You poured out your heart, and I had hope again. And still everything just snowballed into a terrible time to have this talk. So I thought, after the monument. We'd see Nirah and have a great dinner alone, finally alone, then I would ask you. As you may remember, that failed. So now, at last, I'm telling you what I should have so long ago." He smiled. "I love you. I'm sorry I'm an idiot, and I love you."

Jaea started to say something, but Tharen cut her off.

"Before you say anything in response to, well, all of that," Tharen said. "You may want to first know that while in Silverhaven, I learned that I am not really a Shaper. I'm a dragon apparently. Technically, a True Dragon Shaper."

"Uh huh," Jaea managed. "Which means what exactly?"

"Basically, the only difference between me and a normal dragon is that I had a human father, so technically I am a Shaper. However, since my mother was a dragon, I am a dragon. Hence True Dragon Shaper, as in completely dragon but also Shaper," Tharen explained. "Also, I may or may not live about five thousand years," he said sheepishly. "Little longer than the Shaper average of two or three hundred."

"Oh."

"But please consider my proposal. Preferably, consider answering it. Seeing as you are already wearing the ring and all."

Jaea looked down at the ring on her left hand. "Hadn't

realized I put it on," she mumbled. She was silent for a long time. Part of her wanted to yell at Tharen for all the time he had let go by without telling her all this. Part of her wanted to drag Tharen to a church before he could change his mind. Still another part of her wondered how they could be together when he would outlive her by thousands of years, assuming the Stones didn't kill them. All of her was freaking out a little bit. "I don't know where to start responding to everything you just said," Jaea admitted.

"If it's okay with you, a solid yes or no to the marriage thing would be great," Tharen suggested. "I'd be happy to hear your thoughts on everything else once that is out of the way and I can breathe properly again."

"By marrying me you would practically be volunteering for heartbreak and life as a widower. I don't know how I feel about that, Tharen."

"As opposed to a life of regret for not getting to spend what time I can with the love of my life? I've thought this through. I wouldn't have asked if I weren't certain this is what I want."

"Are you sure?" Jaea asked seriously. "Even knowing you'll likely outlive me by centuries?"

"Positive," Tharen assured her. "And let's be honest, I'd never survive that long without you. You are simply too big a part of my heart."

Jaea wiped a tear from her eye and nodded. She looked at the ring and then back to Tharen. "Yes, you ridiculous man. I've only loved you my whole life. Of course I will marry you."

Tharen let out a shout of joy and swooped Jaea up. He spun her in a circle and gave her a quick kiss before he set her back on her feet.

"We still have a lot to talk about," Jaea warned, jabbing him in the chest. "And I need to go home and hit my dad. Then hit you. Then yell at you both for thinking I can't make up my own mind. Then maybe hit you both again for not just telling me about this."

"Maggie already did." Tharen smiled. At Jaea's confused look, he explained, "That is why I borrowed the messenger pen. To ask your dad's blessing and to inform him I was going to ask you with or without it. Maggie saw it and yelled at both of us. I'll show you the pages if you want."

"Good," Jaea said. "I'm glad to know I have an ally."

"In my defense, I didn't want to cause any sort of rift between you and your parents. I know how much they mean to you."

Jaea put her hand against Tharen's cheek. "I'm glad you asked him. It shows me that you had courage enough to do so, and that you respect my family enough to consider their feelings about having you join it." She shook her head. "You still should have told me."

"I couldn't. No matter what I did, things between you and your parents would have been strained. And even without your dad's refusal, I couldn't be sure you would say yes. I guess I lost my nerve."

"You thought I'd say no?" Jaea asked incredulously.

"We had discussed the topic of marriage before," Tharen reminded her. "You always seemed uncertain about getting married. You didn't want to risk passing Shaping onto your children."

"You and I remember that conversation very differently," Jaea informed him. "As I recall, I said I didn't think I could ever marry someone who wasn't also a Shaper, or at least already knew about Shapers. You obviously fall into the acceptable possible partner category."

"Obviously." Tharen laughed. "How silly of me, panicking about proposing," he said sarcastically.

"Oh, shut up and kiss me again. Fiance."

Tharen pulled her close again and kissed her senseless.

"Better?"

Jaea nodded, a loopy smile on her face. She let out a dreamy sigh. "Such a weird day."

"Day?" Tharen asked. "Month. Summer! I'm a freakin' dragon. We are on a planet that isn't Earth. And nearly at war with your college buddy Caleb."

Jaea made a sour face. "Yep. Sit down time again. I've a bit to tell."

"Uh oh."

"Hush and sit," Jaea ordered. "First off. I want to stay in Caeldighn. Live here, permanently. But only if you may want to also."

"I would love to stay here, if you are sure that is what you want."

"It is." Jaea smiled. "I talked to Mom and Dad about it already. Secondly, even more of a question now actually, someone needs to sit Caeldighn's throne, and I am pretty sure it should be you."

"Me?" Tharen asked astounded.

Jaea smiled. "Why are you so surprised? You have a strong presence, it sort of pulls people to you like gravity. You generally think before you act, and you actually listen when someone talks to you. Those sound like good traits for a leader to have. I have seen how much you care for the people here, and they seem quite fond of you as well. You are the best candidate I could think of. Admittedly, I was thinking of trying for it myself if I couldn't convince you to do so. Figured the whole Lost Twin thing might work in my favor if Caeldighn was willing to try another McClanahan on the throne. My family has been pretty entwined with the Stone drama, so I couldn't be certain the people would want to risk it. I guess we are kinda a package deal now though." She wiggled her fingers, admiring the light that played on the diamond there. "Where did you get this?"

288

"Doc," Tharen answered. "Come back to that. You want us to take the throne? Be King and Queen? Not just marry me and live in this cool place, but be King and Queen?"

"Doc? Right, later." Jaea tore her gaze away from the ring." Yeah. That sounds right. What do you say?"

"Do you think we really could?"

Jaea nodded. "We love this place and its people already. We are both fed up with the state of disrepair due to lack of a ruler. Someone needs to step up but nobody is. And I think something of an outside perspective could be a good thing. I'm rather terrified at the thought, but it seems right. Like this is why we found the key, to help Caeldighn. Not just to find Maya."

"Okay," Tharen said. "Wow. Okay. Have you told Maya any of this staying and ruling business?"

"No. Just Lily. And only she and Kaylee know about Caleb."

"What about Caleb?" Tharen asked suspiciously.

"Oh. Right. Well." Jaea paused. "He is here. I've seen him twice. He warned me to leave so that we wouldn't be assassinated by his father's men."

"Assassinated," Tharen repeated.

"Yeah..."

"We really may not live very long here. Pending war and assassination for taking the throne from under the Stones." Tharen nodded decisively. "I'd like to amend my proposal. Marry me tomorrow?"

"Tomorrow?"

"Yep. We can have a little ceremony now and something bigger when your parents can attend." Tharen nodded again. "That could work, right?"

Jaea felt a grin spread across her face. "I think I'm free tomorrow. I never pictured myself having a big fancy wedding anyway." *Besides*, Jaea thought. *What about their lives so far had been normal?*

289

Tharen lifted Jaea into his arms and started walking back toward the castle.

"Where are we going?" Jaea laughed.

"To get Maya. I need to know where to find a priest in Caeldighn."

Tharen, still holding Jaea in his arms, followed a practically bouncing Emily and Lily into Maya's office.

"Company again, ma'am," Emily said. She and Lily shared an excited glance.

"Just a quick question," Tharen said.

"Fire away," Maya replied without looking up from her reports.

"Where is the nearest priest?"

"There is a church on Ironbound Road. Father Mathew is usually there when he isn't in the chapel here at the castle. Wait, why do you need a priest?" Maya looked up.

From her perch in Tharen's arms, Jaea wiggled the fingers on her left hand to show off a ring.

Maya jumped out of her chair. "You are getting married?"

Jaea squirmed out of Tharen's hold to go to her sister. "I'm getting married! To that loon!" She pointed at Tharen.

The burst of feminine squeals and giggles emitted from the four ladies in the room almost made Tharen regret coming with Jaea and Lily to tell Maya.

"Oh my stars!" Maya exclaimed. "Let's move out that way where there's more room," she said. She led them out of her office and over to the plush chairs that horseshoed the fireplace. "Do you have any idea when? Mercy, or on what planet!"

"We actually wanted to talk to you about that," Jaea said.

"Certainly. How can I be of service?" Maya asked.

"Well," Jaea began. "A few things to run by you, really. First off, can you be my maid of honor tomorrow?

"You want to get married tomorrow?" Maya asked. "As in the day after today? Isn't that rushing things a bit?"

"Nope. Not when you take into consideration the fact that we would have married already if we hadn't both been idiots," Jaea said. "Especially not after you factor in the other things."

"Other things?" Maya repeated.

Jaea nodded. "We would like to stay. Live in Caeldighn. Permanently."

"Really!" Maya cried happily. "You are sure?"

"Very sure," Tharen answered. "But there is more."

Maya looked at Jaea nervously. "Such as?"

"We think we would like to become candidates for Caeldighn's throne," Jaea said quickly.

Maya and Emily stared at the couple, dumbfounded. Lily shrugged when Emily looked to her for an explanation.

"You want to be King and Queen?" Maya asked slowly.

"We want Caeldighn to have a King and Queen. And for them not to be Jakob Stone and whoever he snags as wife," Jaea said adamantly. "As I have been unable to locate another willing candidate, due in large to the murder of the previous rulers..."

"We would like to offer ourselves as an option," Tharen finished. "With your permission."

"You realize that makes you a serious target for the Stones?" Maya asked.

"We are already serious targets," Jaea said. "The lost twin Dragon Shaper and the True Dragon Shaper. We may as well get to do something to deserve the attention."

"Whoa. True Dragon?" Maya repeated.

"Yeah. We have a lot to catch you up on," Tharen apologized. "But how do you feel about all these plans? Staying, marrying-"

"Maid of honoring?" Jaea added.

"Right," Tharen said. "And what else was there? Ah, and the

291

trying not to get dead while running for the crown bit."

"I love these plans." Maya laughed. "Admittedly, you caught me by surprise. I am touched that you have come to care so greatly for Caeldighn in so small a time. I would be honored to work with you to restore Caeldighn to glory, and beyond honored to be your maid of honor." She smiled at her sister. "Just promise you won't die."

"I'll do my best," Jaea said.

"Ditto," Tharen said when Maya looked at him expectantly.

A knock at the door reminded them all of the hour. Emily rushed to see who it was while Jaea pushed Maya to her bedroom to quickly change into a dressier shirt. With Michael installed in the seating area, Emily and Lily joined their mistresses in Maya's bedchamber. Michael and Tharen eyed each other distrustfully.

"You could have told me it was Maya you were sweet on," Tharen said finally.

Michael barked out a laugh. "And have missed you squirming like a worm on a hook? Not a chance."

"Thanks ever so much," Tharen said sarcastically. He still wasn't sure what he thought of the tall redhead.

"Michael!" Jaea called cheerfully. She nearly tackled him with a hug. "Did he tell you?"

"Did who tell me what, Spitfire?"

Jaea just bounced in place and held her hand up for Michael to see.

Michael shot Tharen a sidelong glance. "About time," he said approvingly. He kissed Jaea on the cheek. "Congrats, sweetheart. My brothers will be heartbroken. Mother will try to adopt you anyway."

"Thanks." Jaea grinned. "Tell your mother I am sending her Maya for a daughter-in-law in my stead," she whispered.

Michael's laugh boomed through the room.

"What's so funny?" Maya asked. She stuffed a handful of files into a leather bag that looked completely out of place next to her garnet dress and the delicate gold earrings dangling from her ears.

"These two." Michael jerked a thumb at the happy couple to his right. "Ready to go? I think I may be under dressed."

"Oh. Blame Emily," Maya said, smoothing a hand down her dress nervously.

"Thank you, Emily," Michael called. He held an arm out to Maya. "May I escort you to the library, Chief Maya?"

"You may, Lieutenant Black," Maya replied cordially. She turned to Jaea and Tharen. "You two, breakfast here tomorrow. Lily, you may come too if you like. I'll have Kaylee come as well. I can take you over to the church after. As to the other request, we should plan a tad before we take the matter any higher."

"Sounds good," Jaea agreed.

"What request?" Michael asked.

"We better get to the kitchens or Gwena will have our hides," Tharen remembered suddenly.

"Oh!" Jaea exclaimed. "Come on, then." She pulled him out Maya's door. "Bye!" She called over her shoulder.

CHAPTER TWENTY-FOUR

The next day was hands down the busiest of Jaea's life so far. She and Tharen had sat down with the messenger pen the night before to tell Jaea's parents, Opal, and Doc. All morning the pen had been blinking as the four responded. All of them were thrilled with the wedding news and praying Jaea and Tharen stayed safe in their ventures to the throne. Doc wanted to know how Jaea liked his mother's ring, finally cluing Jaea in to how Tharen had come into possession of an antique Tiffany's diamond ring.

Maya and Kaylee showed the happy couple to the church to speak with a priest about having a wedding that evening. Father Mathew agreed to do the ceremony, but only if his two conditions were met. The first condition being that the couple complete some form of premarital counseling, as was required by all who wished to be wed in the church. His other term merely pushed the ceremony to the following day, to ensure each of them had slept on the matter and knew their own mind. For while he agreed it would be best to marry the pair prior to their announcement of jointly running for the crown, he wanted to be certain Jaea and Tharen were ready to be married.

A couple hours of discussing the meaning of marriage and sketching out a small wedding followed, as Father Mathew condensed months of marriage prep into a day. Then Maya and

Kaylee brought Jaea and Tharen before Aurora to nominate them for regency. This prompted Aurora to immediately send word via messenger pens to tell the Council members of the nomination, though she decided to wait until the following Thursday to have the candidates make a formal announcement, to give the newlyweds a few days to themselves before embarking on a campaign.

Jaea wasn't certain if she had eaten lunch, but vaguely remembered overhearing Maya and Kaylee making plans for a dinner of some sort. A very prim servant arrived at Jaea's door to confirm that Jaea would be preparing for the wedding at the church. Once Jaea confirmed this, the man informed her that Jaea's belongings would be moved into the quarters assigned to the McKenna newlyweds as soon as she left for the church. The idea of sharing a bedroom with Tharen set off a riot of panicked butterflies in her stomach, so she did her best to squash that line of thought. The day had been overwhelming, but understandable. That is until Lily quit.

"What do you mean you can't be my maid?" Jaea asked, sinking dejectedly into her chair.

"You need to hire on someone of more experience, especially after you are approved by Nirah to rule," Lily said sadly. "You'll need a whole fleet of people. And I don't believe I could bear to take orders from someone else in regards to how to do the things I managed just fine before they arrived. So I thought to resign now to give you plenty of time to hire on a staff."

"No," Jaea said firmly.

"No what?"

"No to all of that. If you don't stay on as my maid, I won't go any further with this queen business."

"Jaea!" Lily said shocked. "That's downright addled. You'll need more than just me, as I have already explained."

"Fine," Jaea said stubbornly. "Only if you are in charge of

them all. Be, whatever head maid is."

"What!" Lily shouted. "That's a huge promotion. I'm just a common personal maid, that's not how it usually works, Miss."

"Is now." Jaea returned Lily's glare with her own. "I trust you, Lily. I will not sit on a throne and worry about being killed by my own maid on top of everything else. You and I have a good friendship building here. I need your help. If you don't come with me to the Royal Wing, then I'm not going!"

"You're serious, aren't you?" Lily asked.

"Completely," Jaea said.

"You really are going to have to hire on others though," Lily persisted. "At least two for now."

"Deal. Maya told me the same thing. But the moment they don't do as you ask, we give them the boot."

"I can live with that," Lily said smugly.

"You wouldn't happen to have anybody in mind would you?" Jaea asked hopefully.

"I may actually," Lily realized. "Michael's younger sister was asking after castle work last week. And I have an older cousin who has been trying to find work as a maid."

"Perfect!" Jaea clapped her hands together. "Let's invite them to dine with us as soon as possible, and we will see how we all do together."

"I will write them tomorrow." Lily smiled.

"Good. Can we get back to the moving and wedding prep now?"

The morning of August 3, found Jaea in the bridal suite of St. Andrew's, holding her dress and staring at her reflection in the tall standing mirror. She had decided to wear the pink gown she had worn to the ball for her wedding dress. Months of wearing short sleeves and playing Shaper tag had allowed the Caeldighn sun to tint Jaea's complexion a shade or two darker. She was wondering about tan lines of all things when a knock sounded on the door. Lily rushed to open it, admitting Mrs. Lind to the large room.

"No, no, no. You can't wear that, dear," Mrs. Lind said, seeing Jaea hang up the ball gown. She placed what looked like a large, shallow basket on the table and beckoned Jaea over. She set aside the lid and folded back a few layers of undyed cloth. "This is a wedding dress." She pulled a dress of flowing ivory silk from the box. "If there had been time, I would have made you a brand new dress. As it stands, I altered this one just a smidgen to fit you. No one else has worn it, mind you. I made it years ago, and this seemed like the perfect time to bring it out of the depths of storage."

"Oh, it is beautiful!" Jaea said. "Are you sure?"

"Am I sure?" Mrs. Lind laughed. "Of course I am. Now let's get you ready. The other girls are on their way. They are bringing a dress for you as well, Lily."

Jaea wrapped her arms around Mrs. Lind in a quick hug. "Thank you."

"Yes, yes. Get a move on." Mrs. Lind shooed Jaea behind the dressing screen as Lily dashed to answer another knock at the door.

"Jaea? You in here?" Maya called.

"Yes!" She raised a hand above the screen. "Over here. Who all came with you? Sounds like a regular party out there."

"Kaylee, Gwena, Terra and her mother, Emily, Michael's mother and sister," Maya answered.

Mrs. Lind fastened two small buttons. "All done."

Jaea came around the decorative dressing panel, much to the delight of her waiting friends who clapped and giggled happily. "Well this is unexpected." Jaea laughed. "What are you all doing here?"

"I have your flowers," Michael's mother said. "And my Marie

is here to help you girls do your hair."

"I just stopped in to say hello real quick," Gwena said. "And drop off some bubbly." She winked.

"I certainly wasn't going to miss out on this!" Kaylee said with hands on hips. "Especially now there is bubbly involved."

"I'm here to keep you all on time," Emily said. She had already separated the dresses and was now dispersing champagne with Lily's help.

"I have your ring!" Terra said. She skipped over to Jaea and held up a wooden box with sets of rings in rows of velvet. "Tharen made me ring bearer, even though I'm a girl. He didn't know which one you would like though, so I'm to have you pick a band, and he will take the one that matches it."

"I'm with the rings and the bouncy lass there." Teresa smiled. "She may want to sit down, Terra. Or say hello to her friends before picking a ring."

"Oh. Sorry." Terra hung her head and shuffled her feet.

"That's okay. I know exactly which one I want." Jaea squatted down to be more on Terra's level.

"You do!" Terra brightened immediately. "Which one?"

"The one that best goes with this." Jaea held up her engagement ring. "What do you think?"

Terra scrunched up her face, comparing the bands before her to Jaea's ring. "Either of these would look good." She pointed to two silver pairs on her left. "But this set looks more like you and Tharen."

"I agree completely," Jaea said. "One more thing? Would you be flower girl as well as ring bearer?"

Terra nodded excitedly.

"Great!" Jaea hugged Terra and gave her a quick kiss on the cheek before standing up again. "Mrs. Black? Do you have a couple flowers to spare for my flower girl?"

"Mrs. Black, she says. Like she doesn't know my first name."

Michael's mother chuckled. "I actually brought supplies for a flower girl, just in case you found one after we spoke yesterday."

"Thank you, Ruth," Jaea said, emphasizing the name. "Well folks, what do we do now?"

"We get you all ready!" Emily said, waving Maya to the dressing screen and Jaea to a seat before the mirror.

In what seemed an eternity and in no time at all, Jaea stood between two wide oak doors with a flower strewn aisle before her. Maya and Terra had already gone ahead of her to stand at the front of the church with Tharen and George. All that was left was to walk it herself and say her vows. She rested her hand in the crook of Michael's arm and took a deep breath. The organist began the wedding march.

"You ready?" Michael asked.

"Yes." Jaea smiled. "Just don't let me trip in these heels."

The handful of guests stood as Michael escorted Jaea down the aisle. Jaea only had eyes for Tharen. She thought he looked more handsome than ever in his black jacket and kilt. Michael kissed Jaea's cheek and placed her hand in Tharen's. Then the priest led them through the timeless words, binding Jaea and Tharen to each other before God and family.

"I now pronounce you husband and wife. Tharen, you may kiss your bride." Father Mathew smiled.

Tharen dipped Jaea back and kissed her soundly, earning applause and laughter from their small audience.

CRLF

A vase full of flowers crashed into the wall, shattering the evening's silence and startling Caleb from the book he had been reading. Caleb's mother shot his father a disapproving look before rising to clean up the mess. His father, red faced and pacing the room, barely noticed. Caleb set his book aside.

"What's happened, Dad?" Caleb asked.

"We should have killed the brat when we had the chance!" Baer Stone bellowed. "She and that other Dragon Shaper announced their intent to rule! After we were kind enough to explain our claim to the throne, the wench plans to pull it right out from under your brother!"

"Jaea and Tharen?" Caleb tried to clarify. "They are Dragon Shapers?"

"Yes! Who else would I be talking about?"

"Hang on," Caleb said. "Isn't one of the main reasons behind our claim to the throne the fact that we descend from the last known Dragon Shaper in Caeldighn?"

"Our claim to the throne is that it belongs to us," Baer said madly. "And it will be ours," he vowed.

"That doesn't make sense. They just invalidated half of Jakob's claim," Caleb tried to reason.

Jakob rose from the couch across the room. "They can't be a threat to my rule, if they don't draw breath."

The idea must have had appeal to both Jakob and Baer, because they shared a rather terrifying grin over it.

"She will be harder to get to now," Baer mused.

"Better guarded," Jakob agreed. "Didn't our man say the castle staff moved Jaea and Tharen into new quarters a few days ago?"

"Yes, yes. Hmm. So we will draw her out," Baer decided. "Randal! Hornby! Get your sorry hides in here!"

"Father? What are you planning?" Caleb asked suspiciously.

Baer ignored the questioned and instead gave his men their orders. "We have located the Harbours on Earth. Randal, you will notify our men to take Ben and Maggie, as well as that Opal woman and her brother, hostage. If they do not come willing, just dispatch them. We don't have time to tiptoe around this.

Hornby, get in contact with our Keeper allies. We will take the Harbour family to draw out the McClanahan girl and then blast the gates we marked to draw out the Keepers. Jakob, you should speak with our troops here. Ready them for action. Once Caeldighn's gates are secure, we make our move."

Caleb watched in horror as everyone jumped to do his father's bidding. "You can't be serious." Caleb pleaded. "This has been your grand plan? Taking innocent civilians hostage?"

"I am perfectly serious," Baer warned. "And you had better be as well. People may begin to question your loyalty to the cause, to your family."

"Yes, sir," Caleb said, hanging his head. "May I be excused?"

"You may," Baer said gruffly. "Don't stray far. I need you by your brother's side this evening. For some reason both he and our troops draw encouragement from your presence."

"Yes, father," Caleb replied dutifully. He forced himself to walk calmly to his room. Once behind his closed door, he hurriedly packed a few items into a Shape Stay bag. He opened his window silently and Shaped into a raven. He spared a backward glance over his shoulder before launching himself into flight. This was insane. If he did this, he would be deserting. He tried to talk himself out of it as he flew toward the capital. But his family had finally gone too far. And Jaea needed to be warned.

☙❧

Jaea sat sipping a cup of tea, admiring the morning sky and reflecting on how incredibly happy she was. She had been a married woman, Mrs. McKenna, nearly a week. Her husband and Charles had stepped out to interview some gentlemen in hopes of hiring on one or two. When Charles had threatened to hire an additional servant without Tharen's input he gave in and agreed to a trial by breakfast, figuring he'd know who he could tolerate by the end of his favorite meal. Husband, Jaea thought with a laugh. She looked dreamily at her wedding band. Such a nice ring to the word husband. There was certainly a lot to be said for being married, she thought with a smile. She was quickly jolted out of her reverie when a raven suddenly collapsed on her window sill. Concern abruptly changed to full fledged confusion when the bird Shaped and Caleb was left sitting in her window.

"Morning," Caleb croaked out. "Bad news." He coughed. "Also, pretty sure I swallowed a bug." He clambered off the sill and slid into a chair at Jaea's table.

"Caleb!" Jaea yelled, bringing Lily running into the room. "What are you doing here?"

"Bad news," Caleb repeated. "Bad, bad news. Urgent." He downed Jaea's forgotten cup of tea. "Get Maya, Kaylee, and Tharen," he told Lily. "Fast."

Lily looked to Jaea for confirmation. When Jaea nodded, Lily scowled. She handed Jaea her staff and ran to gather the requested people.

Jaea pushed the water pitcher toward her guest. "Caleb, what is going on?"

"Father is irate. Plans to draw you out so he can have you killed," Caleb began. He poured a cup of water and took a gulp.

"How does he plan to do that?" Jaea asked.

"Your parents." Caleb shook his head. "Jaea, he has sent men after Ben and Maggie. They are under instruction to take Opal and her brother, too."

Jaea felt the blood drain from her face as ice cold dread shot through her veins. "What?"

"It's true. I left right after I heard him give the order. Jaea, do you have any way to contact them?"

"Pen!" Jaea said desperately. She hurried to the desk and scratched a message telling her parents that hit men were on the way and that they needed to leave fast. With Doc and Opal, she added.

They are already outside. Maggie's writing scrolled back. *Ben and Doc are baring the doors as best they can. We are lucky we were all together for breakfast today, had planned to make jam this morning. Don't worry about us, dear. We can hold out fine until the police get here.*

Caleb shook his head when Jaea read him the response. "No cops are coming. Dad has a number on payroll. He added more when we learned who you were."

Jaea stared at Caleb in disbelief. She racked her brain for some way to help her family. "Ransley!" she exclaimed.

Lily returned with Tharen, Maya, and Kaylee in tow. Emily filed in behind them all.

Jaea turned to Tharen. "Ransley can help them!"

"Help who?" Tharen asked, coming to her side.

"Not if he doesn't hurry," Caleb told Jaea. "Dad is gonna blow the gate."

"What is this fool doing here again!" Kaylee yelled, advancing on Caleb.

"Who is he?" Maya asked confused.

"Quiet!" Lily screamed.

Everyone turned to her, shocked that she had raised her voice in such a way.

"Get Ransley then," Lily told Jaea. "Now."

Jaea nodded. "Ransley!" she yelled. She waved her hands at Tharen and the others.

Still confused, the rest of the group joined in. "Ransley!" The combined cry echoed strangely.

"What? What! I heard you the first time!" Ransley popped into existence at Jaea's table.

"Stone's men have surrounded my house and intend to take my family hostage," Jaea explained in a rush. "I need you to get them and bring them here quickly, before the Stone's blow the gate."

"On it!" Ransley jumped to his feet and disappeared with a flash.

"What!" Maya, Kaylee, and Tharen yelled together.

"Ah!" Jaea exclaimed. "What I just said. Caleb! Explain!"

"Caleb?" Maya asked.

"Stone," Kaylee grumbled.

Lily pointed at the whole group threateningly. "Talk fast," she told Caleb over her shoulder.

Caleb needed no further encouragement. He tossed back the rest of his water and brought the group up to speed.

"Oh no," Maya said quietly.

"It's started then." Kaylee pursed her lips. "Tharen, guard this idiot Stone. We have to get the word out and see what can be done." She hurried out the door, yelling for the nearest castle guards.

Maya hugged Jaea tight. "I'm so sorry. I have to go."

"I know. Be safe," Jaea said.

"You too," Maya said. She glared at Caleb. "Tharen, if he does anything remotely threatening, eat him." She followed after Kaylee at a run.

The look on Tharen's face as he moved protectively to stand in front of Jaea made Caleb lean back in his seat.

"Shapers don't eat other Shapers," Caleb argued weakly.

"I'm a dragon." Tharen smiled.

"Yeah. Shaper."

Jaea shook her head. "Dragon dragon," she said sympathetically.

"Oh." Caleb swallowed. "Huh."

A few minutes later Ransley returned with Jaea's family. He and Opal appeared to be arguing.

"Never rush a packing woman!" Opal scolded him. She glanced around at her new surroundings and whispered,

"Merciful heavens."

"You're welcome," Ransley said wryly, handing Opal a bag.

"Jaea!" Maggie and Ben called as one and nearly crushed her in a hug.

"Hi guys," Jaea squeaked.

Doc moved to stand next to Tharen. "Interesting day so far."

"I have to warn the other Keepers," Ransley told Jaea.

Jaea ran to Ransley and wrapped her arms around him. "Thank you. Be careful."

"I'll be right back. Hardly know I was gone." Ransley winked and was gone again.

"I must admit," Opal said grudgingly. "That's quite the trick."

"Alright, little one," Ben said, taking a seat at the table next to Caleb. "If you could be so kind as to fill us in?"

"Do you have any coffee?" Doc asked, pulling a chair out for first Opal then Maggie at the table. "Mine was interrupted this morning."

Lily laughed and set about preparing breakfast for the crowd now in Jaea's quarters. "You don't seem the least bit unsettled by all of this," she accused Doc.

Doc shrugged. "I was a soldier, a long time ago. You learn quick to appreciate a good cuppa Joe and to take your days as they come. Eventually, you may get answers." He arched an eyebrow at Jaea and Tharen.

"Right," Jaea said, taking the hint. "Well, first off, welcome to Caeldighn."

Jaea and Tharen settled in to get the newcomers caught up on events. A page came by at one point to inform them that Maya had requested they all remain in Jaea and Tharen's quarters for the time being, so that they could be located quickly if necessary. A page was soon assigned to stay with the group to keep them informed and in contact with Maya. Jaea began to dread the blinking red light of the page's messenger pen. Every report the young man read, Jaea could feel apprehension wrap more firmly about her. The gravity of the situation was sinking in more and more. By evening, most of Maeshowe's residents had filed into the castle, fled to the countryside, or joined the increasing number of Stone men gathering outside the castle walls. Royalist patrols were kept busy in small skirmishes around the capital. Tension was at an all time high as everyone waited for the main battle begin.

CHAPTER TWENTY-FIVE

Jaea and Tharen did their best to convince Maya and Kaylee to let them fight. They could both Shape into dragons after all. But the Junior Chiefs declared the royal candidates too valuable to risk in combat. Like most of Maeshowe's residents, Jaea and Tharen had been pushed to the inner and lower parts of the castle. So when the Stones attacked in earnest on Sunday, Jaea and Tharen were well away from the smoking hole that had once been the Southeastern gate. They were told they could help in the kitchens, the hospital wing, or anywhere that kept them out of harm's way. Jaea couldn't imagine there was such a thing as out of harm's way, not with the Stone's occasionally pelting the place with black powder explosives.

Tidewater, the main trade port and the second largest Shaper city in Caeldighn, was bogged down in an attack of its own and unable to assist the capital. The dragons had been hit with some sort of aerosolized pepper spray the same day Maeshowe was besieged. Robbed of sight, with many in a panic, the dragons had effectively been trapped in Silverhaven and cut off from the battles raging across the country. Who knew how long the Stones could really be kept out?

Caleb had told Kaylee everything he could think of that could be pertinent, but Baer had not kept his younger son appraised of many details. He soon exhausted his knowledge of the Stone plan. Of the handful of spies he had named, two were found and detained in cells below the castle. Caleb himself was placed in Jaea and Tharen's custody.

Jaea tried to convince her family that their help wasn't needed. The last time Jaea suggested they keep to themselves and stay in the library, Opal had threatened to lock Jaea in a closet until she could be trusted to talk sense. So Jaea had ushered them all into Gwena's kitchen and pleaded the head cook to give them jobs. Gwena happily agreed to employ the two older women and Lily in the kitchen. Doc joined a group headed to the infirmary with hopes he could be of help there. The remaining men, Caleb included, Gwena assigned to carts. Jaea was sent with them to help handout food and drink, as well as keep an eye on Caleb. At first, the knowledge of Caleb's identity made people reluctant to accept anything from him. When it became apparent that to refuse Caleb meant to be ignored by Jaea and Tharen, thus being passed over and left hungry, most people were much more accepting of the ex-rebel.

Between meals, Ben helped with kitchen prep or wandered to the infirmary to help Doc. Jaea and Tharen, always with Caleb in tow, seemed to be everywhere at once. They would check in with Aurora to see how the siege progressed and if there was news from the rest of the country. They helped plan evacuation routes and kept people informed of the signals that would cue when it was time to go. The three of them visited with soldiers and patients. Jaea led them in organizing a room just for younger children to play out of the way and found the older ones chores to keep them out of trouble. The end of each day found the trio in the library, hoping for good news. By Monday evening, it was clear that the capital would soon be lost.

"Is there nothing else we can do?" Tharen asked in disbelief. "Let me Shape and hit them with a bit of dragonfire."

Kaylee shook her head. "And see how those weapons of theirs

fare against dragonhide? I'm sorry. We cannot risk it."

"I still can't understand how they managed to bring them through the gates," Maya muttered. "Guns shouldn't be able to cross through the gates. But the materials..." she realized looking at Caleb. "They must have assembled the guns here. What else have they been sneaking in?"

"I wish I could tell you," Caleb said earnestly.

Maya and Kaylee looked at Caleb suspiciously, not yet willing to trust the Stone traitor completely.

"Any word from Ransley yet?" Jaea asked.

Maya shook her head.

"The Chiefs? You know, the senior ones?" Caleb asked hopefully.

"Won't get here in time," Kaylee sighed. "Like many of our allies. We have waya and centaur patrols at the ready to aid the evacuation. If we leave tonight, our people can be through the tunnels and safely in the depths of the Great Forest before dawn." She pounded her fist on the table. "Maybe if we had less civilians or more actual soldiers... Stones picked a good time. A large portion of my forces are still scattered all over from that rash of attacks last week."

Aurora put a hand on Kaylee's shoulder. "You could not have known. And you are doing an exceptional job with the resources at hand. Even Adrielle could not have done better."

Kaylee managed a small smile. "I just wish we didn't have to leave the castle to the Rebels."

"It is just a building." Aurora shrugged. "It's no good to us if we are all dead. Besides, we are coming back for it," she said determinedly.

"We are agreed then?" Kaylee asked.

Maya, Aurora, and a couple of military men nodded in response.

"Alright kids, let's get this plan into action," Kaylee said.

Hours later, Jaea and Tharen stood at a large wooden door. The long, dim hallway behind them filled to bursting with Maeshowe refugees. Maya and Kaylee stood before them, part of the circle of guards surrounding Aurora. Soldiers were scattered throughout the crowd, with a large number bringing up the rear. Caleb stood quietly beside Tharen, who was promising Terra a thousand of her favorite cookies if she went back to her mother and promised to run as fast as she could to the safety of the forest when her mother said to. Jaea went over the plan in her head, bouncing back and forth between complete confidence and something akin to total panic. Michael and his men would go out first and ensure that the area outside the tunnel entrance was secure, then help the centaurs and waya keep it that way. Aurora would follow with Maya and Kaylee. She would start doing spells to silence the group's traveling sounds and help keep them hidden. *And then, you know, the entire castle flees for their lives,* Jaea thought grimly.

"Time to go, folks," Michael announced. He looked around at those near him with a smile. "I'll have you know that if any of you get yourselves killed during this lovely midnight jaunt, I will never speak to you again."

A reluctant chuckle swept among those that had heard Michael's comment. Then the large door was pushed open, and Michael's men moved through it silently. Moments later Jaea followed Tharen through, her hand clasped tightly in his. They wound their way upward through the wide tunnel, finally emerging into the cool, clean night air. Thousands of stars glittered between wisps of clouds above them, but quickly disappeared from view as the group followed two centaurs deeper into the woods. After what felt like years later, Jaea and Tharen met Maya and Kaylee again near a small clearing.

"Alright you two, you know the drill," Kaylee said.

"I know you don't like it," Maya said before Jaea could protest. "But you aren't in charge yet, and thus are under our orders."

Ben and Maggie walked past just then. "Get a move on it, girly!" Ben told her. "Or so help me I will ground you." He kissed Jaea's cheek. "Be careful."

"You too," Jaea told Ben and Maggie. She turned to Maya and Kaylee. "See you soon."

"As soon as we possibly can," Maya promised.

"Go!" Kaylee urged. "And remember, fly as high as you can and give the castle wide berth."

Tharen nodded. He walked a few feet away from the crowd and Shaped into a dragon once he was far enough that his tail wouldn't knock anyone over. Jaea gave Maya a quick hug before running to Tharen and climbing onto his back. Then they launched toward the heavens and set course for Silverhaven.

ᘓᘔᘓ

The Rebel troops pushed hard the next morning and were elated when the Royalists fell back, farther and farther, finally retreating through the main gate. It occurred to some of them that the fight had been much too easy, and that the castle was much too quiet. Overall though, it was a cheerful group that scanned the castle halls for stragglers and clapped each other on the back for a job well done.

Jakob, the future King, and even his father seemed pleased with how the battle had played out. Until they found the note propped against the seat back of the throne. It read: *Welcome to Maeshowe! I do so hope you enjoy your brief stay. All my loathing, Aurora Buchanan, Queen Regent of Caeldighn.*

Baer Stone bellowed curses on the pretend Queen and on all those dimwitted enough to follow her. Jakob only laughed loudly and settled comfortably on the throne.

"Come now, father, we've won the capital," Jakob reminded him. "We control all of Caeldighn's gates. All of Caeldighn's ships. And the Royalists are on the run, afraid of what we may have in store next."

"You are right," Mr. Stone relented. "Today has been victorious. Not even the nerve of that woman or your traitorous brother can dim my happiness, to at last see you seated on this throne." He stood beside his son and proudly placed a hand on Jakob's shoulder.

"I have no brother," Jakob said. "Caleb is just another Royalist now and as good as dead." He grinned evilly. "But I want Aurora alive. I have plans for her. All others that return to the castle still breathing will be an added bonus. I look forward to seeing them kneel before me, begging for their lives."

◌੪੪◌

Flying with a passenger was more of a challenge than Tharen had expected. Even so, he refused to set down until well into the day and a long ways from Maeshowe. Finally, he had no choice but to land or drop out of the sky. He and Jaea ate a quick meal of bread and cheese and washed it down with large gulps of water from their canteens. As soon as she was finished eating, Jaea Shaped into her dragon form and crouched low to the ground so Tharen could climb on.

"Let me know if I get off course," Jaea said, craning her head around to look at Tharen. She flapped her massive violet wings and they were airborne again, just in time. Three men with bows and one with an old fashioned rifle materialized out of the tall grass. Jaea was faster, and she quickly drew out of range.

"That was too close!" Tharen yelled.

Jaea bobbed her head in agreement and pushed ahead.

It was night again before they reached the mountains. Jaea landed next to a stream and plunged her head in it. Tharen's legs gave way as he dropped down, sending him sprawling into the cold creek.

"Brrr!" Tharen shouted jumping out of the water. "Well, I'm certainly awake now!"

Jaea laughed as she Shaped back into her normal self. "You okay?"

"Fine," Tharen said. "Cold, but fine. Let's get flying. Nearly there." He Shaped and bowed to Jaea. "All aboard!"

Jaea vaguely remembered Tharen landing at the University. Mostly she just remembered that kind people had helped her to a very comfortable bed shortly after they landed. She reached across the bed trying to find Tharen. When her hands found only rumpled sheets, she forced her tired eyes open to look for him. As she woke further, memories of Maeshowe's battered walls and wounded men rushed back. She sat up abruptly, eyes darting around the room.

"Take it easy." A woman with chocolate colored hair rushed over. "You are probably pretty stiff. Don't want to go fallin' on your pretty face trying to get out of bed too quick." Her smile tried to reach her eyes, but was hampered by the swelling around them.

"Have you been crying?" Jaea asked before she thought better of it. She shook her head. "Sorry, that was rude. Brain is still waking up. Filter takes longest to reboot."

The woman waved the matter away. "Stones hit us with something that burned the eyes. It wasn't pretty. Many of us are still a bit puffy faced. You'll be wanting to see Tharen I imagine?"

"Yes, please."

"This way, ma'am. He is with Caspar and Raja." She turned

and led Jaea into a large hall, orange skirts and cloak billowing behind her. A few turns and corridors later they came to a large open door. "Master Caspar?"

"Maria, come in," Caspar ushered. "And this must be the Jaea I have been hearing so much about."

Tharen came to stand by Jaea. "Morning, my love."

Jaea smiled up at him. "So it seems."

"Caspar, I'd like you to meet my wife and fellow crown candidate, Jaea McKenna." Tharen chuckled. "Not sure which takes more getting used to saying, wife or potential Queen."

"Both are equally wonderful news." The short, white haired man grinned and gave a small bow. "As I am sure you have gathered by now, my name is Caspar. I'm the head of the Dragon Council. I believe you know our member of the Caeldighn Council, Raja?" He motioned to a woman seated at the table.

"Yes," Jaea answered. "Although she looked a bit different when last we met."

Raja smiled. "Good to see you again, Jaea Shaper."

"We were just going over some things," Caspar said as he led Jaea to the table. "I hope you will accept our offer of breakfast while we get up to speed. We should be heading out shortly."

"Tharen has filled us in on the information we were lacking in regards to Caeldighn's battle plans," Raja explained as she passed Jaea a bowl of fried potatoes. She set other platters in front of Jaea. "Eat up. We have a long flight ahead of us."

Tharen took a seat beside Jaea. He set her messenger pen and journal within her reach. "I let them know we arrived safely."

"Thank you," Jaea said around a mouthful of eggs. "So how soon do we leave?" she asked Caspar and Raja.

"An hour," Caspar answered. "Our patrols are preparing to mobilize as we speak. We will join them when we finish here."

"We plan to follow the mountain range north, stopping about

half a day west from the Heart of the Land. Jayla and Adrielle are to meet us there and give us further instructions," Raja added.

Jaea nodded and continued eating, not sure what else to say.

"Under less hectic circumstances, I would have a good many questions for you, Jaea. In regards both to your nomination for the crown and your relationship with a dragon," Caspar said cautiously. "But we do not have the time, and rumor is you've a knack for speaking your heart to the point of offending your adversaries. So perhaps it is for the best." He smiled affectionately.

Jaea blushed and stared into her tea.

"I have heard many good things about you, Shaper," Caspar continued. "So, before your face can fill with any more worry about what I am saying, I will get to my point. On the matter of your marriage to a dragon, you have my blessing as Tharen's parents are not alive to give theirs. A belated formality, but an important one nonetheless. On the matter of your intent to rule Caeldighn, I am happy to say that it has already been put to the dragons, and we support your and Tharen's campaign."

"You have already spoken to the Dragon Council?" Tharen asked surprised.

Raja laughed. "We took the liberty of presenting it for a vote as soon as we received word from Aurora that you were nominated for regency. It was perhaps the quickest anything has been voted on by the Dragon Council, due in large to Emil. You both made quite the impression on our historian."

"I know it sounds pompous, my giving you permission to marry this young fellow," Caspar apologized, "especially after the fact. Dragons believe such words should always be spoken, to ensure that all parties understand the lay of the ground. Both Shapers and dragons take marriage seriously."

"I am honored for both your blessing and your support," Jaea said truthfully.

Caspar nodded decisively. "Good. Glad that is out of the way. When you are finished we will head to the courtyard."

"I'm ready if you all are." Jaea folded her napkin and pushed her plate away.

"Well then, let's be off," Caspar said.

CHAPTER TWENTY-SIX

The sun hadn't even crawled across the horizon when Jaea and Tharen were summoned to the command tent Sunday morning. It had been nine days since Caleb had arrived at her window to warn her of his father's plans. While Jaea and Tharen had flown north with the Silverhaven dragons, Maya and Kaylee had led their forces west after evacuating Maeshowe. It had only been the afternoon before that both parties had regrouped with what could be gathered of the Royalist military. They were all under her aunts' command now, placed halfway up Caeldighn's western coast just inland of the mountains. The Chiefs must have decided on a plan of attack to call for them so early. Through the still, dawn air she heard Caleb and Kaylee happily insulting each other. Turning, she saw them plodding along behind Maya, heading the same direction as she and Tharen.

"Command?" Tharen asked.

Maya nodded.

"What's up with them?" Jaea motioned back at Kaylee and Caleb. "Are they friends now?"

Maya frowned. "I'm not certain. Possibly." She shrugged. "He may have saved her life on the way here. And they fight very well together. Kaylee has even found him a few weapons to call his own. It is very strange. I've not seen her behave this way with other men."

317

Jaea raised her eyebrows. "Really? Hmm."

"What?" Maya asked.

"Nothing." Jaea smiled. "Just a theory."

Maya shook her head. Muttering something about couples, she pulled the tent flap back for everyone to pass inside.

"Good, you are all here," Aurora said as they came in. Jayla and Adrielle sat on either side of her. Jayla worried at the waya claw she always wore around her neck. Adrielle looked grim. "Please, take a seat. I'm going to give you all your assignments before I leave."

Jaea saw her confusion reflected on Tharen's face, but she kept quiet.

"First off, I would appreciate if you allowed me to inform you each of your duties before you all begin to comment on them. Jaea and Tharen, you are to remain near the command tent or the temporary hospital at all times unless told otherwise by Maya or Kaylee. Caleb Stone, you are to remain under Miss Buchanan's supervision. If you are smart, you will do as told, when told, without question. Maya and Kaylee, you are to oversee the upcoming battles from here. I have a number of scribes with messenger pens at the ready to allow you to keep apprised of the situation. Adrielle will be commanding troops on the ground." Aurora looked at the determined faces before her. "Lastly, I should inform you that Jayla and I are leaving directly after this meeting. We will go, with a large number of dragons, to encircle and protect the Heart of the Land." She nodded at the group to let them know she had finished.

"You are positive that we will be able to oversee things from here?" Kaylee asked.

"And that you want us in charge?" Maya added.

"Absolutely. On both counts," Aurora assured them. "I wish that Jayla or I could remain to assist you, but you two are more than ready for this." She looked at Kaylee. "The Rebels have already begun to march on the monument. And we have reports of Rebel troops headed this way from the south. We believe the major battles will take place somewhere between the monument and the mountains behind us."

"From this area you have a good vantage point of the fields below. You also have a good escape route into the mountains from this hill, should we need it," Adrielle told her junior counterpart.

"The Stones know we are here," Jayla said plainly. "Rather difficult to miss. Our army camped along this region, dragons flying in. The Rebels are anxious to expel the Royalists from Caeldighn. They will certainly be coming here."

"Remind me why I must hide?" Tharen asked, frustrated.

"Because you are the future King of Caeldighn," Aurora said forcefully. "Jaea is the future Queen. You cannot be risked. You are the first candidates since I had to take over from Sarai. And you have already been approved by all the races of Caeldighn to seek Nirah's blessing."

"But you and Aunt Jal can be risked?" Jaea demanded.

Jayla gave her niece a sad smile. "I am the Chief of State. I must be at the monument to try to speak reasonably with Jakob when he gets there. We have heard that he will seek the Lady's blessing, to appease the more traditionally inclined among his supporters. Besides, I have a replacement lined up."

"Uncle Alaric surely doesn't approve?" Maya asked hopefully.

"My husband is aware of the risks of being married to a Chief," Jayla replied evenly. "Before you ask, he is at home. He is making sure the town is ready to fend off attackers if the Stones veer that far."

Jaea looked at Aurora. "You are the current ruler. If you get to fight, why are Tharen and I held back? We can fight as dragons. Surely that is worth something."

"I am not the Queen," Aurora reminded Jaea. "I do not have

all the power afforded that office as a Regent. Beyond that, I am the only Shaper among us able to wield magic. So you can understand how I can serve my country best by defending the Heart." She looked at Jayla. "We should be going."

Jayla hugged her sister and her nieces before following Aurora out. Everyone stood awkwardly, uncertain what they should be doing.

"You have nothing to say about your orders?" Adrielle asked Caleb.

Caleb grinned back at her. "Follow a beautiful woman around and help guard her back. No complaints here." In a mock whisper he told Jaea, "She isn't so bad you know. Rather growing on me."

Kaylee rolled her eyes. "Stars have mercy."

☾☽

Jakob Stone rode proudly toward Nirah's monument. He was in very good spirits. Everything had been going brilliantly to plan recently. His personal guards rode with him and his parents. Two long, neat columns of soldiers and cavalry trailed behind him. Hooves clopped steadily on the wide paved road that stretched from Maeshowe to the Heart, and the sound of the men's chatter occasionally drifted forward. The sun had painted the morning sky a brilliant red, reflecting even among the gathering clouds to the west. So far, it had been the best Monday in Jakob's memory. Today he would receive Nirah's blessing to rule Caeldighn or order the destruction of that crystal pillar which only seemed to wreak havoc. Personally, Jakob did not favor one outcome over the other. On one hand, Nirah would grant her permission and the world would know that the Riddle of long ago had indeed lied to his ancestor, and no one in Caeldighn would be able to dispute his reign. On the other, he would have the chance to finally rid Caeldighn of the ridiculous notion of seeking a rock's permission to rule the country. Men ruled the land, not vice versa.

Now that he was closer to his destination, he could see the sad defenses Royalists had bothered to place at the monument. He and his men rode between two rows of widely placed Shapers lining the path. As he dismounted, he noted the Shapers were spread thin to form two large circles around the area. Jakob strode toward the monument and haughtily greeted Aurora and those beside her.

"Fancy seeing you here on this fine day," Jakob said. "Come to witness my triumph?"

"Hardly," Aurora said tersely. "We are merely here to protect Nirah should you disagree with her answer."

"Whatever the outcome, we hope to sit with you and resolve the matter peacefully," Jayla added.

"Peace?" Jakob laughed. "Did you hear that father? After centuries of murdering our kin, a McClanahan humbly extends the olive branch," he scoffed. "Peace cannot exist between us, my dear lady. Not until one of us lies dead."

"There have been days I feared that was true," Jayla said sadly. "Thankfully, I have recently had the pleasure of meeting some very remarkable young people, one being your brother Caleb."

"Caleb is no brother of mine!" Jakob spat. "He deserted his family. Betrayed us to that Jaea wench. Never underestimate the power of a whore over weak minded men. No matter, they shall both be dead soon enough."

"Surely you realize that your brother is the only reason you have been allowed this far alive." Aurora fought to keep her voice even. "My future queen seems to believe he is a good and just man. And I owe him for saving the lives of so many in Maeshowe. His advanced warning allowed us to empty the city before your men ransacked it. It is only out of respect for the one intelligent Stone in existence, and the woman he befriended, that you continue to draw breath and will be permitted to approach the monument."

Ransley materialized suddenly at Aurora's left. "I greatly dislike when my friends are called names," he told Jakob ominously.

"No one cares about your feelings and likes, Keeper," Baer Stone growled. "Now if you would all excuse us, we have business to attend."

"Very well," Aurora relented. "Riddle, they are ready," she called over her shoulder. She stepped aside just enough to let Jakob and his parents pass.

Jakob walked up to the woman standing at the foot of the obelisk. She wore the long brown robe of her office, and her hands were clasped tightly around a small book.

"You have a request for my Lady?" Riddle asked.

"We do," Baer answered.

"Speak it now before the Heart of Caeldighn."

"We petition that The Lady accept my son, Jakob Stone, as King," Baer said formally. "To rule over this great country and end the war that has so long plagued its people."

Riddle ignored the mist swirling in the crystal beside her at this announcement. She studied Jakob with an foreboding stare. "This is your request?"

"It is," Jakob responded solemnly.

"Are you prepared to accept the consequences of the answer granted you?"

"I am."

"Do you accept that Lady Nirah's word is final and beyond dispute?"

"I do."

"Then kneel and ask if you wish to seek an answer."

Jakob knelt before the monument. "May I go with your blessing to ascend to Caeldighn's throne?"

Everyone watched the glowing stone, waiting. No one moved. No one hardly dared to breathe. The monument filled with dark smoke. Its usual radiance dimmed, and the gathering clouds seemed to darken in response.

Riddle broke the eerie silence. "Please rise and hear the Lady's ruling."

Jakob stood. He knew the answer already. It wasn't hard to guess Nirah disapproved, what with the ominous clouds and darkened crystal obelisk.

"Lady Nirah has denied you the crown," Riddle announced. "By Caeldighn law, you will not be allowed to rule. Any attempt you take to ascend the throne without Nirah's blessing will be fought against bitterly. You are bound by your words during your petition to the Lady to step down peaceably and relinquish you claim to Kingship."

Jakob smiled. Without a word, he returned to his horse, his parents and guards following closely. They rode back through the columns of Rebel soldiers toward Maeshowe. Two of Jakob's captains galloped to his side.

"Kill them all," Jakob ordered. "Then tear down that oversized paperweight."

The captains nodded and wheeled around shouting orders out to their men as they rode at the monument and the feeble forces gathered to defend it.

Rebel troops rushed forward. Then to their great surprise and dismay, the entire front line burst into flame. The Royalists that had been so sparingly placed to protect the Lady, the ones the Rebels had assumed were Shapers, were, in fact, dragons. Horses panicked and threw their riders, trampling anyone unfortunate enough to be in the path of escape. Men balked at the idea of charging giant, fire breathing creatures but were

323

spurred forward by their commanders.

One of Jakob's guards looked back at the commotion. "They were dragons!" he said in horror.

"It makes no difference," Jakob replied. "They will fight for their King."

∞

"This is going to be awful," Jaea summed up. She glanced down at the map on the table before her, then looked back out at the gentle slopes and fields beyond the command tent. A deep red sunrise spilled ruby light over the land below reminding Jaea of a saying her Dad often repeated. *Red sky in morning, sailors take warning.* She shivered. A different type of storm was coming at them today.

"I should be out there with Adi," Kaylee said for the hundredth time. "With my men."

"You are of better use here," Maya reminded Kaylee for the hundredth time. "I really don't like the size of their army. There must be off-worlders among them to be so numerous."

"I could go roast a few hundred," Tharen offered.

"You can stay put, as per your orders," Maya chided.

"Guess I'm not allowed to go either?" Caleb ventured.

"Absolutely not," Kaylee confirmed. "Why can't we attack first?"

"No sense in picking a fight if our enemy only plans to sit and stare at us," Maya said. "Also, because Adrielle told us not to," she added when Kaylee opened her mouth to argue.

"Chief?" one of the scribes called. His messenger pen was blinking rapidly, and its black ink was spilling words in a rush onto a thick pad of paper.

Maya and Kaylee hurried over, closely followed by the rest of the group.

"What's happened?" Jaea asked anxiously.

"Nirah denied Jakob the crown," Kaylee answered cheerfully.

"They attacked the monument!" Maya yelled.

"What!" Jaea and Tharen shouted together.

"I didn't think they would actually dare to harm Nirah's stone," Maya muttered unbelieving.

"Uh, guys?" Caleb called from just past the open tent sides.

"What now?" Kaylee asked impatiently.

Caleb didn't have to answer. The sounds of battle began to reach their ears, and the three scribes manning messenger pens were suddenly very busy.

"You three should probably head up to the field hospital," Kaylee suggested hollowly. "I imagine they will be needing assistance shortly."

"I'm staying with you," Caleb said determinedly.

Kaylee seemed surprised but pleased by his response. Maya looked more confused than ever, but she quickly turned her attention to the reports flowing in. Reports Maya understood and could do something about.

"Tharen and I can go help the hospital," Jaea told Kaylee.

"They have pens up there too," Maya said with a quick glance at her sister.

"We will check in occasionally." Jaea nodded. "Stay safe, you lot."

The nurses at the field hospital were glad of the extra hands and put Jaea and Tharen to work almost immediately. It wasn't long before teams of griffins were landing outside with stretchers laden with wounded men and women. A while later, the head nurse called Jaea and Tharen away from bandage making and sent them to watch those wounded that had already been seen to. This freed up the nurses in that section of the huge tent to aid where they were more needed. It also had the added bonus of seriously increasing morale among the injured Shapers, humans, and even Caeldighn's other races. Imagine! Getting a glass of water from the future King and Queen!

True to their word, Jaea or Tharen wandered to the back doorway every so often to check in with Maya and gather what news was to be had. Neither side appeared to be really gaining ground as far as Jaea could interpret. After a few hours of battle, Jaea had nearly given up trying to make sense of the reports Maya scribbled out for her. Only knowing that the others in the tent wanted to hear of the happenings kept her at it. On one such trip, Jaea noticed a handful of stretchers being carried out the back door and toward the line of trees just beyond the tent.

"Frank, what are they doing out there?" Jaea asked the scribe she sat with.

"More seriously wounded," Frank told her. "Take 'em to the unicorns." When Jaea only looked more confused, he tried again to explain. "Unicorns can't be on battle fields, see. Or in the midst of a lot of pain. They've healing powers, you know, and can do a lot of fixing and mending that our nurses and doctors can't. But if a unicorn walked in here, all of its magic would rush out of its body to heal every little scratch and dry every tear of hurt. And the unicorn would fall down dead at our feet."

"So they wait out there, for cases that need them most?" Jaea asked.

Frank nodded. "That way they can help, but not so much that we lose a unicorn. They're few in number, those precious beasts." He handed her a page of Maya's writing. "Any chance you can send a mug of coffee with Master McKenna when he comes in a bit?" he asked hopefully.

"I'll send him out with one right away." Jaea smiled. "You hungry at all?"

"I could eat," Frank admitted.

"We will see what can be rustled up."

"Thank you, ma'am."

"No problem," Jaea assured him. "See you later."

Jaea and Tharen returned to the command tent that evening when the battle appeared to be winding down for the day. Looking at the maps Kaylee had been moving pieces around, it was hard to discern whether the Royalists were pushing Rebel troops back or if the Rebels were trying to purposefully draw the Royalists away from their hilly vantage. The crack of rifle shots and the muffled bangs of black powder explosions had thankfully stopped once the light began to fade. It seemed both sides were ready to call it a day.

"So this all just starts over again tomorrow?" Jaea asked.

"More or less. Though we aren't completely done for the day," Maya said tiredly.

"Tomorrow we hopefully push through their line better," Kaylee amended.

"What battle plans remain to conclude this evening?" Tharen asked.

"Waya have a few tricks up their sleeves," Kaylee said gleefully.

"We arranged to have most of the injured moved to Tidewater," Maya added. "They will start moving out this evening. There is an actual hospital in Tidewater that will be able to better tend the patients. Though the wounded dragons are heading to Silverhaven instead."

"Wounded dragons?" Tharen repeated in disbelief.

Maya nodded sadly. "We lost two today. Three more are injured enough to need serious medical care. Those scales are tough, but their wings are not as durable. And that wretched powder..."

"You are awful quiet over there, Caleb," Jaea observed.

"Just going over the day," Caleb muttered absentmindedly.

"The Rebel tactics don't make a lot of sense, makes me think they are up to something."

"Think he is after my job," Kaylee joked to Jaea.

CHAPTER TWENTY-SEVEN

Jakob lounged in the ornate high backed chair that had seated so many of Caeldighn's kings. Aurora and Jayla were due in the throne room any minute now. He had known the pretend Queen and her Chief would seek him out here if they survived the battle at the monument. When he had received word of how Aurora had massacred his men, he had nearly forfeited his plans to spare the woman's life. She had eliminated them, turned every last one into a pile of salt. Even their bodies were long gone now, scattered on the winds.

The doors opened to admit Aurora, Jayla, and a woman Jakob knew was really the dragon Raja. Guards escorted them to stand before the stairs at the foot of the throne.

"Well, well." Jakob sneered. "I must say, I do so enjoy this view."

A muscle twitched in Aurora's face. "We would like to extend our gratitude for taking time to speak with us."

"I could hardly resist the chance to hear you three groveling and begging me to end the war, now could I?" Jakob smiled. "Besides, I wish this conflict to come to a close as much as anyone else." He looked at the men bustling into the room, three carrying chairs and a fourth pushing a cart. "Aha, here we are. I took the liberty of readying tea for us. Could I offer you a seat?"

Jakob's servants placed chairs beside the women.

Aurora, Jayla, and Raja remained standing.

"Perhaps later," Jayla said. "If we could please attend to the business at hand?"

"Very well." He waved a hand at the four men, and they immediately scurried back out of the room with their load. "So, have you decided to back my campaign at long last?"

"No," Raja answered bluntly.

"The Lady has already denied you the crown, so we cannot by our laws pursue the idea of you as King," Jayla clarified. "We do have a recommendation that would keep you in a high position in Caeldighn and bring a quick end to this age old feud."

"Just for kicks." Jakob laughed. "What is it that you propose?"

"A position in our government," Aurora explained. "There are a number of choices that could be made available to you which would allow you a hand in Caeldighn's day to day. Ambassador, judge, secretary, head of one or more of our many committees, a position in local government in a town of your choice, possibly even Council member."

"All you would need to do is step aside from the throne and allow others to seek Nirah's blessing," Jayla added.

"Why would I step down from the throne?" Jakob's jovial expression vanished, immediately replaced with undiluted loathing. "It is my birthright!" he shouted. "It is rightfully mine. No one will take it from me, least of all a chunk of glowing rock."

"You have no claim to kingship, you miserable whelp," Raja growled. Smoke was starting to pour out her nostrils.

"Nirah can see into your heart, just as she saw into your ancestor's," Jayla said tersely. "You are not worthy to wear the crown."

"I wouldn't try to Shape into your true form here, dragon," Jakob warned. He snapped his fingers. Men in armor and the Stone colors filed into the room through both side doors, aiming long rifles at the three Royalists. "My guards really wouldn't like it." He stepped down from the platform the throne sat on, advancing on the group with his sword drawn. "Here is my proposition." He pointed the tip of the sword at Aurora's heart. "You, the current Queen, will marry me and help solidify my position as rightful King. Shame you are past childbearing years," he tsked.

Raja and Jayla made to step in front of Aurora, but she waved them off.

Jakob shrugged. "But I'm certain plenty of young legs will part willingly for their King. I foresee no real trouble procuring an heir, or ten." He laughed. "No reason I shouldn't live up to my reputation and ravish some fair maidens occasionally." He ran the flat of his sword down Aurora's body, outlining her figure. "I promise you won't go unattended though. A husband must fulfill his duties, after all. And if we are outrageously lucky, maybe I can plant a seed in your womb despite your advanced age." He tugged Aurora forward. "As a matter of fact, I think I'll get started on that right away."

"Not a chance," Aurora growled. She clapped both hands to Jakob's face.

Jakob shoved her away, screaming with pain as Aurora's spell covered his face in blisters. His eyes streamed with tears trying to douse the horrendous burning. With his vision hampered, he could just barely see Aurora crumpled on the floor. With a bellow of rage, he surged forward and thrust his sword at her. He felt it sink into flesh, but knew something was wrong. It was Jayla standing at the end of his sword, her face blood-splattered and pale. He noticed the sticky warmth trickling down his neck when he saw the bloodied claw Jayla held in her hand. How could he have been beaten by such a ridiculous trinket? He could feel the life fleeing his body, a terrible wetness gushing from his throat, before he fell to the ground, an empty shell.

Tharen and Jaea Shaped into dragons while Maya, Kaylee, and Caleb mounted the three dragons that stood nearby. The tide of the battle had changed, and the Royalists were at an advantage. Adrielle and the Junior Chiefs had decided to use it to make their way back toward the capital. Not liking the idea of trying to protect the young monarchs-to-be while pushing through the Rebel troops, Adrielle was sending them ahead of the army. There had been no recent reports of Rebel activity at the Land's Heart, and the Chief thought it would be safer for Jaea and Tharen to wait there, where the land was flat and it would be hard for attackers to hide. The dragons and Junior Chiefs she was sending as a precaution, to guard the royal candidates. Caleb, not feeling altogether welcome by many of the Royalists, had volunteered to go as well.

"Fly high," Adrielle reminded them all. "Be careful. Wait at the monument for the rest of us."

"We will, Aunt Adi," Jaea said.

"Good! See you as soon as can be." Adrielle waved them off. "Godspeed!"

The dragons flew high above the battlefield, hoping they were out of range for the Rebels weapons. They followed the wide gap Royalist forces had made in the enemy's lines. Below the odd mix of races forming the Royalist troops were obviously making a big push, funneling their numbers right through to the opposite side of the Rebel army. Tharen did his best not to focus on the bodies that lay on the ground unmoving. It didn't seem like long before the entire battlefield was out of view, replaced by empty fields with the monument growing ever so slowly into focus.

Unburdened with passengers, Jaea and Tharen landed at Nirah's circle before their companions. They Shaped back into their normal selves. Jaea stared toward the glowing obelisk, a look of awe on her face. It was quickly replaced with an expression of horror when the wind brought them sounds of fighting. A man seemed to be trying to pull down Nirah's stone, which was shooting sparks easily seen even at their distance. Without warning, Jaea ran forward. Tharen took off after her, his only thought keeping her safe. He wondered if she even registered that Ransley and Riddle were back to back, fighting off four men and trying to edge closer to Nirah. The man tugged again on the chain wrapped around the monument, and the earth trembled beneath their feet.

"Stop!" Jaea screamed. "Stop it!"

Tharen surged past her, closing in on the Rebel. He ducked under the man's wild swing and threw a returning punch that landed on his opponent's jaw. Jaea immediately began trying to rid the monument of the heavy chain.

"Jaea, get out of here!" Ransley yelled.

Two of Ransley's opponents broke away, presumably to go after Jaea, the main threat to Jakob's regency. The man Tharen fought gave up and scrambled to get away after Tharen managed to take his sword. Tharen turned his attention to the two men headed for Jaea. He had just met one's sword when the now familiar retort of a Stone rifle sounded through the circle. A second shot rang out as Tharen tried to push the men back so he could see where the shot had come from. Suddenly, two large green paws wrapped around his adversaries and carried them off. Tharen realized the other dragons must have caught up. He turned to survey the field and locate the rifleman when he heard a third shot. The man Tharen had wrenched the sword from was kneeling in the grass next to a handful of rifles laid out on the ground. He was shooting toward the monument. Toward --

"Jaea!" Tharen dropped the sword and spun around. Fear like he had never known before filled his entire being in the second it took to turn. Another loud crack split the air as Tharen ran to Jaea, who was already sliding down the monument, dark streaks of her blood staining the pale stone behind her.

"Jaea. Jaea, please," Tharen whispered. He cradled Jaea against him. "Please, Jaea." Blood gushed from a hole in her right thigh and her entire left shoulder was crimson. *Not her heart. Don't have hit her heart*, Tharen prayed.

Tharen was dimly aware that the dragons dispatched the remaining Rebels. He could hear their fire and the beating of their wings. The Shapers and Ransley joined him at the monument, out of breath and faces full of fear. Riddle knelt over Jaea, tearing strips of her cloak and pressing them against Jaea's wounds to try to stem the bleeding.

Maya sank down beside them, hands pressed to her lips. She caught Tharen's eye. "We can't treat this," she sobbed.

"We can. She will be okay," Tharen said determinedly. "We just need to get her to help." He looked up frantically for someone to tell him what to do to help.

Kaylee shook her head. "Three shots found her. She is losing too much blood. She wouldn't make it to Maeshowe, let alone Tidewater." She wiped at the tears spilling from her eyes. "There is nothing we can do."

"Ransley?" Caleb asked. "Could you take her somewhere?"

"The gates are still blocked or down. I had to take a bit of a back way here, and that certainly wouldn't help her," Ransley answered sadly.

"What about the unicorns?" Tharen asked desperately. "Jaea told me they can heal."

"There is no way to get her to them," Maya said hopelessly, "or them to her. She would die if we tried to transport her that distance. The unicorn would die crossing the battlefield to get here. It would take too long for a unicorn to get safely around the injured without their magic sapping from them. By the time they got here..."

"We can't just sit here and let her die!" Tharen yelled. He glared at the nearest dragon. "What about Silverhaven? Could someone there heal her?"

The dark green dragon shook his head. "I am not certain. Regardless, you would never make it there in time."

"No!" Tharen shouted again. "I will not just sit here and let her die!"

The ground beneath them began to shake. A loud grinding rumble was emanating from a spot just beyond the road that circled the monument.

"She can't die!" Tharen repeated wildly. "I won't let that happen!"

A jet black arch sprang out of the earth with the sound of a sword being sheathed, magnified a hundredfold. Most of the group looked to see what had happened. Maya and Tharen kept their eyes on Jaea, willing her to keep breathing.

"Unbelievable!" one of the dragons cried happily. "McKenna!" he called. "Try the arch!"

"What?" Tharen asked uncomprehendingly.

"The arch!" the blue dragon repeated excitedly. "It is a longshot at best, but it is better than doing nothing at all."

Hope surged through Tharen. "What do I do?"

"Just walk through it. Focus all your thoughts on getting to Silverhaven." The dragon cocked its head. "I think it will transport you there."

Maya looked up excitedly. "I read a paper on that. The arches as internal gateways. Do you think it will work?"

"It was my paper," The dragon answered proudly. "We can't be certain it will transport us. But since this is the first one created in maybe thousands of years, I'm willing to bet it will work for him."

Tharen pushed to his feet, holding Jaea carefully. "I have to try something." He strode toward the strange black arch. When he stood before it, Tharen glanced back at the rest of the group.

"I will meet you in Silverhaven!" Maya called as she climbed back aboard the dragon that had flown her to the monument. She looked down at Kaylee. "You stay here, all of you. Guard the Heart. Let Aunt Adi know what's happened."

"We will," Caleb answered.

Tharen clenched his jaw and stepped through the arch. A brilliant violet light flashed all around him. His body felt strangely weightless. His stomach seemed to have disappeared altogether. And then he was suddenly stepping forward into a large courtyard that looked as though it were carved into a mountain side. The bright purple light must have attracted attention because a number of people were peering at Tharen curiously.

"Help me!" Tharen called to them. "Jaea McClanahan is injured!"

Tharen was led to Silverhaven's hospital wing. Two capable looking women took his charge and quickly set to cleaning her up and stemming the blood still leaking from her wounds. Tharen was bustled out of the way and settled in a comfortable chair nearby. More people looking like doctors and nurses flooded the room. One pushed a strong cup of tea heavily laced with more than just honey into his hands. He sat dejectedly watching the scene, wishing there was more he could do.

"McKenna?"

Tharen startled. He looked up at the doctor before him. "Yes." He took a quick drink in hopes it would revive his voice and coughed. "Is she okay?"

"No," The doctor answered honestly. "But she has the barest sliver of a chance to pull through this, and that is an infinitely greater chance than she had before you brought her here. All of her wounds have been cleaned, treated for infection, and bandaged. There is a deep groove on her arm to show the path of one bullet. This has been cauterized. The other shots passed through her thigh and chest, leaving a good deal of damage on their way out. Those wounds have been stitched up. Unfortunately, the bullet that struck her just below the collarbone broke her shoulder blade as it exited her body. We have done what we can to repair and set her shoulder. We have utilized some spells to help her heart continue beating and hopefully encourage an increase in her body's blood production. It is really up to her and the Father now."

"Is there anything I can do to help her?" Tharen asked.

"Yes." The doctor smiled. "You can sit with her and talk to her. Many cases that looked bleak were only turned around by the presence of loved ones. If you need anything, or have any further questions, I will be in my office just down there. You can always send a nurse for me, too. Just ask for Seth."

"Thank you, sir."

Seth nodded and turned to go. "Oh! I almost forgot." He quickly turned back around. "We have a team scouring our records for further treatment. And I received word a moment ago that Merlin and some of our elder dragons are on their way here. When they arrive we will conference near your wife's bedside and see if we can come up with a solution to improve her chances."

"Alright. Thank you again," Tharen said.

While Seth returned to his office, Tharen moved to the chair right beside Jaea's bed. Jaea's face was whiter than the un-dyed sheets she lay against. Even her hair seemed to have lost its luster. "Hey there, beautiful," Tharen tried to say lightly. "The doc says you are on the mend. Should be up and about in no time." He took her hand in his. "You just focus on getting better okay." He hung his head. "Don't leave me, my love. Don't go."

Fifteen minutes later Merlin took a seat next to Tharen. "How are you holding up? How is Jaea?"

Tharen rubbed his hands over his face. "I've been better. Jaea has never been worse. They tell me that her heartbeat is weaker than they would like. And they keep having to change the bandages on her leg and stomach. They think the spells may not have taken."

Seth and an elderly couple came to stand beside Merlin. All three peered down at Jaea, assessing the situation. Nurses hurried over with more chairs as well as a cart laden with tea things and food. One nurse took Tharen's still full mug away and shoved another steaming mug into his hands.

"Drink this one," she warned. "Or I dump the next one on your head, lad." She swiped a biscuit and a generous wedge of cheese from the tray. "And you'll eat this while you're at it, if you know what's good for ye."

"Yes, ma'am," Tharen promised.

"There's a dear." She patted his cheek and set about serving the others in the group.

"What do you think, Solvieg?" Seth asked.

"I think she is in a mighty bad way." Solvieg sighed.

"You have her charts?" the elderly man asked, his snow white mustache nearly dipping into his tea. "I'd like to glance back over what has been done, so I do not suggest something already applied."

"Right here, Marvin," Seth replied. He passed the man a clipboard.

Marvin scanned the papers and passed them to Solvieg. She looked through them and handed them off to Merlin.

"It appears you have already done everything that can be done to aid this woman," Marvin told Seth. "That was good thinking with the blood spell," he complimented.

"Her heart rate is still this low?" Merlin asked anxiously.

"I'm afraid so," Seth answered. "I checked it last just minutes ago. Though I wouldn't object to all of you checking again now on the off chance I had a false reading."

Solvieg took what looked like a stethoscope from a peg on the wall and listened to Jaea's heartbeat. She then passed this to Marvin as well and moved to set her fingers against Jaea's wrist.

"It's as the chart states," Solvieg concluded. She moved to the foot of the bed and began to massage Jaea's feet and calves. Tharen could see wisps of faint blue light streaming from her hands. "This may help her circulation," she explained when she noticed Tharen watching.

"I am afraid that there is likely nothing more we can do for your wife," Marvin told Tharen quietly.

"Please," Tharen begged. "You are dragons. You are older than anyone else in Caeldighn, and you have knowledge of magic. There must be something that will heal her. Some dusty, half forgotten spell?"

Marvin shook his head sadly. "Even magic has limits."

"And yet events continue to happen beyond those supposed limits," Merlin said wryly. "Like me."

"You were an incredibly rare exception," Solvieg reminded him. "You don't even classify as a shared-" She broke off abruptly, eyes wide.

"No!" Marvin said firmly. "Absolutely not. There is no guarantee it would work, and if it failed Caeldighn would be left without even one royal candidate."

Tharen was looking back and forth between Marvin and Solvieg. "What?" he asked hopefully. He looked at Seth, but the doctor seemed equally confused.

"Nothing," Marvin said quickly, avoiding Tharen's eyes.

"I will tell him if you do not," Merlin warned. "He has a right to know."

"He wouldn't be able to complete the spell," Marvin

339

shrugged. "He does not know how."

"I do," Solvieg said simply. "Tell him."

Marvin cleared his throat. "There is an old spell that allows a dragon to share its life with another. Actually sharing their life force with another being, forever linking the two. It is rumored to be capable of conquering nearly every injury and sickness so long as the being in question has a heartbeat."

"Why didn't you say so earlier!" Tharen demanded indignantly. "How? What do I need to do?"

"First, you need to understand that this spell is not without danger," Solvieg said calmly. "Nor is it without consequence."

"Yeah, yeah." Tharen waved his hands impatiently. "Such as?"

"Such as linking your lives," Marvin explained. "She would unwittingly trade a Shaper lifespan for that of a dragon. She would live to see her sister, her sister's children and grandchildren, pass into the stars. Her human parents would have long been dust before she were able to rejoin them in the heavens."

"That is not all," Solvieg continued. "Beyond what it may mean for Jaea, it would also have the chance to lessen your dragon lifespan. For were one of you to die, the other would immediately follow in death. And as Marvin said earlier, it may not work. It is only rumored to have the ability to heal so completely. If you managed to link yourself to this woman, but the spell did not heal her..."

"You would both die before the morrow," Merlin concluded.

Tharen let out a deep breath. "If I do nothing, she dies?" he asked Seth.

Seth nodded. "I'm afraid so."

"Then we do the spell," Tharen decided. "At least she will have a chance."

"Sir, we must alert the troops."

"No," Baer Stone muttered. "We can still win this."

Mr. Stone's wife glared at him. "How dare you!" she screamed. "Our son is dead, and all you can think about is who else you can force into Kingship!"

"Alissa," Baer warned. "Now is not the time to fall apart." His voice shook a little, betraying him. "Jakob would want us to fight on, for the cause."

"No!" Alissa yelled. "This is the perfect time to fall apart!" She cradled Jakob's head in her lap. She hadn't allowed anyone to move him from the floor of the throne room where he fell. "My eldest son is dead because of the cause," she spat. "My youngest fled from you and your evil schemes before it could kill him. But will I ever see him again? No. Now is the time to mourn, husband. Both sides have lost this day." She pointed to the floor not far from where she sat, where men were trying to clean the lifeblood of Jayla Campbell from the flagstones.

"I will not be beaten by a McClanahan again!" Baer Stone bellowed. He spun toward the General that had suggested notifying the men Jakob had commanded. "All you are to do is order our troops to annihilate the Royalist forces or die trying!"

The General's face showed a strange lack of emotion. "It is possible, perhaps, that you forgot," he offered. "We swore allegiance to your sons, not to you. I did not take orders from you, but from Jakob. He is now dead. Your other son, Caleb, appears to be in league with the Royalists. However, as he alone of the men we swore our swords to remains alive..."

"What are you saying?" Baer demanded. "Traitorous scum!" He grabbed the general's arm. "You will do as I say!"

The General punched Baer full in the face without hesitating. "No, Mr. Stone, I will not," he informed the unconscious man laying at his feet. He turned to his Captains. "Alert the men, our King is dead. The King's parents are mad with grief. As this leaves us with no clear leader, they are to cease fighting immediately and await further instruction from Caleb Stone."

CHAPTER TWENTY-EIGHT

Jaea woke to see Tharen asleep in a chair beside her. She smiled when she realized he was holding her hand. She tried to raise her other hand to rub her eyes, but someone appeared to be holding that one as well. She turned her head and discovered Maya asleep at her other side. She blinked hard to clear her eyes better and tried to figure out where she was.

"Hey," Jaea croaked. She moved her arms a bit. "Guys?"

Tharen and Maya both jerked awake. "Jaea!" they shouted together.

"Ssshhh!" a nurse scolded as she bustled over. She helped Jaea sit up and take a drink of water.

Seth hurried over from his office. "You're up!" he exclaimed happily. "How are you feeling?"

"Fine," Jaea answered. She took another drink. "Where am I?"

"Silverhaven," Seth told her. "Do you remember being wounded?"

Jaea narrowed her eyes thoughtfully. "Yes," she said reluctantly. She looked at her left arm and felt her thigh.

"They've healed." Seth grinned. "And you can thank this young man for that." He pointed at Tharen.

"Long story. Tell ya all about it later," Tharen dismissed. "Do you really feel alright?"

"Yes," Jaea smiled. "Hungry, but otherwise fine."

"Oh, thank heaven!" Maya cried. She threw her arms around Jaea and didn't bother trying to stop her tears.

"Maya!" Jaea exclaimed, concerned. "Hey, it's okay. What's wrong?"

"I thought I'd lost you!" Maya sobbed.

"Sister of mine." Jaea laughed. "Oh, not you too," she said when she noticed a tear rush down Tharen's face.

"We nearly lost you, Jaea," Tharen said soberly.

"Good grief. Would somebody please tell me what's going on?" Jaea asked.

"Certainly," Seth answered. "You said you are hungry? If you like, we can have some things brought in and get you caught up over some food."

"That sounds lovely," Jaea said.

Tharen helped Jaea to a nearby table while Maya wiped her eyes on a handkerchief a passing nurse handed her. Tharen kept an arm around Jaea. Even though she could walk steadily, he only let go when she was settled in a chair. As soon as a steaming cup of tea was in her hands, Jaea looked pointedly at Seth.

"Well," Seth began, "to start, you arrived here in Tharen's arms Tuesday evening. From what I can gather, you were shot while trying to protect the Lady. Today is Thursday. And since Maya is the one with the fancy pen, I believe I will let her fill you in on the goings on since you departed the monument."

"I was out of it for days!" Jaea exclaimed. "What's happened? Is everyone alright?"

"Slow down, sister dear," Maya said. "Our group secured the monument. The Captain that shot you had an unfortunate meeting with a burst of dragonfire shortly after his last shot. Tharen carried you through an arch here to Silverhaven for treatment. I tried to follow, but couldn't get the arch to work. So I took the longer route here and arrived yesterday. By that time,

Tharen had already done the Shared Heart spell, and you were healing quickly, though you were still unconscious, and we feared you may not ever fully wake."

"You did a spell?" Jaea asked Tharen.

"Later." Tharen smiled. "Maya has a lot left to tell."

"My messenger pen was blinking more than a lost firefly," Maya continued. "So Tharen and I took turns keeping an eye on its reports. The war is over, Jaea. Jakob died the same day you were injured. Almost his entire army turned to side with Caleb, who led the Royalist and Rebel armies back to Maeshowe. All fighting has stopped. The war is over." She smiled.

"Jakob died?" Jaea asked. "How?"

Maya's smile quickly faded. "Aunt Jayla slashed his throat with the waya claw she wore around her neck. She jumped between Jakob and Aurora. She saved Aurora's life. But Jakob's sword struck her. Aunt Jayla has gone to the stars, Jaea."

"What?" Jaea whispered.

Maya nodded sadly.

The news of her aunt's death didn't seem to be sinking in. Jaea wondered if it would hit later, when she was alone to cry her tears. "How is everyone else? Are Aunt Adi and Kaylee okay? Michael?"

"They are just fine." Maya answered. "Aunt Adi may have a scar or two from the battles. Kaylee is still arguing with Caleb, but emerged from the fighting unscathed. Michael too, is safe."

"Good." Jaea sighed. "Do we know how many we lost?"

Maya shook her head. "Not yet. Reports are still coming in from our hospitals. It could have been so much worse, Jaea. If you hadn't trusted Caleb, hadn't made us seen the good in him...it would have been a much different story when the troops met at the monument if Caleb had still been a Rebel."

"Poor Caleb," Jaea said. "How strange everything must be for him now. He turned his back on his heritage and lost a brother

345

in the process."

Maya shifted in her seat. "Your parents should be here tomorrow night or the following day."

"Really?" Jaea asked relieved. "It will be good to see them."

The room fell silent. Everyone pretended to drink their tea.

"Maya?" Jaea asked.

"Yes?" Maya stopped stirring sugar into her mug.

"I am sorry about Aunt Jal. I know you two were close."

"We will see her again." Maya smiled weakly and took Jaea's hand. "We all meet again in the stars."

A week later, Ransley brought the Harbours, Doc, and Opal through a gate back to Earth. Not quite two weeks after that, Jaea and Tharen stood before Nirah's monument, surrounded by the Caeldighn Council and many friends. Alaric, Jayla's widower, stood with Adrielle and the Junior Chiefs, all of whom wore black to mourn the fallen Chief.

When Riddle gave the signal, Aurora stepped forward and spoke loudly. "We are here to back our candidates for the Crown as they seek Nirah's blessing. Would the representatives of each race step forward and declare your people's say."

Raja moved first. "The Dragons approve," she said simply.

"The Waya approve," Tsagi declared.

"The Centaurs approve," Twil added.

"The Pegasi approve," Dayun said.

"So do the Griffins approve," Gale followed.

"The Unicorns most happily approve," Zorya said.

Adrielle, Maya, and Kaylee stepped forward. "The Shapers also approve," Adrielle concluded.

"Then will the candidates in question please present themselves to the Lady." Riddle beckoned Jaea and Tharen forward. "Speak your heart before the Heart of Caeldighn, Nirah, Lady of the Land."

"We seek the Lady's blessing to rule this beautiful country," Tharen said formally.

"Are you prepared to accept the consequences of the answer granted you?"

"We are," Jaea replied.

"Do you accept that Lady Nirah's word on this matter is final and beyond dispute?"

"We do," Tharen answered.

"Kneel and ask, if you seek an answer." Riddle guided them closer to the monument.

"Will you extend your blessing," Tharen began.

"That we may ascend Caeldighn's throne," Jaea continued.

"To guide Caeldighn in continued peace."

"And keep its people close to our hearts," Jaea finished.

Immediately Nirah's stone filled the clearing with a brilliant white light. It was as though the sun had decided to stop in for a quick visit before returning to its usual place in the sky.

Riddle laughed. "Lady Nirah says yes. Very much yes." She waved the crown bearers forward. She crowned first Tharen, then Jaea. "Please rise and greet your people, King Tharen and Queen Jaea."

Jaea and Tharen stood. Amid a great deal of applause, they bowed to Nirah, then turned and bowed to the crowd.

"Long live the King!" someone shouted. "Long live the Queen!"

Soon the cry was taken up by everyone present, quieting only when Aurora called for the crowd's attention.

"There will be a banquet held in the castle Saturday, a week from now, to further celebrate this joyous occasion," Aurora announced. "King Tharen and Queen Jaea will also begin to address some of their most pressing concerns by naming the Chief of State, Chief of Military, and approving new Council members should any of our current members wish to resign."

"We beg your patience as we settle into our new roles and sift through the mountains of paperwork I glimpsed yesterday," Tharen added, sending a ripple of laughter through the audience.

"We feel truly blessed for this opportunity and look forward to working with you to make Caeldighn great again," Jaea said. "And most of all, we hope to see you Saturday because Gwena has already started cooking, and there is no way we can eat all that delicious food without your help!"

More laughter and applause followed as Tharen led Jaea through the crowd. It is tradition that the King and Queen walk to the castle after receiving Nirah's blessing and being crowned. So Jaea and Tharen began the long walk home to show, as other Kings and Queens before them, that they were humble enough to walk with their people and willing to work for their country.

"We did it!" Jaea cheered quietly.

Tharen chuckled. "If the banquet goes as well, I'd say we were doing pretty great already."

After a few minutes Maya, Kaylee, and Caleb caught up with them. Others straggled along behind, following their new rulers back to Maeshowe. Jaea glanced over her shoulder and saw that Aurora, Adrielle, and Alaric weren't far behind.

"So," Kaylee said. "Since we have this nice long trek back to the castle where you can't yell at me for fear of everyone behind us hearing, I'd like to speak with you all about something."

"Spit it out," Jaea said. "You are making me nervous."

"Okay. Right." Kaylee cleared her throat. "I will stay on until things settle down more, but I don't want to be Chief of Military."

"What!" Jaea, and Tharen shouted at the same time.

"Sshh!" Kaylee admonished.

"I wondered how long you would keep the position now that we are at peace," Maya said.

"You knew she wanted out?" Jaea asked.

Maya simply nodded and looked at Kaylee.

"I want to live a nice quiet life," Kaylee said wistfully. "Maybe even marry and start a family. I would like to visit my mother's people without worrying I am putting Caeldighn at risk by leaving. That is what I have always wanted. I just thought I would always be desperately trying to keep Caeldighn from completely falling apart. So I can't be acting Chief," she summed up. "I will be an advisor to whomever you appoint to the position if you like."

"I don't suppose you have a recommendation for Chief of Military?" Jaea asked hopefully.

"I have a few ideas," Kaylee said.

"I think it should be Caleb," Tharen said suddenly.

"Say what now?" Caleb asked.

"Think about it," Tharen said, excited now. "You are at least half the reason the war finally ended here. The fighting stopped because the Rebel armies turned to you for orders, even though you had sided with the Royalists. There are still people in this country that wish to see a Stone in power in Caeldighn. With you as Chief of Military, a Stone as Chief, even those who were on the Rebel's side will be happy with the war's outcome. It's perfect!"

"Actually, that makes a great deal of sense," Maya admitted reluctantly. "Especially if you act as advisor," she told Kaylee. "Smooth any feathers that may get ruffled, ease the transition over to a new commander."

"Caleb?" Jaea asked.

"You really want me to?" Caleb asked.

"Yes," Jaea and Tharen said together.

Caleb grinned. "Alright. I'll do it. It would be an honor to serve as Chief of Military under your reign."

"Surely even your parents will be glad to hear it," Jaea

349

ventured.

Caleb's grin disappeared. "Doubtful." He let out a breath. "What are you going to do about Dad?"

Tharen shuddered. "Monday's problem. Today is only for happiness."

CHAPTER TWENTY-NINE

The next day, Jaea woke to see Tharen staring at her from his side of the bed .

"Good morning." Jaea smiled sleepily.

"Good morning, beautiful." Tharen replied. "I was just counting my blessings."

"Oh yeah?"

"Yep." Tharen grinned mischievously. "I had to count you about a thousand times, you are that great a blessing."

Jaea laughed and swatted his arm. "It's too early for you to be flirting. I haven't even brushed my teeth."

"I fail to see how teeth brushing impacts morning flirting."

"It does because I say so." Jaea grinned back. She stretched luxuriously, hit Tharen with a pillow, and rolled out of bed. "Oh man." Jaea slouched. "It's Monday, isn't it."

"Drat." Tharen agreed. "It is."

A knock sounded on the door. "It is Lily, ma'am. Are you ready for breakfast?"

Jaea glanced at Tharen. "Yes. We are decent!" She laughed and pulled a robe over her nightdress. "We are coming."

Lily and Charles had the table set for breakfast in the adjoining room.

"That smells amazing." Tharen praised.

"Gwena seems to have pulled out all the stops." Lily smiled.

"It'll be a miracle if the both of you don't gain a hundred pounds by midwinter."

"Good." Tharen approved. "Only if that means I get to hibernate the other half of the winter."

"Not likely, sir." Charles guessed.

"Worth a shot." Jaea shrugged.

Jaea managed to eat a little, but the dread of their audience with Mr. Stone weighed in her stomach like lead. Jaea abandoned the breakfast charade after Tharen kissed her and left to get ready. With a sigh, she walked into her dressing room to pull on the fancy dress Lily had set out. Today was Jaea's first appearance since being crowned, and Lily and Mrs. Lind had wanted to make sure she looked the part when she faced the Stones.

"It'll be over soon," Lily assured her. She fussed with Jaea's hair, arranging it in a graceful knot.

"I know." Jaea sighed. "I just feel for poor Caleb. I hope this goes well."

"There," Lily said proudly. "You look perfect, ma'am."

Jaea squeezed Lily's hand. "Here goes." She left the royal quarters and headed to the throne room to meet Tharen. It would be only the second time she had been there since Jayla and Jakob had died. The first time had been with a long procession of people, all of whom placed flowers around a handful of candles in memory of her aunt. Today she saw the long black cloth bearing the Stone emblem that Caleb had requested be placed in memory of his late brother. Jaea hoped it would bring some measure of peace to Jakob's parents.

"Hello again, beautiful," Tharen greeted as she took her place beside him. "Ready?"

"No," Jaea admitted. She shifted in the high backed chair and smoothed her skirts. "But let's get on with it anyway."

Tharen nodded to the man at the door. The guard opened it

to allow Aurora, Adrielle, Maya, Kaylee, and Caleb inside. Once they were all in place around the throne, the guard opened the door again, and Caleb's parents were escorted in.

"You are aware of the reason for this audience?" Tharen asked them.

"To sentence me to death, I presume," Baer Stone sneered.

"Hardly," Jaea chided. "Do you understand that action must be taken against you for your crimes against the Caeldighn crown?"

"Yes, Lady," Alissa Stone answered. She pointed at the shroud set out for Jakob. "But first, may I offer my gratitude for this show of respect for our mourning."

"Everyone is loved by someone," Tharen said. "No one's memory should be trampled if it can be helped."

Baer Stone barked out a laugh. "If you are done with the pleasantries to ease your conscience?"

"Very well," Tharen complied. "We have reached a sentence. However, it comes with a choice. One each of you may make separately. You may remain in Caeldighn if you like, though it would be under supervision. If you choose this option, you will be allowed your family home in the foothills, south of the First Queen's Forest. You will be more or less under house arrest. You may have visitors, and perhaps occasionally, with escorts, be allowed to travel to certain areas. Obviously, a number of restrictions apply to this choice."

"The other option?" Baer asked.

"You will be banished from Caeldighn," Tharen answered. "There are several worlds you would be allowed to seek refuge on. Earth is not one of them. You should know that with this choice are severe consequences. For if you were ever seen in Caeldighn again, you would be killed on sight. The people cannot bear the thought of you wandering freely in this land."

"You have heard that Caleb is to be named Chief of Military

on Saturday?" Jaea asked.

"Yes," Alissa said. "I was most surprised to learn it."

Baer snorted.

"You may each choose differently," Tharen reminded them. "But you must choose now."

"I will not remain here, a prisoner in my own house," Baer said angrily. "A subject to a false King and Queen," he added. "I choose banishment." He looked at his wife, clearly expecting her to voice the same.

Alissa avoided her husband's stare. She looked at Caleb. "I have missed so much of your life."

"You did what you thought was best," Caleb said.

"Jakob has been buried in the old family plot?" Alissa asked.

"Yes. It seemed most fitting," Caleb answered.

Alissa nodded. "I will stay. I agree to your terms of house arrest."

"What!" Baer shouted.

"I will not leave the land that holds one son's bones and the other's future!" Alissa shouted back. "I stay! With or without you."

"So be it," Baer spat.

"Would you like to change your answer, Mr. Stone? Now that your wife has made her choice?" Tharen asked.

"No," Baer answered resolutely. "When may I leave for my new home?"

"Immediately," Tharen said. "Ransley?"

The door opened again, and Ransley strode across the room. "You called?" he asked Tharen with a smile.

"Mr. Stone has chosen banishment. Would you accompany the squad bringing him to the gate and see him safely through it?"

"Yes, your Majesty," Ransley answered. He turned to Baer. "Would you like to say farewell to your wife and son first?"

"They have bid me farewell already," Baer said viciously. He stalked out of the room, guards flanking him.

Ransley nodded to Jaea and Tharen before following his charge through the door.

"Mrs. Stone," Tharen said kindly. "I know you are going through a difficult time, but please allow me to express my gratitude. I am very happy that you have chosen to remain in Caeldighn. I think that your presence and continued relationship with your son Caleb can only bring good things to our country. Caleb and Kaylee have asked permission to accompany the squad that will see you safely to your home. Would you permit their company?"

"Yes. Thank you," Alissa said with a small smile.

"I am afraid you will find the house in a less than ideal state," Jaea apologized. "We had to be certain it was free of weapons and the like. Should you need anything, within reason, to set it right again, please notify your guards, and we will see what can be done."

Alissa stared at Jaea. "You two are rather unusual monarchs thus far."

Jaea laughed. "Perhaps."

"There was a rift in this country," Tharen said. "There was plenty of fault to pass around. And it wasn't helping anything. In fact, it made everything worse. We have only just started to mend that tear, and we hope you will help us to do so."

Alissa smiled. "I am glad my son will be working alongside you to achieve that goal. I am ready to go home, if my escort is ready."

Caleb and Kaylee moved to stand with Alissa. "Our bags were already packed," Caleb told his mother. "Just in case."

Caleb and Kaylee bowed to Tharen and Jaea. Alissa offered a small bow as well. When the door closed behind them, Jaea let out an audible sigh of relief and sank low in her chair.

The rest of the week passed with few incidents. Mrs. Lind set a small army of tailors and seamstresses to work, finalizing the garments for the formal banquet on Saturday. Even Lily and Charles were fitted for new things. Jaea thought time seemed to be playing hopscotch. Parts of the week rushed by as though she had skipped a day, while other moments it seemed time was dragging and the next day would never dawn. Finally, it was Saturday, the day of the first big gathering in the castle since the coronation. In the midst of the mad rush to get ready, Ransley pulled Jaea and Tharen aside.

"I have a present for you." Ransley whispered as he pulled them away from the preparations. He shooed everyone but Lily, Charles, and Maya out of Jaea and Tharen's quarters. "Come over here." He led them to a closet door. "It is a wedding and coronation gift. Open it."

"You put our present in the living room closet?" Jaea asked suspiciously.

"Just open the door, girl," Ransley insisted.

"Opening the door." Jaea laughed. When she saw what was beyond it, she let out a cry of surprise. Hand over her mouth, she looked at Ransley for confirmation.

"What?" Tharen asked, peering around her. "That..." He pointed. "Is that?"

"Home," Jaea whispered. It was her room in Ben and Maggie's house. Her Caeldighn closet led to her Harbour closet on Earth.

Ransley, wearing a huge grin, nodded. "Anytime you want to see them, or they want to visit you." He handed her and Tharen each a bright blue key. "That was the old man's idea. Said it was an inside joke," he explained.

Jaea threw her arms around Ransley's neck. "Thank you! Thank you! Thank you!" she shouted.

Ransley laughed and hugged Jaea back. "You are most welcome."

"Best present ever," Tharen said, staring at the blue key in awe.

"It was a pretty good idea huh?" Ransley agreed. "Maya thought you would like it."

At this Jaea ran to Maya and gave her a huge hug too. "You are the best sister in the universe."

"I'd say we are tied." Maya smiled. "Now, go give your mom and dad a quick hug." She pointed to Ben and Maggie waiting anxiously just on the other side of the door. "We have to finish getting ready yet."

"Okay!" Jaea ran back to the open door, grabbing Tharen on her way through.

Maya, Lily, and Ransley laughed watching Jaea bounce happily around her childhood room. Jaea kissed both her parents, talked excitedly for a few minutes, and then followed Tharen back through to Caeldighn.

"Bye!" Jaea and Tharen waved. Ben and Maggie waved back. Jaea and Maggie closed the doors after one last smile at each other.

"Let's do this banquet thing!" Jaea cheered.

Her earlier bravado quickly fading, Jaea walked with Tharen toward the entrance to the ballroom. For tonight's occasion it was set up for feasting instead of dancing, but Jaea knew the hall was just as decorated now as it was the night of the ball.

"Well, here we are," Tharen announced when they reached the door.

"Yep," Jaea said. She patted her hair and made sure the delicate crown was still in place atop her head.

"We really have a lot to do, don't we?" Tharen asked suddenly. "Getting Caeldighn back on track. This is just the start."

Jaea nodded. "That's alright, though. We will do it together."

Tharen leaned down to give Jaea a quick kiss. "Together," he agreed.

The doors opened, and they could hear the herald call for the crowds attention. Jaea set her hand in the crook of Tharen's arm. Then, side by side, they stepped forward to greet their people.

ACKNOWLEDGEMENTS

Thank you to all my friends and family for not committing me when I kept talking about writing a book and for believing such a thing to be possible.

Thank you Rebecca Williams for dragging my butt to a writers' group, many moons ago.

Jeanna Vanessa-Pink, without you no one would have a name.

Casandra, all my sisters, Jenn W, and anyone who happened to call me during this process- thanks for answering some very random questions and offering your opinions.

Thank you Dr. MacLeod, for pointing me towards Maeshowe.

NaNoWriMo! You are phenomenal, just so ya know. Thanks for the pep talks.

Kevin O'Reilly, many thanks for the fine cover you designed and your assistance with Caeldighn's map.

Laura Hannon, thanks for your tremendous help editing both grammar and story.

Zoe Douglas. For everything. Just everything. Prayers, support, writing aid, and co-misery. For your belief in the impossible and the crazy.

Husband! Thanks for putting up with this chaos, and me, and me with this chaos. And for all your insights and help. Love you!

Above all, thank the Lord! For inventing stories in the first place, and for putting this particular one in my head and heart.

ABOUT THE AUTHOR

Jennifer Leitzman is a full time author and stay at home mom. She and her husband make their home in Virginia with their daughter and a dog. Before she decided to try her hand at writing, her love of stories led her to a Bachelors in History.

For updates on her newest projects, visit her website:
http://www.JenniferLeitzman.com

Made in the USA
Middletown, DE
17 July 2015